About the author

Tony Bury, born in 1972 in Northampton, England, has had a passion for writing songs, poems and short stories since an early age. He has taken it more seriously since having kids, writing several children's books and screen plays as well as the Alex Keaton series of crime novels. *Edmund Carson is The Alphabet Killer* is the third book in the Edmund Carson series.

EDMUND CARSON IS THE ALPHABET KILLER

Also by Tony Bury

The Alex Keaton Series:

Intervention Forgiven
Intervention Needed
The Intervention

The Edmund Carson Series:
Inside Edmund Carson
Edmund Carson – The ONE. The Only.

Tony Bury

EDMUND CARSON IS THE ALPHABET KILLER

Vanguard Press

VANGUARD PAPERBACK

© Copyright 2018
Tony Bury

A CIP catalogue record for this title is
available from the British Library.

ISBN 978 1 784654 62 7

Vanguard Press is an imprint of
Pegasus Elliot MacKenzie Publishers Ltd.
www.pegasuspublishers.com

First Published in 2018

Vanguard Press
Sheraton House Castle Park
Cambridge England

Printed & Bound in Great Britain

For Peanut...

Chapter 1

"So, sir, may I ask, when is the wedding?"

What? What wedding? I look down at him as he is standing there with his tape measure in hand. What is he going on about? I only came in here for a suit. Well, not just a normal suit; His suit! Come to think of it, it does look like they have a lot of stuff to do with weddings in here. I never noticed that. I didn't even know that they had such things as wedding shops. I suppose it makes sense to have them as most people do it a couple of times now. Get married, that is.

Although I am pretty sure this guy isn't married. Maybe that is why he works here? To see if he can pick up a passing best man?

Why do they call them the best man anyway? And why wouldn't the woman marry the best man? The clue is right there in the name. Instead, she marries the groom, and groom sounds like someone that you have to, well, groom, to make better, when there is already a best man there, standing next to him? Women are strange. They would rather have the damaged goods and fix them, than the finished article.

Maybe he is married. I shouldn't have presumed that. Everyone can get married now. Although he definitely isn't the faithful kind if he is married. He felt the inside of my leg in these trousers for far too long. He knows what I keep in my trousers and he wanted some of it. I could tell by the look in his eyes. I know when someone is hungry for me. I see it all too often. I bet if he is married his husband doesn't like him working here.

It has been a while. Wait, why did I say that? That sounded like, oh, it has been a while, maybe I should? I meant a while since Brighton. It's been what, ten days? That thought is now in my head. Ten days. Ten days, but I am calmer now. I was mad. I was really mad. I shouldn't have… Oh, what is done is done. It is not about what I should or shouldn't have done… It was a zoo, she was a keeper and thanks to the fucking Blackout nobody is ever going to know it was me. Wait, has it really taken ten days to make a plan? That is not like me? What have I been doing for ten days? Other than zoo keepers. I can't waste time now. Now it is more important than ever that I work on being heard by the world. Even if they don't want to report on it! I have a lot to do, and a lot, a lot of places to visit.

Twenty-five… wait, twenty-five, is that right?

A–B–C–D–E–F–G

H–I–J–K–L–M–N–O–P

Q–R–S–T–U–V

W–X–

Y and Z

Twenty-six. Twenty-six places to visit.

I always have to sing a tune in my head to remember the alphabet. I think everyone does. Isn't it odd how you remember a tune as well? Music has a habit of making you remember the words. I remember rehearsing it with my nan all the time. Maybe that is why it makes me smile. It reminds me of the good old days. I even sound like her now. The good old days, as if they were decades ago.

He is looking directly at me now. Why is he looking at me? Just finish measuring the suit. He is thinking about my inside leg again, isn't he? I wouldn't be surprised if he isn't thinking about just getting it out and going down on it. A quick unzip then. Fuck, why am I even thinking about that?

Does he think we shared a moment? He is looking into my eyes like he thinks we did.

No, wait, I think he thinks he knows who I am. He doesn't know who I am. Does he? Beard, shaved head – I look like those trendy types now. A hipster, that's what they are calling them. I am just a hipster looking for a new suit. They do have them out here as well, don't they? It is not just an English thing, is it? Why is he still looking at me?

"The wedding, sir, when is it?"

Oh, that's why he was looking at me. The wedding thing again. Didn't I answer that already?

"It is in a few weeks." I don't even know why I said that. It just came out of my mouth. Sometimes I swear my mouth speaks before my brain. It should keep him quiet though.

"Is it your wedding, sir?"

I spoke too soon. Mine? Why would it be mine? Surely I don't look that old, do I? I mean, how old is marriage? Like thirty? I don't look thirty! Is it the shaved head? Wait, does he think I am bald? I should tell him I did it on purpose, shouldn't I? Save the confusion.

Come to think of it though, I did promise her that we would one day. She is probably off planning it now. Women do that, don't they? You say one thing to them once and they take it as gospel. She has probably been planning it since our first night together in front of the fire. I might even have said it that night. I think I would have said anything that night.

She will understand this. I know she left me with the choice, and I was so close to calling it a wrap. I did think of stopping and spending the rest of my days with her. I will spend the rest of my days with her. But it is not done yet. This chapter of my life is not done yet. I would be disappointing to many people. Too many of my fans would be devastated to see me walk away just because of them. The fucking press. I am not doing it for them; I am doing this for my fans. After this, it will be done. This challenge, this is something that will sign off my career. This is something that will go down as a masterpiece. Legendary, that is what they will call it.

Then we will discuss getting married. Maybe having a family, a little boy called District Carson. I can see my son's name in lights too. It will be good for my fans, if nothing else. Good for them to know that one day he may go into the family business. Aiming to be as good as his dad.

I could wear this at the wedding too. It would be like Miss Walker was marrying one, ha! One of my characters. I am the ONE, in more ways than one. There are so many things I can do with that name.

I must be a merchandising dream. The T-shirts in Camden are only the beginning. I can see it all: aftershave, clothes and TV deals. None of the others put this much effort into it. I mean, Jack didn't bother. The Ripper, hardly original, is it? Just because he ripped open the people he worked with and then sewed them back together. They could have easily called him the Sewer. Jack the Sewer. I bet that would have pissed him off. At least I am reinventing myself all the time for them. No, not for them, for the fans.

She is a lucky woman. I am sure she knows that. She will actually get to marry all of them. Wait, maybe Father Harry could marry us. Not sure how I could do that, but I definitely need to do something like that for the fans. Maybe I need to put it out on the big screen. Cinemas, that type of thing. They are all screening live shows now. If I time it right, it would be amazing. That would stop this Blackout nonsense. Every magazine in the world would want to cover the wedding. I would get millions in royalties, endorsements...

They must know they are only hurting the country, the people, by not reporting on me? I must bring in thousands of tourists to the UK. I am like the royal family. Reporting on me must be made a law or something.

Someone will have to step in at some point and realise that revenue in the UK is down. Maybe the issue will be raised at the Houses of Parliament? Or the House of Lords? They will make me a Lord one day. Lord Edmund Carson.

I am sure they will lift the Blackout as soon as they see the capabilities of the Alphabet Killer. Killers, what they can do for the UK. What fame and fortune really looks like. I can see the headlines now.

I do wonder how long it is going to take for them to pick up on the Alphabet. D? My guess is D, unless it's that Sarah woman. She is the one behind this Blackout, I am sure of it. Ever since she has been editor of *The Times* it has gone to her head. I should find out where she lives and pay her a visit.

I am not sure what her problem is with me. She probably fancies me. I don't remember rejecting a Sarah, but there have been so many women. I am sure I might have broken her heart at some point. I mean, look at me. I haven't forgotten that guy in York either. He was bad-mouthing me on Twitter and on that radio show. I am going to save a letter for him.

He is looking at me again. It is his eyes, they are burning into me. I know I am good-looking, but this is ridiculous. I only came in for a suit! I think I am going to have to… Oh, no, it is about the wedding thing again.

"No, sorry, it is my sister's wedding. She wants us all dressed in the traditional top hat and tails. Full works, she calls it. Handkerchiefs and cravats. Do you sell canes? She definitely wants a cane."

He always had a cane. In the pictures when he was lurking around Whitechapel, he was always coming out of the shadows with his hat on and cane in hand.

"We do, sir."

"Yes. Good. I would like one of those as well, and I would like to see coats. A long black coat. I think it will go well with the grey, don't you?"

"It is very trendy at the moment, sir."

I love the fact that I can be trendy. It is really important for famous people to know what the latest trends are. That's how they get all that stuff for free. People should be sending me free stuff. Maybe I need an address for people to send it to, along with all the fan mail? I am sure the post office must be full of letters with nowhere to post them to. It must be sitting somewhere between Santa and the Easter Bunny with the amount of letters they have for me. When all this is over, I will spend some time keeping up with my correspondence. It keeps the fans interested. Social media will lift the bans too so that I can recap all my adventures to my fans. I wouldn't be surprised if that's not a slogan somewhere. Lift the bans for the fans. Yes, someone will have come up with that one.

I take another look in the mirror. This is pretty much how Jack looked when he was at the top of his game. So, that is what I want to look like. Well, what I want him to look like, the Alphabet Killer, as I am just getting to the top of my game. A whole new level of professionalism. That is what the fans want.

This outfit was the trend back then. He really was the first trendsetter. I am going to have to get used to people comparing us when I launch this character. Compare how we are changing the face of fashion.

Compare us just on the clothes though. I am far more famous than him already. He only worked with, what, less than a dozen people? I am sure that's not right. I think it was more. They just covered it up.

Fuck!

That is it, isn't it! Jack the Ripper had a Blackout too? I never thought of that. Maybe that's why nobody ever heard of him again? Is that what they are trying to do with me? Make me disappear? I have already told them who I am. Don't they know it will just make me into a legend? Well, more of a legend than I am already. That is what it did to him.

I am not sure about a hat. I am not sure I am a hat person. How am I going to carry it around with me? What if I need to run away from fans? What if I am mobbed? Surely it will just keep falling off? I am going to need to carry a box or something, and they are so big. Hardly travelling light, is it?

I will need the hat for selfies, for the full effect. That is all. Although I need to think about walking down the road wearing a top hat with a cane at ten o'clock. There is no way I can do that and not be recognised.

That's why Jack kept to the shadows. Problem is, there are no shadows any more. Every street is full of lights, neon lights. It must have been so much more fun by lamplight. Spooky, like how they have done the Edmund Carson walk in Brighton. Cobbled streets and lamplights, I need to remember that for the films. That is a director's eye.

He is back and passes me the coat. It fits. It's a good fit. He must have really been looking me up and down as he can tell my size without a tape measure. It will be part of the job, being able to tell a man's size. I am afraid to ask for underpants. Imagine how big they would come. He will go one or two sizes even bigger just to flatter me and get on my good side. I like the coat though. It covers the suit as well and makes me look bigger, like I have more muscles than normal. That will be great for the photos.

The Alphabet Killer, a force to be reckoned with. That is what they will say.

That is why Jack wore it, I am sure now.

"Do you want to try with the hat, sir?"

I nod at him. I put the hat on. Perfect. Maybe I do want the hat. He knew the size of my head too. Probably knows the size of both of my heads.

I look so good. This was a great idea. This is going to be a great launch of a new character. I love launch days. They are the best.

I am really liking this triple mirror thing. Looks like there are three more of me. What a buzz my fans would get from that. I can see it now. Picture me standing here, as me. Well, Edmund me. I am looking at three of the most famous characters in history: the ONE, Father Harry and now the Alphabet Killer. Picture them all smiling back at me. All in their costumes, ready for work. I am on fire today.

One day I am going to need a house of mirrors, like they used to have in those old fairgrounds. A house full of mirrors just for all my characters. I can visualise everything. That's what makes a great film director, isn't it? Visualisation of all of the scenes. I am going to be such a great film director.

I really need to start to thinking about writing my screenplay. These movies take years to make. Maybe I need to call up one of these film studios and get the process going before someone else tells my story. They are always ripping off these movies with cheap versions of the truth. Mine needs to be quality, and in my own words. Universal and Disney, they will be queuing up for the rights. It will be the biggest bidding war in years. I need to get on with it though so that the movie is released when the ban is lifted. With the Blackout, all these dodgy film-makers are probably working on it already.

"What type of cane would you like, sir?"

I turn, and he is holding one. It looks very simple. It's not me. I am not a simple type of person. I need to be more flamboyant. Jesus, where did that word come from? It's a good word, but I am not sure I used it correctly.

"Do you have anything a little more, well, more…?" I didn't want to use that word again, in case I sound stupid. Especially if I didn't use it correctly in the first place. I nearly said, well, more me, but he doesn't know who I am.

"Yes, sir."

He disappears around the corner again. I look back at myself in the mirror. Yes, this is me. This is the return I have been planning. This will get them back up and noticing me. This will make the press and the fucking government think about who I am again and what they have done by telling the world not to report on me. On me! My fans deserve this.

"How about these, sir? Are any of these to your liking?"

He is back again. He is the little shopkeeper that could, isn't he? He is good at his job. It's like he appears from nowhere. He hands me over the canes. One has an egg on the top. Looks like a posh egg, but an egg all the same. That is not me. Then a snake in the shape of a handle. I like that. I like the snake. The last one is a lion's head. That is cool and it is golden. The head of a golden lion on a cane!

Am I a golden lion? Or a silver snake? Now that is the question. That is the question. Okay, not a hard question.

"I will take the golden lion head." It is who I am. I am a leader, a strong force that shines in the darkness. A lion, that is the type of person I am.

"It is a good choice, sir."

I know. That is why I chose it. What an odd thing to say? I hand the other two back to him and turn to look in the mirrors again. I can't take my eyes off me. It is no wonder that I am adored so much. I was destined for this. Yes, this is me. This is really me.

"I will take it all." I head back to the changing rooms. Takes me about five minutes to undress and redress in my normal clothes. I walk back out and go to the counter and hand the clothes over to him. He is smiling again.

"Do you have the whole outfit again?"

"I am sorry, sir?"

"Do you have the outfit again? My twin brother is exactly the same size as me and I just thought it would save him a trip?" I give him a smile back that will make his day.

"Oh, I see, sir. Yes, I am sure we do. Other than the cane, sir, they are one of a kind."

"That's fine. I will take the snake for him. He will enjoy that." I don't really want it. I can wash a cane. I am not a snake type of person. The last thing I want to do though is not have a spare to put into the dry cleaners. Just like Father Steven from the Lake District. He always kept a spare suit hanging in case of emergency. I do hope they are all okay? I should really take a trip back up there. I am not sure whether it is an L or a D though. Is the Lake District even a town? I am sure that place was a town. What was it? Something to do with a cake? Mint cake? Kendal Mint Cake, that was it. That must have been a town.

I wait while he wraps everything up. He takes ages. You would think he would be quick at this by now. Maybe he isn't as efficient as I first thought. I pay in cash and head out of the shop. It's a five-minute walk to the car. I am glad it is only a five-minute walk. These things are heavy. I throw them in the boot and drive to Amie's house. It was so nice of her to lend me her car. I park in her driveway and take my clothes into the house.

"Hi, I am home."

There is no response. I am sure she hasn't gone out. She said she wasn't going out. That's why she lent me the car.

"Amie, are you still here?"

Still silence. I go upstairs to where I left her this morning. I knock on the bedroom door before going in. I don't want to catch her half-naked, or fumbling with herself. Although I am sure she will have been doing that this morning. She is still in bed. She is still fast asleep.

"I can't believe you are still in bed. It is like eleven a.m." I lean down and open her eyes for her. I knew she was pretending. She is smiling at me now. She knows she has had a lazy morning. Lazy. Waiting for my return, no doubt.

"I know, it is not even that I gave you a good excuse." I knew she would mention that, she is a straight to the point type of woman. And hungry for it I can tell.

"It was a long night. Sorry about that. I'm, sorry, we, we will be making up for it." I give her the money, making smile.

That has her really smiling now.

"It was just that it took me ages to get here. I was over in East Anglia. I thought because there was an East Anglia there would be an Anglia… Turns out there is not. Hence, I am here, but it is not really local. Come to think of it, it is not local to anything.

"Yes, I know. Even more reason to take advantage of superstars when they are in town."

She has me smiling now, I like the fact that she calls me a superstar. Even out here.

"I was so tired. So tired! Believe me, I must have been. Look at you." That is a line. They always fall for that line. She is so nice. Hot in a mum kind of way and nice. I really found it easy to talk to her last night. It really helped me fall asleep as well. Just knowing you have someone warm to sleep next to always helps.

"No, nothing else was bothering me." That's a lie. I don't think I want to lie to her.

"Sorry, that was a lie. If we are being honest, I wasn't really over the whole Blackout thing. It still hurts and I still reach for my phone fifty times a day. I am coming to grips with it though. Besides, you were hardly up for it yourself, were you? I mean, even you deserve a night off, given how hard you must work in this house."

That has her smiling again. She knows I care about her feelings. I do care about all my fans. Especially the ones that are besotted with me. They are my favourite kind.

"Really? I think you did mention that last night. I was number one. The ONE! Yes, very good. And you are sure he is, I mean, he will be, fine about it?" I am amazed how many husbands are happy for me to sleep with their wives.

"Everyone has one of those lists now. Because of some TV programme that made it famous. Even I have one. Top five celebrities you are allowed to sleep with, no matter what."

Best not to drop the Miss Walker bomb. Some women don't like to know you are in a committed relationship before you sleep with them.

"Mine? Okay, I will share, as you were so kind to. Sandra Bullock, a clear number one. She always has been. Hayley Atwell, Agent Carter, have you ever seen that? There is something about her smile. Then Julia Roberts, she is a classic beauty, I would say. I do keep having a dream about Kylie Minogue in a black wig. So, I think that she may well make number four. Well, as long as she wears the wig, or dyes her hair. I am sure she will. For me, that is." I pause. It is completely on purpose.

"I can't say I have found a fifth though. Maybe it didn't need to be someone famous. Maybe it needs to be someone that lives out by the coast?" I give her the wink. She knew what I meant. I am so smooth. I have used that line before. It always works. They always put out in the end. Besides I couldn't just say Gillian Anderson that would have really pissed her off.

"I am so glad I am on yours too." I can sense what is coming. There is a mutual consent there. I can feel it. I just need to check one thing that is bothering me. I walk out of the room and check in the bathroom. Then go back to Amie's room.

"He is fine. Still taking a bath. He has been in there a good while now, hasn't he? He must have been very dirty? Does he normally spend that much time in the bathroom?

"He does? Really? Hope you don't mind me saying, but it is a little weird. Anyway, shall I show you what I have bought?" That will get her in the mood. It will get the old juices flowing, seeing me dressed to the nines. That is my nan again, dressed to the nines. Why wouldn't you be dressed as a ten? Or in my case, an eleven or twelve?

"I will just go next door and change. Give you the real effect.

"I am sure you wouldn't mind. But trust me, it is worth it." Women generally don't like to see me get dressed. For obvious reasons. Getting undressed, now that is another matter. They love that.

I go and fetch the clothes and then go into the bedroom next to Amie's to get changed.

"You are still in bed too? What is it with this family today? So sleepy!"

Mandy smiles at me. She is hot. She has the same smile that Seventeen had back in the school. First thing I noticed about her. She has a smile that hides all her secrets. Secrets that you really want to know. No shame either, that girl. With her mother in the next room and her father in the bathroom she still wanted it last night. It wasn't her first time either, I could tell. I have had virgins and she wasn't one of them. I think I have had virgins? Haven't I?

"I had to go shopping for some clothes and then I was just talking to your mother.

"No, no, she is not like that. She is a lovely woman. She has been nothing but polite to me." I am not really sure what a shrew is, but I am sure she isn't one. She is doable. I mean, I will be doing her, so she must be.

"No, not as lovely as you. That is a given." Needy, she is starting to sound so needy. I do hope this isn't going that way again. For some women once is just never enough.

I walk over and give her a kiss. A long kiss. She deserved it after what we did last night. I am surprised someone that young knew about the other stuff. I mean, she isn't even twenty and she is taking it in there. I thought that was more an older woman thing. A way of trying to keep you man faithful.

"I was just going to show her, and you, the suit I bought." That was a good save. I start to get undressed. She can't take her eyes off me. I think I must be giving some kind of vibe out today. People are really into me. Even more than they usually are! Maybe it is the confidence. I feel like I am turning a corner. My rage has disappeared and I am going back to my very best. Today I feel like I could be doing this forever.

Maybe it is because of the Blackout. Maybe, what did my nan say, absence makes the heart grow fonder. Maybe this Blackout thing is going to be good for me. That's what it is.

Look at her eyes. They are almost sparkling at me. Hunger, pure hunger. I do have time, and she is really cute.

No, I do have time, but all I can think about now is that shop guy measuring my inside thigh. His eyes were sparkling at me too. He certainly had a feel. I don't blame him. It's not every day he feels one that size. It would get anyone excited. I can't do that while thinking about that, it would be like, well, I would be doing him. And I don't think I like that. Now I am doing him in my head. In exactly the same way as I did her last night. Come to think about it, it must be about the same. I mean, it's used for the same thing. Everyone's must feel the same…

Fuck!

Think nuns, Edmund, think nuns. That always clears your mind. Think nuns with stocking and suspenders and, and… I take a moment and breathe. That's better. I am back, focused on the suit. Focused on getting dressed.

As I do up the last button, I can see the disappointment in her eyes. She didn't want me to get dressed. It must be hard for her. Probably followed me on Twitter and Facebook and now here she is with me in her room and they won't allow any pictures of me on the Internet. She must be gutted. Imagine being this close to your idol and not being able to tell anyone.

She must be dying for a selfie. I will have to leave her some on her phone. Something she can share with her friends and on social media once they lift the ban on me. She will be the most popular girl in the town. Not just for what she can do in the sack. Why do they say that, the sack? It is not like you sleep in a sack? Maybe it is better in a sack? Maybe I should try that?

"So, Mandy, what do you think? How do I look?" As if I need to ask.

"Thanks. I think so too. Yes, I am loving the cane. Gives me a bit of class, don't you think?

"Yes. That is exactly what I wanted to hear. Very, very Jack the Ripper. I think we spoke about that last night, didn't we? He is my all-time hero. He is the one who showed me the way. I now even think he may have had a Blackout too. He probably had the first one. He probably is the only other person in the world that the government has given one to. How cool is that? We will go down in history together for that."

There is a sense of pride about that. Miss Walker was right. A stigma attached to it. Wait, did she mention this before? That has just come back to me. She is a clever woman.

"I know, but I think when I write my autobiography I will still put him as number two of all time. He deserves it. Not that couple or the doc. They were just nutcases. Jack was the first legend. The one we need to benchmark our careers on." In the future, they will use me. I will be the benchmark for all future stars. I will have them. The copycats. Without doubt I will have them. I will!

"I just need to go and show your mum."

She doesn't look impressed at me showing her mum. Jealously can get you like that. I walk out of Mandy's room and back into Amie's. She is nearly wetting herself as I walk in.

"I know. I think I should have done this a while ago. I really suit it. A suit, that is. Not something you would normally wear unless you were at a wedding or a funeral. But on me it just works.

"Wow, straight to it! I would, but I can hardly get this dirty. I need to look my best for the first, well, you know, outing of him. It is very important. The launch, I mean. If you mess up the launch you have to spend so much time getting everyone onside. Look at what happened with the ONE. Took me weeks to get that back on track.

"I know."

She is right I really need to make an impression.

"You know, I have been thinking about it a lot. I am just not sure? There are so many things I could do. So many things I have already done. The first thing I thought of was a party. But it will never top my eighteenth. It was amazing. I had a pineapple hedgehog and everything. People just don't make them anymore. I am not sure why. Cheese and fruit, it is a good combination, right? Then I thought dinner, but I have already done that. I have done the movie scene thing, although I have to tell you some men are hairy. I mean, really hairy. No word of a lie, this guy he was Gorilla-like. Tim, his name was. Yuk. So, I am a little stumped, to be honest. What do you think? Do you have any great ideas? Being one of my all-time biggest fans." They were her words after all, not mine.

"Do you know, I will! It sounds like a great idea. Let me hang this up, and we will get to brainstorming." I leave Amie contemplating ideas and go back to Mandy's room. I start to undress.

"You are so right, that is very rude, Mandy. Sometimes I get lost and forget it is all about my fans. I didn't show them. I can't keep this look to just us."

I go to the bathroom. He is still there. He is still in the bath. I think he has a thing about water. He has been in the bath for like twelve hours. He must be freezing?

"Do you want me to put some more warm water in for you?"

I walk over and turn on the taps. He can't take his eyes off me either. I bring out all the sexes today, don't I? It's amazing how many people would turn for me. I guess that is why he is not that bothered, as it is a bit weird. Not sure I would be that comfortable that my hot wife is lying in bed at the same time that someone as good-looking as me is walking about.

I test the water it is warmer. I turn off the taps, dry my hands and leave him to it. He looks happy enough. He is probably going to be using the loofah really hard in there now. Give himself a good rubbing.

Time to pop in to see the twins. I need to get everyone's opinion. I go into their bedroom.

"What is it with this family? None of you want to get up today."

They are giggling under the covers, I can hear them. I can just about see their faces where I tucked them in last night. I walk over and pick up some of their toys and put them on the bed.

"Yes, I am sure your mum will get you a suit like this too." I am not sure, but you have to give the little ones hope, don't you?

"As a Halloween costume? That is a great idea. I never thought about Halloween. I should really do something for that. It is only a few weeks away. I could make it a whole event." That is a great idea. Kids today are so sharp. These boys are really sharp. They must be a credit to their mum.

"Or maybe you could go as the ONE? Yes, he is another great one. One of my favourites."

That got another laugh from them. I am great with kids.

"Really? Father Harry is your favourite? That's good to know. I thought being twins would mean that you both like the same thing? It's good for me to always know who appeals to whom. Makes me think about what is to come. How to appeal to all ages, that is always on my mind. You are always on my mind. My fans." It is good to always tell your fans that.

"No not really," I lie. I can't tell them how expensive it is. It is only natural for people to want to dress like their idols. I mean, it is exactly what I am trying to do. I am just not sure their parents will be able to afford it.

Maybe I should send it to the boys as a present. On the anniversary of us working together? Or for Halloween. That would be good for the local press, wouldn't it? It would be a heart-warming story of remembrance. Celebrities are always doing things like that. I sit on the end of the bed and look at the both of them. I am really going to make a great dad one day. I just get kids, and they get me. I leave them to carry on playing. They will be taking turns being me, I am sure. Just need to remind them not to run with knives. Kids are probably doing that all over the world now, pretending to be me.

I go back and undress in Mandy's room. I hang everything back up as I don't want it to get creased. This is a bit mean, me undressing in front of her. They really need a dressing room as I am sure she is anticipating some quality time with me. I put my T-shirt and jeans back on, much to her disappointment, and then leave and go and lie next to Amie. She is really cute. I can see where Mandy gets her looks from, although he really is punching above his weight with her. Maybe that's why his beauty regime means a day in the bathroom? Trying to make himself look more appealing. I don't think he will be able to do enough to keep her. She has a wandering eye. Well, it is always wandering all over me.

"So, Amie, why don't you tell me all your ideas? What have you come up with while I was showing everyone the suit?

"No. I said I have done a family dinner before.

"I am not sure about a family trip. I would need to help you all into the car. It is not a problem, but it would be at night and I am not sure what I am trying to say. This is a launch. You are only the third – third, is that right? Third, or fourth – group of people that are going to be able to claim that you were there at a launch. The birth of a new character, that is." Stars often use the words birth of a new character. I will have to remember that for the film.

"Singing? Yes, you lot are quite famous for that, aren't you? I mean, my nan used to say it was in your blood. She said something to do with your accent made you sound like you were singing to God. Made it sound more powerful, she used to say.

"Ha ha ha! I think it is very cute. That's a shame though, it would be good if you had a piano.

"No, I don't think a recorder gives the real effect. Although I am sure Mandy is really good at it." She certainly knows how to blow. I found that out last night.

"Ha ha ha! I think that is so funny. I used to have bazookas as a kid too. No, it has to be something they haven't seen. Something that gives them the wow factor to the new me. Well, not to me, to the new character. The fans are very demanding, you know. Especially now, with the government and the Blackout. They will be demanding something special.

"Now that would be good. But I am not sure that they would print pictures like that either. What would your husband say if they did? Besides, where would we get a sex swing and a whip?

"Really? In the attic, you say? Do you know, I got that vibe from him? I don't know, something about being in the bath for so long. It is a little weird." I keep saying that. I don't know why. The whole thing is a little weird.

"That's not fair. Everyone's bits shrink when they are in the bath. I am sure it is not his fault.

"Okay, not mine, clearly. But when you are this well-endowed it doesn't change that much. Plus, I am always a little horny. So, I think I have a permanent semi, well, half semi. Is that like a quarter hard-on?

"You are so bad. It can't shrink that much that he looks like a girl.

"Concentrate, Amie, we need something."

I do love her laugh. It has that cute but sexy sound to it.

"Okay." I lean over and kiss her, her demand for a good idea. Plus, I still need to thank her for the loan of the car at some point. I mean, really thank her.

"Yes, I have done a picnic kind of scene. It wasn't a garden one though, more of a beach effect, wasn't it? At night."

"You remember Brighton with Carl?"

"Yes, surely you remember? Under the pier? I thought you were my biggest fan? They were your words."

She told me she was a real fan last night. Or was that just a ploy to get me into bed? Why would she lie about that? I mean, it is not as if this was the first time she had ever heard of me. I am world-famous. I am not sure I like lying here now, not if she is going to try and trick me...

"Oh, shit, you are right! That never came out, did it? They decided to swim to France after I left. Sorry, I forgot all about that." I had forgotten about that.

"You work with so many people you forget sometimes what the world does and doesn't know.

"I am sure they do. All famous people forget about how much work they do. I mean, that Jackie Chan fellow – I was watching something about him on TV yesterday – you know, the one that does all that fighting? He has made over two hundred and fifty movies. Surely he can't remember them all, can he? There are only so many punches you can throw before you forget who you threw one at?" I sometimes forget how many girls I have thrown one at. Not a punch of course. It must be the same for all stars. So many actresses, so little time.

"Really? Is this just an idea to get me to give you more kisses? I kind of like the last idea though, I must admit. It is hardly a chore as well." She will like that.

"You promise?"

I lean in. A full-on make her weak at the knees kiss. I can sense it has been a while. Her tongue is huge. It has clearly had no exercise lately. I mean really swollen. I am not sure I would fit in there.

"Okay, what's the master stroke?"

"That is genius. It is pure genius. It reminds me of the school. You could, you could make it so obvious, but they still wouldn't get it. I assure you, the police in the UK today... well, all I am saying is that if I was American I wouldn't have made it past the first month. Do you know how hard I had to work to become famous? I tell you, it felt like forever."

"Really? You have one more? And it will be really worth it? Like how worth it?"

I can tell by the giggles she is excited about it.

"Okay, but if you are telling me fibs... you won't get the goods. And I know you want the goods, Amie." Even I am nearly laughing at that. I lean in again. Full-on, all-over rubbing experience. She moves like she hasn't been touched in years. Nervousness is pouring out of her. Anticipation and the build-up is everything to these women, isn't it? I think that is why they made up that foreplay thing. They didn't just want one man; they wanted four to like worship them for a while. It must have got lost in translation over the years. All men need is for women to start getting undressed and we are good to go. Not always, and not all the way undressed either.

"So, tell me then?"

"Oh my God! I… I am lost for words. And I can't believe I used the words oh my God. That is worth it. It is so worth it. You are amazing." I jump up.

"I am going to get it right now. I will be back."

I run down the stairs and head out. I am at the local supermarket just at the end of the street within five minutes. It is where they were last night when I met them. I followed them home. They looked like such a fun family. Shit, why did I only just think of that? I should have looked at what shopping they had already. I bet they have some of this stuff. I pull out a trolley. It takes me fifteen minutes to pick up all the items. I love some of this stuff. It reminds me of my nan's house. I head into the house and leave everything on the side in the kitchen. Still nobody has made it downstairs. He must look like a prune by now.

I have plenty of time. I can't set it up till nightfall. The garden isn't really overlooked, but I don't want to risk it. I need to get them all dressed for a summer's day. I know it is nearly winter, but they will look better in summer clothes. Then I need to take a shower before the big unveiling.

"Yes, it is me. Yes, I got everything. That is a really good supermarket. I can see why you shop there." I should really thank her properly. She does deserve it. I run upstairs to fulfil my obligations. I quickly check the bathroom, but it's not like her husband is getting out of the bath anytime soon.

An hour later and she is exhausted. Hell, I am exhausted. I didn't expect her to be that good. I am sure she expected me to be. Been dreaming about it since I first chased her up the stairs.

Okay, I have paid my debt for the car. I paid her twice, just to make sure. Although I am sure she feels as if I paid her multiple times.

It is time to get this show on the road.

"I am sorry I am late, Mandy. I had to shop and then I had to get your brothers' mum and dad ready. You know, I had to help him out of the bath in the end. I think he had been in there so long that he lost the use of his legs."

"Yes they are all dressed and downstairs already. I saved the best for last." Oh, I am going to regret saying that. I just can't stop myself, I see a pretty girl and all the lines just keep pouring out. It is a gift and a curse.

"Yes, in the garden. It looks really nice out there. I have put some Christmas lights up also that I found under the stairs."

I knew that was coming. I knew that is what she was going to ask. The best for last comment works on them every time.

"We don't have a lot of time." I kiss her on the forehead as I continue to dress her. She doesn't like the fact that I am getting her dressed. Not helping me at all, but finally it is done.

"Okay. That sounds like fun." I take her phone and start to take selfies of us on her bed. Her hands are wandering, but I can't blame her. I am sure she is just amazed by me. I mean, I do look amazing. I leave her phone on the side and help her down to the others in the garden. I can hear them. They are all laughing. I guess it's been a good day for them all. In the last twenty-four hours two of them have been laid, the dad has had a day to himself and the boys have played in their room all day. I am sure they are hungry though. Pity I couldn't find a real picnic blanket, but a cover does the same thing. We are only in the garden.

"Okay, there you are. Everyone is together. It is a glorious evening. It is really warm too, which is strange for this time of year. I don't think that it will rain tonight. So, this is perfect."

They all agree with me. It is nice.

"That was actually my next job." I throw Amie a smile.

"Good idea. That's a really good idea. You are full of them today, aren't you?"

I can tell that look in her eyes. A good idea, you say. I really need to be careful what I say to my fans. She thinks she is going to get this, I mean, me, again for every good idea she has. I walk into the front room. There is an old chair there. Looks like it could be something out of that *Game of Thrones* programme. I carry it into the garden and place it on the blanket.

"It's like I am lording it over you all. Like a proper gentleman would. I think that is really the look I am going for. I want to keep it casual but a little regal."

"No, not like that. I am not posh. It's not me, it is about the character. Wait here, I will get the food." I fetch it, tray after tray. That will show them I am not posh. I can serve my fans. There is a lot of food. I think I may have gone a little overboard with this. I needed to be to ensure I got everyone of them though. They are hungry, I can tell. I can't tell if I am though? I did think about it after spending time with Amie. She did taste so good. It has been a long time since I had a real meal.

"So that's the last one. It looks good, doesn't it? I mean, I can't take all the credit. Amie came up with the idea."

They all give her a round of applause. That is a really nice touch. You should always appreciate your mum.

"It's okay, tuck in when you want. We have apples and bananas and cucumber and Dime bars.

"Yes, Dime bars, I was stretching a bit there. My mind went blank."

"Doughnuts? Of course, doughnuts! Why didn't I think of that, Jacob? I should have taken you shopping with me."

"Eggs, fish sticks... not really sure what a fish stick is? It jumped off the shelf at me. A stick of fish, I guess. Doesn't sound like something I really would eat, but I will give anything a go once."

The dad is looking at me now. I need to be careful what I say.

"No, they are not fish fingers. They are still raw. Yes, Jacob, it is a little weird." As I say that I look directly at him. He doesn't notice. But those words keep coming into my head. A little weird. A little weird like spending the day in the bath while a hot guy is walking around your house with your wife and daughter?

"At last, very good, Christopher. They are all the letters of the alphabet. You got it. I am not sure the police or press will, but you are a very bright lad, I can tell."

"Wait a minute, I almost forgot the magic. The one thing about all this that is pure magic." I run into the kitchen and open the microwave. I take out the big bowl, place a ladle into it and bring it out.

"And this, ladies and gentlemen, is the icing on the cake. Alphabeti Spaghetti."

There is another round of applause. It is amazing, simply amazing. I start to take pictures of all of them and then set my phone up on the windowsill for a major selfie of all of us. I run back to my chair and the phone flashes.

"Damn, you are right, Mandy… sorry about the damn thing. I meant darn, boys, I meant darn!" I run back in and fetch my hat. I knew this thing was always going to cause issues. I walk back into the garden. There is another round of applause. I like this family. They have been nothing but supportive from the very beginning. Given the last week I have had, I am so happy about that. I guess they have missed their Edmund fix in the news, and this is a real treat for them. Probably dine out on this for years. Especially being the first after the Blackout to make the press.

I go to my phone and set it off again. I run back to the chair and lie back in it, putting one leg on the arm and tilting my hat with my cane. Flash! That was a really cool photo. I think I will make that my profile pic for the new guy. I sit and watch them for a while as they all have fun. Smiling, laughing and happy, just how a family should be.

"I am going to have to love you and leave you now, guys."

That is a very disappointing groan from all of them.

"I will try. You are not the easiest place to get to, but I must say, one of the best families that I have ever worked with. I mean that." I actually do. It feels like being back to my best.

But I am not sure I will ever come back here. I have so much to do.

"Yes, I promise I will try." I didn't mean that. I am probably not going to try.

"Still it's been amazing. It has been really amazing."

"That is so generous, thank you so much. If you are sure you don't need it?"

"Okay, it will be just for a few days. I am sure wherever I leave it, they will bring it back to you."

"Yes, I will be heading back east. Although I must say, everywhere is really east of here."

They smile at that.

"Unless I want to go for a swim?"

That got a chuckle from the boys.

I get up and wave goodbye. I think both of the girls were hoping for a little more. I can see the disappointment in their eyes. I thought about it, but I could hardly go and kiss them there. Not in front of each other. Besides, they have both had their turn with me. Amie had two turns. I leave by the front door. My hat is still on head and cane in hand. I throw my bag in the car and then stand and look at the street.

This is the beginning. It took me a while to work it out, work out what would get the press back on side. What would delight my fans, what would excite my fans so much they will be looking for me, hoping for me, waiting for me at every turn. This is it, the whole country is begging for it I can feel it. I have that feeling, that feeling that something great is about to happen. That the whole world is on tenterhooks in anticipation for my return. I can actually feel the blood boiling under my skin as the excitement builds.

A guy walking his dog walks past me. He gives me a little glance, probably too scared to look straight at me.

"Good evening." It is always good to be polite to potential fans.

"Good evening, sir."

He called me sir. It must be the top hat. It does make me feel a bit like a sir for sure. Either that or he can tell. He can tell by the way I am standing here that they are probably going to knight me for this. Lord Edmund Carson is a national treasure. That has a ring to it.

I am going to enjoy this, enjoy every minute. There is no turning back. With twenty-five in front of me. There is no turning back. I feel like I have stepped up in class, but maybe some of that is the suit. I guess you could say I have escalated to upper class. The press will love that. Edmund Carson is on another level.

It is time to go, I don't want that guy fetching his camera and running back for a selfie. Well not yet, the press can have their field day tomorrow with the return. The return of Edmund Carson the Alphabet Killer.

Aberystwyth, done.

Chapter 2

Two days. It's been two fucking days. How is this even possible? How is it that they can still blackout my work? This was a launch. They have to want to report a launch. Not even the local press reported anything. They were a popular, fun family. I am sure they would have had friends who would have visited them by now. They would have been on the phone the moment I left to tell their friends I had visited. Word of mouth would have alone done the job for me. Let's face it, there is little else going on out there.

I make people famous. It is what I do. There was even a witness as I left the house. He called me sir. He would have recognised me and run straight to the press. What else is there to report in Wales? A sing-song in the local church? A leek-growing competition. There is that and rugby. It is all they have. It is why I chose it. Bring fame to the town and the country. That is the type of star I am.

I switch off the TV. I am fed up with TV. All they do is report politics, or who is in and who is out. Fame is so fickle. I am not sure what fickle means, but I know that is what they say. Why don't they report the real news? Like me. I am real news. I am the stories people want to listen to. I am the story maker. I like that, the story maker. The maker of stories! That is who I really am.

What is it going to take to get rid of this Blackout?

I hate that Sarah woman. How would they even know that it is me? How do they know that I worked with them? It could have been anyone? They are not having a worldwide Blackout on news. It is just an Edmund Carson Blackout. I mean, it's not as if…

You fucking moron, Edmund!

Of course they know it is you. You are the only true professional working at the moment. You practically left your signature on their door.

Fuck!

Mandy's phone. I took fucking pictures.

Why did I stage the scene? This was supposed to be someone new. When the ONE and Father Harry launched, I didn't tell people it was me.

That is my problem, I get carried away. I need to stop working for the people. It needs to be more about me. I am such a giver. I give too much. I mean, I know I am their hero. I am the only artist that is trying to do the best for all of us. Fans and the artist. It is time to stop, time to be more about my needs. It can only be about me from now on.

The Alphabet Killer. Killers? No. Killer. It can't be you, Edmund.

Alphabet Killer, is that the right name? It's not a silly name, is it? I can call myself that? The ONE is the ONE, Father Harry is Father Harry. Do I need a name as well as a title? Like movie stars do?

Edmund Carson is the Alphabet Killer?

Edmund Carson is Father Harry?

Edmund Carson is the ONE.

Edmund Carson is the ONE, the ONLY.

No, it is fine, the press will get there in the end. Maybe I should leave a few signs around the place. Just to help them on their way. Not now, maybe sometime around G or K. Some graffiti. I could have been an artist. Hey, graffiti, that starts with a G. That is perfect. If they dare to black me out then, it is almost telling the world that it was me. My fans will then be up in arms about the whole thing, even more than they are already. The pressure of the country will sway the newspapers, I am sure of it.

I need a plan though, another plan. A better plan that makes sure I, well, not me, but the work, hits the news. I need some randomness to my actions. I need to stop trying to be so creative. It's about the work first. I need something that will have to be reported, but also it needs to not look like my work. The press won't think it is me if I don't work, work with them.

It will be hard for them, I know, but they will understand. When I have retired, I will make sure the books and the movies all ensure that everyone gets their fifteen minutes of fame. I wonder why they always say fifteen minutes. It seems a little excessive for normal people to me. Maybe they should all get their ten minutes of fame. Some, five at best. Then there is more for people like me.

I lie back on the hotel bed. This bed is hard. Hotel beds at airports are always hard. I guess they don't care how comfortable it is because you aren't staying long. Nobody ever notices you here though. They must have millions of people coming through every week and always a new face. Especially now I have mastered an accent. I mean, I could be South African. They really believed it downstairs. As long as you are paying cash nobody ever asks questions. I do need to get some more money. I need to go back to London at some point. I should really go down and visit Miss Walker as well. I can't make her come to me all the time. I take out my phone and text her. Not that she remembers to reply. It just helps her know I am thinking about her. It is a school night so she is probably still marking results for the girls.

I miss the girls. That was a fun night. I still owe Seventeen. I should really go back and pay my debts. I don't want to get a reputation of not fulfilling them. It is funny how she has always stuck with me. Both of them have really, Seventeen and Seven. Seventeen the most. There is just something about that girl.

I get dressed for work. I am getting quite good at the cravat thing. As long as I carry the hat in my bag and wear my coat nobody really notices. I head out of the hotel and towards the train station. I need to head into the centre of town. There is bound to be something good to do there. Maybe even someone good to do. It is supposed to be the country's second city. I am sure I read that on a sign on the way in.

I head into the station and to the kiosk – closed. How is it closed? It's like seven p.m. The trains run till at least midnight. I look around. There isn't even a man to help. There is just a self-service machine. Everything is self-service nowadays! It's like technology is replacing people everywhere we look. I go to the machine. After three attempts I manage to get a ticket. I swear they do it on purpose. They don't pay for someone else's time, they just expect you to use yours. It is like supermarkets asking you to scan your own food. What is that about? How fucking lazy. Profit, I am sure. All about profit. The rich get richer. We need to stop doing that.

The ticket I bought isn't even the one I wanted but it will do. I am not going all the way to Northampton. I just wanted to get into town. I get on the train. I think there are two choices: New Street or Snow Hill. They seem to be the ones in the centre. Why would you have some place called Snow Hill in the middle of town though? New Street sounds like somewhere lots of people would go. I need somewhere that is only semi-busy if I am going to work. I head to Snow Hill. What do people do in Snow Hill if it is not snowing? Surely eleven months of the year it is just called Hill?

I love trains. I think it is the motion and the rocking. It is almost as if it is building you up to something. I love to work on the train. I can't believe how much I have missed it. I look around the carriage. I can feel the ONE going through my head. I can feel like he feels. He really wants to come out to work. He is not retired. I know I said that back with Al at the hotel. He is not ready to retire. Like me.

The feeling must be a side effect of having so many famous characters inside me. They are so close to you at all times. I know exactly what he would be thinking. I know what he would do next. He would dive forward and cut the lady's throat next to me. She looks miserable. It would be doing her a favour. She must be at least forty. That's a good age to get to. Then the two guys to the left of me would start to panic. The ONE would take them both out with two swift blows; one to the side of the neck and the other dragged straight across his throat, almost taking his head off.

I can feel the knife in my hand as he is trying to show me the way.

I can feel the moment when you know not to go too deep. A really sharp knife would do that. Cut really deep into the bone. The blood would be strong by now. Only takes a moment to get that smell in the nostrils.

I reach behind my back with my hand. I should be doing this. I owe it to the ONE. It was him who launched me. It was his fame that made all of this possible. My knife isn't there. I hunt around. It must be there. It is not. I pull my hand back. I am sure I bought it. I would never leave home without it. Wait, it's in my inside pocket. The Alphabet Killer is more professional. I read somewhere that all gentlemen carry a knife and a handkerchief at all times. I can feel it through my coat. It almost feels like it is burning against my shirt. I am sure the knife is calling me. If I undo the coat people will see the cravat. They will know. I should do it though. I should. It wouldn't take long. These three will be down in less than two minutes. That just leaves the two girls at the front of the train. The blonde would have to go first. She has nothing to offer me. Blondes never do.

I wonder if I could pull the emergency cord. There is no way to get between the carriages. It would give me a little more time with the other girl. She is a bit on the older side. She must be nearly thirty, but a doable thirty. She has that Nigella look, the TV cook. Older, fuller, but hot as fuck. I don't like chocolate, but I would let her drizzle it all over me and lick it off. The more I look at her, the hotter she is getting. I think it is Nigella. You know she would taste so good. Sweet and rich! I can smell the blood in my nose now. I have to do this. Her blood would taste amazing, I can tell. I bet everything about her tastes so good. Everything.

I could lay her on the floor of the train. Undress her slowly as she shivers with expectation. Then we would get to it. She would know what to do. I can tell she would know what to do. She is experienced. She would know how to do me, slowly at first and then hard. She would like it hard. She could manage to take all of me, easily. Take me in all kind of ways. I am looking directly at her now. She turns and smiles at me. She knows. She knows who I am and she wants this to happen. I check the cabin again. I can do this even in my suit. I can do this.

"The next stop is Snow Hill." The voice comes out of the monitor.

Shit! The train starts to slow down. We are here. They are all standing at the door now and about to get off. As we arrive at the platform I can see that the platform is full. There are a lot of people here. I am not going to be able to do anything now. I wasted too much time thinking about it. Too much time thinking about Nigella. I need to be more of a man of action.

I should just follow her. Let her live out the fantasy she has been having about me all the time she has been sitting on the train. It is the least I can do for her, for my fans. Maybe leave her covered in chocolate and cream…

What the fuck, Edmund? Concentrate!

The Alphabet Killer. The ONE is not making his return tonight. This is a relaunch of the Alphabet Killer.

She gets off the train with the blonde girl and walks into the distance. I should have done her. I don't like unfinished business. I head out of the building. It doesn't feel like a station. This isn't even a hill. It's a kind of square, and it is flat. Unless this is the top of the hill and I can't see it? There are buildings to the left and the right and then it is out to the road. The place is full of shops.

What do you find when you walk out into Snow Hill? About two hundred people fire-walking. Fire-walking in Snow Hill, with no snow? Maybe they thought there would be snow too? That would make sense, somewhere to put their feet down afterwards. Although it is barely October?

I walk over to the crowd as they all cheer at each other. There is a long queue of people lining up to do this. They must be mad. Who would want to walk on hot coals? I am sure that is some kind of torture, isn't it? That is what you do to prisoners.

I look up at the banners. It is all in aid of charity, a children's charity. They are calling all the heroes. I am sure that was a song that my dad used to play. Be a hero and raise money for charity. Explains why a lot of people are dressed in fancy dress costumes I guess.

I am a hero. I wonder if anyone is dressed as me. That would be so cool. This is something I could do. There are a lot of people taking photos. Wait, they even have some real press. You can tell by the long lenses on the cameras. They are here to cover the event. This charity must be some kind of big deal. They could get a picture of me without even knowing it is me? Most of the people are dressed as superheroes as well so I won't stand out. Yes, I should do this. I mean, the Alphabet

Killer should work here. Not with the children, that's just sick, but with someone, and not stage it. Whatever happens, it has to look random.

Children's Charity Chaos. Now that is a headline, maybe with the death of Wonder Woman? Catwoman? That hot black outfit. Haley Berry, she would so get it. I need to squeeze her into my top five just in case Miss Walker finds out when I do her.

Tragedy at charity fundraiser as Batman bites the dust! "Tragedy", another record off of my dad's playlist! These are the sort of things that will make the headline news.

Is it the wrong headline news though? Doesn't paint me in a good light, does it? I don't know why, but the press didn't like the time I spent with Tim and Verna. We had a perfectly nice evening. I helped them work through one of their fantasies and then I cooked. I don't see what their problem was. When I left them they were cuddled up on the sofa reading a book to the little one. Little Edmund Carson.

That was the last news they reported on me. It wasn't good. If I work here they will make me sound... What the fuck am I worried about? They won't make me sound anything. That's the whole point. This isn't me.

It's the Alphabet Killer. As long as I don't work, work with them, they won't know it was me. This could be...

"Hello, sir, could I interest you in donating, or maybe even taking part in our fundraising event?"

I turn to see a guy looking straight at me. He is dressed as Batman, the old Batman, not the new modern Batman. To be fair, he doesn't have the body for the new one. Hardly a six pack under there.

He may be Batman, but he is smiling like the Joker. How many teeth does he actually have? I have never seen a smile so wide. They all look pretty crammed in his mouth. I reach into my inside pocket and pull out my wallet. I drop a few hundred into his bucket. That should make him happy, well, happier, if that is even possible. He doesn't seem to stop smiling. I think he is on something. They say drugs make your teeth itchy. That is why his gums won't go anywhere near them.

"That is so generous, sir. That's beyond generous. Why don't you come and do the walk, sir? All of this is in aid of the children and it's people like you that make all of this possible. You help our little stars shine bright, sir." I like being called sir, and did he call me a star? Maybe he has recognised me. I am sure he knows what a celebrity can do for a charity. I could really get used to being called sir and a star. He did call me a star, right? Stars like me make things shine bright. He said something like that. He is looking at me again. He is far too happy. Nobody smiles that much. Yes, he is definitely on something. Oh, yes, doing the walk, he asked me to do the walk.

"I am not sure, walking on hot coals and all that. Can you tell me a bit about the charity first?" I can't make it seem like I am too interested in just the press. If they discover who I am this could turn into a real circus. It will be good for him though. Probably get some big donations from my fans.

"Okay, sir, it will be my pleasure. We work with disabled and underprivileged children throughout the UK, while trying to raise as much money as possible nationwide. We do various sponsored events such as this and others. For instance, we have climbed mountains, walked the Great Wall of China and cycled the length of the UK in the past few years, to name a few. The showpiece though is an end-of-year Celebrity Ball where all the proceeds go to the charity." Did he say celebrity ball? He knows the words to get me interested.

Nobody is that happy though, I don't think I can get past that. How can he talk and smile so much at the same time? I am fixated with his teeth, this guy's teeth, he keeps showing them to me. Maybe he is a vampire or something. Maybe he should have thought about that before picking his costume.

"When you say Celebrity Ball…?" It has just occurred to me. There are celebrities and celebrities. It depends which list you are on. The word is so over used today.

"Yes, sir, Celebrity Ball. Over the last few years, Jessie J, The Jacksons, Tom Jones, James Cordon, David Walliams, just to name a few." As I thought, it is the nearly A-listers. Although my nan would say that Tom Jones is an A-lister. She had a thing for him. I think they were the same age.

"That sounds amazing." It doesn't really.

"It must be a very rewarding job?" They say that about poorly paid jobs, don't they? To make up for the money I guess. Sounds like I am interviewing him. I would make a great reporter. Is there nothing I can't do?

"We try to do as much as we can, sir. It is for an amazing cause. Hopefully we will raise circa four million throughout this year, but we are always striving to do better."

Four million! People give this guy four million a year? No wonder he looks like he is hopped up on something. Maybe I should start a charity. Save me going back to London to get some more money. Four million pounds! That is insane, and he just goes and gives it all away? What is up with him?

"Tell me about the name. Why is that the charity name?"

"It is the family name, sir. Simple as that. It is named after the family who run the charity." Somebody taps him on the shoulder and gives him a nod.

"I will be back in one second, sir." He disappears and gets the photographers together for a picture of someone walking on the coals. He must be important as they are all clapping and cheering as he does. Once the photos are done he heads back to me.

"Sorry about that, sir. He is one of the bosses and I needed to ensure that he had his picture taken. We have quite a lot of press for this event." That is the magic word. Press! I am surprised not one of them has noticed me by now. The world is looking for me. Can you imagine how they are going to feel tomorrow when they exit their darkrooms with pictures of me? I don't even know if they have darkrooms any more. I am sure they do. Real photographers don't just use this digital stuff?

He is looking at me again. Oh yeah, I need to stop having a conversation in my head. I have to play the words through though. You have to be careful as one wrong word could lose you a million fans overnight. Imagine if they thought I was sexist or racist. That would be horrible. These people must think I am rude. I am never rude. I always try to be polite to everyone... I am still doing it. What is wrong with me today?

"Not a problem at all. And he is one of the bosses, the bosses of the charity?"

"He is one of the major contributors, and family, sir."

"He must be a very wealthy man if he is a major contributor and you raise four million a year?" I don't think I can get over that. Four million. Is that normal for a charity? I mean, they do those things on TV, but they have lots of stars and stuff. This is in Snow Hill on a school night? And I am pretty sure that I am the only real celebrity here.

"He is, sir. He is a self-made millionaire. He works really hard."

"He is a self-made millionaire because of the charity?" I knew they wouldn't be giving all the money away. These charities never do.

"Oh, no, sir. His fortune comes from food mainly. If you have eaten today, he is probably responsible for whatever it is that you have eaten." I haven't eaten today. Well, other than some dodgy scrambled egg and bacon for room service. I really need to remember to do that more.

"He can't be responsible for all of it?"

"I wouldn't put it past him, sir. Restaurants, pizza, chicken, beef… Trust me, you would not go a day without eating something he has made. He is quite the food celebrity." Oh, a food celebrity. There are so many of them. Not a real celebrity. Not even a celebrity cook. He probably has one of those reality TV shows though. Everyone has them nowadays. Maybe I should have one? Maybe I should hire a camera crew to follow me around. That will get rid of the old Blackout. I can make my own TV show and I am sure I can get people to subscribe to it. I could have my own TV channel. They can't stop me then as it would be the people's money they would be wasting.

Self-made millionaire though. I bet that is how he made his money. A reality TV show, I can see him on the big screen. Minted and celebrity at a charity do, every headline you can think of right there. It is beginning to feel like getting off at Snow Hill was fate.

"Where is he going?" I watch as the guy disappears into a building to the right of me.

"Oh, just to have his feet looked over. We are doing that with all the walkers. We don't want any of you to hurt yourselves." He is giving me that look as if to say I know you really want to do this, sir. Notice how I said any of you? Yes he wants me to do this.

I take out my wallet and drop another two hundred into his bucket.

"Seems like a very worthwhile cause. If I do this, I need to get going as soon as possible as I have a meeting in thirty minutes across town."

He smiles again at me and escorts me over to the front of the queue. Money always talks. There is another guy there giving me and a few others a pep talk about it not hurting. I am half listening and half watching the door on the right as I take my shoes off. I need to get into there. He is a big enough event to get me on the front page. The front page of all the newspapers.

"I think we are ready, sir. Off you go then." He has finished his pep talk and is now looking directly at me. I stand looking at the hot coals. Suddenly I am aware that I have to do this in order to get through that door. I have to walk on hot coals. What was I thinking?

I was thinking that I need The Alphabet Killer to become famous. I look back at the hot coals. There is something wrong with me, isn't there? Who would walk over hot coals for their job? Who does that? I bet none of these idiots have done it? Well, some of them have. But that is for fun. I look up at the crowd as it starts to chant. I just wish they all knew my name. That would be so much better. They really do support this charity. The noise is great. It is really building up my confidence. It makes me want to do it. But I am not insane. Think I will just put my shoes back on. There are more fish in the sea. My nan used to say that. That works with people to work with as well as girls, doesn't it? Although some fish are better than others.

It can't be?

I am sure that's her. I am sure I saw Miss Walker in the crowd. Long dark hair. It is her. I would know her anywhere. I would know that figure anywhere. I start to walk towards her. She has the black dress on and everything, which means I know exactly what she has under there. I have missed that sight. Stunning! She is only here for one thing and we both know what it is. She must have read my text. How did she get here so fast? She must have been close. She must have been in town? The crowd continues to chant at me. I like that. I would like it more if they called out Edmund. I mean, the Alphabet Killer. She would like that too. To hear her boyfriend's name chanted in front of a crowd. Wait, I've lost her. She was just there. She was just right there. I am looking everywhere for her, and I can't see her now. That was her, wasn't it? She wouldn't just wander off? I can't see a black dress in the crowd anywhere now?

It can't have been her. It must have been someone that looked like her. I think it was just a dark-haired girl in a black dress, running for the train, no doubt. The smiley man is tapping me on the shoulder again.

"Well done, sir. Let me take you through to where the doctors are waiting." Wait, what? What is he talking about? I look back. I did it! I just walked across the coals and didn't even notice. How is it possible? I mean, I know I am hard, but I didn't feel anything on my feet. I still don't feel anything now? He ushers me into a reception area. The rich guy is still sitting there with someone washing his feet. I sit next to him. A lady comes over and starts to do the same to me. He smiles at me. I smile back. It's a bit awkward to just sit here smiling at each other. But the silence continues. I don't like his silence. Something is going on in his head, I can tell. He has that I am about to bite your head off look in his eyes. I have seen that before. The woman finishes with his feet and puts his shoes on. He walks over to the bathroom opposite and goes in. I rush the girl on with mine and follow him. As I walk in he is washing his hands and face at the sink.

Before he looks up I have buried the knife deep into his neck. He fits as I drag it across his throat. I pull him away from the sink as there is too much noise and drag him back into one of the cubicles behind me. As I do, I place him on the toilet seat. He is done. There is an obvious scene that springs to mind. That is my problem right there! I am a director so everything I do feels like a scene in a movie. I could... No, I should just leave now.

Don't do anything with him. The Alphabet Killer doesn't care about his fans. For the Alphabet Killer, it is all about the work.

"Sir, it is me Gareth. I just wanted to ensure that you had my card. And I was just checking you hadn't left without all our details for further events? You would really love our Ball, sir, it is only a few weeks away."

Fuck!

Happy is back. Why is he following me in here? Who does that? This guy must be the salesman of the year for his charity. I can hear the door close. He is in here. He is actually waiting for me to finish on the toilet. I can feel him breathing. Now I can hear him moving. I wait at the side of the cubicle as I hear the footsteps get closer. As I see the glimpse of his shoe I jump out. I plunge my knife into him in the stomach three times and then straight into his neck as he slumps backwards. There is no fitting. He is out cold on the floor. That was fast. So fast he didn't make a sound. I will have to remember that move. Works well. I walk up to the sink and wash my hands and face. How didn't he notice the blood on the sink as he walked in? It must be the drugs he is on. He needs to pay more attention to his surroundings in future.

I go back to Gareth. Even as he lies there, there is still a fucking smile on that guy's face. Maybe it was me. Maybe I was so fast he didn't even have the chance to stop smiling. I am good. I don't have the time to sit around and find out why he is always smiling though. There are too many people. I pick up his business card.

I should work with charities more. I bet it is so rewarding. I don't think I have ever been to a real ball, so that could be entertaining. I leave the bathroom and head back into the street. They are still cheering at everyone as people continue to walk over the hot coals. They must be mad. I slip back into the train station and back to the hotel.

I am in my room in less than two hours. I never understood these people that work eight to ten hours a day. If you can do your job in two, why bother? I lie back on the bed. I can't stop thinking about the girl on the train. Maybe I should get the ONE to make a comeback? Soon! That excited me. I think I was born to do the girl on the train.

It is popular. People like it. But it's the old me. The new me is going to be bigger. Bigger and better than just a girl on a train. The Alphabet Killer – now that's a headline. That's a worldwide phenomenon.

The sound of the TV wakes me up. I must have been more tired than I remember. It's still on the movie channel. I check the time. It's three minutes past seven, Nan-time. That gives me the warm feeling that I am still close to her. I can't believe I slept that long. I click the TV channel over to BBC One. The news will definitely be on.

"Local billionaire business tycoon found dead in offices." I jump off the bed at the news.

Yes, yes, fucking yes! Wait, he is a billionaire now? Finally, a news story worth watching! I sit on the edge of the bed and watch as the news unfolds. Gareth wasn't kidding. This guy kept this whole country in food.

Shit, what if people starve now? And that is all to do with me. What happens if there is no food in the supermarket? What if people are starving in the streets? What happens then?

Do those numbers count to me? How would we calculate them? Will the government keep a record of people that starve to death? They don't seem to care about the ones on the street now. How will they know the difference and how will I get acknowledged for it? They don't even know it was me? Are you fucking kidding me, he did that too? What if there is no more finger-licking chicken? My fans won't be happy with that. That will really piss them off. He fucking does pizza! I love pizza. I think I may have fucked up. I need to research these people better. I may have upset half the population in the matter of two hours. The press will have another field day with me.

The police are looking for a man in a long black coat. They didn't see the costume. What is the point of the costume if I am not going to be seen in it? Now I am not sure if I like this or not. It is one thing to be noticed, but you have to be noticed for the right reasons. It is the whole point I got this morning suit. I am not sure why it is called that though? Is that because people are mourning when they wear one? I didn't know you mourned at a wedding? Maybe you do. That's a little weird? What the... a little weird? Again? It's like I have a new catchphrase. Well, the Alphabet Killer does. Why is it not just called top hat and tails? I am sure that's what my dad used to call it.

At least I am on there. I have returned to TV. I am sure I will be back over all the papers tomorrow. They wouldn't have had time last night. But I am back, back in the public eye. I lie back on the bed. I think the smile on my face is one I stole from Gareth. It is hurting my mouth.

Admittedly, they don't know it is me, not yet. But they will and, I am back! That is the main thing. The Blackout of Edmund Carson is no more!

Birmingham and this fucking blackout. Done!

Chapter 3

That was easier than I thought. I don't know why I was nervous about it.

It is my money. I honestly thought that they would be keeping an eye out for my money. Thinking I would be coming back for it at some point. These places are discreet though. That's why they are private security boxes. They must have some famous people's money in there. Probably ones that don't want to pay tax. Not that I have ever paid tax, but I know that it is bad. The taxman is always after your money. I will have to get one of those offshore accounts when this is all done. So I can keep all my royalties for the films and the books. I am sure that my dad used to say that would be the best way to deal with it. Yes, the government would be after my millions too. Probably after this. Even though my dad must have already paid tax on it once? How does that work? How many times do they want the tax? If my dad paid tax on it at work and then you have to pay tax on stuff you buy and if someone leaves you money you have to pay tax again?

Melanie would have probably sorted it all for me already. Laundered it through one of those offshore accounts to try and impress me. I did mean to ask her that when we were at the bank. She did look very trusting as well as hot as fuck. Yes, she would have sorted everything. She would have told the government everything that they needed to know. Well, not everything. I think there was one night that she would want to forget. Forget is a little strong. One night where she would have liked to have done better, shall we say! It was with me after all.

I haven't thought about her in such a long time. She was hot. The more I think about it, the more I am convinced she was just having a bad night. May have just been nerves. Nerves of knowing who she was about to sleep with, it can happen to anyone. It was me. Fantasy to reality must be hard for normal people. I suppose I just have to get used to that.

I really should go back and see her at some point, see if she can do something about the rest of my money. Maybe give her another chance to prove herself. She would appreciate that.

I have left so much money in the bank for my retirement. I should really be investing it now. Investing it in either my movie or property. A little nest egg or whatever they call it. Love nest that was it, not nest egg. Somewhere we can stay when I retire. Needs to have a lot of land and security as fans will be trying to get in to see me all the time. Probably need to get some security to look after us as well, especially for Miss Walker. The women aren't going to like her. The jealousy will be massive and worldwide. She needs to expect stalkers and hate mail. I need to prepare her for that. I need to make sure I even prepare her for the fantasy women. The ones that will be making stories up about me. The ones like that Gail girl. Who believed they met me. Believe we are in love or had sex. There will be thousands of them living in a made-up world where they are Edmund Carson's girlfriend. It is going to be hard for her to deal with.

Something about carrying a bag full of money though makes you feel nervous. Nobody knows the fact I have a big bag of money. It could be washing, for all they know. It could be washing, so why I am nervous about it? What if the security box people tip someone off though? They would do that. That is in a lot of films, so it must happen. I should really stash it before I head off. It will not be a good thing if I lose it en route. I go back to the car and then head back to Hendon and pull into the car park. Parking in a shopping centre is always a good idea. Anywhere where there are a lot of people around. Nobody is looking for me in a crowd. I then head back out and onto the northern line. Out of all the Tube lines I think this is my favourite. I guess it is where it all began for me. Nostalgic I think the word is.

It always takes me to my favourite place in London too. I feel I have a relationship with the people there, kindred spirits, I think my nan use to call them. A little… Wait, is that what this is all about? Am I starting to think I am a little weird? That is why it is in my head all the time? Or is it that the Alphabet Killer is a little weird? Yes, that's what it is. That is his thing. He is not like the others. It is my subconscious creating the new character. I guess all great actors have this. It has created a quirkiness. I need to be a little weird. The difference with the Alphabet Killer is that he can be whoever he wants to be. Or he can be everyone. A was a little Edmund. B was completely random. I have to be a little weird. He has to be a little bit weird to keep them on their toes.

I am amazing. I am an amazing writer, director, visionary. Visionary, that is a good word for me. My mind is always working. Unique that is a better word. There must be more unique people there, in Camden, than anywhere else in London. And I am one of them. That is why I feel at home there.

At last, I am in Camden. I head up the escalators and out onto the street. There is always someone preaching the good word of the Bible as soon as you get off the Tube here. Maybe I should start writing my book. I keep saying I am going to. I am on fire lately. They will be preaching the word of Edmund soon. I really need to start thinking about that. Come up with some profound stuff. That will get people to stop and put a fiver in his donation tin.

A real book to read from! Not with all the numbers, Corinthians 11:14, Peter 5:8, what is that all about? I turn right and head towards the market.

I love the market here. Both markets: the normal one and the horse one. That's what makes this place special. That and the people! That's what makes it its own town. I am sure it is its own town. I am not cheating by being here, am I? Camden Town is what it says on the map. I am not really sure of the difference between a town and a city? The press will still get it though. They will be looking for it. They are on tenterhooks, I know it. They must have been on tenterhooks since the day I started work.

As soon as I reach the first market on the right I remember why I love it here. There is no Blackout of Edmund Carson in Camden. In fact, since my last visit the place has got more Edmund Carson. Walking through the stalls there must be twenty different T-shirts now with me on them. They still have "You are the ONE" T-shirts. "Father Harry will take your confession now" has to be my new favourite. And, "Go with God, I will help you", that's a great quote. I don't remember saying it, but I must have so they printed it on a T-shirt.

I stand corrected. They do have a Blackout, "Shh there is a Blackout" "The Blackout is coming" "Hashtag Blackout". I love that they have Blackout T-shirts too. The press have to see how much the world loves me? They must make a mint out of me here. It is all good branding for the future, for future sales of the books, and TV and movie rights. It is all good branding. They are keeping me in the public eye which is more than the press have done. I think they deserve anything they make. They are my people. My fans.

When the time comes, and I live here with Miss Walker, I won't be after a cut. I may even pop down and sign some every now and again for them. That will fetch a pretty penny for them. Become collector items, no doubt.

I come out of the market. I cross the road and head towards the horse market. It is starting to get dark and I could do with some food. They always have great street food there. I stop on my way at the tattoo parlour where I nearly had my first tattoo. They actually have tattoos of me, well, "the ONE" and "Father Harry", in the window. People are actually inking me onto their bodies. That is amazing. That is just amazing. I should go in and get it done. I mean, if I am ever going to have a tattoo what would be more important than to have it of myself?

I watch through the window as a blonde lady is sat in the chair. It looks like she is having a love heart on her arm. She is crying. I am sure it doesn't hurt that much that you have to cry? It is just a tattoo. I watch a little longer. No, she is definitely not enjoying that.

Maybe I will have one later. Not just now. I am still hungry, I need to have some food first.

I carry on walking to the market. I head to the pizza man. It has been ages since I had a pizza. The Mexican is great here too. I always think about trying the other stuff but am never sure. It does look and smell amazing. They always say Indian stuff is far too hot. I eat the pizza and wash it down with a bottle of Coke. I really need some good food.

It has been far too long since I have cooked with company. That is a good line. I need to remember that. I may even drop that line to one of the people in the market so they can make a T-shirt. Edmund Carson cooks with company. It would make a great cookbook too. That is what all famous people do now, isn't it? Actors, presenters and even DJs sell cookbooks now. Can you imagine the Edmund Carson's cheese and onion sandwich? My liver and onions, they would be a worldwide hit. I could get myself some of those Michelin stars. Maybe a dozen of them.

I walk around the horse market, looking at all the weird and wonderful knick-knacks that they have on show while waiting for dusk to settle. Knick-knacks, now that is my nan's saying. She loved her knick-knacks. Most of it just looks like stuff nobody else would want to buy, but she loved collecting it.

The last time I was here, when I crossed the bridge, I remember looking down at the canal and there was a light mist over it. I remember thinking it looked very Jack. I am hoping for the same again. As soon as it is time I head back to the bridge.

It is perfect. I knew it would be. This is so a scene. I should start to take photos of these scenes for the movie. For the storyboard or whatever it is called that they do. I need one of those lens things that directors look through.

I head down. It is too busy here. You can hear so many people talking in the bars and heading towards the comedy club. I carry on walking until I find a quieter spot. I take my hat out of the bag and put it on. It's dark and misty enough that if I stand off against the wall nobody will see me. I do just that. This is exactly how Jack must have felt as he stood waiting for Sukey or Jenny. It is so exciting. He would be honoured to see the world number one emulating him. I should be filming this.

I can almost feel the adrenalin pumping through my veins. I wait. I wait some more. Okay, it must have been what, like fifteen minutes and nobody is walking up here. Surely people walk up the canal of a night-time? I am all dressed up and everything. I wonder if Jack had to wait or if he had someone waiting for him. He was supposed to be royalty. That is what some of the reports say. He was royalty or a doctor. If he was royalty though, surely he would have got one of his staff to fetch people to work with. Then his staff could place them back at the scene.

He would have had an assistant, an assistant to do all the work? Probably paid them two bits, or a shilling to do it.

Wait, I have money. Maybe that is what I need, an assistant. I should place an advertisement in the local shop or something. If I am going to find one, I am going to find one here. It would need to be worded properly. I can't just say

Edmund Carson needs an assistant. The queue would be around the block. Local gentleman requires a squire. Yes, squire for world-renowned works of art and general assistance. Something like that should get them interested. That sounds really good. I would apply for that.

Fuck!

I nearly missed that. Someone is coming. Sounds like two girls. They are close. I stand as close to the wall as I possibly can. I can't breathe. I am Jack. Yes, it is two girls. I can see them giggling to themselves as they walk. It sounds like they have been out drinking.

I need to time this just right. I will be able to take both at the same time. I watch as they get closer. I am shaking with excitement. It must be the Jack thing. It has me so excited. I pounce from the shadows. Exactly like Jack would have. I grab the first girl by the arm. She turns and screams. As she does she knocks the second into the canal. They are both screaming now. The one whose arm I tried to pull away, I plunge my knife into her neck. I dig it in deep. The blood is oozing out of her. That smell, oh, that smell in this place, dressed as I am. It is the best, really the best. I can feel my eyes widen. It's like taking a breath for the first time. I pull her close as the blood continues to ooze. I can feel it dripping into my mouth. I take a huge lick. That is so good. That is just so fucking good. I haven't had that taste for days. The warm sweet, almost juicy…

Oh my God, is that woman ever going to shut up?

"I can't swim! I can't swim!"

I am having a moment here and you have totally ruined it. I take one more lick and then leave her in the shadows. I go back to the canal.

"Hi! I am here to help. Where are you? I can't see you?"

"Over here! Over here! I think my friend was attacked."

"Okay, I am coming to get you. We can help your friend too." I can hear that she has moved about ten metres south from where we stood. As I get closer I take the hat off and place it on the ground. That way I can lean over and help her out.

"Give me your hand."

She does and I pull her up and on to the bank.

"Oh my God, thank you! My friend, she is down there. Someone came out of the shadows at us. I think it was him. He had a knife. He had a hat. I think it was him, he—"

I lean over and cut her throat as she sits there.

"It was me. Who else would it be?" I push her back into the canal. I swear, some people just don't know when to stop talking. I was really enjoying that. I go back to the girl I left in the shadows. I lift her up to try and recreate the moment. But it is no good. The moment has gone. She ruined it. I lay her back down on the floor. It is good she is only wearing a flimsy dress. Given the time of year I don't understand why young girls don't dress more appropriately? I cut it open and then cut her open. I take out as much of her insides as I possibly can and place them in my bag. That is what Jack would have done. I use the staple gun I have in my bag to close her back up. It is times like this when I wish I knew how to sew better. I mean, I know how to sew, my nan taught me. But I can't do it in a hurry. I lay her out. They can't mistake the similarities now.

Can they? I guess that they can. The press could do anything. I think it is worth leaving the hat. I think that will be a nice touch. I place her hand on the hat and then step back. This is how he must have felt leaving the girls. I smile at her. I want that to be a lasting memory for her. He would have been proud of the work I have been doing.

I leave her there. When she comes round she will be elated. She will see what I have done and know what fame that will bring for her. Her friend will get a mention no doubt. But not as much as her.

I head back towards the main streets of Camden. It's dark and when it's dark in Camden, you see all sorts hit the streets. I love these people. They walk their own paths. I don't want to go back to the Tube. I could go and visit Tim and Verna. They only live up the road. They would have had that baby by now though, wouldn't they? Little Edmund, I am sure. Yes, they would. Maybe that is not a good idea then. I don't think I could be doing with all that changing nappies business. Then there is the whole conversation about godfather. I am sure they would want me do that for them? I just don't have time. I could continue with my night. Carry on down the list. Although there's a surprising lack of Ds London. I am not sure Dollis Hill is a town. It is just a hill and I have already done a hill in Birmingham.

Sod it! I head back to the car. I jump on the nearest Tube and head back to Hendon. I watch as people get on and off the Tube. They are all oblivious to the world around them. There is not even one person in a black hoodie. Have they all forgotten about the ONE? Or they just don't want to dress like him anymore? There was a time on the Tube you couldn't move for people wanting to be me.

Have I made that disappear? Have I diluted my brand? Is it the right thing to do to invest only in the new characters in my life or should I keep the old ones alive at the same time? Do people only want new characters to keep it fresh? Keep it real? Is that what the people really want?

I suppose… No, I don't think that is all they want. Surely it is like when you go to a concert: you like the new songs, but they take time to grow on you. But a classic will always be a classic. When they are played that is when the fans make the most noise. That's what I need, I need the noise. By the time I am back to the car my mind is made up. He returns tonight.

I switch my clothes and place my knife in the back of my pants. The ONE deserves to be kept alive, and when I am in London he needs to come with me. I get back on the northern line. This feels right. My hoodie isn't up. Not yet but it will be when I start. Nobody is even looking at me. They certainly aren't expecting the ONE to return. That makes it even more exciting.

I can't even remember how long it has been since he was released onto the public. I know I need to travel towards the end of the track, back past Camden. Maybe I will hear the sirens as I go past. The click of the cameras could probably be heard from the train as well. The press will be there by now.

I need to watch the stops, not like Birmingham. I need to get to the point where there are about five or six people to work with on the Tube. It has to be worthy of the return. The fans love that. They love a challenging return…

"Excuse me, mate."

I turn to see a group of lads. They are all holding cans of beer. Are you allowed to drink on a train?

"Do me a favour, mate, and put your hoodie up so I can take a selfie."

What? He recognises who I am? How did he do that?

"You know, the whole black hoodie thing, the ONE. People will think I met the real Edmund Carson."

Fuck! He doesn't know who I am. He just recognises the costume. His mates are all laughing. They love the idea. I just pull my hoodie up. They all take turns in taking photos with me. They don't even know that it is me. Why don't they know it is me? I have been off the TV for so long they have forgotten what I look like.

"Thanks, mate. You are a star."

They move further down the carriage. I am sure I can hear them laughing at me. Laughing at the fact that I dress like the ONE.

I am the fucking ONE!

That is why I dress like this, you dicks. I am the one. The ONE, the ONLY!

I watch them drinking and laughing as we travel further up the line. Should I consider it an honour or not that they wanted to take a picture with someone who looks like the ONE? Or should I take it as an insult that he didn't recognise me? I mean, it is not as if my face isn't... Wait, it isn't. It isn't everywhere. Not since the Blackout. Have people really forgotten what I look like? That can't be right? It has only been a few weeks. I mean, I haven't seen George Clooney for a few weeks, but I still know what he looks like. They know I am still here. I am hardly hiding in the shadows, am I? Or is that what my fans think I am doing now, hiding in the shadows? Surely they know me better than that?

How am I going to get my face back into the limelight? I can't have people forgetting about me.

It is the fucking beard! The beard! That was it. It was the beard. That is why he didn't recognise me. I am in disguise. That's the whole point. That's why I grew it; I didn't want people to recognise me. I need to start not taking everything so personally. I forget my own plan sometimes.

Fuck!

There are only three people left in the carriage. I didn't notice. When did that happen? One of them is the selfie guy. I am glad about that. None of them are taking notice though. All three have earphones on. When did that happen? When did people start to ignore everything around them?

I almost run up the carriage. I am not sure how far we are away from the next stop. I need to pay more attention to these things. Two girls and the guy! I head towards the first girl. She is a blonde – hardly worth savouring the moment. One quick cut of her throat and she is down. With the earphones they can't even hear her as she hits the floor. I am behind the next girl within seconds and I plunge the knife into her neck. This time I savour it. The blood is rich, a little spicy. She smells like Camden, like the food market. I check again. She could be Indian. She looks Indian. I have one eye on the guy who still hasn't looked up from his phone. I take a lick. She tastes Indian. Warm and spicy, the taste is great. Why haven't I tried Indian before? I need to remember that for my cookbook. The fans will like that. I drop her quickly as his head moves. I need to get to him. I am in front of him, plunging my knife into his neck. His hands were up. That was close. Another couple of seconds and we would have been fighting, I am sure of it. I rip the knife through his throat. I grab him before he falls and then I pull the earphones out.

"It was me. It was me you took the photo with. You're welcome." There is a look of shock on his face. Probably didn't realise how great this day was going to become for him. He wanted to tell people that he met me. Now he really can. His mates are going to be so mad they left the train.

I suppose the plus point is that on all their phones they have marked the return of the ONE without even knowing it. They will have posted that all over social media. I am sure of it. I drop him on the floor. I go back to the Indian girl and pick her up again. I want some more. That taste was, was something I had never experienced before. I really need to eat more Indians. I like chilli, I like garlic. There are definitely more spices in there. I take another lick. I wish I had a glass or something to take some of the blood and swill it around. Like the real experts do with wine.

The carriage is slowing down, I can feel it. I place the girl back on a seat. I mouth the word thanks to her. I don't say it to loud as I didn't say it to the others. I always like new things, and I like people that introduce them to me. There is nobody waiting to get on. The end of the track is always good for peace and quiet. I get off and exit the station. I hail a cab back to my car. Nobody is looking for me yet so I don't need to worry about it. The press probably don't even know that I have returned to London. Think that is enough for one night.

The Alphabet Killer's tribute to Jack. Then the return of the ONE. Yes, that is a good night's work, and the press will have a field day tomorrow. So many stories to tell.

Camden Town is my favourite place in London.

And it is. Done.

Chapter 4

It was a good idea to stay down in the London area. At least I can pick the papers up this morning, hot off the press, without anyone bothering me. I have given it a day. So, there is no excuse that it was too late to hit the morning news. I know how it works now. I would only be winding myself up otherwise.

I could be a journalist. Really feels like a nine-to-five job. They are hardly pushed when all they need to do is a bit of writing.

I love London. It is very much like the airport hotels. People tend not to look at you. I swear you could hide out in plain sight here every day. The papers will be buzzing about the new Jack the Ripper. They love Jack. I mean, they really love Jack. I need to understand why they do? It can't be just because he was never caught? I know he made London famous again. I have done both those things. I will retire like Jack, into the shadows. Well, the shadows with a few guest appearances, of course; I am still young. He was like forty.

Maybe it is all about the time. I am still young in my career. Jack has been around for hundreds of years. Hundreds of years from now they will probably still be making movies of me? That is good to know. Good to know that what I have been doing will be remembered forever. My children and grandchildren will be dining out on my fame for years to come.

Add to that the return of the ONE all in one night and they must be ready for a big news day. This will see the end of any Blackout, I have no doubt.

I go and get the papers and bring them back to the guest house. I have already sneaked a peak at one of the headlines: "Ed smashes London". I am not sure about Ed? Ed makes me sound like a duck. Ed the duck? Why is that familiar to me? I suppose it is young and trendy though to be called Ed. Like me, so I can see why they would do it. Also, I guess, when two characters have an outing in the same night then it is a problem for them to decide who should make the headline. I wonder if all three, four including me, should make an outing one night. Imagine how well that would go down. The costume changes would keep me on my toes. It would be fun though. The fans would love it.

I head back to my room. I am having a déjà vu moment. Carrying arms full of newspapers back to my bedroom. I have done this a lot over the last few years. It's the excitement of sitting alone with the world's press talking about you. If I read them in a coffee shop or something I am sure people would be constantly getting up and asking me to sign something, or taking selfies.

I look at the headline again. "Ed smashes London". It is not their best work. I didn't actually smash anything... Wait a fucking minute... that's not me. I am not the Ed they are saying smashed it. It is some ginger-headed singer. Apparently he smashed a performance at the O2! How is it that singers get more publicity than, well, than me? What the fuck is the world coming to! There are so many pictures of him. That's hardly news! Some guy on a karaoke machine. He doesn't even have a band. Just some dodgy old guitar. It is not even a new electric one. I throw that paper down, I have always hated that paper. *Star*, my arse. Wouldn't know a star if it punched you on the nose. I start to search through the rest of the papers. There is nothing!

Fucking nothing!

There is nothing about the return of the ONE? Or the Alphabet Killer. There isn't even any news related to the finger-licking chicken guy. How is that possible? There was like one news report on TV, only one. They never put anything in the paper about him and he was a big deal. The world is going to starve without him and yet they have reported nothing.

Wait, wait, no, balls. For fuck's sake, how many people are called Ed nowadays? Are they Edmunds or Edwards? Who knows, but there seems to be loads of them. I throw the papers on the floor. Fucking papers.

Fuck it!

I stamp on them as hard as I can.

Bastards!

Whatever I am doing, it is still not enough to shake this Blackout. I am going to have to take matters into my own hands. I am going to have to deal with the Blackout Queen herself. If I visit her, her paper will definitely report it. Then whoever gets her job would lift the ban. I need to find out where that Sarah woman lives. I am going to have to do something that they have to report on. I sit back on the bed and put my head in my hands.

That's the fucking point, isn't it! Having the Blackout is still negative press. No press is negative press. They are trying to get me to go to her house. They are lying in wait for me. Well, I am not going to fall for that shit. How stupid do they think I am? No, not me. I need to do something else. Something so newsworthy they won't be able to ignore it. They will have to sit up and tell the world, or they are going to look pretty stupid. Something that makes their investors question whether they are a news outlet or not. Something to make them sell the fucking paper. Then I will deal with her.

I lie back on the bed. I take a deep breath. That is what my nan used to say when I was mad. Take a deep breath, Edmund. I am not mad; I am disappointed. I am not shocked but disappointed. If I am honest with myself, I knew there was a chance they would not want to report it.

I am right though. I know I am. I think all of this is a cry from the press for something. They want me to do something as big as the school. Something that makes the world stop and think about the UK. The press know I am the only person that can take on the Americans. The greats: the Freddies, the Jasons, and the Michaels. I mean, they are not real, which makes me even more special. They are my movie competition. No, they know I am the only person who can remind the world how great this country is.

The hotel was big enough, but clearly the world didn't see that. I don't understand why? I can only think it was the fault of the people I worked with. Maybe they weren't as appreciative. They weren't as into it as the girls at the school.

They probably didn't give good interviews to the press. They didn't tell them what a remarkable night it was. Maybe it was because they were on different floors. The excitement wasn't building into a frenzy between them. The girls at the school were all together in one room. They would have been drunk on the excitement.

Maybe that is what my work needs: an audience. The girls were appreciative, they knew what it meant for them. They knew that this was the start of fame which would never go away. Probably reality TV stars in their own right now? I know Seven and Seventeen will be, and they won't forget where they came from. They will still be talking me up, keeping my legacy alive. I think it needs to be something as big, as creative and as good as the school to be able to break the Blackout. It will be something that the public will demand to know about.

Okay. I need to get my head in the game.

D. Something to do with a D? I look down at the papers. "Ed heads to Derby for the next leg of the tour". Ed, the headline stealer! Maybe that's it. Maybe that is the plan. If I take the headliners out, who else would they have to report on? I stand up and go and look directly into the mirror on the back of the bathroom door. It is time. It is time that I worked with celebrities. It is time that I take my rightful place in the world's press. It is time to join the A-list. Derby it is then.

Fuck that was quick do I know how to make a plan or what!

I pack all my stuff up and head out of the hotel. I am leaving the car and going to take the train. Within the hour I am on the train. It is a bit of a trek to Derby. I am so glad that

I found a direct train, can't be doing with all those change overs.

Edmund vs Ed.

Now that is going to be a headline. It is also going to be a challenge. There will be protection. These singers always have a lot of protection. I suppose they will have their fair share of crazies too. It won't be easy, but fame is not easy. Not many of us can handle it. It is time I mixed in my own company though. We are very similar people. Although he looks like he is a bit older than me, and ginger.

Adored by millions and can pack out stadiums. Yes, we are very similar. It said in the paper his whole world tour was sold out. Not for people like me though. I am sure there is a VIP area for people that have money. Those ticket people are always outside selling tickets so they can't be sold out.

Maybe that's something I should consider though. I mean, really consider. A stadium is a big place, a lot of people to deal with.

I need to consider whether or not when I retire I should be doing things like stadium tours? I will sell these things out, without a doubt. It will boost all the T-shirt sales, and they'd be able to print my face on mugs. I could even charge twenty quid for a selfie, maybe even fifty quid? I am not sure what the going rate is now. I would make a killing. An absolute killing!

We finally pull into the station. I can see the stadium as we approach. It's not that big. Maybe this guy isn't as famous as the papers make him out to be. I get out of the station and straight into a cab. I need an operation base.

I use Google to search for local hotels on my phone. I wonder if Google would want to do some advertising together. I need to look into that.

The Stuart Hotel looked the most unassuming. Who's ever heard of The Stuart Hotel? Stuart's Hotel is one thing, but putting "The" in front of the name is just stupid.

The cab driver drives me the five-minute journey. I check in, and I am in my room. I was right, it is nothing special. That's a good thing though. I could stay in luxury, but I am sure people will be expecting that. Probably have police at all the five-star hotels, where all the stars stay. I use google again. He isn't coming for six days. I should have really looked at that before I came here. What am I going to do for six days in Derby? I type that into Google. What can you do in Derby? I can visit an abbey, museum and a cathedral. Derby and Brighton must be practically the same place. Where old people go to die! This is going to be fun for a whole fucking six days. Other than football, they have a dairy, a park and Pickford's House. Honestly, why do people live here? Although they are playing Manchester United tomorrow. Even I know who they are. That must mean something to the people around here as that is sold out as well. Maybe I don't have to stick around. Maybe this Manchester thing is a bigger event than the ginger singer. I wonder if he calls himself the ginger singer. Has a good ring to it. It would raise his profile a bit if he did. Probably help him sell songs around the world. Advertising is just a gift for me.

I am sure those scalp people will have a ticket for the football too. Why are they called scalp people? Weren't they Indians? The people who used to scalp you? They are not normally Indians? Most of the scalp people I come across are Londoners or Liverpudlians. Why are they called Liverpudlians? They don't stand in puddles? I suppose it might rain a lot in Liverpool? The scalpers are all over London. Always trying to flog you tickets. I am sure it is the same up here. Anywhere people will pay over the odds to see something, they will be there. I will get in. I am not worried about that.

I flick on the TV. I still go straight to the news channels. I don't know why, I am not on there anymore. It must be a force of habit? I carry on flicking. It is their loss. The news programmes must be boring now. They can probably downsize the hotness of the reporters now that nobody is watching. Move them all to the sports channels.

At least you can always bank on Sky to have a marathon of *Criminal Minds* and *CSI*. Maybe that should be my day, a bit of research. I could do with a few new ideas to help me get rid of this Blackout. I kick off my shoes and settle in.

I open my eyes. There is a clock on the TV. I can just about make it out. It is three minutes past seven. Nan-clock has clicked in again. How weird is that? The TV marathon of last night didn't feel the same somehow without her. I missed her blanket, and her cheese and onion on toast. I did order it from room service, but it wasn't the same. There were no burnt edges, she was always good with the burnt edges.

Kick-off is at lunchtime today although I haven't really worked out what I am going to do at a football game. There were no new insights from the marathon. I had seen them all before. Emily is getting hotter in *Criminal Minds*. If JJ had black hair she would be hotter, but she keeps insisting on the blonde. Once I get to Hollywood I will have to talk to her about that. These actresses will change for the chance to work with me. Well not just work.

One of the episodes is sticking in my mind though. I do like the idea of taunting the police, a little like mixing with celebrities. They seem to make it look fun. I need some fun. I like the idea of a game of cat and mouse with the police. They would be the mouse, clearly.

I feel a bit odd today. Something doesn't feel right about being here. I get up and dressed and head down to breakfast. Normally I would call room service again, so that I don't bump into any fans. But I need a change of scenery and a baseball cap is a good distraction from my face so nobody will recognise me. It must be a big game; nearly everyone in the hotel is wearing a football shirt. Football is very tribal, isn't it? Everyone here is standing by their teams in their team colours. Almost feels like a war. It is just a costume on a big stage. Everyone playing their part, even the guys in black. It is just a costume.

I finish up and head back upstairs. I get into the lift. There is a guy next to me in a Derby shirt. It looks a little bit big for him. Maybe he has been ill or something.

"Morning."

"Morning."

Oh crap, he is one of those talk in the lift people. I prefer the silent ones that just look at their shoes. It is not like we are going to become friends or anything.

"Are you here for the game?"

"Yes." Well, I am going to the game. It wasn't a lie.

"Cool, you a Red or Rams?"

Am I a Red or Rams? What does that even mean? He is looking at me. I guess he wants me to pick one? Am I a Red or a Ram? What the fuck is the difference?

"Rams." As good a guess as any, I suppose? I guess, I am more of a ram, in a world of sheep. Yes, I am a Ram.

"Up the Rams!"

He punches the air. Up the Rams? Why did he shout that out? Who is he shouting to? Does that mean he is a Red or a Ram? What does he want to put up the Rams? Was that what he was doing with his fist? I am regretting saying I was a Ram now. He does look the type, but I am sure the weirdo's do it with sheep, and he didn't sound like a shepherd?

"Ian."

He holds out his hand. I guess that is his name then as it's not mine.

"Ed... ward."

Fuck that was close. That was a good save.

"I am going two–nil Derby. What about you?"

Two–nil? Two–nil? Oh, the score! He thinks Derby are going to win the game by two goals. I think this bloke may have some kind of special needs. It is a good job I can read people's body language.

"Yes, I hope so."

"You have got to love our team, eh? We all chose that hill to die on. This is mine. Rams on tour!"

What the fuck? Why is he shouting Rams on tour now? He is punching the air again. We are in a lift, for fuck's sake? And what, he wants to die on a hill? Who chooses a hill to die on? He kisses his hand and then touches the badge on the shirt. We get out of the lift and head to our rooms. He is in front of me. Our rooms must be close. He stops and puts the key card in.

"See you later, mate. Up the Rams!"

As he turns his back and pushes the door open I am behind him. I stab him four times in the back while I hold my hand on his mouth. I push him forward and kick the door closed behind me. I hold him there, lift my knife up and cut his throat. I wait until his legs give way. I am not interested in sniffing him. The smell hasn't even affected me. I don't want it to today. Is that odd? It is not like me? I lift him into the room. I take his shirt off. I needed a costume for the game. If I am going to do anything in the football ground, I need one of their costumes.

It means the Alphabet Killer suit isn't going to be used, but I can't turn up dressed like that, I will stand out too much. I can't have forty thousand fans looking for an autograph. People will notice that.

Is that what is up with me? I am sensing the whole Alphabet Killer costume is wrong. I shouldn't dress like Jack? I don't make wrong decisions, but this is feeling like one.

No, no, it is not a wrong decision. The suit is a great idea. What is up with me today? It is something about this place, Derby. I don't know why it is making me question things. There is a feeling at the bottom of my stomach that I knew not to come here? I will just have to use the suit for E. It is not like they are reporting on it yet anyway. My fame will gloss over a few blips. The press will apologise to me and say they reported it wrong once the book is out. Either that or I will put them on a timeout. See how they like it. They are not reporting on me, but I am sure someone will have taken the hat home as memorabilia. I can't see them leaving it down by the canal in Camden. They probably have a rule where whoever is first on the scene gets first dibs on the stuff. As long as you are there before the world's press turn up, or they will have to barter for it.

They will all be building their archives for when they finally lift the ban.

I need to start saving all the papers too. It will be good to build my scrapbooks.

I go into the bathroom and wash the shirt. It is never going to all come out. I will be wearing a coat anyway. It is going to be tight, but it is a good job that I am ripped like a model. I go back into the room and use the hairdryer on the shirt to dry it off.

"Oh, sorry you are awake. That was quick. Was it the hairdryer waking you up?"

"Yes, yes I am. Sorry about the Edward thing. It is Edmund. I nearly said it. Force of habit, I am afraid."

"No, no, it is nothing like that. It is not a personal thing. I just like to reward people randomly. Well, I say randomly. I was sitting downstairs thinking about costumes and then there you were wearing one. It was too good an opportunity to miss. For both of us I am sure. I need to blend in, you see."

Is he going to shut up? I am trying to dry his shirt here. I can hardly hear him over the hairdryer.

"I am not sure I would be able to work with the whole United team. To be honest, I don't even have my plan yet. I just thought I needed to be more adventurous. Push the boundaries more, you know, mix with more celebrities."

He keeps naming football players to me. I have no idea what he is on about. The only footballers I know are David Beckham and that Spanish guy that everyone thinks is hot. Ron something?

"We will see, Ian! It sounds really important to you?"

"Really? You were going to run around the car park naked if they won? It is that important to you?" Who says that? It is not even as if we know each other? He is very forward for a small guy.

"If you don't mind. I understand that you would want to wait around here for the press now. Have your fifteen minutes of fame and all that." I look around the room until I find his ticket.

"Thanks for this. You never know once you are famous we may even catch a game together" he likes the thought of that.

I leave the room. What an odd little man. He seemed to love his football though. I go back to my room and start to get my stuff together. I change into the shirt.

Fuck!

I didn't think this through. I now have a suitcase and a bag that I have to take to the game because I need to check out of the hotel. All because I worked with a guy down the hallway. It wasn't even enjoyable.

Fuck it!

What the fuck is up with me? I go back to his room and knock on the door. Nothing. He doesn't fucking answer. Now I can't get in. I need one of those access cards that opens the rooms in the hotel.

Fuck!

This wasn't how today was supposed to start. Now I have to move. Stash my kit somewhere. This has really fucked up my already shitty day.

Fuck, fuck, fuck!

I go back and finish putting my gear together. I head out of the room just in time to see the cleaner knocking on his door.

Fuck!

This isn't getting any better. I walk along the corridor and watch her push the door open. She walks in. I have dropped my suitcase and bag and followed her in too. My knife is out and in her neck. The blood is oozing everywhere. I am kicking the door shut behind me for the second time in less than an hour.

Fuck!

What am I doing? Now I have two of them in the room. What the fuck am I doing? This morning is really going to shit. Now what do I do with them? What the fuck do I do with them? I need them not to be discovered yet. The press will be everywhere. I can hardly move them somewhere more discreet, it's the middle of the day! Wait, it is not even the middle of the day yet.

I walk back to the door and put the Do Not Disturb sign on. That is a start. I pick up the cleaner and put her on the bed with him.

"I am sure you will have a lot in common."

What the fuck is he complaining about? Not many people get to see me twice. He should be honoured.

"Listen, women just don't fall on your lap this often. Give her ten minutes, and she will be a lot more talkative. She may even put out. Trust me, women get all wet and weak at the knees around me. They will do anyone."

What is up with this guy? I have no idea what I am doing here. Think, think, think, Edmund!

Fuck!

I grab the card. Al said the master key records all the rooms it has opened, and this was the last door she opened. I leave the room and click all the doors down the hallway. I then go back to the room and push her trolley back into the room that they are in. I stand frozen.

I turn, then open the door and push it out again and put it at the end of the corridor. She may have gone missing, but the fucking trolley wouldn't have. I need to give the impression that she may have just quit. I am sure with a job like this people quit all the time. I go back to the room.

"Fuck!"

I keep using the card to go back into the room. What the fuck is up with me today? I prop the door open and then go and click all the doors again. Go back to the room and close the door. I think that is all I can do to keep them from hitting the press before the game. This is not what I do. It is not fair to them either. They should be excited about talking to the press.

I am just not at the top of my game today.

"I am sorry, guys, I seem to be off my game a little. I didn't plan any of this."

"No, you will still have your fifteen minutes of fame. It will just be later today, that is all. I wouldn't take that away from any of my fans."

"No, I hope the Rams aren't off their game today either. Up the Rams!" The cheer will make him happy. Show him I am one of them.

"Of course I will. I will come back and tell you the score. If they win I won't be doing the car park thing though. I can imagine what kind of press that would attract. It is nearly winter."

I leave the room. He will get the scores later, I am sure. I won't be coming back. Something about being here is bugging me. I am starting to feel like I really shouldn't have come.

What a difference a day can make. My nan used to say that all the time. The difference one day can make in your life. One minute Jack and the ONE are making a return of epic proportion, and now I am here. I pick up my bag. I turn and go back into the room for the fifth time. I caught sight of my reflection in the hallway mirror. There is blood sprayed over my face. I am just not thinking this morning. Imagine if I checked out like that. Even the receptionist would put two and two together and know who I am. I wash my hands and face. That is better. I go back into the main room. They are talking to each other which is nice. I am sure he will convince her to put out. He has all day. I go over to the backpack that he had placed on the side and open it. There is just a shirt and a waterproof mac in it.

"Do you mind if I borrow this?"

He just nods at me. Too engrossed in his conversation with the cleaner. I pick up my go-bag and empty some money into the rucksack. I place some in all my pockets too. I just stand there looking at the bags.

Why am I doing this? Something isn't right? It is like I am not myself. I am not leaving them here am I?

I feel like something is about to change. Something is coming. I say my goodbyes, head downstairs and check out. I get in a cab and then head back to the train station and stash everything in their locker centre. These things are everywhere now. I would not be surprised if they are used for drug and cash exchanges. The police should watch these places, to help keep the criminals away.

I lock everything in, apart from the backpack I just filled up. I am going to keep this with me. I don't know why, but I think I am going to need it? I then get a cab back to the ground. This morning has been wasted. First the hotel and then an hour to stash my kit. Given all of that I am still here early. I take a big breath, I can hear nan telling me too. Now start again. I have an hour to kill till kick-off. It is filling up though. There are police everywhere. I need to put this morning behind me. What happened has happened.

This is exciting. I do like the thought of walking among the police and the press. These games are all over the TV nowadays. Millions will be watching the crowds. Imagine how many of them would be thrilled to know I am here. I am sure they are. None of them would be expecting me. Especially me in a Derby shirt. I don't think anyone would ever expect that.

I walk past two policemen. One even nods at me. Nothing. This shirt must be like the father thing. If you are wearing a Derby shirt no one notices you. I wonder if it would be the same if I had a red shirt on.

I have that feeling again: déjà vu. I feel like I have been here. It doesn't feel new to me. I feel like I have been to this football ground. I have walked around this stadium before. Which is really odd as I don't really like football? I head into the ground. Why have they got a scanner at a football game? What do they think that I am going to be carrying here? I give the guy my bag and he puts it through the machine. Money won't set it off, will it? I mean, there is a metal strip. Wait, won't they think it is funny that I am carrying some money? Can they see that it is money on the scanner? I guess it could just be paper? I scan my ticket and I am in. The guy checks my bag but not me? I could be carrying. I am carrying something.

What the fuck is wrong with me today!

If I was caught with that they would have put two and two together. Two and two together? Why do I keep saying that? They would have recognised me and after a while of taking selfies and giving signatures called the press I am sure of it.

I am on the east stand so I follow the directions. I am still early. People are drinking beer and eating a lot of pies and burgers. There is a lot of singing. They are not singing about being on tour? That is probably because they are at home. What was the guy in the lift on this morning? Why would he shout Rams on tour? Maybe he was on tour? I am sure people come to Derby on tour? Okay, I am not sure. Wait, I have walked here before. I have walked under that sign, I am sure of it. I look around again. Am I losing it? Have I already worked at a football ground? Is that why it was in my head? If I did, what did I do? How did I stage it? I am sure I would have remembered. I really need to start keeping a record of all the work I have done. I need that scrapbook. I also need to seriously start thinking about that assistant. I need someone who can document all this for me.

I queue up and get a cold beer and a steak pie. It will help me fit in with the crowd. The police are just walking everywhere. It is like they have free rein of the place. I wonder if they have to pay for a ticket. Probably get in for free. It wouldn't be a bad Saturday job. Better than working at the Golden Arches.

I walk up to my section of the ground. I can see my seat, but I don't sit down yet. I am not sure what I am going to be able to do. It looks like I am in the middle of everything. Maybe I could work with the people around me. I am sure they won't be cheering anyway; they are in the Derby end. I keep walking around while I eat my pie and drink my beer.

They all look excited. I wonder if they are that excited every Saturday. Or is it just because it is a big game? I finish my pie and go and take my seat. Takes a while but the place starts to fill around me. Everyone is laughing and joking. Not really paying attention to me. They were probably expecting the little guy from the hotel.

I am not sure what I am doing here. There are eleven people to my right and eight to my left. I have nine rows in front of me and lots more behind. I can't do anything here. I am trapped in. I am trapped in to watch a game of football which I don't like. I can't work with anyone. I couldn't get through them all before attracting attention to myself. Then the Sky cameras would be all over me. I wonder if I should talk to them about a TV series whilst I am here. Get ahead of that game.

The football game starts.

I have watched football before. I have watched it live before, I am sure of it. I just can't remember when. There is a feeling as the whole crowd sing as one. That is what I remember. It is very end to end. I can hear them talking about it. Apparently, Derby are playing some good football, not that I would know anything.

Fucking hell!

The whole of the crowd has erupted. I am looking around everywhere. They are screaming. The guy next to me grabs me and hugs me. Hard! What the fuck is going on? I am looking everywhere. Derby scored. Fuck, they are going mad. I jump up and down with them. I don't want to stand out. They are all doing it, everyone in this section. This must be what it is like to follow the crowd.

That is not something that I would normally do. But I have never seen so many people so happy in one place. I think I am going to enjoy stadium tours. This many people. Cheering you on as you do what you love. I will probably pick a few special girls out of the crowd to work with on stage. They will be begging for it, thousands of them. That will look so good on the big screen. One of those forty-foot screens behind me.

Hold on! Where is everyone going? They are all trying to get past me. The players are leaving too? The screen in front of me flashes up. It is half-time. Derby one; Man United zero. They will be happy about that. I move with the crowd till we are back in the tunnels around the stadium again. I queue and get another drink. It is a lot warmer in here than I thought it would be. This shouting is thirsty work.

Everyone starts to go back. I do too. I am back in the crowd. They are all singing again. Derby! Derby! Derby! They do love their town, or city, or whatever it is. It all starts again, all the running end to end.

I need a wee. I knew I should have gone before. I knew when I was out there in the tunnels, but the queues were huge. I am trying to watch the game so that I don't think about it. Now it is all I can think about. I shouldn't have had two drinks. Wait, wait, wait!

"Yes!" I actually watched that one.

Two! That is two. I hug the guy next to me now. Everyone is jumping. I am really getting into this. I mean, really. It is two–nil to Derby. I really need the bathroom now. All that jumping can't help. People are starting to move already. I am not sure how long this game lasts, but it's only at eighty-four minutes. They must go to a hundred or something. I move with them. It will get me to the toilet quicker. I get to the stairs. People are walking down them slowly as if they are still watching the game and don't want to leave. If they don't want to leave why didn't they stay in their seats?

Fuck!

There are police. They are coming from everywhere. Looks like a hundred of them from every corner of the ground. I have seen that on the telly. That is normal, isn't it? They are here for the end of the game?

Or are they here for me? Do they know that I am here? I start walking a little bit faster, only because I need to go to the toilet. I pass all the people on the stairs. They aren't looking up at me. They are looking at everyone. I am out of the stadium and back into the tunnels. Lots of people are leaving. The queue to the toilets is already out the door. The police are here as well. They are everywhere, aren't they? I need to leave, don't I? Should I wait for more of the crowd? If they are here for me, should I wait and hide among them? Wait, did I really say hide? I don't hide! What is wrong with me?

I am walking straight out the front door. I keep walking. There aren't as many police out here as there are in the stadium. Some are looking this way though. I keep walking, and I am out of the ground. I can hear sirens now. That is not normal. I can hear lots of sirens. That is not the sound after a football match. They know I am here. They know that there are going to be huge crowds chasing after me. I think I am walking towards them. I get to the roundabout. I keep walking. The A6, isn't that a car? I didn't know it was a road as well. Why is it called an A road? I mean, I know it is a road, but do they have B, C and D roads as well? Do they go all the way to M for M1? That is not normal, is it? It is not normal, that many sirens heading towards a football game. Maybe they are expecting trouble? Maybe they are rioting after the match. The Manchester fans won't be happy I am sure of it. I keep walking although I do seem to be walking a little bit faster. It is because I am keen to finish D and get out of Derby. There is no other reason. It is not because the police are coming. I keep walking. As I do, I see them coming over the hill in front of me. Police cars, and lots of them. Lots of them, they have the vans and everything. I pull my cap down a little further and keep walking. I am counting. There must be what, ten, fifteen cars. They all go buzzing past me and head towards the front of the ground.

I keep on walking. I turn left up into the housing estate. I take the second road to the right. I had to take the second road to the right. Somehow it is where I wanted to go. I carry on walking then go left again. Feels like instinct. I walk halfway up the road and stop.

Why am I stopping? I look around. There is a house to my left.

Fuck me!

I know why I stopped here now. It has all come back to me like one of those flashbacks. I know why it all fell into place at the football ground.

This isn't the first time I have been to Derby. I walk up to the house and knock on the door. It takes a while, but finally it opens.

"Hello, Uncle George."

He looks very surprised to see me.

Chapter 5

"Edmund…"

He has said that twice already. At least, I think he is has. His mouth is wide open. It is like he is one of those ventriloquist dummies. Either that or he has forgotten my name.

"Yes, it is me, Uncle George. Are you going to invite me in?"

He is nodding, so I will take that as a yes. I step past him. I am so tempted to close his mouth for him as I do. If my nan was here she would have done. She would have told him he would catch flies if he didn't.

"I thought you would have been at the game. It was a good one. We, I mean, Derby, won two–nil. So, it is a good one if you are a Derby fan. You are still a Derby fan, aren't you?"

I walk into the living room. It is like it is all flooding back to me. Nothing in his house has changed. It looks like it did what, four, five years ago? Maybe even longer.

"The old place hasn't changed much?"

I stick my head back into the hallway to beckon him. He is just standing there. I walk up to the door and close it. Finally, he follows me into the living room. He almost looks like he is in shock? Maybe he was at the game and just left before I did. Either that or I suppose he never expected I would visit him. Not now I am famous. Even though he is the only family I have now. Other than Miss Walker. She is family too. But he is the only blood family.

"So, how have you been, Uncle George? Tell me everything. It feels like ages since we last met."

He is nodding his head again. I sit down and make myself comfortable. I look over at him. He is just standing there looking at me as if he has seen a ghost or something.

"Are you going to sit down?"

He nods again and sits down opposite me, really slowly as if he had forgotten how to sit down. What is up with him?

"Do you know, I have had this feeling? This feeling, all the time I have been in Derby that I have been here before. Something wasn't right. I was off my game a bit. Even when I went to the actual game, I was still off it. I had this gut feeling I knew I had been there before. You know, just walking around the ground, it felt, it felt familiar. And then I ended up here. I don't know how. But I did. Isn't that weird? In my head, I wasn't intending to visit you today. I was going to be popping in at some point clearly, because we are family. But not today, is what I mean."

That was close. I don't want him to feel that I had got too big to visit family. He is still nodding his head. You would think that he would be excited to have me here? He doesn't seem to be that excited. I stand up. He almost puts himself flat back against the chair.

"Uncle George, are you okay? You are acting a little weird?" Good use of the catchphrase right there. I am so back to normal. He is still nodding. Only ever so slightly. But there is a little nod.

"You don't seem okay? Is this still about the break-up? Nan told me. She told me about you, and I want to say Carole? Was that her name? Aunty Carole – it sounds about right. She left you, didn't she? Nan said it was for a football player."

Yeah, that it is it. I can tell by the look in his eyes.

"Oh shit, was it a Derby one? Is that why you weren't at the game? That makes sense now. I wouldn't support them if one of their players went off sleeping with my girl."

I walk around the living room. I feel full of energy all of a sudden. I don't know why. Maybe it is due to being home. Wherever family is, that is home. He is watching me. He is probably building up the courage to ask for a selfie. It must be hard to ask your nephew for a selfie or an autograph. He is supposed to be the one I look up to.

"Something I needed to ask you, Uncle George. I say I needed to, I mean, I really wanted to, but I didn't have a number for you and until five minutes ago I couldn't remember where you lived. So that was lucky. Great how these things work out. I wanted to ask you… I know that Nan was living in Brighton, you know, to keep all of my fans away from her. I also know she sadly passed away." That stuck in my throat. I don't think I have ever said that before.

"It hit me really hard, I can tell you. They were dark days. What I don't know is how many people attended the funeral? Hundreds, I am guessing? Maybe thousands. It was thousands, I knew it. Was the church lit up with orchids, white and pink?

That's how I imagined it would be. I mean, I knew it would be. They were always her favourite."

He is nodding his head again. Just how I knew it would be. I am glad that was her special day. Her day in the spotlight.

"Oh, I am so glad, Uncle George, so glad."

There is silence again. I swear, if I wasn't talking nobody would be. I always remember him talking more. He is probably thinking about the funeral now. I have dragged that all up again, haven't I? I should have been more thoughtful. He was probably just getting over it. I didn't mean to bring it back to him. I am sure he loved her too. Maybe it is time to change the conversation.

"Oh shit, I forgot I need a pee. How I forgot, I don't know. I was nearly bursting. It is the same place? Of course it is. Why would you move the toilet?"

I head out of the living room. I thought he would be more pleased to see me? Maybe it was because I didn't bring a gift. A bottle of wine. My dad always brought him a bottle of wine. I walk back into the room. I need to apologise for that. Then we can move on. I will get two bottles next time I come to visit him.

He is standing in the corner of the room, looking out the window. He must have jumped up the moment I left. He is probably getting his energy back too. Now that he knows I am here for a while there is no need to worry about when he can ask for a selfie.

"Hello, police please…"

I am behind him within seconds and cut his throat from ear to ear. He didn't turn around. I whisper into his ear.

"Oh, you can talk?" I grab the phone before I drop him to the floor.

"Hello, yes, police, sorry I dropped my phone. I was just at the train station in Derby and I am sure I saw that Edmund Carson fellow getting on a train. Heading south I think… Oh, it is no problem at all. I am happy to help. My name? My name is… Jake. Jake Summers!"

I hang up. I knew that name would come in handy. He served me the beer and pie at the ground. Cool name.

"Now why did you go and… No, I still need to pee…" I head out of the living room and into the bathroom. Oh, I needed that. I think when you drink beer it goes straight through you. That is better. So much better! I feel like I have drunk two pints and peed four. I wash my hands and face and go back to the living room and pick him up and put him back into his chair. I give him the disapproving look. He knows what he has done. I suppose I can't stay mad for long. He is family. He did call the police first as well to help with the press so that is one thing. I head into the kitchen and pick up a bottle of wine. I grab a couple of glasses and the bottle opener. It will be good to catch up properly. I sit back down. He is not with me yet. As I sit here, I can see my nan in him, and my mum. It is funny how they all look similar. I wonder if when I get old I will start to look like them. I don't really think so. I am too good-looking. I guess it must be the mix of my mum and dad that has made me look this good. I open the wine and pour us both a glass. It is good wine. I remember that about him now, he used to love his wine. Dad used to say that he spent far too much money on it. Snobby he called it.

"Oh, there you are.

"Yes, sometimes it takes ten to fifteen minutes for people to come to terms with working with me. I think they call it star-struck. It happens when normal people meet stars. But it shouldn't have happened to you as we are family. No need to be nervous."

"Yes, Edmund. You do like saying my name, don't you?" I think he is still a little star-struck even now.

"I sensed you weren't expecting me. Not many people ever are... I don't like to say it because we are family, but is that what this was? Is that why you couldn't get more than my name out of your mouth?

"I thought so..."

I top up his glass although he hasn't drunk a lot of it? Lack of confidence. I don't want to tell him, but it is probably why his girlfriend left him.

"So where were we? Oh yeah, Nan's funeral. Was it amazing? It was, wasn't it? I knew it. I have been thinking about it for ages now. Was there a church big enough was my worry? I presumed there was. I have been to Brighton a few times. It is nothing but churches. Just tell me it wasn't ruined by the police? I knew they would need some to keep the crowds and fans out. But I presumed that they were also in plain clothes on the off-chance of making themselves famous. Sorry, so many questions. I have hardly given you the chance to reply."

"I wanted to be there. I really did, but you know, work just got in the way."

He will understand. Well, not totally. He is not famous like me. He will understand that working away from home mean's you are not always available for the family stuff.

"I am so glad. I thought that you would have made sure of a good send-off. I thought that the flowers would be a nice touch. I can pay you back for them, if you like. I have money now, and I am about to come into a whole lot more. You know, when the book deals and the movies kick in."

Finally there is a trace of a smile on his face. That is because he knows my fame will spread to him too.

"Yeah, I know she was your mum."

I think that makes him feel closer to her. He hasn't been living with her for the last couple of years though, has he? I think everyone knows that I was her favourite. I was her blue-eyed boy.

"Every day. I miss her every day."

"No, I don't think you do ever recover. It is the little things. Someone told me that once. I can't remember who. But it is the little things that you miss and it's the little things that are important. The smell of the flowers she would have around the house. The food. If I eat a bad sausage sandwich it always reminds me of her. You know, in a good way of course. If I walk past a homeless person, I think of all the people she helped. She was all jumble sales and soup kitchens. She was just that kind of nan."

She was that kind of nan. The only nan anyone would ever want. Being this close to Uncle George is making me miss her a lot today. I wasn't expecting that.

His phone rings. I walk over and pick it up off the side. You would think he would have a better phone than a Huawei. When I am sponsored by Apple I will have to send him one. It is a withheld number. I put it back down.

"I never answer those, I don't know about you?"

I go back and sit down opposite Uncle George. I am looking at him. He called them, didn't he? He called them. What if that wasn't the first person he spoke to? What if he had already called the press? I was out of the room for a little while. Was it a little while or a long while? I almost got all the way to the bathroom before I turned back, didn't I? There could be film crews and everything heading here straight from the ground. There would have been loads of press at the ground.

The withheld number could be them phoning him back. They would have the number, wouldn't they? What if they got to the station and I wasn't there. I wasn't there. They would check where the call came from.

Fuck!

Why did I say the station? That is where all my gear is. I didn't mean to say Derby station. Why didn't I say London or Scotland? Then they wouldn't have been there. They will probably have footage. They will have seen me stash my stuff in one of those lockers. I have lost the clothes. I need my clothes. Why didn't I put it somewhere else? Like a...

"I think I am going to have to cut our visit short, Uncle George. But do you still have the safe under the stairs?"

He nods at me with his eyes.

I knew he would still have it. Why would you get rid of it? I go back into the hallway and look in the cupboard under the stairs. When I was a kid he changed the code to my birthday. I used to keep my sweets in here. It is funny how it all comes flooding back. My dad used to say that only idiots have a house safe though. He kept all his money in the bank. I am glad of that given the accident and the leaking gas pipe that burnt our house down. I enter the code. It is still the same. I am a little shocked by that, but I guess there was no need to change it. I open the safe. He has money. That is pretty much it. Well, money and... I open a little black box. There is a diamond ring in there. It is beautiful.

"Uncle George?"

"Thanks. I guess you are right. You don't need it any more since she left you. It is a lovely ring though. It is her loss, Uncle George. Her loss."

Miss Walker will love this. This will get me so laid. I grab the money and the ring and put them in my backpack and go back into the room.

"Of course, I will come back and visit. I won't leave it as long next time. Thanks for the loan too. As soon as I get to a bank I will transfer over the money."

I need to be out of here before the world's press descends on me. They won't remember me as the Alphabet Killer if I only get to D. I go back into the hallway and look at the key rack on the wall.

"I will if you are sure you don't mind?"

It is so nice of him to lend me his car. I will need to change it soon. If he has called them, they will do their research and know what car he drives. They will be looking for it. They will think it is stolen, and probably report it to the police so that they track it for them. The press are very sneaky like that.

"Bye, Uncle George. I will remember to bring a nice bottle of wine next time. Two, two bottles of wine."

I grab the door handle. There is a lump in my throat as I turn it. Why would that be? I haven't felt like this since, since the lift in Al's hotel. I open the door slowly. It is just a normal street. I am not sure why I was nervous about a normal street. I leave and get into Uncle George's car. He is so generous. An Audi Q7! A seven-seater and automatic. This car must cost a fortune. I pull out of the driveway and head down the street. This car is amazing to drive. Within fifteen minutes I am on the motorway. I need to be careful. This thing drives like a tank but at a hundred miles an hour. I can't be pulled over by the police today. Not today. All in all this has not been a good day. Not what I thought a trip to Derby was going to be like.

I don't think I have ever felt like this. I have that feeling at the bottom of my stomach. That feeling like something bad is about to happen. I feel like I could mess up all the good work I have done in a moment of madness. The pressure on us celebrities to be perfect is far too much. People just don't realise that. To be perfect all the time is a lot of pressure.

I can't be seen to fail my last quest. I can't fail. I need to make sure that I complete the Alphabet before I move on. I have told the world now. They will know from the picnic what I was planning. They will have seen A, B, C and now I am sure they will have found Ian and the cleaner by now. That is a good title for a romance novel. Ian and the cleaner!

Nobody has ever done anything like this before and I need to be the first one. I pull into the services. I need to fill the car and get some water to help me sober up. I could do with some food too. I fill up the car. It doesn't just drive like a tank; it must carry a tank. It cost a hundred and twenty to fill it up. It is funny how I just started to think about money when I left two hundred grand in a locker in a train station. The police will probably be having a night out on that tonight. I pick up some water and snacks for the drive. I need some distance between myself and Derby. It has not been my favourite place. I need to clear my head and then get back in the game.

I get back into the car. I pull out of the garage. Then I stop. There are four girls with backpacks standing on the side of the road before the motorway. They are holding a sign saying "John o' Groats". John o' Groats? I am sure that is not someone they are waiting for? They are waving and holding out their thumbs. Isn't that what you do when you are hitch-hiking? Four small, petite, dark-haired girls hitch-hiking on the side of the M1 heading north? At exactly the same time as me? Heading north and waving at me to give them a lift? Feels like a trap. It must be a trap. They will be press, I am sure of it. They will have tape recorders and cameras in those bags.

Derby is done, and the press are hedging their bets that I will continue north.

I haven't used that name, have I? John. I don't remember being a John. They can hardly hold up a sign that says Edmund Carson, can they? Yes, it is a trap. Ignore them, Edmund. It is a trap. They don't want you to be the Alphabet Killer. The bitches are trying to catch you on camera!

Chapter 6

"So, let me get this right. Susana, Raquel, Rocio and Ebay? Ebay... eb, ay." That is an odd name. I wonder if she is loaded and her parents started the whole eBay thing. If she is, I need to wonder what impact working with her will have. I don't need another Chicken King fiasco. They don't sell food on eBay though, do they? More bikes and washing machines – the world can survive without them.

I do admire the name thing though, like District Carson. They are giggling like schoolgirls. I think they may have been drinking already today. Excited about the possibility of meeting me I am sure of it.

"So, you have to tell me how do you spell that?"

"E–V–E."

Rocio is definitely the boss of them. They all look to her to speak. I love her accent I can imagine those lips at work in other areas. Wait what did she say?

"Oh, Eve!" Why didn't they just say that in the first place? They are giggling again, must me lost in translation, the v's sound like b's. I bet she gives a good Vlow Jov. All the giggling has to be because they are all thinking about me. Can you imagine you are stranded on the M1 and someone as good-looking as me is willing to pick you all up? They must think it is Christmas.

"So what were you holding a sign for what was it? John o' Groats?" I needed to ask. I am sure I haven't used that name before. If they really wanted my attention they should have probably used my real name. Or been wearing bikinis. That would have got my attention too. Yes, black bikinis on brown tanned skin....

"It is a charity hitch-hike, the Halloween Hitch-Hike for Vets for Pets. We started in Land's End and we need to be in John o' Groats before Wednesday. You know, Halloween."

I love her accent. It is very cute. They are not English, I am sure of it. Their names don't sound English either, but you never know nowadays. They look like those Brazilian models you see in magazines. The ones Uncle George had in his bathroom.

"And where exactly is John o' Groats?"

They all look at each other.

"It is right at the very top of Scotland."

Probably should have known that. Given I am the only English person in the car. She is cute, Raquel. My dad used to have a thing for a girl called Raquel. I think she was a Welsh girl. I don't remember him visiting Wales very often though.

She has that look in her eyes. To be fair, they all do. They all have that pull over to the side of the road and do us all look. I mean, I could, but I am not sure how that would go. Four hot girls and one hot guy, would they just play with themselves waiting for their turn? That could be hours. Although I suppose that if you see your friend having multiples then you would wait for the man giving them to her. Or maybe they would just play with each other for a while? Really work themselves into a frenzy. Yeah, a frenzy. That is a good word for a group of friends all getting it on together. We should be doing that, we should be having a frenzy at the side of the road. Maybe one of those lanes that people are always talking about. Although why they take their dogs to I don't know… Wait, are they talking to me?

"Sorry?"

"Your name, silly."

Oh shit, yeah, my name. My name is… Think! I can't use Jake again. I just used that. I should have kept that one for the girls. Jake Summers sounds like a ladies' man. Think. I look down at the floor of the car.

"Matt… Matthew." That was close. I am sure they didn't notice me looking at the mat on the floor of the car.

"Yes, Matt Cot… ter." What am I doing? I was overstretching with the first name. Why did I try and give myself a second one? They didn't give their surnames. I really need to think about the name thing before I start to engage with people. I am always a breath away from telling them my real name.

"So, can I ask, where you girls are from as I am guessing you are not English, are you?"

"Spain." They all speak at once. I sense they are proud of that. It is probably why they all have good tans. I wonder if their tans are all-over tans. I am sure they are. At some point I am going to check it out. On all of them. I just have to choose who goes first. That is a really hard choice ahead of me.

"How far do you go?" I look in the mirror. That's the Susana girl. How far do I go? Baby, all I can think is I go all the way. For you I go all the way.

"To er, Edinburgh?" That is in Scotland, right? And an E. Where did that come from? I wasn't aiming to go there. I did say I needed some distance. They are all clapping so they are happy I said that. It must be in Scotland. The Rocio girl leans over and kisses me on the cheek as I drive. Yes, she wants me. If her friends weren't in the back then I am sure she would have leant over straight into my lap as I drive.

She said Halloween Hitch-Hike, right? So, Halloween is Wednesday. That has come about so fast. I need to do something about Halloween. That is the big thing that I need to do. I need to make it my own day. Like the bunny has Easter and Father Christmas has Christmas. Halloween could be mine. How cool would that be? They would probably change it to Edmund Carson Day. Something like that. Or make it a Bank holiday. They need it; those poor guys only get like half a dozen holidays a year. Even my dad got more holiday than that, not that we went anywhere nice.

Maybe I should do something with the girls. They can be like my Halloween stars? Although, that is a few days away! I am not sure these girls will hold out a few days to be with me. They are only human.

They are all whispering in Spanish now. They are only doing that to discuss how hot I am. How each of them would like to do me. I wouldn't be surprised if it is a debate about who is going to go first. Not that they will want to. They know the second time and third time is longer. They will have read the papers. The girls will have told the papers what a great lover I am.

It will be Rocio. I can tell. It is why she jumped into the front of the car. She is struggling to contain herself now. It's not the first time they have shared a man. I can tell that. I wouldn't be surprised if they start pulling straws or something. They must be wondering how to do that without making it too obvious to me. I put my foot down. The sooner we get to Edinburgh, the sooner they get the opportunity to impress me, enough for me to give them all a go, one by one. I will consider the frenzy thing while I drive. It is not a threesome so it might be good, nobody will feel left out if they play with each other while they wait. I am such a thoughtful lover.

We pull into the campsite. That was so much fun, even if it did take us eight hours to get here. I am not sure why they have the smart motorways. I think there are more delays now than ever. Well, from like last time I came to Scotland. Although I don't think I came this way. Don't remember seeing the Llama Café before. I don't even think they are real. They were just in that Dr Dolittle film. Talking to animals – the bloke was mad as a hatter.

The girls are so funny. The stories they have about the beer festivals and fairs. I knew they had shared men before. Is that all they do in Spain? Drink and party in bikinis. Every time I look at them I can see them in bikinis. I really should visit Spain. It sounds amazing. The hot weather and the even hotter girls, sounds perfect. If they are all small and cute with dark hair it would be a bit like heaven.

I get out of the car. I promised to help them set up in the dark. I don't mind. It will give me time to decide which one of them deserves my attention. I mean, they all deserve my attention at some point.

It is important to them who I take first. I am thinking Raquel. Some of her stories had that darker side to them. I am sure, but I think that she plays for both sides too. I mean, I don't mind. I am sure I will probably ruin her for other men now. Although I thought Macarena was a dance? Sounded more like some hot girl she made out with at one of the beer festivals. She was very keen to tell me she liked men though. There was only one reason for that.

I thought this place would be busier. Edinburgh is a popular place. I suppose a campsite at the end of October is not going to be that popular. I have never put a tent up before so I am not sure how good I will be. I took one down once. I say took it down, was more squashed it down. That was a bunch of girls too. Not my best day, if I remember correctly. This day has considerably got better though. Where the fuck was that? It seems like ages ago. I remember there was a field, and a well? And it was dark. I mean, real dark. It is a good job the Q7 has great big headlights. At least we can see what we are doing here.

Twenty minutes later it is done. The tent is up. That was easier than I thought. I can turn my hand to just about anything, can't I? I get a kiss from each of them for the tent and the lift. Susana's tongue did hit the back of my throat. I am not sure how big that thing is, but I bet she has kept a few boys happy with it.

They are all going to shower in the public showers. They are all braver than I am. I had a look at them on the way in. They are really small and I think I would rather wash in the

116

stream. The council need to keep these things in better condition. It is not a good impression to give our visitors, especially the ones from another country.

I leave them to it. It has been a long day. I say my goodbyes and get back in the car. I need to find somewhere to stay myself. That is going to be tough this time of night. Most of the hotels will be full by now, I am sure. Although I am sure if I needed to, with these seats down I could fit in the back of here. Sleeping in the car would be okay. It is just a tent on wheels, isn't it? I pull out of the campsite and turn right. I guess that is why people have caravans so that they don't need to worry about where to stay. Maybe I should do that for a while. It will keep me off their radar and I won't lose my fucking stuff in some train station. It will give me a place of operations. Nobody would think of me as a caravan type of person. That is for really old people with little dogs and deck chairs. I would make it cool again. I could probably get sponsorship from caravan monthly or something like that.

I turn right again. It would give me somewhere to take girls back to also, like a love nest. Most celebrities have one of those. It doesn't matter to them then whether they have a wife or a girlfriend. It is somewhere to take the fans back to. Show them how much they mean to you. It is the least you can do for them. I have to give that some more thought for when Miss Walker and I live in Camden. I am not sure she would like me to bring fans back to the house to show my appreciation.

I don't see Miss Walker hiding in the closet like Tim so that she can get a look at me and another woman going at it. Tim was a little weird like that. Who does that, watch there

Mrs with someone else? No, she wouldn't like that at all. Maybe I can rent a flat on the side. Somewhere she doesn't know about. Above one of the tattoo places. I imagine that would be good for business. The fans would probably go straight downstairs and get a tattoo of me. The sale of the world's greatest lover tattoos would go through the roof. Tattooed under a picture of my face to remind them of the night. I will have to patent that. Make some real money. I turn right again.

Yes, I need somewhere. That is a great idea. If I had somewhere now I could have taken each of them, one night each before Halloween. Think I would have started with Susana now. That tongue action. She really has my motor going. It is all I can think about now. What she could have done with that. She would have been first. Then Rocio, Eve, and save Raquel for last. Raquel had that sweetness about her. Not sweet as in sweet, as I bet she could get a bit freaky but sweet as in tasting sweet. It is all about diet. Girls who sleep with girls probably look after themselves more? I could smell it on her. She has something that would keep me going through whatever I needed to do for Halloween. Wait, what am I going to do for Halloween? I need to give it more consideration.

I pull over. This is as good as place as any. It is still dark, but hey, it is about eleven thirty. I think it gets darker the more north you travel, doesn't it? Must be pitch black in this John o' Groats place. Not sure why they would want to go there?

The more I think about it, for Halloween, they all need to return. That is the kind of event which will get the press buzzing again. I will need a new costume for the Alphabet Killer. I am just not sure it needs to be the same costume. I have done that. Jack has had his moment of glory with me. Should I keep it fresh, changing all the time? Besides, it was hardly the easiest thing to get around in. It was all right for him. Probably had a carriage drop him on the street corner and pick him up again. You can't do that nowadays. Can it be different costume each time? It is a different letter each time. Can I even think of twenty-six different costumes? Although, the finger-licking guy is done now. So, technically, I worked with two people in Derby, three if you count the maid, without the costume getting a shout.

Fuck!

Fucking hell. What is wrong with me? I didn't take a single selfie! How am I going to be able to keep track of all this if I don't start taking selfies with every one of them? It is because I am not posting it straight away it feels like I have forgotten about the fans. What is that all about? It is all about the fans. I really need to work on this assistant thing. It can't always be down to me to do all the work. I need someone who chronicles my diaries. Jesus, where did the word chronicles come from? That's not something that just springs to mind, is it? I mean, Chronicles?

At fucking last!

I was wondering how long it would take. Good job I noticed the slip road to the back of the shower block. They won't be able to see the car from here. But at last, I can see the torches coming up to the shower block. They must be coming two at a time. There are only two lights coming in this direction. As they get closer I can see who it is. It is Susana and Rocio. It is like I can predict the future. I said I would have worked with them first. If you had asked me an hour ago, I was doing Raquel first. Then bang! I change my mind and it falls into my lap. I should try and predict other things to see if I can summon them up too. I think I may just be one of those people who live a charmed life. Someone good things always happen to.

I get out of the car and head towards the shower block. Rocio is standing outside. They must be clever girls. I think they said they were all vets or something. That must take forever at school, like medical school. Mum always wanted me to be a doctor. Can you imagine another five to eight years in school? Who the fuck would want to do that? Although five more years with Miss Walker as a teacher does have its appeal.

It is wise to have someone stand guard when you are in public showers. Anyone could walk in and see them naked. How embarrassing would that be for them? I stand around the corner waiting for the shower to start running. It does. All I can think of now is that Susana is naked. I am sure she is the type to shower naked. Even up here. She is naked and soaped up. For some reason I see her licking her lips in the shower. It is that tongue, I am getting obsessed by it. Now that is turning me on. I take a quick look. Rocio is looking at her phone. That is not good; she is supposed to be standing guard. What if some weirdo is looking to get a peek at her friend? Or worse. She is facing the shower room so I suppose that is one thing. She is probably trying to get a look herself. Getting herself all worked up and ready for the frenzy.

I am behind her with my knife at her throat within seconds. One swift move and the smell explodes into my nose. I drag her back around the corner from the main door and just hold her close to me. I lean her head back so I can get the full effect as I hold her even tighter. She must be enjoying this as much as I am. She can feel how hard I am in her back. All fourteen inches or more right in her back. She must be thinking I knew it was him. I hoped he would work with me and now she can feel how much I want her. I pull her closer so I can whisper in her ear.

"You are welcome."

I have missed this moment. I just need to appreciate it. It was ruined in Camden by that girl screaming that she couldn't swim. How insensitive can one woman be? God, she smells good. It is all I can do to stop myself from doing her here and now against this wall. She would love that. That smell, that smell is something, something sweeter than I have ever remembered. I wonder if it is the Spanish thing. Maybe the diet is so much better in Spain. Maybe they are all going to taste this good. That makes me so happy, happy and fucking hard.

I have to stop myself. I still have three other girls dying to work with me. I drag her back to the car and place her in the back seat. She is not awake yet, but I give her a little kiss on her forehead. Just so that she knows she will be getting the good stuff. I close the door and compose myself. I don't want to miss out on Susana in the shower. She wouldn't want me to either. I am sure she will be washing some places more than others as she is thinking about me.

I head back to the shower block and enter slowly. The shower is still running. That is a good sign. I get past the shower and into the corner. I stand in the corner. I almost have a full view from here. She is still covered in soap. Exactly the way I imagined it. She must have been really dirty for the time she is taking. Either that or she got carried away with herself.

The thoughts of eight hours with me would have done that to her. Probably started rubbing down there and couldn't stop. It is nice to think you are giving a girl multiples when you aren't even in the room. I must be doing that all across the country.

That's it, make sure you are clean everywhere. Lathering up that soap as it gently rubs against the chocolate-coloured skin. She really does have an all-over tan. I can't see a single white mark. It looks amazing with the white soap though...

What the fuck am I doing standing here!

I thrust forward and head straight into the shower. I am on her and before she knows what is happening my knife is in her throat. There is another explosion of smell. It is the Spanish thing. It has to be. The blood is so fucking...

Fuck!

I dropped her!

Fuck!

I slip on the shower floor.

Fuck!!

I hit my head on the shower door.

Fuck!

That hurt. The blood is everywhere. She is spurting everywhere. It's a waste. It should be spurting into my mouth not down the drain.

We are both now on the floor. The shower is still going. I am getting soaking wet. I try to get up, but it is slippery. I hold on to the side and manage to stand. I manage to turn the shower off.

Fuck, I am soaked!

I wipe my eyes. Somehow I got soap in them. Must have been when I was standing behind her. At least I can see now, and I mean all of her.

"That's better."

I look at her on the floor. Even there she looks amazing. The smell is sweet, so sweet. She is going to taste amazing, I know it. I am even hornier now though. I am surprised my trousers haven't ripped open. I can hardly contain it in there.

How long would you give it before coming to look for your friends who have gone to shower together? Ten, maybe twenty minutes? What has it been already? If they heard us going at it in here surely, they would just walk away. Give us the moment – they are friends, after all – especially if they spotted the car. No ten, twenty minutes. It is not enough. I think I could go all night at the moment. Go all night with each of them. I have to think about her as well. She wouldn't get the best of me in that time if I had to try and rush. She deserves to savour the moment. Maybe I should just knock one out myself. Try to calm myself down. I can normally do that in ten minutes although the way she looks on the floor, maybe five. My hand wanders down to it. I can feel it throbbing to get out...

Fuck's sake, focus, Edmund.

I am back to this I could fuck this all up in a moment of weakness. I am better than this and I have a quest to complete. It is the work that is important. I am going to have to write that somewhere. Maybe get a tattoo of it just to keep refreshing myself.

I pick her up off the floor. My God, she feels good. Wet and hot, like most of the girls I pick up, but she feels really good. How long has it been since I have had any? It has been far too long. I grab the towel off the back of the door and then throw her and the towel over my shoulder. It doesn't make any difference. I am already wet. Her body is covered in blood. I give it a little lick, and then another. I am so hungry, hungry for her, hungry for the blood, hungry for everything.

I check the doorway first. There is nobody about. I carry her straight to the car and place her next to Rocio. I don't give her a little kiss. I don't think it is fair when there are two of them together. Jealousy is a strong emotion in women and I wouldn't want friends to fall out over me. I will ensure what we do is kept between us.

"Yeah, sorry it took so long. She had a little accident in the shower. She slipped over. She is fine though. Maybe a little concussed but she will snap out of it soon."

"No, I assure you, you were always first on my list." That made her smile. I am safe as Susana isn't awake yet. I have half a mind to lay them both down in the back of this car and take a turn with each of them right now. I am that horny, I think I would even consider a threesome with them. That would be a good enough end to what I thought at one point was a really shit day.

I need to think about the bigger picture. How far am I going to get if the other two go running to the police because I didn't include them in the night? Yes, jealousy will make women do strange things.

I use the towel quickly and try to dry my face and hair. It will have to do. I don't want to miss the other two girls coming back to the shower. I stand by the car. It is not that cold for October. I think I will dry off better out here too. Besides, I am not sure it is safe to be this wet with heated seats in the car. I might electrocute myself. They will come in handy later just to warm me through though. It takes another ten minutes before I see the torch. There is only one light heading in this direction? I can make out it is just one person as well. I guess one of them wanted to stay a bit dirty. I bet it is Raquel. The torch gets closer. I knew it. I knew Eve would be the one to come looking for them. I get to the shower block just before she does. I come around the corner before she goes in.

"Hey!" That shocked her. She wasn't expecting to see me. "Hey!"

I know that look. That look is an immediate am I wearing the right clothes? Is my hair good? That is why they toss the hair. It is the, I can look a mess, but a hot mess look.

"I was hoping I would bump into you." That will have her weak at the knees. If it doesn't. My knife is in her neck. She doesn't even move. There is a look on her face as if she was expecting it. The smile is still there. There in the corner of her mouth. A smile that says thank you, I know what is coming next. She knows that she will be coming and so will I. She will be coming at least once.

"You are welcome." I love the fact that they are all small. I can easily throw them around, and I will be doing a lot of that. I pull out the knife. Blood is spurting everywhere. I pull her closer and let it hit me straight in the mouth. It is like drinking from a fountain. A rich, dark, sweet, heavenly fountain! I lean in further and take another lick around the neck. This is an amazing night after such a crappy day. What a difference a day can make. I should really pick up hitch-hikers more often.

I am suddenly aware I am standing in front of the shower block with the lights on. It is probably not the best place to be. Besides, with only Raquel left to work with I think I finally have some time. I take Eve back to the car. I borrow Susana's towel again and clean myself up the best I can. She must have bumped her head as she is still out. I think that Rocio has been preparing herself for me though as she has one hell of a smile on her face now. I will have to take care of her. She deserves it. The wait must be agonising for her. For all of them.

I leave them all cuddled up on the back seat. The excitement for them is going to be overwhelming, knowing they are halfway to the time of their lives. I head back to the shower block. Maybe she just isn't coming for a shower? I should just take a walk and pay her a visit. I pick up Eve's torch and head back towards their tent. It is good that we pitched it by the road. It gave us easy access. Plus it didn't disturb anyone on the way in. Not that there are many people around. She is still awake. I can see the torch moving inside the tent.

"Knock knock." Why am I whispering? Nobody else is really close enough to hear us. I suppose you don't know who is lurking in the woods though. You can't be too careful there are some weird people out there. Some psycho probably went for a pee and saw a group of hot Spanish girls pull up and place a tent. Could be spying on them. I should check that out later for them. Make sure they are safe.

The zipper to the tent opens and Raquel leans out. Hardly lingerie, more teddy bear PJs but still doable. There is still a very doable body under there.

"Hey, I thought you had gone."

"I had. Eve left her coat in my car so I came back to return it. I bumped into them at the shower block. Believe it or not, there are quite a few other campers up there. In the middle of October. There is a fire and a few bottles of wine being passed around. They are settled in for a while, I guess, so I thought I had better come back and get you. You know, just in case you wanted to join them? You know, with me." I try to say that as slowly as I can. To point out that there is another option. There is a better option. A really better option.

"That is, unless you can think of something better we could be doing?" I can't make it any clearer than that, can I? We could be doing each other!

Fuck!

No, I didn't need to spell that out any more. She is out of the tent and her tongue is in my mouth. She must have been gagging for it. That is why she didn't go for a shower. She wanted some alone time with herself. The thought of me does that to a woman. She pulls me down and back into the tent. She certainly doesn't mess about, does she? She is pulling at my top. She hasn't even closed the zipper. Anyone could walk past us.

"You are wet?"

Shit! Forgot about that. I am sure I am not the only one in this tent who is wet though.

"Yes, it was raining a little."

She doesn't care. I manage to take control of her hands and start her on undressing herself. I need to see flesh not PJs. As she is undressing I quickly place the knife into the side of the tent. Last thing I need is her undressing me and finding that. What would she think then? She is pulling at my trousers

127

now. She just can't wait to see the goods. She pulls them off. She is just looking at it now. She has never seen one that big before, I can tell. Her eyes are rolling at the thought of it.

Fuck!

She tries to swallow it. What the fuck is she doing? I am sure she is trying to eat it. All I can feel are her lips and tongue and teeth gnashing against it. That's not right! That's not what it normally feels like. I pull her off. That was just weird. I then throw her onto her back. She likes that. She likes that I am back in charge. That stuff she was just doing didn't feel normal. In a split second, I am on top of her. I am in her. That is what happens when you are as hard as a rock, and she is dripping wet. You just go straight in.

Fuck!

That is warm. I mean really warm. I haven't felt anything that warm since, well, since Mrs Green and I figured that was because she was old and probably going through the change. Raquel makes the loudest noise, as if someone had stabbed her with a sword.

It wasn't a sword. It was big, but maybe she is only small down there. I do it again to make sure it is me. It is me. She is making that loud sound every time I enter her. Something is wrong. This doesn't feel right. She is moving all wrong, wriggling and she is grabbing at me. She grabs my bum. What is up with her? Why would she do that? Doesn't she feel that I am big enough as it is? Why would she try to push me further into her? And the kissing, it doesn't stop. I think she is trying to suffocate me with her mouth. I am going at her. I am doing everything I would normally do. That should be enough, more than enough for most girls, but she wants more. It is like it is all about her. That is not what this is supposed to be about. She really is pushing me into her. I don't like it. It makes me feel like…

Fuck!

They are some fucking sharp nails digging into me. I grab at the side of the tent and grab my knife. I put one hand over her mouth and give her something sharp of my own, again and again into her ribs. She is fitting now. That feels a little better. That is more of the movement I remember. Better than it was before.

At last she has relaxed her grip on my bum anyway. I pull the knife up and cut her across the throat. The blood is so strong. So strong! I can feel myself get even harder. I am probably fifteen, sixteen inches now. That will stop her trying to push me in more. I wouldn't be surprised if it is sticking out of her bum now. I just needed the blood. That is what was missing.

That is so much better. She has totally relaxed now. That is what I needed. I needed her to relax and enjoy it like anyone else would. I lie on top of her. The smell is overwhelming me. I lick at her neck. The taste is amazing. I lick again. I take a little bite. Not too hard, just enough to ensure the blood in my teeth, on my tongue. I let the flavour roll around my mouth. I have just realised that I am still inside her. I am still as hard as a rock.

I shouldn't really carry on though, should I? I don't think I have permission. But I don't want to pull out. It won't be nice for her. It will make her feel like I don't want to continue, but I really do. I take another lick at her neck. It is sweet, sweet and rich. There is definitely something about Spanish girls.

They have a taste all of their own. Maybe I should think about that when I work on my cookbook. Different flavours from around the world. Like the Indian girl on the train. The world will be surprised how different the taste of nationality is. My fans will like that. It shows that I am not racist or anything as well, as I will work with anyone. Well, anyone except blondes unless I really have to.

"Hey." That didn't take long. Not long at all. I guess she could still feel me inside her. All of that throbbing would have given her a reason to come straight back to me, which is good for me too. I need to remember that in future if I want to help them wake up quicker. Keep fucking them.

"I wasn't going to without... you know." I didn't need to worry about it. She is still gagging for it. I start again. This feels better. So much better! Although... she is still really warm down there? That feels a little strange. I do hope it is not warm for another reason. Something, you know, disease-ridden. No. She was just so excited to get me back in the tent. It might be because she is Spanish as well, as it is hot in Spain. I suppose their bodies must be hotter in more ways than one. Makes me think about shagging an Indian now. They must be hot as fuck.

I keep going. I can tell she is into it now. This is how lovemaking is supposed to be. Both of us relaxed, and she is letting me do all the work. At least then when she has multiple orgasms she will know that I did that to her. And hopefully she'll be able to tell the press reporters how many times I made her come. I sense it will be three, four times, at least.

I wonder if she has ever been with an English man before. She will definitely want to be with one again. I should probably warn her that they are not all like me. This is not the normal experience. This is a master class in lovemaking. On a scale of one to ten she needs to know that most men are a five to six compared to me. I can tell she is close. I know that look. No matter what nationality you are. That look, when they bite their lip so hard a little bit of blood comes out of their mouths. She must have really bitten her lip as there is blood everywhere.

There she goes. The eyes are rolling and the body is giving multiple shivers. I go too. I was just being a gentlemen and waiting for her to go first. That feels good. Oh, that feels good. It feels like it has been forever since I had that release. The other girls will have helped with that too. Helped to build up all that excitement, I will have to thank them later. She is still going, I can feel it. She must have had at least three orgasms by now. I pull out and lie back next to her.

"I know how you feel. I needed that too." She is trying to speak, but it is hard for her. I can tell she is still tingly all over. She finally manages to get the words out that I was expecting.

"Ha ha! I bet the girls will be a bit mad that you were first.

"Eve? Really, that is who you decided would have the first go? I wouldn't have said that. Not that I wouldn't be tempted as she is a pretty girl. But I always had an eye for you." That will keep her happy. Not a bad thing either. Keep them sweet so that they tell the positive side of everything. I am sure now that was the issue with the hotel. I didn't make it personal enough. I treated it more as a job than the art it really was. It feels like I let them down a little. I wonder if that was what finally turned the press against me? They believed that I had started to neglect the people that I work with. Maybe the press felt I was getting too big for my britches. That is what my nan used to say if you were showing off. Maybe the feedback from the guests told them that. I need to show a bit more interest in my fans and the people who are helping me on this journey. Give them something back. Spend some quality time with them so they know they are appreciated. Because they are, I really do appreciate their support. They are after all who I do all this for. I look over at Raquel. She is hot. She is an eight or a nine in anyone's book. I think she has finally stopped. See, I do appreciate her. I gave her time to finish her multiple orgasms before engaging her in conversation. I am that type of lover.

"So, this Halloween thing, is there a party at the end of the hitch-hike?

"Really? That is good to know. At John o' Groats? Not that I have ever been. Is it going to be costumes or just a how can I say this, boring one?

"Costumes. You know that is the best type of party. My type of party! Can I ask who you were going as? I presume you have your costume already? You know, just in case you were running late.

"Me? What do you mean you were going as me?" I am playing innocent. I know exactly what she meant. It is Halloween. I am sure there are a lot of me on Halloween.

"Ha, ha, you knew? How did you know? Did the others know?

"Really? You all knew as soon as you picked me up? Didn't I pick you up? It doesn't matter, I just got that. Yeah, it was a sight to see four hot girls on the side of the road. So who were you going as then?

"Father Harry. He was your favourite? I am shocked. I didn't see you as a churchgoing type. What was special about him? I would really like to know as I am always on the lookout for another character. For instance, what was your favourite Father Harry event?

"No way! And you were going to try and visit it while you were up here. I didn't even think about it till just then. I suppose we are close enough. The fact I got us to here today must have been so exciting for you also.

"Yes, it was in Glasgow. Can I tell you a secret? It wasn't really planned. To be really honest, I was just hungry. I was really hungry.

"No, not hungry for that, although I must say, you have wet my appetite again. I was hungry for food. Sometimes I forget to eat. You just get so wrapped up in your work. I had been working with a couple of friends. About three streets up. Ana, her name was. She was cute. No, more than cute, she was hot." From the way she is looking at me I can tell this is not a good time to pause.

"Yes, a couple of friends. Her boyfriend's name was… I want to say Antonio. I think he was actually Spanish. At least I think that was his name. That is a Spanish name, right? She did call out to him at one point. She may have said she wanted him to join us. Or that she wanted me and was asking permission. I can't blame her, of course. We did share a few moments together. She was sweet too." Shit, need to change this. She doesn't look happy about me talking about another girl. Although the more I think about it she was sweet too. She tasted really sweet. I wonder if she was Spanish. Ana can be a Spanish name, can't it?

"After I had finished working with both of them…" That was good. I was keen for her to know I worked with both of them

"He was downstairs in the kitchen and she was upstairs in the shower like…" Shit, this is supposed to be engaging. I very nearly said Susana then. That wouldn't have gone down well. I am supposed to be leaving her happy and content so that she can tell the world's press what a great lover and person I am. Caring, considerate lover. That is what she needs to tell them.

"Like nearly in the shower, she was heading to the shower." I look at her face. I think I got away with that. She is smiling at me again now.

"Someone kept knocking on the door and shouting through the letter box. I mean, who shouts through the letter box? Just because they knew they were in. It got me in a bit of a panic, to be fair. I had to climb over the back fence to get out of the house. Thing is, I had followed them back from a restaurant. They had been having dinner in one of those BBQ places, I think it was one of those all you can eat places. I walked past the window and the food looked so great. They were just leaving with a big doggy bag full of ribs – at least, that is what I imagined them to be. I am partial to a little bit of spare ribs. I thought, that looks good and I imagined those ribs with a few more of Ana's delicacies.

"Yes, I am fit. Getting over the fence wasn't an issue." I sense she was trying to change the subject. That is fair, I need to stop talking about Ana and her delicacies.

"Anyway, I digress. When I followed them home I parked round the back of the house. Now I come to think of it. That was lucky really, especially as I had to make a quick exit.

"No, you are right, back to the McDonald's story. I still can't believe how famous it has become. As I said, I wasn't intending it. I went into there as I didn't get the BBQ ribs or anything else to eat." Let's just leave it at that. I don't think she is ready to hear what I really wanted for dinner.

"I am partial to the odd Big Mac. McDonald's has actually been significant in a few moments in my life. My parents wanted me to work there. I am considering letting them being one of the first companies to sponsor me. I mean, I know I will have to do a few TV adverts for them, but that is fine.

"Yes, really, they wanted me to work there. I am sure you understand that wasn't for me. Anyway, I watched as the staff shuffled around a lot behind the counter. It was gone midnight on a Tuesday night in Glasgow. I am not sure why they were open for twenty-four hours in Glasgow. I was the only person in there. I had been the only person in there for about twenty minutes until someone went through the drive-through. I could see them from where I was sitting.

"It was still the old-fashioned drive-through. The one with the three stops. So, money, drinks and then food. The thing that made me laugh was it was the same person at all three windows. There were only three of them on site and the other two were cooking. Well, I say cooking. One was microwaving and I guess the other was the supervisor.

"I know, right. I said I guess he was a supervisor as he had about three stars on his shirt. The others didn't have stars so he must have been in charge.

"Thanks. I think you just gave a five-star performance yourself." I sense she is ready to go again. Flattery will get her everywhere. I think the press will have probably leaked that fact about me somewhere. The fact that I am good to go very soon after the first time. Women like that in a man.

"When they had finished serving the guy in the drive-through, all I could think about were the monkeys. You know, the three monkeys as there were three of them running around behind there. Three monkeys and three windows, it was too good an opportunity to miss. It was more Edmund than Father Harry, I do agree. The whole staging the scene is Edmund's thing. But I couldn't shake the feeling. So I waited for one of them to wander off. They went to the bathroom. I made sure none of the other two watched me as I followed them in there and then I worked with him as quickly as I could. I knew if I waited long enough another one would follow. They did. By the time I came out the third was on his way to look for them. It was so simple. I sense they all wanted to be worked with. Probably knew who I was as soon as I walked in.

"Yes, I suppose I am good at my job. Sometimes it may just feel simple as I am so good. I then just went behind the counter to find the light switches, and turned the big M off outside, and all the lights inside. I then went back outside and picked up my go-bag.

"Yes, then I made the windows." She really is a fan, isn't she? I do love it when they are a true fan.

"It took me about an hour or so. But to be fair, nobody came into the shop or the drive-through. I am sure it was because the lights were off. People must have been driving straight past.

"I am sure they wouldn't if they knew what was happening inside. The chance to watch a master at work would have pulled quite the crowd." I do like her. She is really talking a lot of sense. Calling me master as well is good. It tells me that this is the type of thing she will say to the press.

"So, I made the first window. Hear no evil. I taped the girl's hands over her ears. Then see no evil, the guy's hands over his eyes. Then finally, speak no evil. It was a nice touch to fill his mouth with a Big Mac before taping his hands, I must say. That went down a bomb online. It was actually his idea. I guess it was why he was a supervisor. He was always advertising the business. Come to think of it, maybe he was part of the family. I mean McDonald is a very Scottish name, isn't it. I would expect the next day it probably got him two extra stars. There would have been a huge demand for Big Macs. I hope there was. The boy needed to be promoted after that.

"No way! Really? It has hit twenty-three million? I must admit, I haven't seen it for ages. But it wasn't just the hits on YouTube. The pictures went viral worldwide. I wouldn't be surprised if they were in all their stores worldwide. I am sure I read once that they have something like thirty-four thousand outlets.

"I know, I switched the lights back on and drove through the drive-through myself. It looked great. They reckon it took the Glaswegians – that's the word, isn't it? – about three hours after me opening back up to call the police. They thought it was a stunt for advertising by McDonald's. I heard actually they are thinking of ditching the clown in favour for the ONE. They were going to go with Father Harry, but they didn't want to be associated with just one religion. Makes sense, I suppose, they are worldwide. Besides, there is so much you can do with advertising as the ONE. Number ONE. Only ONE. That type of thing. The ONE will probably become a burger at some point.

"Really? Thank you." She is not wrong. I probably could have worked in marketing. I would have been great at that. I imagine it to be a boring job but creative. I am creative.

I know that look in her eyes. She is ready again. It is a good job I am always ready again. I think I have shared enough as well. I think I have taken time with her to show her this is about the work as much as it is about her. That was the main thing. Plus, she doesn't have to ask me twice. I am back on top of her.

"Just once more, for me, of course. I will ensure I leave you multiplying. I have to get going. Besides, your friends could come back at any time?" I doubt they will as they will all be waiting for me. It will make it a little more exciting for her though. I take a little lick. That does the trick. They should bottle this stuff. It is better than the little blue pill that those old guys take. Maybe I should start marketing that as well. The EC pill. I will make a killing.

Thirty minutes later we are both spent. She is exhausted, I can tell. That must be what, nearly a dozen times in under an hour? Most women don't get that in a lifetime. She is not going to be giving me any negative press.

"If you like I will go and check?" Thank fuck for that. I was wondering how I was going to get out of here without upsetting her.

"I am sure they are having too much fun. You just relax and see if you can get your strength back. You really did earn that extra sixth star tonight." I get dressed as best I can in a tent. I lean over and give her a kiss on the forehead. She is going to sleep those orgasms off, I can tell. I don't blame her; she must be really light-headed now. Wait, that is the sack, isn't it? She is lying on a sleeping bag. That is what they refer to as the sack. Good in a sleeping bag. We should have tried that.

"I will be back soon." I get out of the tent and zip it up for her. I take one look at the trees. I don't see any weirdo's out there. Seeing me around will keep them away as well. They won't want to attack a bunch of girls when they have a protector like me. She will be safe.

It was only a small white lie. I won't be back soon. Not that I would mind seeing her again but it is time to get out of here.

Besides, Edinburgh is… I undo the zip and go back in.

"Just a quickie." I lie next to her and take a photo. A couple of them. She is really hot. It is good for my fans to see the type of girl I can get. Good looking people are meant to be with good looking people it is nature or something.

I am back out of the tent and zip it up again. I have to remember to take photos. Always take photos.

Now. Edinburgh is done.

Chapter 7

Crap! I must have dozed off for longer than I thought. I only pulled over for a quick siesta. Siesta? See what happens when you spend time with Spanish people? You start to think in Spanish. Siesta is Spanish, I am sure. I watched it on the programme with the Spanish waiter. Little sleep, siesta. My dad loved that programme, especially the one about the Germans and not mentioning the war. He laughed at it, no matter how many times he had seen it.

"Sorry, ladies, you must think me so rude. I nodded off. I just saw the little road and thought we wouldn't be disturbed down here.

"Oh, you all did too. That is good. It was a late night, wasn't it? Such a long drive yesterday as well."

Really should have given Susana a blanket, she must have been cold last night. She is still smiling though. I suppose the excitement must keep her warm. The thought of having me this close would have kept all their motors running.

"What do you reckon then, what shall we do today?

"Ha ha ha! Eve, that was fast. Funny and fast! I am sure we will get around to that later." Do me is a great answer. They must have been thinking about the friends' frenzy all night.

Although I am having this feeling deep down that I need to ditch the car. There aren't many of them around and if we are going to have quality time together I don't want any interruptions. The press will be looking for a Q7 I am sure of it.

"So, things to do today include ditch the car, plan the Halloween fest, and have fun while we do. I mean, real fun." They are all smiling at that.

"Oh yes, and do Eve. Sorry, Eve, nearly forgot."

She is gagging for it this morning. Blatant as well! In front of her friends.

I click on the sat nav. I am somewhere near Livingston. I am sure that he was an explorer or something. I learnt about him at school. He was probably Scottish. They have quite a few famous people up here, don't they? I zoom out the screen. The sat nav on this car is amazing.

"Sorry?

"Yes, I am sure we have." I am sure we have time. It is only Sunday and Halloween isn't until Wednesday.

"Yeah, I didn't really think about that." She has a point. I love the fact that she is hot and intelligent. So many girls are just about their looks nowadays. There has to be more to a woman, even a woman who is just wearing a towel. It is going to be so much harder to ditch the car as a foursome. I really should have got her some clothes.

How am I going to do all of that today? Where do I start? I am looking directly at the sat nav.

Maybe I can do all of that in one day. Well, most of it. It is staring me straight in the face. If I do this, it still counts though, doesn't it? They don't know the girls have been worked with. They are barely missing by now. They are probably not even reported as missing. Raquel would have put two and two together by now. She will know they are all with me. Although she won't be mad. She got to go first and twice. Well, twice for me, multiple for her. Nobody will be missing these girls until Wednesday, I am sure of it.

I set the sat nav. They were so close together I would be stupid to miss the opportunity. Then I need to decide where to go. But first I need to think of something for each of the girls. I am going to have to perform for each of them today. That is for sure. I need them to have something special. They deserve it. They have been so much fun over the last day. I start the drive. Should only be thirty minutes to get there.

The roads are good in Scotland. I don't know why, but I always imagine them to be more like Cornwall. More countryside with narrow lanes. It is a good job they are not, not in this car. Thirty minutes and I am here.

"Okay, Eve, this town is for you. Any ideas about what we can do? I am open to a scene. Even though it is not the Alphabet Killer style I am happy to do anything for you girls? Any position you like?

"Doggy style? Really?" Poor girl has been dreaming about it for the last twenty-four hours, it has fried her brain. I pull into the next little lane I find. Looks like the entrance to a big house. It is still early. It is only ten thirty. How the hell did it get to ten thirty? I back up against a tree.

If I am going to keep the girls happy I am going to have to give them everything they want. I get out and open the back of the car. I then fetch Eve. I whisper into her ear as I carry her out of the car.

"We could go a bit further into the trees or we could just go to the back of the car? It really depends on how shy you are?

"It will be cleaner, but we will have to be quiet. It is not fair on the other two. I don't want them to get overexcited. They will never make it through the day without me."

She will keep the noise down. I don't see her as a screamer. Rocio, on the other hand, I don't think she is going to be silent. I move her round to the back of the car and bend her over it. This car is great. She is just the right height. This feels a bit missionary, which is odd as it is more doggy fashion. There is something missing. There is a lack of excitement and passion. For me, that is. For her, it is probably all her dreams come true. I can feel her quivering with anticipation. I lean over and take a lick of her neck. It is cold? I don't think she is frigid so why would it be cold? She has been practically begging me for it since the moment that we met. It tastes nice, no, not nice, okay, but it is not the same.

I need something to warm it up a little, give it a little heat, which is bound to get this party started. I take another lick just to be sure. Yes, it needs something. That reminds me, I haven't had breakfast. I thought about packing up the stuff from the campsite that could have come in handy this morning for some real breakfast, and I could have done something with the camping stove. Nice piece of liver or something.

I wonder if heat is like garlic. My nan used to say that if you rubbed garlic on your foot you could smell it on your breath within two minutes. If I set fire to her foot, the heat might work its way all the way through the body in minutes? Surely it is a little bit like boiling water.

"Yes, everything is okay. I was just distracted for a minute.

"No, we are certainly getting down to business. I was just thinking how I can make you a little hotter. If that is even possible?" That is a good line. I will have to remember that one for the film. If she wasn't soaking wet before, she will be now.

"Oh, that is a great idea. I am sure it will work. Not sure why they would have one of them back here though?" I look. It doesn't have the connection so I go and get the one from the front of the car. It fits. I click it on.

"It shouldn't take more than a minute."

I finish getting her prepared to receive me. I should really start to get some feedback for the book from them. How they feel when I am close and ready to take them. All of it will be great. The girls love to read about this stuff as well. Gets them all excited. That can only be good for business. It clicks.

"Looks like we are ready. This may tickle a little." I place it on her neck. It sizzles. That is going to warm the blood up. I am not sure why every car has a cigarette lighter nowadays. It is not very PC to smoke. I think it is actually banned in the car now isn't it?

I lean over and take a big lick, and then another. That is the stuff. That is what was missing. I take a little bite at her neck. I get a piece as it comes off in my mouth. I didn't mean to do that. It doesn't taste that good. I think it is the coldness of it. I am sure if it was warm it would be better. I am so hungry this morning. For real food, not appetisers. It helps though and makes me hard as a rock in seconds. I was hard enough, but this just gives it the extra wow factor. That will impress her. I am in her. Straight in.. I just slide straight in. If she has been this wet since yesterday, she must be worried she is dehydrated. I need to ensure she at least drinks some water after this. She does feel good. I do love it when they have those hips, the ones you can hold on to as you enter them over and over again. They are like handles built for your pleasure. Her pleasure clearly, as she is the one getting me. She probably has never been done like this before. Not by someone as big as me anyway.

Is this technically doing it outside? She is half in the car, although if I keep entering any harder she may find herself in the front seat. Yes, I think it counts as outside. This feels good. She feels good. And she is keeping her word, hardly a sound. I can hear the faint oh my god in Spanish but that is expected. The other girls don't even know we are still here. Her lip must be bleeding, the amount she is biting down on it.

I really don't do this enough. It just feels like I haven't had the opportunity lately. I think I may be working too hard again. I need to remember to take some downtime. Some more me time.

I do wonder if Miss Walker hasn't gone off me. I haven't seen her for ages, and she isn't replying to my texts? I know that is not a sign as she always forgets to reply. I know I said I would make a decision on my future when we were in Brighton. In fact, I don't think we have spoken since then. Is that right? Maybe she wasn't as happy about that as I thought. The decision I made to carry on? She said she would be fine with it. She said whatever I decided was going to be fine with her. I know she knows I am not doing this for me. It is for them. The Eve's, Rocio's and Susana's of the world. Oh, and the Raquel's. Almost forgot about her.

She is shivering now, I can feel it. She is close. All that build-up over the last twenty-four hours has made her get to the point really fast. I don't think I am ready. Am I? I need a little inspiration. Miss Walker in a, no, wait, she can't be my inspiration, not if she is going to ignore me. Nuns, nuns with all the gear on. That always does it for me. Nuns in a meadow, in a field, lying down on a white blanket all dressed in stockings and suspenders. Black, no, red! Red stockings and suspenders, now that isn't something you see every day. The red with the whiteness of their skin and the little black dress they always wear. They always go so well together. I am catching up with her quickly. Yes, yes, yes. We are done. We both come at the same time. I am really getting to be a master at that. Maybe I should make a career out of it. I could be in those types of movies! They seem to always be able to hold it until the camera is ready, and the cameras love me.

She is still going. I can tell it must have been a while. I pull my trousers up and leave her to it. I go and put the cigarette lighter back in the front of the car before I forget it. Uncle George wouldn't be happy if I lost it when they return the car to him.

"No, we just went for a little stroll." They clearly didn't hear her. She was quite quiet considering the pleasure she just had, not many women could be so constrained. I go back and sort her out.

"Don't smile too much when you get back in the car, it is a dead giveaway. Especially as you have been so clear that you wanted it from the beginning" I am not sure she will be able to contain herself, but let's see.

I place her back in the car and then get back in the driving seat and continue up the lane. I was right, it was a driveway to a house. Quite a big house although there are no cars in the driveway. Maybe they are all out. I pull up outside the front door and go and knock on it. No, nobody is in. I walk around to the back of the house and try the back door. Still nothing! I can hear a dog barking though. So they must have a pet. I go back to the front door and try it. It is not going to open.

It is not nice to leave the dog alone in the house. I feel sorry for the poor thing having to spend its day all alone in there. I look at the front of the building. They haven't even left a window open for the dog. How is it supposed to breathe in there? I get back in the car.

"No, nobody is home. That is a shame. I did think they might invite us in for a bit of breakfast or something? I bet you are all as hungry as I am.

"Yes, it do's sound like they have left a dog in there. All on its own!

"I am sure they will have left water and food. They haven't left a window open though. You are supposed to do that, aren't you?" Vets are so caring, aren't they? They are always thinking about the animal first. That's why they got the job I am sure of it.

"I don't know how long they have been gone. We were down the road for a good twenty minutes or so. So I am guessing they have been gone for a while." They don't seem to be very happy about that.

"Okay, I will have another look."

I leave the car and try to look through the front door. I can't see a water bowl or any food. They have a point. Owners shouldn't leave their dogs on their own. I need to ensure it is okay. I go to the back of the house. I can see the key in the back door. It is only a small window. I could break the window, open the door and check that it is okay. I fetch a small rock and break the window. The dog is there straight away. It is barking, but it is not mad, I can tell. It looks a real softy, to be honest. It is a big dog with a golden coat. It looks like one of those guide dog types, which is a bit worrying if the guide dog is at home and the car is missing. Is there a blind man driving around the estate without his guide dog to help him? How do dogs help them when they drive anyway? Do they steer? I am sure I have seen that on the Internet. I turn the key and go into the house.

"Here, boy, here." I walk towards it. He is reluctant at first but starts to warm to me. I look around. It was okay, they left a big bowl of food and some water. That is good. We don't need to worry any more. I go back and tell the girls.

"The dog is fine. There is a little window open too now.

"I don't know when they will be back?

"Are you sure, Eve?" She sounds serious about it. I go and collect her. She is such a kind person, wanting to stay with the dog till the owners come back. That will be a nice surprise for them as well. I guess she is just keen to tell someone about her last twenty-four hours. I don't blame her. I take her round the back and into the living room. I sit her comfortably on the chair. The dog really likes her already. He is already up and licking her. He is a friendly dog. I run up the stairs and look in the wardrobes. It would be handy if I can find some clothes for Susana. I am never sure where we are going to end up. I go through the wardrobes. They are all a little fuddy-duddy. Susana seems a little trendier to me. I think she will be able to pull anything off though. Good-looking women can wear practically everything and still look hot. I find a summer dress and go back downstairs.

Vets are great with dogs. It must be part of their training. They are now wrestling on the floor. The dog is licking her all over now. I swear she is trying to put her head in his mouth. I am sure he is making all those growling noises with her just to make it entertaining. Just like the lion tamers do. That is what it reminds me of. Head in its mouth. Lion tamers have to be vets as well. They must be just naturally good with animals.

"Enjoy yourselves, you two."

I head back out the door. I quickly turn back into the kitchen. Open my wallet and leave fifty pounds on the kitchen table. I then walk over to the fridge and write on their chalkboard. "Sorry about the window. Love Edmund Carson." They will love that. Nice piece of memorabilia and I am sure Eve will give them all the low-down about how much of a great guy I am.

I go back to the car.

"So, I have some clothes, Susana. Eve and the dog are rolling around the floor having fun together. I swear the dog was licking so hard her ear may actually come off." They start giggling at that. They probably know how good she is with animals.

I head out of the driveway. Next stop, Glasgow. That was a lot easier than I thought it was going to be.

Falkirk is done.

Chapter 8

Glasgow again! It is close to lunchtime and I am still starving. I think we should go to the drive-through. It would be great to see them all again. By now they probably have a plaque or something on the wall. Maybe I could sign it or something. It is as much a photo opportunity for them as it is for me. Besides, how else will they name a burger after me? The ONE or The Big E or The Big C. They are all good names for food. I can see the advertising banners now. I head towards the drive-through.

"Ladies, do you eat McDonald's?" I have to ask as they are both so slim they must keep themselves fit.

"Really? There aren't that many in Spain? They seem to be on every street corner here in England. Well, every street corner in Scotland as well.

"I think they do fish as well, if that helps. Filet-O-Fish. I suppose it is like a fish burger. Hey, it is probably inspired by John o' Groats. That must be where the fish comes from. That makes sense.

"No, I don't think it is that fresh. It can't be if they have to deliver it all the way from there. It will be frozen and reheated."

I sense Spanish women eat a lot of fresh fish. I suppose you would if you live by the sea. I wouldn't but I suppose they would. I drive straight there. I know exactly where the McDonald's is. It was straight off the M8. I must have eaten here at least three times before I worked there. Still makes me smile to see the...

What the fuck!

It was here! I know it was here. I pull over to where the McDonald's was. I remember seeing the sign from the road. There is just a great big space here now. It is all fenced off. I pull up next to it and get out. Nothing. There is nothing written on the fence. It is just been taken down. No mention of a statue or a monument in my honour. Why would they do that? Why would they lose such a money-making opportunity? I get out my phone and google McDonald's Glasgow. I wait. It comes up with nothing. How can it come up with nothing? How have they managed to wipe me from the history of the Internet? How is that even possible? I keep searching. I can't even find the YouTube clip. Twenty-three million people watched that. Twenty-three million! Don't they understand that it is themselves they are letting down? They are the ones who gave their time to support me. There is nothing. This government and press will have to realise that sooner or later they are not going to keep their jobs. Not if they keep upsetting the public like this. The country will have its say. I get back into the car.

"I am sorry, ladies, they seem to have taken it down." It is my turn to bite my lip. I don't want to ruin the day for them. But I am mad.

"I don't know. My guess would be that they are probably in the process of building some kind of monument to me." I give it a second, they seem to have bought that.

"Something tasteful, I hope. I always liked the thought of a bronze statue.

"Edmund, I would guess, although now that you mention it, I think the ONE would look good as a statue. He would almost look like a knight." He would look good. I am going to have to remind people of that when they are trying to honour me.

"You are right. The last time I was here I was in my Father Harry phase. That would be good too. With my Bible open and a big cross held out in front of me." I wonder how many statues there are of me around the country already. It is not as if I can look it up though, is it, since they have tried to wipe me from the face of the earth? Did Jack disappear before he reappeared as a legend? I mean did they stop talking about him. They must have. I need to look that up.

"I am sure we can find another McDonald's, don't worry."

I start driving again. There has to be another McDonald's around here somewhere. Takes me about fifteen minutes, but I find another one. I go through the drive-through. I order far too much food. I always get overexcited. I mean, who can eat a burger and twenty nuggets? I drive a little down the road before pulling over to eat. I make sure that I lean back and I fold the middle seat for them so that they have a little table.

"See, that's better." This car is amazing. It is a shame I won't have it after today. I will have to leave a note in the glove compartment so when it gets returned to Uncle George he knows how much I enjoyed borrowing it.

"It is good. I hope you like the chicken. I was sure they did a fish burger. Maybe they just don't do it in Scotland any more. There is probably no need for it. It is far too healthy. Do you know last time I was here they were deep-frying chocolate? Mars bars. Deep-fried? I tell you, with that and the drinking I am not surprised they don't live long up here."

I finish up. They hardly touch theirs. I suppose when you have a hankering for fish and you get chicken it is not the same. What now? What now for Rocio? It needs to be something special. I have built up my energy so it needs to be something special. I grab my phone. There is Glasgow Green. They are hosting something called Oktoberfest. That has to be something to do with Halloween, doesn't it? It doesn't look very Halloween. It looks more Heidi than Halloween. What is it with Glasgow? It seems to be all parks and museums.

M&D's is Scotland's only theme park. I say that, but that address isn't Glasgow. I think it is going to have to be something in a park. In fact, I think it is something in Kelvin Grove Park. I am sure I used to go to school with a boy called Kelvin Grove. He sat behind me in Mr Smith's maths class. Bit of a dork, if I remember. Always did the robot moves as if it was still cool and… that is it! That is what I can do. Genius!

I set off towards the park until I find a row of shops. I need to pick up some supplies. This is going to be great. It is genius. I am going to need somewhere to pay attention to her first. I need to ensure she is fully satisfied before I leave her. This is really going to be testing my stamina today. Three in one day. Four if you include Raquel. It is a good job I had a break for some food.

I drive around the outskirts of Kelvin Grove. There is not really anywhere we can stop and get down to it. I am going to go a little further afield. It takes me about ten minutes to find somewhere deserted enough for a little quality time.

"Rocio and I are going to take a little walk. It is just to discuss her scene, and what she is looking to get out of it." Susana doesn't care. She knows what all of this means. She knows that as soon as Rocio has gone it will be just me and her. She has probably been thinking about that since I told them the order in which I wanted to work with them. I think she deserves some real quality time together. She did put the effort in, in the shower scene. I take Rocio around to the back of the car. The bonnet lifts up on its own. It reminds me of those doors on the *Back to the Future* car. That is so cool. I really like this car. I sit her on the back of the car. I was thinking that, wait, she is slipping. I sit her up again. I was, wait, she is slipping again. Is she doing that on purpose? She is now on her knees in front of me. Oh!

"Are you sure?" She is trying not to look up at me. She is looking directly ahead at it. She can probably see how big it is through my trousers. She wants to do this for me. It is probably her way of thanking me for the night.

"If you are totally sure…" It has been a while since I have had one. I unzip and place myself in her mouth. That feels good. There is even a little heat there. There is something about grabbing the back of a woman's head to help her with the rocking motion. That motion is so good, controlled. It is quite tight in there, feels like her tongue is swollen. It will be something to do with all the excitement. Can your tongue swell with excitement? Is that why they call it tongue-tied? When you can't get your words out you are tongue-tied. It is because it swells up. That makes sense. I keep saying that. That makes sense. Make sense why all the girls in school struggled to talk to me. I said it again. Why do I keep saying that makes sense? It is true. They were probably too excited to speak.

She is really good at this. She must do it a lot. I am nearly there already. I am there, but she doesn't stop. She is still going till she gets every last drop out of me. I lift her up and sit her back on the car. She has that look in her eyes. As if she got everything that she wanted. That can't be right, can it? She wanted to, wait a minute, I make sure that she spits. She could have been keeping that stuff in her mouth and when my back is turned put it in a little jar and taken it down the clinic. Yeah, I can see that now. Nine months from now a knock on the door. A little Spanish Carson. She is still smiling. She knows I know what she was up to now. She is a cheeky so-and-so.

"Thanks. You didn't really need to. I was looking forward to, well, you know, with you…

"Really? You would consider it cheating. And what just happened is not cheating? I didn't know that.

"Just so that I get this right, it is only cheating if it is the full-on sex thing? So blow jobs, hand jobs. Even, you know, if I flipped you over to the other side that would be okay?" I never knew this.

"And all Spanish girls think like that? It is not only you.

"I can't really ask Susana as she will then know what we have been up to. But I do know something: I really need to go to Spain." The more I think about it the more I think this place must be heaven. Small, dark-haired, hot women in a hot country who like lots of sex. Sounds perfect.

"No, it is okay. I have a plan. It is bold, bold and brave, but what can I say? You girls have inspired me. Scotland has inspired me too. They love my work up here so I think it is the right place for it. I have been thinking about it for a while actually. I love London and I see it all the time there. I often wondered if I could get away with it. If I don't try now, I never will."

I pick her up and place her back in the car. I go back round to the boot and pull out my supplies and make the sign. I sign the sign. My signature is really coming on. Someone will want to keep that. I can't imagine what my signature is going to be worth in the future. I hear some celebrities are worth a grand. I could probably sign that a thousand times a day. A million pounds a day, just with a pen.

I get back into the car and head to the park. I pull into the car park. I go around to the side of the car and get Rocio out and throw her over my shoulder. I then head into the park. Fuck this feels good. It is packed. Everyone is looking at me. I head towards a park bench. There are lots of them around the park. I can see them everywhere, artists. People must come here to relax often. I place Rocio on the bench. I lean her to one side and close her eyes. I put the sign around her head. Lay the blanket on the floor in front of her and place a hat on the blanket. I then take some money out of my pocket and place it in the hat. I stand back.

"Edmund Carson loves Scotland, signed by the man himself, I see."

I turn. A woman with a pushchair is standing beside me.

"Yes. I couldn't stop him once he saw my work."

She starts laughing really hard. Opens her purse and throws a couple of quid into the hat. Then she takes her phone out and takes a photo.

"Would you mind being in it?"

I smile at her. "Of course not." I sit down next to Rocio. She takes another photo. Photo, fucking photo. I stand up and take a photo of my own. Again I forgot. I forgot about Eve. I am never going to keep track of all this. I don't have time to go back now do I. Fuck. That would have been a great photo with her playing with the dog.

"It is so lifelike."

"Thank you."

"You know, even he would have been proud of that one."

She laughs and walks on. It is lifelike. I am such an artist. People are all smiling as they walk past Rocio. This is going to go down a storm here. She will make a real killing. I lean over and kiss her on the forehead. I still can't believe she didn't want the full-on Edmund Carson experience.

I head back to the car. It is only two thirty in the afternoon. I am killing this Alphabet thing today. If I tried I could do this in a week, I am sure of it.

"So, Susana, it is just you and me for the rest of the day."

I don't think I have ever seen anyone smile so much. Other than Batman back in Birmingham, but he was on drugs.

"Yes, I am totally yours." I can imagine those were the words she has been waiting to hear. I must remember to get her some water before she really dehydrates. Poor girl must be so wet for me that there is nothing left inside her.

Rocio is going to be making a fortune in the park. I can tell. I can see there is a crowd forming around her right now.

Glasgow. Done!

Chapter 9

"It is a beautiful day in the park for Rocio, and Eve is probably out walking the dog. So what shall we do? I mean, I know where we need to end up this evening, but we have the rest of the afternoon together." That smile is intoxicating.

"Oh, we will definitely be doing that. I mean, you haven't even got dressed yet? I can only think of one reason for that." She is giggling now. It is the proper schoolgirl giggle. I suppose it's the nervousness of being alone with me. That is understandable. They have all had a little alone time. Susana will get the most. She is going to taste so good, I can just tell. The thought of it is making me hungry again.

"Hey, I know, we should drive towards that theme park that came up. That could be fun. I haven't been to one of those for ages. It's only worth going in if we have time though." I head towards M&D's. It looked okay. Not Alton Towers okay, but still we could have some fun. There was a zoo too, that is always a good alternative. Especially given she is a VET. The zoo will impress her. Show her I care about her profession and animals. I care about what she cares about.

I am amazing boyfriend material. I need to sit and discuss this with Miss Walker. She needs to understand what she is missing out on when we are not together, especially when she is clearly ignoring my texts now.

I am sure she is mad about the going back to work thing. She was probably already at the settle down stage in our relationship. I don't blame her. It is only natural to want to see me more. I have been working so hard, so hard. I need to ensure we have some time together and soon. Maybe I need to take a break. Somewhere around M and go and see her, or I could just text her now. We are not moving anywhere. Traffic is a bitch up here. I take out my phone and text her. I just say "Missing you, why don't you come and see me? Love Edmund." That should be enough. She knows where I am.

Come to think of it, she always knows where I am. What if she is tracking my phone? You have those Apps now. I should speak to her about that though. Imagine if my stalkers got hold of that App. I would have people following me everywhere. I take out my phone again and text her. "We need to talk." Yes, we need to talk about that. This traffic is not moving anywhere. Sunday afternoon and the traffic is not moving. Wait, she isn't going to think that "we need to talk" is we need to talk, is she? That might have got her upset. She is probably crying her eyes out now, the poor woman. I text her again: "I didn't mean we need to talk in a bad way, just missing you. See you soon. E." I end it with a dozen kisses that should stop the tears. I hope she wasn't out somewhere when she got the message. I wouldn't have wanted her to have a breakdown in public.

"Oh, it is just my uncle. I was thanking him for the use of the car." For a second I forgot she was behind me as I was texting. I am sure she can't see my phone from there though. It was quick thinking on my part. Keeping women happy is just one of my gifts.

"I don't know. It is a Sunday as well so you would think it would be quiet. Traffic is just a pain.

"I don't know." She is right. I don't know. Is the traffic slow because they are looking for me? The press are everywhere. We are moving but almost one car length at a time. Do they know the Alphabet Killer is at large in Scotland? If they were close in Derby and they have found Raquel, D and E would link it.

How would they know I am heading towards Hamilton now though? Eve is out walking the dog and Rocio wouldn't have told them yet, would she? She would, wouldn't she? She would be singing it from the hilltops. Have I told any of them about the Alphabet Killer? Did I tell Rocio? That hat will be full of money by now, I know it. Why wouldn't she? She just gave the greatest blow job to a superstar in a back street and then I made her famous in the middle of a park. In front of the world!

Fuck!

What is up with me? I am doing too much for everyone, again!

They may not have caught up with Eve. But they will have figured it out. I knew it was risky, too many letters in one day. They were to close together. I should have learnt from that. I can see an exit. If I go down the hard shoulder for a little bit I can make it.

"I think you are right. Maybe we could go somewhere different." I don't want her to think that we are running. That is the last thing I need, her telling the press that I ran when she has her moment.

"I am not sure. I will figure that out once we have a little distance." I start to drive. I go through some back streets and just keep going. The more distance I can get between myself and Glasgow or Hamilton the better.

M74, that's the one. That's the one that gets me back down south, isn't it? I take the road. We are motoring now. That's not a bad thing.

I am looking at the sat nav. It is such a shame as there are so many places up here. I could cover half the alphabet in half a week. That would make a lot more sense. Makes sense. I am at it again as if I don't always make sense. I could have covered a lot more in a couple of days and get to Miss Walker for a break. This car is worrying me now though. I don't know why. I just know I need to get rid of it. I feel like I am sending a beacon to everyone. Showing the world I am here, which isn't normally a bad thing, but now I have a mission. Now I have something to accomplish. It was easier when I could have given up at any time, but now I have to complete the damn alphabet.

Now this is how the roads are supposed to be. Clear. I keep heading south.

It is beautiful, all the way from here to, oh yeah, to the Lake District. I love the Lake District too. I should go and visit my friends there. That will be a better place for me to regroup and think of things. I can change this car there as well. I will need to drop Susana off before then though, as I did say to Father Steven that I didn't have anyone special in my life.

"How are you back there? Are you sure you wouldn't be more comfortable sitting in the front with me?

"Ha ha! I suppose you are right. I would be more comfortable in the back with you." I probably need to get that out of the way. She has been waiting long enough. I just thought we could have done something before, before getting down to business. I need to make it special for her. I need all the girls to be saying nice things about me. I need all the people I work with to be saying nice things about me. It will help with winning the press back.

Besides, all work and no play makes Edmund a dull boy. My nan used to say that. One of her million little sayings. She always knew what to say to put anyone at ease. She could talk to anyone at any level, nothing ever frightened her. I think I get a lot of my skills from her. My people skills that is. I don't think she was ever cut out for this fame thing. She was just happy as long as I was happy.

"Really? That is all you want? The only reason you haven't got dressed yet?" These Spanish girls are very direct. There is no messing around. If they want something they just tell you. I do like it.

"I am all about giving my friends what they want." She is laughing now. It is such a cute laugh. She does the hair toss as well. That is a sure fire way to know she is up for it.

"Shaw.

"Sorry, Shaw, Hangingshaw, it is someplace five miles away. I just saw a sign. Susana Shaw, isn't that a singer? Yeah, I am sure she is... something about a puppet on a string "

Hangingshaw, Susana, puppet! Surely that's a sign. It must be a sign. I am supposed to go there, aren't I?

"I think that is the place. Something tells me I am supposed to be there. It is odd too, as when I stopped to pick up the hat and the stuff to make the sign, I picked up some rope as well. I had the idea to have Rocio by a tree. Not have her, you know what I mean. Place her, for the art of it." That was close. I think I got away with it. I don't want her to think that I was thinking about doing another woman.

"Then here we are, heading towards there. Do you believe in fate, Susana? I have started to think a lot about that now. You know, that we were meant to meet. I was meant to be who I am and you were meant to be who you are. Rocio Shaw or Raquel Shaw wouldn't have worked, would it? But Susana Shaw. Hangingshaw and a puppet on a string! It is all fate. We were meant to be." She will love that. The fact that we were meant to be.

If this is all fate she will probably get a record deal out of this. I mean, she is pretty enough. She has that Spanish Latin look about her as well. Guys go for that.

I pull into Hangingshaw. There is nothing here, nothing but a truck stop and a farm. I pull over on one of the side roads by the farm. There is no activity going on. I suppose most farmers are finished by end of October, aren't they?

"So what do you think? Go to the farm and pet some animals or go to the truck stop for a bacon sandwich?

"Really? You can think of something more exciting to do?" It is time. I can't hold out on her any longer. The poor girl is begging for it.

I go to the back of the car and fold down all the seats. Then I lay Susana down. I stand and look at her from the back of the car, remembering the shower scene. That was a good shower scene. In all the great movies there is a shower scene. I have had my fair share. What with Melanie, Ana and Susana that means there will be a shower scene in each of the movies from the trilogy. That will keep the fans happy. It will probably be better if they have me shirtless while doing the shower scenes too though. Exactly like I was when I was with Ana. That was a real shower scene. I am so thankful for the shower mat else I would have slipped and slid everywhere. I climb into the back of the car and close the boot behind me. These tinted windows are perfect.

"I do like what I see. I think you can tell that, can't you?

"It has been said before, I am bigger than most. Let me just take them off so you can fully see how excited you have made me."

I should have taken my boxers off when I was standing outside. Although I must say, there is a lot of room in here. This car could be used as a tent.

"It is always at attention. I will say, it has been at attention since I picked you up." Another amazing line. I am such a natural at this. It is not surprising how much I get laid.

"No, you were always my favourite. That is why I left you until… until I had dropped all the others off."

That was close. I nearly said until last, meaning that I had done all the others. No, that was good enough, good enough to make her feel special. Although I must say, her scent has changed. She was the sweetest-smelling of all of them even through the shower. And now there is a, a mustiness about her.

The blood is dry, I can tell, otherwise the smell would be richer. I should do the lighter thing again, but it gave a bit of a smoky taste. I think Uncle George actually used it for smoking. I don't like the taste. I reach into my bag of tricks and pull out my knife. This will help. I drag it across her stomach. She is ticklish, I can tell by the way she moves.

"You know, sometimes the blood is like a Viagra.

"Viagra. You know, the little blue pills that they sell to old men. I have never had to use it myself, of course. I am sure you have never had a man that has ever had to use it either. I mean, look at you.

"Hey, you do understand me. I was only going to use a little. Just to see if it was going to enhance the situation. It is not that I need it."

I slowly put the knife into her side. The blood trickles out. It trickles as if it doesn't want to come out. I take out the knife and plunge it in again, slowly. There is something about the way a sharp knife enters the skin. It is so sexy. Especially if you have time to do it slowly. She doesn't move. She can clearly take a lot of pain. In fact, I think she is actually enjoying it. I pull it out and place it in again. I wiggle it more this time. I tear at her side a little. The blood is very dark. I shift down so that I can lean in and take a smell. It is strong, it is dark and rich. I lick at it. It is cold. Not freezing cold but not hot. The taste is there. I prefer it warmer. The taste is good though. It is making me even harder, if that is possible. I bite at the wound in her side. She flinches, not a lot but enough to tell me she liked it. I taste her again. There is really nothing like it. It is strong and full-bodied at the same time. The blood is like a meal. It fills me. It fills my stomach as if it were food.

I nibble a little bit more. I think that is enough. I am up and inside of her. That was exactly how I imagined it to be.

She is perfect. I knew she was going to be the best out of all of them. The taste is swilling around my mouth, little pieces of her are between my teeth as I enter her over and over again. God, I am hard. I want more. More of her and more of her! I pull out and go down to the wound again. I take some more. A bigger bite, something I can move from cheek to cheek in my mouth. Then I am back in her, pumping her as hard as I can. It is not enough. I need more from her. I grab the knife at the side of me and cut across her shoulder. It gives me something to bite into as I do her, over and over again. Now that is a love bite. I swallow. I swallow as if it is the best food I have ever tasted in my life. It is the best. Something takes over me. It is like a thirst for more. I think the hotness of her, and her taste has me so worked up. I look her straight in the eye. She smiles. She can feel what I feel. She knows what I need and she wants to give it to me. I full on bite at her neck. I bite it like a vampire would. I tear at it. It opens up everywhere.

Fuck, it's good!

I am really fucking her now. Fucking her harder and harder, the blood from her neck is spurring me on. I bite again. I can feel the bones crunch in between my teeth. They are not big bones. They must be tiny bones in the neck. They feel like chicken bones. I keep going. I can feel her building up to explode. That was quick. I thought she would be able to go longer, but the anticipation must have really made her want it. I make myself get there quickly, just for her. To make sure that she doesn't feel bad about not being able to last. It helps with a mouth full of her. I need to make sure we come at the same time. I hold back a little and go when I know she is having multiples. The thought of me inside her is helping her have multiple multiples, I can feel them as she shivers. I lift my head and catch my reflection in the car mirror. I look hot. I mean, really fucking hot. Admittedly, a little bit vampire hot which is always good. The fans will like that look from me. I reach over and grab the phone from my pocket. I take a couple of selfies before I get off Susana. They will be great for the movie. I move and lie next to her. She is still going, I can tell. I take a moment's breath, I deserve it after what I have just given her.

"What the fuck was that?

"I know, right? I am not sure where all that came from. It got a little crazy for a minute then. I have never done that before." I have never done that before. I feel a little light-headed.

"Yes, yes, I have clearly done that before. I meant the whole biting at the neck bit. I mean, I have nibbled, but that is all. Nothing like what just happened. You really got me worked up. All I could think of was devouring you. Devouring all of you. I didn't just want to be inside you, I wanted you to be inside me.

"You have never done that before either? Never let anyone do that to you?" I find that hard to believe. She seems all kind of kinky to me. There is that look in her eyes that says she is up for everything and anything.

"That must be a first for us both then."

I have thought about it. There are just too many similarities for me not to, but I never really thought I would do it. Bite at someone like that. But the more I bit, the more I wanted. I wonder if it is even better if it is hot, the blood. I wonder if it is better if it is still pumping. That blood hitting the back of your throat.

I really need to find that out. I need to know before...

"Really? Still going? I knew they were multiples. That is what I wanted for you." It was the biting thing, I am sure of it. She will be having dozens. I think I even had a couple that time. Men can have more than one right?

"Yes, me too." I did have multiples I am sure of it. I don't think normal men have multiples. Only professional lovers like me do. They just have good ones and not so good ones, but it is good to let her know she would have been capable of giving me them. She will be telling all her friends that. She will be telling the press that.

I need to know before? Before what? What was that about? It is not before anything. I was just new, exciting, or is that why I did it? Finally is that why I did it? Did I want to know what it was like to lose control? So I did. Well, I did a little. I wonder what it would be like if I really lose control. Lose control so much that the press think that I have actually lost complete control? They will then think I will slip up. That will excite them, the thought of me slipping up may even excite them enough to publish it. Now there is an idea... I will never slip up. They should know that deep down.

"Sorry, Susana, I was lost in a thought then.

"The thought. The thought. It was about losing control. For a moment then you had me losing control. Something that has never happened before. It is why I am still working. I have always been in control of everything. Professional. Calculated. Everything I do, I do for a reason,

"Yes, like you. I did you for a reason because you are so damn hot and probably the most beautiful Spanish woman I have ever seen." I have only seen five if you include Ana. And Ana is a close second. Maybe first now as she has her whole neck and everything intact. Although I don't think it will leave a scar.

"Yes, I suppose we do need to get on." She is right. I could lie here all day with her, but I have to keep moving. I still have to do something about this car.

"The hanging thing? Yes, although I am not sure about the hanging or the puppet thing. You know, with the name and everything. Seems that both would be a fitting tribute to you and, you know, the other Susana."

I hit the button and exit the back of the car, grabbing my trousers and getting dressed as I do. It is getting dark already. How long were we actually at it? It only felt like minutes. I think I was carried away more than I thought. Saying that, it does get dark earlier in the winter, never really understood why? Maybe it is due to the cold; the sun doesn't shine as bright.

The one thing I always remember about Scotland – I am still in Scotland, I think – is that there is never a shortage of trees. Trees and land and hills, they are everywhere.

It needs to be one that I can easily pull her up on. I don't know how many times I have said it, but I am so thankful for small girls. Although I am now thinking, imagine what a bigger girl would taste like. Imagine all that extra meat around the neck area. The blood will be pumping twice as hard around the body. Imagine all the goodness that would be in that blood as well. Sweets, chocolate, all those foods that you are not supposed to eat. I bet I have been on a diet of fish and salad for years through the girls I have chosen. That is probably why I am still as fit as fuck. I am basically a fucking vegetarian.

If this is nearly all over, if I am about to step down from the limelight and retire, maybe I should treat myself a little more. Try a different type, not just for me, but to give the larger girls a bit of hope. Let them know that I am willing to consider anything. It could double, triple my fan club. I bet they are more comfortable, there's more to grab hold of. Yeah, I should consider it. I should maybe consider a blonde as well...

What the fuck is wrong with me!

Talking myself into thinking that that is normal? A blonde. What am I, a fucking monster?

I take the rope from the back of the car and tie it to her wrist. I then untie it, remembering that she is still naked. I grab the clothes and dress her while she is still hot. I think it is going to be cold tonight, and I am not sure how long it will take for the press to get here.

"With every touch you are still going? I am a natural giver, it is true." Poor girl is going pass out if it doesn't stop soon.

"It must be something about the neck thing. I have never had a girl going this long before. Well, not one that has told me." She is so open about all the sex stuff. I do like that about these Spanish girls. I have probably had girls going for weeks, but they would be too embarrassed to tell me. I understand that. I really need to think about that more. How I have ruined so many girls for other men. Once they have been with me, there is no going back to another man. It will never be the same for them.

Now I think about it, I have probably made a great impact on the lesbian world. Probably increased their numbers in the hundreds. Wait, have I slept with hundreds of girls? I must be close to that number. I need to remember the number for the film.

Fuck!

The number? I don't even remember my number. The number of people I have worked with. I can't believe I have forgotten it. I was so focused. I don't even remember the last time I counted. When was it? It may have been in Cornwall. That was when I was only at the one hundred mark. I don't even remember the two hundred mark. I must be well over that by now, must be two twenty, two thirty, at least. Maybe even three hundred. It is the fucking press thing again isn't it. Making me forget the important things.

She is dressed. It is a shame. She is hotter naked. I think all women are hotter naked. I start with the rope. I tie her hand and then her neck and then her other hand. That's good. I can just throw the rope over the branch and she will look like…

She will look like she is holding on to the branch. I tie back around her neck again. I am worried now that is a lot of rope for such a little neck. Especially given part of it is missing. I really need to plan ahead. It is not going to look great, but I am going to have to tie it around the body as well. There is an obvious way. But it is not very ladylike. Straight down and then up again around both shoulders as well.

"Really? I hadn't thought about that. I am sure you can't have too many. So if it does keep you going as you swing, you know, because of where the rope is placed and the rubbing, then I say just enjoy it. Really enjoy it.

"Ha ha! And, yes, think about me while you are there. That will help no end."

I get her out of the back of the car and head towards the tree. This doesn't look too hard. After the fifth attempt, I manage to throw the rope over the branch.

I had spoken too soon. I pull. She comes up easy. I then tie it on to the trunk. That was easy in the end. I go around and look at her. She is looking good. Her head is a little to one side. That could have been better. I could have done with my nail gun at that point and a scarf or something to hide it. That would have been better. I need a new nail gun. I miss that. I wonder if Father Steven has a new one.

I should pop in and see him. He is just down the road from here.

Either way... Hangingshaw is done... A, B, C, D, E, F, G, H, and now for I.

I can't think of anywhere with a I off the top of my head. I'll, Is, In, Isle – there were some places called Isle, but that is heading back to Scotland and I don't think that is the best idea. I think my love affair with Scotland is over for a while. I get back in the car and get back on the road. I should just head south.

Isle, Island, there is that place that is all over the news. Callington Island, I think it is called. It is very popular for some reason. Maybe that is a good place for the letter I. That counts as a town too, doesn't it? It is an island, but they are towns too. It is a long way south though. I don't think I have been on an island before? I do like the thought of it, I love the seaside. I will have a holiday home somewhere like that.

I love the sandy..,

Fuck me!

Sandy! Fucking Sandy! Sandy Shaw. It wasn't Susana Shaw. It was Sandy Shaw who was the puppet on a string. I pull into the lay-by and take out my phone. I know Susana Shaw is famous. I know the name. I was sure she was a singer.

I google it. Where would you be without Google, eh?

Hear'Say? A band called Hear'Say. "Pure and Simple" is their biggest hit? I have never heard of it. Susana Shaw "Pure and Simple". I look again to see what else they do. I go through the list. Nothing, nothing speaks to me. Wait, a song called… "Not the End of the World".

It kind of fits. I am not done yet. Not the end of my world. Not the end of Susana's probably just the beginning of hers with all the fame she is going to get. No, not the end of the world I am nearly heading into number nine. They will be happy it is not the end of the world of Edmund Carson. I am already a third of the way through. They will be able to pull that all together, won't they? Make it plausible.

Fuck!

Fuck, it is a loose connection… Fucking Sandy Shaw! I should go and work with her just for trying to distract me.

Hangingshaw is done.

It is not the end of the world.

No, not the end of the world.

175

Chapter 10

I am looking forward to seeing the sign. The Welcome to England sign! Although it is already getting dark, so I won't see it till I get up close. A warm feeling comes over me every time I see that sign. I am English first. Patriotic, I think is the word about my country, because it is mine. I am British as well. I guess. Because I pretty much own that too with all the work I have done in Wales and Scotland. I guess I am European now, although I can't remember if we are either in or out of Europe. I am just a global superstar. I am not sure they have a word for that. Worldwidean, is that even a word? Earth child, I am sure I have heard that one before. Although that might be a Michael Jackson song.

I think "superstar" covers it. They call them A-listers. Maybe that is because you can't categorise them so the A stands for Alphabet listers. They are every letter of the Alphabet.

I am the A-lister of the A-listers. I don't know how I do it. Everything I start is just... I don't even know the word for it. Outstanding? Amazing? How would I describe me?

I am a marketeer's dream. I am sure marketeer is a word, or was that musketeer? Anyway I am a filmmaker's dream.

Product placement in all my scenes. I am very good at that, very good at being able to recognise my own brand. Advertising opportunities in everything I do. I am going to be remembered for the rest of time, just as Jack has been. We are so similar, we must have been related at some point. I really need to do my history, my family tree to make sure... It is like the blood has given me some clarity. I am on fire now. I am feeling so good.

Wait, was that a sign for another isle? I can still do an isle going south. I would like that. My fans would like that. I would like to be on an island. To watch the boats as they sail across the sea. Walk on the beach. That would be nice. It would be nice for my fans to know that I will go that extra mile for them as well. They will probably have dreamed night after night that I may visit them one day. I wish I could be in their shoes when I actually do. So I know what it is really like to meet me.

Isle of Whithorn! Sounds good to me and it is a lot closer than that Callington Island. Although there must be something going on on that island. It is in the news every day. It must be worth a visit. Maybe when this is all over I will take a trip there. Maybe take Miss Walker for a mini holiday. She will love that. I turn towards Isle of Whithorn.

I really need to do something about this car though. I keep saying it but not doing anything about it. I pull over in the lay-by. It is a bit off the road so a perfect place to find some help. There is another car parked in front of me. I walk up to it. There is a family in the car, all eating sandwiches. It is a bit late to be having a picnic at the side of the road, isn't it? Well, the dad is eating a sandwich. The kids have crisps. I miss crisps. I could eat a nice bag of cheese and onion right now. I don't think he has even seen me. The kids have to tell him. I knock on the window. He winds the window down.

"Hi."

"Hi."

He has a cheese and onion sandwich. I can smell it from here. That is my favourite. It is on white bread too. I am really hungry as well. Cheese and onion. I already have the blood taste in my mouth. I wonder if he will let me have half. If he recognises me, he will. Maybe I will have to give him a hint.

"I was just wondering if you could do me a favour."

The guy is nodding with a mouth full of food. He still has half of that sandwich in there, doesn't he? I am looking at the box between him and his wife.

"You see my car there, the Q7? I was wondering if you would trade me for your car."

The guy looks perplexed. Perplexed, another word I don't know where it came from. It is the right word, isn't it? Did I use that right?

"It is a fair trade. I mean, your car is a lot older. It needs a good wash and, okay, the Q7 may need a bit of a clean, but it will be good for a growing family." I am smiling at him. His wife is smiling at me. She knows what a good deal I am offering them. She is kind of cute, a little bigger than my normal tastes, but I have been considering that change. It may be worth a trial. Is it a trial or a taster?

"I am sorry? What are you on about?"

Didn't I express myself well enough? I thought I did. I did say it all out loud, didn't I? Not the bit about the sandwich or doing his misses, I hope.

"Sorry. I may not have been clear. I would like to change cars. I would like you to take the Q7, must be worth like fifty grand, and give me your car which, let's face it, must be worth only what, half of that?" That is me being generous. I wouldn't give you a tenner for his car, but I didn't want to upset him in front of his family. He is still staring at me. I think he has recognised me as he isn't talking. That makes more sense now. Star-struck. Tongue-tied. That and he can't believe the offer I am making to one of my fans. I will sign it if he wants me to. I should make him look good in front of his kids. They will be impressed if they know their dad is friends with me.

"Yes, it is me. Nice to meet you all. Edmund Carson, the ONE, the only. I do like that saying. You see, the ONE, the only meaning the only Edmund Carson. The ONE meaning I can be the ONE and clearly other people." Still star-struck, although his mouth is open now. Just like Uncle George's.

"You have dropped some of your sandwich. Be careful, a cheese and onion sandwich is a delicious thing." I don't think I want a bite of that piece now. There is still some in there, isn't there? In the box. He grabs for the keys in the car. I suppose he is just... Wait, he is trying to start the car. Why would he do that? I lunge forward and grab the keys.

"Get the fuck off!"

There is no need for language like that, is there? I was just doing him a favour. He is screaming now and so is she. I didn't need all this attention. I grab behind me, bring my knife out and through the window straight into his neck. He doesn't deserve me working with him, but it will show his kids that I am not upset about the language. It is good to still be an inspiration for the younger generation.

She is screaming now and trying to get out of the car. I run around to the other side of the car. She is already out and on the embankment. She is still screaming. It must be like meeting a pop star. They are always screaming at their idols, aren't they? For my fans, it must be the same feeling. I manage to get hold of her. She isn't fighting that much. She wants this to happen. I slice at her neck. It oozes out of her. Then I remember, I remember Susana. I remember the crunching of the bones in her neck, the thought of the warm blood as it pumps into your mouth. I climb on top of her as quickly as I can. I have her hands pinned down and she is shaking her head from one side to the other side. It is to show me the best side of her neck, I can tell. She is almost begging for it. I lunge forward and bite through the side of her throat as hard as I can.

Oh fuck!

It is… that is just…

Oh fuck!

All this time I have been nibbling when I can, I can… I bite as hard as I can again on her throat. The blood is pumping hard and fast into my mouth. It is amazing. The bones crunching as the blood oozes. Oozes isn't the word; explodes, erupts… Yes! Erupts is the word. This is why everyone loves a vampire story. I never knew that it was going to be so good.

Oh fuck it is good!

I should have, I should have created this character years ago. I drink as much as I can, I keep biting as I do. I am full. It does fill you up. I drop her down to the ground and stand up. I go back to the car and get into her side as the door is still open. My head is dizzy, I mean, really dizzy. My heart is thumping like it may come out of my chest. I feel like I am a warrior, an actual fucking warrior. He is slumped over the wheel. What kind of example is that to set for your kids, just fucking lying there? They are crying, for fuck's sake! I don't know why they are crying. It is not as if they haven't just seen the best show of their lives. I mean, their mum and dad getting to work with the greatest of all time. Right in fucking front of their eyes! It is stuff that will live with them forever. Oh, I get it now.

I lean over with my knife and cut both their throats.

"You are welcome. Sorry about that."

It is good they have those seats that keep them strapped in. They have to be safe nowadays. They are only little and there are some right weirdos on the road.

They must have been feeling left out, seeing me work with their mum and dad and me leaving them out. I probably should have worked with them first so their parents could see. They like that type of thing. Things for the scrapbook.

Fuck, I am dizzy!

I take a minute of peace to try and clear my head. What the hell just happened? I can feel my heart slowly dying down. I really wasn't here to work. I just wanted another car. I look back at the kids, I am glad they have stopped crying. It is understandable if they thought I was leaving them out. They must be like what, five and three? I am probably their first A-list celebrity meeting. They will be amazed when they wake up. Amazed at how famous they are going to become. My heart is back to normal.

"I wasn't expecting that. I thought I would just come and trade cars."

He is still sleeping and so are the kids. I should probably get going though. I need to find somewhere to stay tonight. It looks like it will already be nine, ten o'clock before I get there... My head is dizzy again. There is a feeling in my stomach. I lean out of the car. Oh no! No!

Urggghhh, Urggghhh.

Where did that come from? No, not again.

Urggghhh.

Sick. I don't remember being sick for years. There is so much of it. How is there so much? I haven't eaten that much, and where did the peas come from? I don't even like peas. I sit back upright in the car. Something is wrong with this. I don't throw up. It must have been something that made me that way. Susana, or her, maybe it was her. I look back at the kids. They are still sleeping. I need to get on. This isn't a good way to see your idols.

I go and fetch their mother after stepping over the sick. It will be good when they wake up if she is sitting with them. It will calm them down about the whole celebrity thing. I pick her up. She isn't as small as the girls. She isn't big but not small. I get her to the back of the car. I try and squeeze her into the back. She doesn't fit. There is just not enough room with the booster seats and her. I suppose the logical thing to do would be to get them all into the Q7, but that defeats the whole point. I came here to change cars and that is what I need to do.

"I am sorry. I think you are going to have to go in the trunk. It won't be for long. Just until we get where we are going." Wait, where are we going?

"Yes, I am sure they will still hear you from there."

I go to the driver's side and get the keys. I then open the boot. It is rammed full. There are lots of bags. They must be on their holidays. I start chucking them out and then stop. I need to keep one, one with his clothes in. I am a bit of a mess today. I open the bags and find the one with his clothes in. I then throw the rest onto the embankment. I will leave her some money to buy the kids new clothes. Stars do that sort of thing. I fetch her and stick her in the trunk and lay the suitcase on top. I don't want the blood getting on all their clothes. It is a bugger to get out and that will take her ages.

I close the case and then close the boot. I then go and help him into the passenger seat. He is not going to be able to drive safely knowing that he has someone like me in the car. I am too much of a distraction. I can't imagine how his wife would be able to drive being so close to an A-lister? Although a hand job as she drives may have been a nice touch. The kids wouldn't have seen from where they are.

"Okay, are we all ready?"

There is a cheer from the kids. I am glad they have woken up to spend some time with me. It will be good for their confidence.

"We are off to the seaside. Isle of Whithorn, to be precise."

The kids are smiling now. At least they have stopped crying for my attention. I still have that sick feeling in my stomach. I wonder if he was poisoning her and now I have some of it in my system. You hear about these weird husbands and how they get rid of their other halves. With two kids though he must have been doing her for at least six years now.

So he must have liked her at one point. That shit has to get boring. Doing the same woman for six years.

I carry on heading down the road. The kids are singing "One Hundred Green Bottles Hanging on the Wall". Just like my dad used to make us do on family holidays. It seems to be a bit further than I thought.

I get to Dumfries. Dumfries. Thick chips? What a strange name for a town. I know they like their chips up here, but that is ridiculous. Wait, actually there is another town. It is another I, Irongray? That sounds like something out of that Thrones programme. The one they are always talking about. *Game of Thrones*, that was it. It is very popular with people. Irongray, it sounds like me as well. King of Irongray. I would be a great king. I was born to be a King.

"What do you reckon? It is a lot closer, and not what I had in mind, but I think the kids are tired. To tell you the truth, I am a little tired too. It has been a very long day.

"Thank you. I will take you up on that. It is lucky we weren't that much of a different size." It is not just me; I think we could all do with a shower and a new set of clothes. I know the kids look like they could do with a bath. Crisps all down their fronts.

I head towards Irongray. It is only ten miles away.

"So you were saying that you and your family are here on holiday, touring the glorious scenery in Scotland? It is a bit late in the year for that, isn't it?

"I suppose autumn is a beautiful time of the year?" I am not sure it is still autumn. It is beginning to feel a lot like winter. Everywhere you go I can feel it is coming, Christmas is coming, i I can tell.

"I guess you spent a lot of time in hotels and B&Bs? They wouldn't fancy camping this time of year? Far too cold for that.

"I suppose it is a bit much with two young kids, and they certainly sound like a handful." That is what happens when you give them too much junk food. Even I wouldn't eat Wotsits.

"You do look like an outdoor type of man. I was just with some friends actually who are camping their way to John o' Groats. They will still make it, I am sure. Just decided to spend a little time with yours truly. You can't blame them. They weren't expecting a little fame on the way, but I am happy to help anyone out like that." He knows I mean him and his family too. I do like it when they start to open up to me.

"Hey, that was quick, we are here already. It took no time at all from Dumfries." I drive through Irongray. Well, at least I think I have driven through it. There is nothing here. I drive back. The Sat Nav is telling me I am here, but there is nothing here. Well, nothing but a deserted old barn.

I need somewhere to stay for the evening. I need a shower. They all need a shower. This isn't the place.

"I don't know. Why would you give a name to a place that has nothing in it? Either that or I am missing something. I didn't see a sign anywhere saying town centre, did you?" Scotland is an odd place. Why give a name to nothing?

"I was just back at Hangingshaw, you know, off the M74. It was pretty similar. It is like they are giving empty land names just to make them look bigger than they are.

"Fuck!" I had a whole *Game of Thrones* thing in my head then.

"Sorry, kids, I mean funk. I said funk. Funk, funk, funk!" I guess I can drive back to thick chips and see about a room for us all. I get out my phone and look for hotels. Yes, Dumfries is the nearest. Although, to be fair, the last thing I want to do is share a room with kids. I don't even want to get a room next to two kids. I need the rest. They will be all excited and jumping on beds and stuff. I look at my phone again.

"St John's Town of Dalry." Saint John, that is pretty much like John, isn't it? The saint is like Mr or Mrs, isn't it? I mean his name isn't Saint.

I check to see if there is anything there. I am not going all the way there to find another field with three sheep in it. Good, there are a few places, quite a few. I choose one and ring. The Lochinvar. Loch is lake, right? Lake in Var, so there must be a lake somewhere nearby.

They have rooms. Things are looking up. Maybe I just go there and then—

Fuck!

I am not going to cheat. I was thinking of letting the mum and kids stay there and then take him down to Isle of Whithorn. They won't keep it quiet, will they? The fact that we have worked together and then it will be in the wrong order. The press will have a field day. J can't come before I…?

Although I don't normally mind if they come before I! The women. That is the sign of a good lover. That is good. I need to remember that for the film. That will get the audience laughing.

"Oh sorry, it was nothing. I have booked a room for the evening." Shit, should have said rooms.

"I was just working through this in my head. You see, I am on this mission, some might say a quest or a challenge, but some days it feels more like a mission.

"Yes, exactly, the alphabet thing." It is good that he understands.

"Hey, hold on a minute, how did you know about it? I don't have any press at the moment?" Is he some kind of stalker or something? That is why he and his family were in a lay-by waiting for me to come past. If so, what was all that screaming and crap about?

"There is? The whole world is talking about it?" What the fuck!

"Where? Where are people talking about it? Tell me more." That is the best news I have had all day. I can feel a buzz in my stomach all of a sudden with that news.

"It is all over the Internet. I must say, since The Blackout I haven't even looked at the Internet. When I can't use social media there is no point." I knew my fans would find a way to keep tabs on all the work I am doing.

"It is all in code, but it is there. I just need to learn the code they are using. Then I will be able to talk to them. Give them the real insight into what I have been doing. The Dark web. That sounds amazing. I could give them little clues about where I will appear next. I don't think I have been this excited for weeks." I knew he was a fan. I knew people were out there talking about me. Worshipping me. He is smiling at me now. He knows how happy he has made me by letting me know.

"Really? You wouldn't mind? I mean, it is hardly The Ritz, is it?" OMG. I can't believe I just thought... OMG.

OMG, what am I a little girl? He is a genuine nice guy and he will stay here as well to help me out?

"Yes, I suppose you would be. Not many of the people I have worked with get the limelight all to themselves." He obviously isn't that much of a family man if he doesn't mind being separated. Probably had the same thought as me. Screaming kids in the room all night. Never get peace and quiet that way.

"Do you know, I was just thinking that same thing. *Game of Thrones*. Irongray. It sounds like it could be the name of one of the families. Mr Irongray." He puffed his chest out at that. He really wants this.

I pull the car up next to the deserted barn. I get out and take the new Mr Irongray into the barn. This is perfect. I lean him against the door and walk over and move some pallets around that were sitting in the corner of the barn. I make a throne in the middle of the barn. It looks really good. They always have the throne in the big halls, don't they? I think it is so that everyone looks at them. I should have a throne for the stadium tours. I take him over and place him on the throne.

I really miss my nail gun. I need to buy another one. He is a bit slumped to one side. I try to sit him up, and again, no, he just wants to lean. You could argue it is a good look. They all look like that in that programme in the end. Dead to the world. I step back and take a good look. Yes, they will get it. Although I have just realised I am back to scenes. No matter what I do, I end up being Edmund. Whether it is Father Matthew or the Alphabet Killer, I keep making a scene. I think it is in my nature. Unless I am the ONE. He is a scene all on his own.

"Now, are you sure you are going to be okay?" That is a weird look he is giving me. Oh, I got it.

"Oh, I am sorry. Are you going to be okay, milord?" He really is playing the part.

I think he is going to be fine. It suits him actually. He has probably been dreaming about that since the programme started. He would have been thinking about the mother of dragons too. She is a blonde that even... No! I can't. There is an actual shiver down my spine. Yuk!

I am going to have to put her on my list to contact about her hair colour when I get to Hollywood. There are a few of those leading ladies that will just do that as soon as they meet me. As I turn to leave the barn I spot it. There is a tap in the corner. I don't suppose it is still working. I walk over. It is and after a while the water starts to clear. I need to change and clean myself up before I get to St John's. I go back out to the car and open the boot. Fuck, I forgot about her. She almost gave me a heart attack.

"Of course. I am sorry, that should have been the first thing I did when we stopped."

I take her out and put her in the passenger seat. She will be a lot happier there. The kids are excited to see her too.

"No, he won't be joining us. He has asked if he can stay here. He is really helping me out, saving me some quality time. He is a really nice guy in the end, your husband. Really playing his part of becoming Lord Irongray.

"Yes, he thinks he is in *Game of Thrones*."

She is laughing. He must have a problem with the programme. He probably makes her dress up in all the gear. She looks a bit like a serving wench. She has the right figure and everything. I take the suitcase into the barn and go through it until I find some clothes. They are a little big, but they will do until I go shopping. I wash my face and hair under the tap. The water doesn't smell good, but it will get me into check-in.

"Yes, they are a good fit." I lie. It is probably good for him to think that he is nearly the same size as a celebrity. I want him to give a good rendition of our time together.

"You know about that too? That I am looking to make movies?

"Really? The public are screaming out for it?" This guy is a delight.

"I am sure they will let you play yourself in my movie." Okay, maybe not a delight. They won't let him, and come to think of it, I won't as I will be the director. I think he watches too much TV and film. It has gone to his head. I think that Snow guy could play his role. Jon Snow. Bit part, too good looking for a big role in my film, not good looking enough to play me.

"Yes, I think it is a great idea." I walk over and pick up what I can only presume is some kind of rake. Or fork. A pitchfork that is what it is. I place it in his hand. I try again. He is a little limp-wristed. She didn't look like she had been satisfied in a while. She needs a real man in her life. I lean it against his hand and the throne.

"Is that better, Lord Irongray?"

That got a laugh out of him. I can't believe this guy is going to give me any bad press. This must be a dream come true for him. Lord of his own… own shed? I leave him to it. He must be so excited about being discovered.

I go back to the car. They all seem to be excited too, I guess, to have me to themselves.

"He is fine. I think he is really enjoying it.

"Yes, lording it up."

She is smiling at me. Not the first time she has heard that. I start the car and head towards St John's. I get a mile down the road and stop the car.

"Sorry, I forgot about you for a second." I forgot to put her belt on. I lean over and clink her in. She has to be safe, besides they pull you over for that sort of thing now. I head towards St John's again. I need a real shower and some food. *Fuck, food*!

I look around. There is still half a sandwich in that packet. Result. It was just sitting between us in the car, how didn't I notice that earlier? I pull it out of the packet. Three types of cheese and onion. That looks so good. I take a bite. I mean, real good. I can't remember the last time I had a good cheese and onion sandwich.

"Sorry, do you want a bite?" It is a bit rude to eat alone. I can tell she doesn't. She is probably worried about bad breath or something with the onion. Women are funny like that. I don't mind kissing a girl who tastes of onion.

"How did you know about that? If you are sure that you wouldn't mind, then sure. That is very generous."

Now she must be a real fan if she knew how I like my cheese and onion sandwich. I dip the sandwich into her neck. I must have tweeted it or something. Either that or someone is making money somewhere out of my recipe. I wouldn't be surprised, but I really need to get my cookbook out there. All these opportunities will pass me by if I don't get on with them.

"Yes, we are heading to St John's. It is not that far.

"They sleep better in the car, do they? My mum used to say that about me. Yes, I think that will be fine. To be fair, it will probably help me out no end if you really don't mind staying with them." I did think about having a little fun with her, but if she is sure. It will give me a break.

"I suppose it will give you an early start as well to your next destination.

"It has been a busy couple of days. In fact, come to think of it, I have gone from D to J in a couple of days. I wish I had this much momentum all the time. Imagine what I could accomplish.

"No, D to J, not a DJ.

"No, I have never really thought about it. Although I am a natural at most things so I could probably do it. What am I saying? Probably? I know I could. I have a good taste in music and my mum and dad taught me all the classics." I should probably do a set at the stadium tour. That will get the crowd going. Bit of an old school disco would go down a storm. Get all the girls to dress in uniform. That would be good.

"No, I think I am going to take a few days to sort something out. Not to give too much away but it is a certain holiday in a few days. Some would say my holiday. So I need to spend a few days researching the best place to be and what to do while I am there.

"Halloween. Yes. You think so too. All hallow Edmund. Hallowedmund. Needs a little work, but I am sure we will come up with something."

The sat nav says we are here. Well, just, on the outskirts of St John's. It is only five hundred metres to the hotel.

"I think I'll pull in here. It is quiet and nobody is going to wake the kids."

I pull the car over to a little side road. This will be nice for them. Out of the way from any passing traffic.

"Thanks for everything." I lean over and give her a kiss on the cheek. That will be something she remembers forever, and all is should really do in front of the kids. I get out of the car. The walk will do me good. It may even get rid of the smell of that water from the barn. That was a mistake. I am sure I stink.

They were nice people. Although it felt a bit forced. I know I wasn't expecting to work with them, but it felt as if... as if I was trying to rush it. As if I was trying to ensure I crossed some letters off the alphabet as quickly as possible. I am glad my stomach has settled down. I think there was something wrong with that McDonald's that we had. It will be better once they start selling the Edmund Burger.

Fuck!

I don't even remember if I asked their names. In fact, I didn't ask their names. That is not like me. What is up with me? Why wouldn't I ask them their names? I am better than that.

I am fast getting the feeling that there is someone or something behind me. It feels like I am trying to rush this in order to complete it. As if I am being pushed into situations that I wouldn't normally find myself in.

It has thrown me off my game. I know I have never taken on such a challenge before. Nobody has. Everything else I have done is done in one night. This is a lot harder than I thought it would ever be.

I get to the hotel and check in. She doesn't say anything. Barely notices me as she gives me the key to the room. I head into the room and sit on the bed. I take out my phone and text Miss Walker.

"J is done. I am heading south." Followed by three kisses.

That should make her happy. I pull my phone back out and text her again.

"I miss you." That should make her really happy. It is true. I do miss her. She would bring sense to the last forty-eight hours.

I lie down. I am too tired to shower. I will do it in the morning.

Chapter 11

I really should have closed the curtains and the window before going to sleep. The last thing I need is sirens going off at stupid o'clock in the morning. I am really tired. They should have a rule or something. That they can't use sirens till what, ten, eleven in the morning?

Sirens!

I jump out of bed. Shit! Sirens are going off. I am at the window and I can see them heading down the road to... to fuck knows, I didn't ask their name. What kind of man am I now? One that doesn't even ask a lady's name?

Fuck!

I wanted a shower. I grab my bag, throw it over my shoulder and head downstairs. There is no one at reception. I look over the counter. Car keys. Perfect. I grab them and get out of the door. Another car goes flashing past. I press the button. The lights of a mini come on. I go and get into it. I look for the keyhole, but there isn't one.

Fuck!

How the fuck do I start the car? I am pressing the button and nothing. It is a round-shaped key buzzer. It must be something to do with that. I look around. I find the place to put it and then press the key. At last it fucking works. The car starts. It is an automatic. That makes it even easier. I head in the opposite direction to the police as fast as I dare without raising suspicion. The last thing I need now is people stopping me for selfies. There is no sat nav in the car so I just drive and drive. After two hours I find the M74 and then I head south. This is not good. The press are on my shoulder. They don't want me to finish becoming the Alphabet Killer. Surely I am already the Alphabet Killer? Or would they say I wasn't because I didn't finish it? Would they brand me a failure? I can't be branded a failure.

It is fast becoming more of a challenge for them as it is for me. They probably think it would make a great story if they stopped me. Stopped me before I get to the end! They would love that, wouldn't they? To feel like they have won.

Fuck!

Have I taken on something too big? Is this a step too far for me? Should I have saved myself for something else? Maybe I should have done another school or another hotel. Have I planned this enough? Do I need to plan more? If they are going to try and stop me from achieving my dream then I need to plan more. I need to make every event something special. Make them want to see what is coming next. Excite the nation that is what I need to do. The last two days have been a disaster. I feel like I have been losing my mind. What was that biting all about? The kids, what about the kids, I left them in the car overnight. What kind of monster am I? What if the girls don't speak highly of me? Or that fucking family? That family. I can't keep calling them that. Why didn't I even get their name? That is it! That is the reason I know something is not right with me. That's not me. There is no pride in just working with people.

Fucking Game of Thrones!

Why would I even reference that? How has a TV programme ever got into my scenes? That is just nonsense. I was just trying to justify leaving him in the middle of nowhere.

I have not even researched the alphabet. I said I was going to at least a dozen times, but I never did. I am sat naving my way around the country, dropping people I work with off like a postman. I went to bed last night feeling I had accomplished something. I have not. I have ruined everything.

Idiot, fucking idiot!

Do I need to start again? I am not happy. Not happy at all.

I need to take some time. Some time to plan my next moves, all my moves. I need to ensure that I bring the fans back onside. The last few days won't show me at my best. Well, other than Rocio. Rocio will show them that I am here. That I am still brave enough to walk out in public. I don't want anyone thinking that I am in hiding. In hiding? I am never in hiding.

I need somewhere to go. Somewhere with no prying eyes so I can work out a plan. Somewhere on my own. I need to work out something that is tasteful, not rushed. Somewhere that shows them I don't hide.

I need to be organised and worthy. Something that needs to be worthy.

I keep driving south. I pass the sign. I am back in England. I am not as happy about it as I thought I was going to be yesterday. I have fucked some of this up. I think I just got too greedy in more ways than one. I don't want to be known for this. I want to be known for pieces of art. I am an artist. An A-list artist.

I am ten down, and can I say, other than A, I am truly proud of any of them? Okay, B wasn't bad. He was a star. C was for Jack, but it could have been better... So it is not as bad as...

Fuck!

What am I doing? I am trying to justify it now. I need to be better. I need to be smarter. I need to be more creative in my thinking. More, just more, and for fuck's sake, I need a shower. What if they did catch up with me today, the press? This would be the picture all over the news. Can you imagine that? The day we finally meet for the first time, I am wearing someone else's clothes. That always has to be foremost in my mind. Today could always be the day.

Gretna Retail Village. That is clothes, right. At least I can do one thing right today: I can get some clothes.

It took me about an hour, but finally I am redressed and have some supplies. That strip wash in the toilets wasn't bad either. They are a lot cleaner than they used to be. Some of those guys were looking a little too hard at me though. Probably never seen a celebrity before.

I still need a shower though. I sit back in the car. I am not happy. I am not happy about what has happened over the last couple of days. That is not me. I set off. I feel like I need to go home, wherever home is now.

Annan! A nan? My nan? That is home. Surely that is a sign of somewhere to go. If I ever needed somewhere to go when I am in need of some direction that is it. That can't be a coincidence that that is here when I need some help. I quickly pull over and look at my phone. I do hope it is not one of those false places again. It is not. It is quite big actually. There are a number of places to stay. There is one. The Corner House hotel. That is perfect. The corner house, like the one I always wanted to buy my nan. That is what I told Melanie anyway. She was going to help me buy it. I should have done that.

Nan was happy where she was though, especially when she moved to Brighton. She would have been very happy there. She would have been happy to wake up and see the sea every day. That would have been nice for her.

I am not crying, but for some reason there are tears rolling down my cheeks. I think they must be happy tears. Tears to show me how happy she would have been. I make my way to Annan. I find the Corner House and check in. The lady seems nice. She let me check in early. I don't suppose many people are visiting this late in the year. I go to my room and look at the shower. It is one of those rainfall ones. Perfect. I so need a good shower. My nan would love this place. It has that homely feel about it. I undress and then get into the shower. It is hot, it is beautiful. I don't remember the last time I had a good shower. Living in and out of hotels you can end up with some really naff ones, especially those showers that are attached to the taps. You may as well just give me a hose. I let the water just hit me. I don't move. It is great. I have been dreaming of this. I need to recharge my batteries. I need to sit down and think about it more strategically. Plot my moves. Create my master plan. They always say it, don't they, in all those great police detective stories? They always have an intelligent master adversary. I am one now, aren't I? The press and the police will have worked the whole Alphabet thing out and now they have my plan, they are on a mission to stop me. Throughout my career there has been no plan. No set agenda.

They can hide behind that. Now, now they have nothing to hide behind. I have told the world my plan and they are listening. They know. It will be all over the Dark Web, and in code like Mr Irongray said.

I really need to sort that. I can't not know their names. That is really starting to bother me. I am better than that. My story is better than that. I get out of the shower and start to towel myself dry. I needed that. I needed a shower and a fresh start. I could really do with…

"Hey, are you finished in there?"

I know that voice. I know it as I have been texting it for weeks to come and visit me. I walk into the room. She is sitting on the bed. Well, almost lying, as she is at the headboard with a big smile on her face.

"Hey." That is the sight I have missed so much. The sight of her on my bed. Smiling, waiting for me.

"Hey, yourself.

"Did you have a nice long shower?" She smiles. I know what she is hinting at. That I would have been playing with myself in there. I wasn't. Wait, why wasn't I? Did I know she was coming?

"Yes, why didn't you join me? Would have been a lot better if you did?

"I thought about it. But I know how much you like the little black dress."

It is true. I do like it. It wouldn't be the same if she turned up any other way.

"This is true." She gets up off the bed walks over and kisses me. Really kisses me. As if she hadn't seen me in months. I let the towel drop to the floor so she remembers what she has been missing.

Wait it hasn't been that long, has it? It has been a month, at most.

"How did you find me?" I want to check if she is actually tracking my phone. Her expression doesn't change. She is smiling at me. She needs to know that it is as dangerous for her as much as my fans if she knows where I am at all times. They will try and get to her. I know they will.

"You texted me that you were heading south from Scotland and then I saw the Corner House. At Annan. Where else would you be when you are feeling low? Just like you wanted to buy her, right? The corner house for your nan."

She is right. I don't remember telling her about that house, but she is right. Where else would I be? She always seems to know when things aren't going in my favour. Or if I am stuck at a crossroads she turns up all the time to help me get through it. It is why I love, whoa, nearly said it then.

I like her so much. I am glad she isn't tracking me though. I don't want to have to have that conversation with her. We sit on the edge of the bed together. I am conscious I am holding her hand already. As soon as she is here I need to be touching her. It feels right. It feels like where my hand should be. In hers! I smile at her. I know what she says makes sense.

"You always know when to turn up. In fact, I thought I had seen you a few times, once in Birmingham. When I had to do this fire walk." She squeezes my hand.

"I was there. The charity thing. You are so giving, Edmund. I just knew that you knew what needed to be done.

And it nearly worked, didn't it? You were almost back in the press. Even if it was for just one day.

"Yes, it did. I am close. Really close." I am not. I need to tell her. I need to tell her how I am feeling about the last couple of days. It will help, I am sure. I am sure I am not going to look like a wimp. She knows me now. She loves me unconditionally.

"I need to tell you something. I am starting to feel, maybe even fear, I have lost my way a little. The last couple of days have not been good and I have become too focused on the task rather than the art of everything that I do. I am not giving enough." She kisses me on the cheek.

"I know, Edmund. That is why I am here. I could tell from your text messages you were undecided. You are too hard on yourself. You have been making good progress. You just don't need to rush it. The Alphabet Killer is a genius." I have waited to hear those words. Don't rush it. I knew that is what I was doing. For her. I was rushing it for her, to get to her. I wanted the prize at the end. I wanted her, and now she is here. I almost feel relieved.

"I thought you would be mad. Mad at the fact that I wasn't finished, after we were in Brighton together. I thought you would be mad that I didn't return to you and just stop working?

"No, I am not mad. I could never be mad at you. I could tell you weren't finished. But this will be the one though. Well, not the ONE!" She is smiling now. I love that smile. I could spend forever with that smile.

"This will be your swansong. They are out there and they are coming for you. The press, I mean. They are so excited about seeing you. So excited. I have faith you will outfox them to the end. None of them are you, Edmund. None of them are you." Sometimes she sounds like my nan. Outfoxing someone, or your swansong. That would have been the type of thing she would have said.

"I know. I was just thinking that in the shower. It is like I have set them a challenge. A challenge to stop me completing my goal. My question, I guess to myself, is should I have done that?

"That is exactly what it is, Edmund, a challenge. They know where you are going. They know if they meet someone you have worked with they only need to look in the vicinity for the next piece of work. I am sure none of your friends would tell them where you are headed, but you only need to look at the last couple of days. You have proved this for them."

I know. Everything she says is making sense. I think I just needed to hear it from someone else. I have been too reckless.

"I know." I give her the approving nod. She knows too.

"Then you also know what you need to do, Edmund. You need to plan it better. You need to set a goal. I am not saying don't get this done as quickly as possible, because they are close, but make it planned. Make it randomly planned." She is almost laughing at that.

"Throw them off the scent as much as you can."

That is very a good point. I need to throw them off the scent. Maybe I could throw in a couple of random appearances. I could include some returns of the ONE of Father Harry. That will mix it up a bit. They won't all be looking for the Alphabet Killer. In fact again… that is genius. Edmund, you are a genius.

"I think you are right. No, I know you are right."

She is smiling at me again. I think she likes being right, even though I came up with it on my own, didn't I?

I think planning it is going to be the key. K to Z. It is just sixteen to go. How hard can it be? Hell, I have done more than that in a night.

"Sixteen, Edmund. You have come so far. Make them all special. Make them key dates as well Edmund. Think about it. Make the world remember you every time they think of a holiday." It is like she is in my mind. Some days we are always on the same page. How spooky is that? I know I should have all the holidays, they should all be mine.

"I know. I can't miss Halloween, Miss—"

She thumps me in the arm. Didn't hurt. It was a playful punch. It has been a long time since she was my teacher. Well, teacher at school anyway.

"Cheeky! No, you can't miss Halloween, and what about the fifth of November? Thanksgiving. Even Christmas, Edmund, what about the twelve days of Christmas, Edmund? That sounds like you, doesn't it? Don't you want people to be thinking of you at all the holiday seasons?"

I do. I do want everyone to think about me at all the holiday seasons. I deserve to be on wrapping paper. I deserve to have those dolls made of me like they do with all the superstars. The Barbie and Ken dolls that have just had a face changed. Imagine the accessories. The costume changes, little toy knives and nail guns. I deserve better.

I also know I need to give better to deserve better. I am not a loony. They are begging me for more and I need to give it.

"I do, I really do.

"Then let's make a plan. We have the whole afternoon, Edmund. Let's plan out the next sixteen. Where and when all of this is going to happen and how you are going to get back to me, full-time back with me."

I do agree with her. We need the plan.

"But first, my darling, first, let's really remember what we are working towards." She leans in for what I know is going to be a real everlasting kiss. Before I know it, the dress is being lifted over her head and she is on top of me. This is what I remember. This is what I am working towards. Nothing brings me back on track quicker than quality time with Miss Walker...

"How is it nine p.m. already?" Time always seems to get away from us when we are together. It is like we are lost in our own little world.

It has been an afternoon to remember though. This was what I needed: time to rest and quality time to make the plan. I just need to stick with it. No distractions. No matter how hot they are. Damn Spanish girls. I blame them. They got me all side tracked. I haven't told her that though.

Next year will be all about us. I have promised her that. Next year we can plan a family. It is time for little District Carson to make an appearance. Maybe even have the celebrity wedding. It will be good for the fans. Before I start work on my movie and books. I am sure it won't take long to write the first book. What, two weeks? Then turn it into the movie. The whole thing shouldn't take more than six months. If I film them all back to back I will get the trilogy done in a year.

"Are you hungry?"

She is nodding. I am hungry too. Last thing I ate was that sandwich in the car.

"Good. I don't think they have room service so I will just go downstairs and get us some food." I get dressed. I kiss her on the forehead as she lies on the bed. She will think that is sweet. I go to the door. I stop and take a look at her on the bed. That is the sight I want to see every day. Her lying there exhausted from an afternoon of sex and fun with me. That is the picture I have always wanted from her. She smiles. I smile. It is perfect. This is our moment. I go over to my bag and pull the box out that was in Uncle George's safe. I go over and kneel in front of the bed. She is sitting up now. She knows what is coming. She has been dreaming of this day since the first time I walked into her classroom.

"Would you do me the honour?"

She is crying. I can see she is too happy to speak. I put the ring on her finger and then I kiss her. I mean, really kiss her. She is stunned, I can tell. I kiss her again on the forehead.

"I will get us some dinner."

She lies back on the bed and I head out of the room. Smooth, Edmund, really smooth. That is movie gold right there.

I go downstairs to the bar area. It is really busy. I order some food and a bottle of wine. There is a ten-minute wait, but that is fine. It will give her some time to catch her breath. She was already exhausted from the sex. I can't imagine how she is feeling now. Excited and knackered at the same time. The man of her dreams has just proposed to her. Probably ringing round all her friends to share the good news. I hope she doesn't tell them all where we are? Well unless they are close, hot friends.

It is good for her that I keep my skills up with other women. It just ensures that I know how to make sure I still ring her bell over and over again when we meet up. I don't think all other men are as considerate.

There are a lot of people in here called Ken. It seems to be every second person, and they are always asking questions too. Do you Ken? Does he what? What is Ken always up to? It is interesting listening to a Scottish accent. I need to try and do one for when I am staying in hotels. It will really throw people of the scent.

Will Langham, I think that is what he said. Do you Ken Will Langham. How does he know so soon? Is it in the press? Has the ban been lifted? Is the ban even in Scotland? I never checked that. They said worldwide. Scotland is a country, isn't it?

They found him in a shed. Game of thrones style. That is what Ken is saying. I carry on listening. His name isn't Ken. Ken must be the Scottish word for know? Do you know? Now I get it. I will have to remember that for the film. It wasn't a shed, it was a barn. He, Will would have told them it was a banquet hall for sure. I bet he lorded it up. I bet Will lorded it up, making the press call him milord. He will have played his part. That was what he wanted.

They found his wife, Mandy, in St John's. She didn't look like a Mandy. I mean, it must have made the news? If not, is it this Dark Web? Is the world watching the Dark Web now? How do I get on the Dark Web? Is there like a dark Twitter, or dark Facebook? I need to look into that. I really need to get back online with the technical stuff.

I have names. That is a sign. I have names. They won't give the kids names out as they are still too young. That is why nobody is talking about them. They will worry about their safety. Fame is hard to handle when you are really young. I have the mum's and dad's names. It was worrying me that I was no longer in touch with my fans. But now I have names. The barmaid brings over the food and drink. It is on a tray. That was thoughtful. I throw her the look. The one that says play your cards right and you could be the one I am wineing and dining. I take it upstairs. I kick on the door. There is no answer.

"It is me. I have food. I have wine."

I kick on the door again. There is no answer. I put the tray down and open the door. I then pick it up again. She isn't there. I stand and look at the bed, remembering what she looked like when I left. Something told me as soon as I put the tray down that she would be gone. She loves her disappearing tricks. I walk over to the bed. There is a note. There is always a note. The little black box is sitting on the note and the pillow.

"Dearest Edmund. Yes, yes, a thousand times yes. But give this to me again when you are done. You will know the time. The day when we can spend every minute together. You have the plan. Next year belongs to us." It is signed with at least three dozen kisses.

She is right. She is always right. The last thing I want her to do is spend all night looking at the ring, dreaming of the day I get there. It will be too upsetting for her, especially around the holidays. I do have a plan now. Some of it is thick and fast.

Some is distracting. Something to mesmerise the press. Some of it will ensure that I go down as a legend, a legend above all legends.

But most of all, as the build-up to the end of every good movie trilogy. They will be holding their breath in the cinema. Wait, a cinema, I never thought of that. That could be fun. As long as it is not a chick flick. I haven't been to the cinema in ages. Nothing good on. Not yet anyway. It is all superheroes nowadays. I suppose I am a superhero too. I need to remember that.

I set the cheese and onion sandwiches and wine on the bed. I am ready. She has made me ready.

Tomorrow... it really begins.

Chapter 12

Setting the alarm for four thirty a.m. That is dedication to the plan. That is me giving dedication to my career. That is what I need now, dedication. There is just me, and the milkman, working this hard at this time of the morning. They do have milkmen now, don't they? I can't remember seeing one recently, other than on TV.

I switch off the alarm and get dressed. I make the bed. It will look better if the bed is made. Shows that I care what people think about my scenes. I mean, they know I do, but I need to be back to my best.

I leave the bag in the corner and head downstairs. I head to reception and lift the barrier to get to the other side of the desk. I can see the night guy that was on reception. He is in a little office at the back. I think he is watching one of those portable TVs. Doesn't he know you can get it on your phone or Ipad nowadays? I walk up behind him. He is not watching it. It is some kind of gambling programme, with a wheel with numbers on. He is asleep. I can hear him snoring, sounds like a train. That makes it easier for me. With one slice I cut his throat. No messing. He is not important. Focus is important.

Okay, some mess. He is a bit of a squirter! I immediately step back. I don't need to get covered in someone else today. I have a lot to do. I need to get south and prepare for the party tomorrow night. I still don't really know what I am going to do. I just know where I am going to do it.

Important dates. Her words are ringing in my ears. She is never too far away that I don't hear her words in my ears. I go to the hat stand and grab the scarf that is hanging there. Good thing about being in Scotland, it is always cold and someone will always have a scarf. I tie it around his neck so he stops splurging everywhere. I then grab him under the arms and take him back to my room. I am glad nobody else is silly enough to get up this time of the morning.

I suppose that was a bit of a gamble. I shouldn't have done that. I need to remain focused. But it did feel good. The thought of moving around freely while I work does feel good. It would have been annoying if someone had woken up and wanted selfies with us. It would have been exciting for them for sure to see me at work though. I lay him on the bed and undo the scarf. It is not spurting any more. I dip my fingers in his neck and start writing on the wall. I think messages look so much better when they are written in blood. Even if you have to keep dipping your fingers in their neck to write it.

I wonder if I should start to carry a paintbrush. Maybe I should drain the body. That way I can make like a small paint pot and carry it around with me. It would save time. I could just string them up like they do in the slaughter houses. That could be quite fun. Also you can imagine the old forensics people. It would freak them out testing the blood and knowing it was not of the person that I just worked with. It would be another twist to my remarkable scenes. I am going to be doing that.

I step back. That looks good. I then grab my phone and take a selfie with him and the sign. Feels like ages since I have taken a decent selfie. I think I have lost the love for them since the government has stopped the world from seeing them. It makes me not think about it.

I need to think more long-term. My fans will be hurting from this Blackout more than me. They will want to know what happened. I need to keep doing this for them.

I must be working quickly as he is still asleep, even now. Probably for the best. He is just a distraction. Still, none of that dipping woke him up. By the look of him he drinks too much. On nights as well so nobody would see him. It is a thing up here. I am almost sure I heard it was an epidemic. I go and wash my hands. I then go back and quickly check his pockets. Nothing. They must be downstairs. I take one more look at the sign.

"Sorry about the last few days. It begins.

Edmund Carson, the Alphabet Killer."

I like my signature. It looks good in red as well. I stop and look at it. It is not right. I read it again, and again. I have it. I walk up and put the word "is" in there.

"Edmund Carson is the Alphabet Killer." Like George is Batman. Daniel is Bond. Brad Pitt is… is? What is Brad Pitt? Ocean Eleven? He really needs to be someone or people will forget he ever existed.

I think I need to start carrying a marker or something as well. It would have been good to have my name in blood and then the title in marker. Makes it look all official.

I look at it again. I am not telling them anything they haven't already worked out. Other than the fact that they now think I am going to begin again. With Annan! Or am I? It may just mean that I am starting again. As the last few days weren't great. They will go with the first, I am sure of it. They will be heading to all the B's which are close to here. That will give me some time. I am so glad that I don't live in America with the *Criminal Minds* team. Hotch would have known what I was doing, I am sure of it. He knows how the mind of people like me works. Stars!

I head downstairs with my bag, and back into reception. I find his keys and head out of the door. I click. The car lights up. It is a bit of a crappy old car. I'm surprised it even clicked. I suppose the night shift job in a small hotel doesn't pay that well. What was his name? Smith. I did make sure I clocked it. I don't want to have another person forgotten in my bio. Is that common for Scotland? I am still in Scotland, right?

It will suit me for what I need. Although as I get close I can tell it could have done with a wash. Inside and out. He doesn't really take pride in his car.

I get into it. The passenger seat has a beer can on it and there are a few empties in the foot well. I am not one to judge but drinking and driving? Sometimes people need to have an intervention with a police officer. I start the car and then start heading south. It is not a long drive to my second stop.

What... what is Devil's Porridge? I can go and see the Devil's Porridge? It has that funny sign so it must be some kind of tourist attraction. It isn't going to be open now at this time of the morning. Will it? What time does the devil get up? Who would want to go and see the devil's breakfast anyway?

I guess the same guy who wants some dumb fries. It will be deep-fried. Deep-fried porridge, now there's a thought. They are mad about food up here, aren't they? I ignore the sign. Next time I am up here, next time I will go and see what all the fuss is about.

I get to the M6 and keep heading south. It does feel like I am heading home. The M6 south leads to home. Wherever home is.

There is a smile on my face as I see the junction. One of the hardest yet most rewarding times in my life. I take the junction and head straight there. It doesn't take too long before I pull up outside the church. I do love the round stained-glass window in this church. Every time I see a round window, it makes me think of this place. If Father Harry were to make an appearance again, I can't think of anywhere better for it. This was a pinnacle part of his history. Pinnacle, love that word. Not sure where it has just come from. I know a lot more words than I let on. Mrs Whitaker, my English teacher, has had a real effect on me. Was it Father Harry? I was Father Harry when I got here last time wasn't I?

No, no, I wasn't. I was Father Darren. That Darren guy had got it my head. He won't be there forever. I will deal with him at some point. I remember I was Edmund when I left. It was an Edmund type of night. In the end!

I am so lucky. Well, as lucky as I always am. Before I even get out of the car I spot him as he is walking over from the vicarage to the church. I look closer. It is not Father Steven. I would have liked to see him again, but I think that is a good thing. It means he has taken some of my advice and is spending more time with the family and kids. She was hot, in a hot unknown way. That hot you only find out when she is naked. Which I am sure a lot more people have done since I left them? My guess would be that he has left Eugene in charge. She is nursing a night out on the town with the girls. Flirting with men at bars. She will be getting laid a lot more, I am sure of it. I did that for her. He may be spending more time with her and the kids, but you can't help who you fall in love with. Those things never change. Love is love. I am glad for everyone that has that.

He is a good-looking vicar. I can see why he fell for him. They always say the best ones are taken. My nan used to say that, about boys and girls. She would have been a best one. My granddad, he would have been punching so far above his weight. That is another one of hers too. I really need to start writing her sayings down. I keep saying it. They will be great for the book.

I suppose it is to be expected that she is close to me when I am here…

I am out of my car and almost following him into the church he takes so long to unlock the door. As he walks in I am behind him. I plunge my knife into him three times in the back until his knees go weak. I catch him, before he falls, by the hair and cut his throat. I then let him drop to the ground. I turn back towards the door and lock it behind me. I don't want anyone coming in yet. I need to get the place ready.

I go up to the altar. I do like this church. I think it was the first one that I really looked at. I mean, really looked at. I took the time to look at the windows and the décor. People really support this whole religion thing. It is like a cult. Although their book is a good read. So really exciting stuff in there if you get past the Shakespeare language.

I find the wine and the daily bread. I don't know why they call it bread. It is hardly bread. The things basically melt in your mouth. Almost like rice paper. I set up the altar, placing the wine in the cup and the wafers in the wafer cup. I think they would be better with a baguette or something. They would probably get more people in on a Sunday too. Maybe a bit of ham and cheese too would go down well. Even a pickled onion. Feed them and they will come. I am sure that is in their book.

I light the candles. That is a nice touch. Looks like one of those midnight masses. Although it is still stupid o'clock in the morning. They will appreciate that when they come to say their prayers.

I go and fetch Father Eugene and place him in front of the altar. I place him on his knees in the praying position. He is really worshipping, isn't he? I borrow a bit of blood from his neck. I will do the draining thing next time. I must remind myself to get some rope. I leave my second sign of the day on the altar.

"Help yourselves. Father Harry."

That should really confuse them. They are going to wonder what is coming next. Wait, should it be Edmund Carson is Father Harry Chapman? Like Edmund Carson is the Alphabet Killer? Does that sound better?

No. I think that is fine. Father Harry is a legend in his own right now. I think once you have your own T-shirt in Camden you are established in your own right.

I love it. The press are not going to know whether or not I am continuing with the Alphabet Killer or if this is the return of Father Harry. Little do they know Father Harry is just helping them second guess. K is K.

I make sure I take a couple of selfies. That is what is missing. I have not been taking enough pride in my work. Two quick and easy scenes and I can be back on track. I have been too focused on the end game and not enjoying what I have done. Selfies, selfies, selfies. I need to ensure not only do I remember everything for myself but for the people who this is really for, my fans. They will like the fact that I am back here. This will have been one of their favourites. This was the first time I used a nail gun as well. Those pictures went down a storm. Now Kendal is making a return into the world of the Alphabet Killer. It is probably the second best thing that has ever happened here. The first being my last visit. The cakes are a distant third. Nice but a distant third.

I leave. It would have been good to catch up with Eugene for a little while to see how things were going with Steven and the family. How all the people in the old folks' home were? Even Fred, the miserable old git. Although I would guess he would be dead by now? He didn't look like he had long left.

It would have been good to catch up. But I need the scenes to be emotion free. Even I may have slipped up speaking to him, letting him in on my plans. I need to be careful. It is about completing the task I have ahead of me. Focus! Now I have left a doubt in everyone's mind where I am going and what is to come. Genius! I am a genius. I knew all I needed was to recharge my batteries. Lock myself away from the world for the day. Some quality alone time works wonders.

I am back in the car and heading south. It is a shame. I love this part of the country. I would have loved to spend more time here. Maybe we will come back. Once we are retired next year, we will come back and spend some holidays up in the lakes like Susan did. Susan and Fred, that is the kind of relationship Miss Walker and I will have. That type of love that lasts a lifetime. She was a lovely woman, that Susan. The biscuits were really good. I don't think I have had shortbread since. I need to treat myself more.

It takes six hours, but I make it to Leicester. I check in to the hotel and head into my room. I feel like I do this a lot. The amount I have paid in hotels I could have bought myself a couple of flats around the country. It would have been good to have a couple of love pads for the ladies.

The party is not far. Bridge Street or something like that.

As much as they can censor what I do, they can't censor what the whole country is doing. The whole country is about to celebrate Halloween. My Halloween. At a time when the world needs inspiration, due to the fact the government has stopped reporting on it, the best inspiration of all time. Who else would have they looked to?

There are Blackout parties everywhere.

It is amazing. Researching them was so much fun. But this looks like the best place to be, the best place beginning with an L. They can't take the whole of the Internet down. I am sure that the costume sales alone would have made a cool million in profit for the people. I really need to start trademarking my characters. I am sure I can do it. I looked it up once, something about postal systems and recorded delivery, if I remember. Miss Whitaker taught us that in class. If we should ever write something so good that it needed protecting, that is what we were meant to do. My book will need that. My books will need that, all of them.

She looked at me through the whole of that class. She knew there was only one student in the room capable of doing something great. I hope I have showed her how great I could become now. I showed her outstanding, the only outstanding pupil in the class. She was so bright when it came to these things.

I throw my bag down and then leave the hotel room and head into town. I need to get a new the ONE costume. This is his type of thing, and I am sure that half of the world will be dressed as him tomorrow. It will be the way to blend in. I find a shop selling black hoodies, T-shirts, trousers and black trainers. I buy two of everything. Then head back to the hotel. Part of me is tempted to go out now. I could be done with L today and move on. There were parties in M. I have that bit between my teeth again now. That let's get on with it again, but we have a plan. There has to be a good mix of anticipation and event. The fans will like that. The media will be even more tempted by it. I lie on the bed and switch on the TV. I go straight to the news channels, but there is nothing on there. I am not surprised. I wouldn't have reported on my last few days either. They weren't my best work. But my best work, it is coming. I can feel it deep down inside of me.

Inside Edmund Carson!

Now that is a good name for one of my books. Understanding the real me.

I settle into the Sky TV marathon of *Criminal Minds* and *CSI*. They are all from season seven and eight, you can tell by the cast members. That is where I get my ideas from. Even they throw in the odd new character every now and again to keep it fresh, I suppose. The key thing is that they never let go of the classics. I needed to remember to do that more. She knew that. That is what she told me. Not to lose touch with myself. Not that I ever would, stop touching myself, that is. I go and fetch some tissues. Time to touch myself over Emily. She is hot…

Three minutes past seven. It has been so long since I woke up at Nan-time. I must have been tired, although the food tray from the room service is still on the bed. I must have slept like a log. I get up and move it over to the side and then jump back on the bed. I am staying here all day. That is the plan.

It is fucking Halloween!

I am going to make it my holiday today. Mine forever. Halloween will belong to me. I am going to need to leave everything for this evening. That is going to be hard. Part of me says that I should just start and now and spend all day on it. Make it amazing. A day people will never forget. That would make more sense, wouldn't it? Although Halloween is at night, isn't it? You have to give people what they want. I stick the TV on. *3rd Rock from the Sun*! Channel 4, I think, is the only channel that ever shows this. This and *The King of Queens* every morning. She is hot. The wife of the big guy, she is very noisy and full of herself. But I would do her.

Nan loved this stuff though. It was always on in the background when she was making breakfast. She used to say the news was too depressing. Lately I would have to agree. There is nothing decent on the news any more, not since me.

I lie and watch TV. It is going to piss me off lying here all day. There is a knock on the door. I get up and open it. It is the room service woman. I send her away. I hang the sign on the door and close it. I don't want to be disturbed again today. I look down. Good job I was wearing boxers. I could have been naked opening the door. I didn't even think about it. I just jumped straight up. Although I am sure that is the best sight she has ever had when she has knocked on a door before.

I am hot. Fucking hot. She will be strumming herself later at just the thought of me. I am back on the bed flicking between the channels. Imagine what it was like before? My dad used to say that there were only three channels. Can you imagine just three? And before that it was all in black and white. What did people used to watch? No *Criminal Minds*, no *CSI*. Not even real cartoons.

He said the best cop show on TV was *Z-Cars*. *Z-Cars* was apparently all about coppers who drove around in police cars. How exciting would that be? Ran for like sixteen years. Longer than anything else that I have watched.

Everything I have seen from that age didn't even have action. It was all talking and stuff. Why would they want to watch it for sixteen years?

No Internet, no mobile phones. You had to go to a phone box to call someone. They even did that on the TV show. The coppers went to a phone box to call the office. You would have thought that they could have pretended to have a mobile phone. It was TV, for Christ's sake. Take the cord off. Get rid of the dialling thing in the middle. It is fiction. That is what you were supposed to do to keep the massed entertained.

People didn't really like TV back in those days, I am sure of it. *Z-Cars* probably only got a dozen people watching it.

I am so glad I am not old. Although they must be amazed now, with the last thirty years of television. The world has changed so much, for the better.

I find the movie channel. It is in black and white. Jesus, things are going back in time everywhere today. A movie called *It's a Wonderful Life*? I wonder if we will get any of the *Z-Cars* coppers in here. I lie back and start to watch it. It looks a bit Christmassy to me. Maybe it will give me some ideas for the twelve days of Christmas. That was another great idea of hers. I really need to explore that a little more. I am not sure I even remember all the twelve days of Christmas. I thought there were only three. Christmas Eve, Day and the Boxing thing. I settle in to watch the movie. Yes, this will give me some ideas.

How the fuck was that a wonderful life?

What is up with people? Why would they make movies like that? About Christmas as well! Who the fuck wants to cry their eyes out at Christmas? Not that I cried, but I am sure some people would have. It is supposed to be a happy time.

I need to find something to take my mind off that film before I go out. It will put me right off working with people. I flick through the channels. Thank fuck for that – a *Criminal Minds*. That should do the trick. Penelope never fails me. I watch a couple of episodes. *It's a Wonderful Life* is clear out of my mind now. Black-and-white movies suck. I bet they all suck. I am sure *Z-Cars* sucked as well. Typical English policemen, they all suck.

It is time. I get off the bed and take out my costume. I lay it on the bed first. This is what an actor must feel like before he goes on stage at a theatre or on a film set. An actor getting dressed to impress his audience. I dress to impress. I move over and stand in front of the mirror. It is so good to be the ONE again. I feel all tingly at the thought of it. I pull the hoodie up. As soon as it is up I feel like him. I feel like he feels. Like a predator. Like a king of the underground. That is a good strapline for him as well. King of the Underground! Unique is a good word for him. This is where it all started for me. This is a classic. How weird that it is not in colour either? Was I thinking that far ahead without even knowing it? Was I thinking about the posters and the advertising campaign? I can see these images in like that *GQ* magazine. The hoodie getting slightly more and more undone, the girls will love that. I think I am just a natural at this stuff.

This will be popular tonight, this outfit. True fans will go classic.

The Blackout and the parties are worldwide. I will not be surprised if Halloween as a title has already gone. I can see the kids running up and down the streets in America now.

There are free drinks in some bars in Leicester if they come dressed as the Blackout. That is what the posters were saying. They do know the Blackout isn't a character, don't they? Or do they think the Alphabet Killer is the Blackout? Maybe the Blackout should have a costume.

They are only saying dressed as the Blackout because if they said dressed as Edmund Carson then the poster would be taken down. That is so clever. My fans, my followers are so clever. How to stick two fingers up at the government and the press, right there!

I check my knife is in place and then head out of the room. My hoodie is still up. I get to the lift. The doors open. My heart skips a beat as soon as it does. Standing inside is the ONE and Father Harry. Father Harry is actually a girl. I guess that makes her Father Harriet? Mother Harriet? It is good to know though that I am legendary across all genders. I feel a little nervous as I get in. It feels like the first time I have met a real fan. When they start dressing like you they are real fans. I am sure I read that somewhere. When they start dressing like you, you have a stalker and someone sends you fan art. That is when you are famous.

"Cool costumes." I had to say something.

"Thanks. Cool costume too, mate."

We are not mates. That is a little unfair. We should be mates. I should be mates with all of them. There is a brotherhood thing going on here. A Brotherhood! I like that. Brothers in hoodies, like brothers in arms but with clothes. I will have to remember that for the T-shirt in Camden. Join the Brotherhood today. That is another great one. I am on fire today. I am not surprised I am worshipped.

She smiles at me. She wants me. It would be a bit weird doing a girl dressed up like me though. I am sure lots of stars have to work with that same dilemma. Except for Brad! They all look like him in jeans and T-shirt. I think he is just too lazy for his fans. He needs to get himself a character.

We all get out on the ground floor and leave the hotel. Oh my fucking God! There are lots of them. I mean, lots of them. Well, lots of me. This is such a buzz. I can feel myself strutting down the sidewalk. I follow the couple from the hotel as they seem to be heading to the same street as me. Must be where all the cool bars are. They are the type of places that I would go. I get there. It is like one of my dreams. In fact, I think I have had this dream. The dream where everyone in the world is me! With every turn of my head I can see me looking back at me. It is all about me. At last it is all about me.

Although there are a few other characters walking about as I head down the street. Some vampires, that is not very original. Some witches, again I think these things are dated. Who but me is coming up with new horror? I quite like the hot witch look though. The short skirt really does it for me. And the little hat. I remember them having long dresses and warts. Not anymore. I go into the first bar. It is free entry for Blackout costumes. That is amazing. Imagine what I would get if they really knew it was me. In fact, shouldn't I be getting some kind of kickback from this? I really need an agent. I go to the bar. A free drink as well. It is just a bottle of Carlsberg. There is a sign above the bar. "The Blackout! Probably the best serial killer in the world". What do they mean probably? My name and probably should never be in the same sentence. Besides, how do you kill serial? I mean, I like my cornflakes, but I don't kill them?

Hold on a minute. Why would they say their beer is probably the best beer in the world? Who thinks that is a good way to advertise something? This Carlsberg company lacks a bit of confidence, is all I can say. You would at least tell people it is the best beer in the world. Even if it isn't! It is too late, you have bought it. This stuff isn't hard. Some people just don't think.

I look around the room. I am at least fifty per cent of the room. That has to be one of the most amazing sights ever. I don't know another star that ever has ever had that. There has never been a George Clooney party. George was Batman though. I think I saw a Batman out tonight. Maybe it is that smiling guy from the walking on the coals. What was his name? He was dressed as Batman. The old type Batman not a George Batman. Gareth, that was it, he was a nice guy. Maybe he took my advice and upgraded to the cool one.

I swig at my beer. It is not good. It is not even probably good, let alone the best in the world. I am realising more and more that I am not a great fan of beer. Stella is the only one I have a little taste for. I suppose it is wet and cold though. So I keep swigging as I want to make sure that I blend in with well, me. The place is filling up nicely.

I am still not sure what I am going to do, but it will come to me. The plan was to come to the party. I couldn't miss the opportunity. Clearly I have to work, but it is still early. I am sure if I get to see every party they are throwing for me, inspiration will take over. Maybe even a scene, leave them wondering who turned up. I am sure the security cameras all over the place will be going mad with the amount of pictures of me they are seeing at the moment. Imagine if they—

What the fuck!

All the lights go out. Have they done that on purpose? Is there a reveal coming? Was it all a trap by the press to get me here? I put my bottle down. If they think that...

"Blackout party!"

That was the DJ. I could tell that even in the dark. He starts playing a song. It is an odd song. The people next to me are saying this is so my song. How is it so my song? I haven't released a song yet? I mean, I will but after the movie. I start to listen to the words.

"I don't know, Why do they treat me so?" This singer really understands me. Wait did I say that out loud? It is a good job it is noisy in here.

"I am a jack of all trades". I love it. I am a Jack of all trades. I am a champion. Oh my God, they have created my own theme tune and I didn't even know it. What else don't I know? Have I won awards already? Oscars or whatever the music equivalent to an Oscar is? I really need to know.

"The devil is inside me?" Why would you add the devil into my song? Wait, did they create this song just for Halloween? Do I already have more than one holiday song? "The devil is inside". It is sending a shiver down my spine. What a line. That is perfect. This guy, the guy who wrote this, must have interviewed all the girls I have ever been with. That would have taken him ages. How didn't someone tell me that? I have worked with so many people. I don't understand why someone didn't mention it? The song ends.

It was a guy called George. It was his song. Everyone is cheering. The DJ says on the hour every hour, "Blackout party". I check my watch. Four minutes past nine. This is the place. I have to work here. That song was the inspiration I was looking for. It was a sign. Fate gave me a sign.

Not only here, because that wouldn't be fair on the rest of the city, but I have to work here. That song was amazing. I need to get it as a ringtone. Probably wrote it knowing it would be the theme tune to the movie, like they do with the *Bond* movies. I am sure there are lots of rock stars trying to associate themselves with me. I am probably number one across the world and don't even know it. I need to listen to more music, maybe a more up-to-date channel for the car. I keep listening to BBC Radio 2 because that is what Nan listened to. I need to switch to a younger, more modern station.

I head out of the bar. It has bouncers on the door of a pub. Is that normal now? I thought they were only for clubs. I head to the next bar. They have bouncers too. It must be natural to have people on the door. If not, they were just expecting such a great turnout that they brought a lot more staff in. That will be it. They do bring extra security in with all stars, don't they? I go into the bar. I have to pay for a drink in here, so I have a bottle of Stella. That is better. It is a stronger taste. I think my taste buds need stronger tastes.

This is a bit of a different bar. They sell wigs and glasses and hats right here in the bar. They are not even my costumes. They look really old. The walls are plastered with old people sayings and for some reason they all want to live in the eighties. Still, there is a fair share of people dressed as me. I guess they think with all the black and white they would feel back at home in the eighties. That was when all the black-and-white TV was, wasn't it? They probably also thought they were getting a free drink in here too. I watch as they party. All shapes and sizes, the clothes as well as the people. I am not sure why some of the larger ladies are wearing some of the smaller ladies' clothes and vice versa. They do like everything to hang out, don't they? The blokes seem to like it though. They are all lapping it up.

This is what the government and the press are keeping from the public. They must be outraged. I would imagine they would party like this every night. Every night, after the press have reported someone new who I have been working with, they would party like this. They could put my friend's pictures on the bar as a type of reward for working with me. Keep a list. Like they do in America. They praise these people, even put them on milk cartons and have posters of them in the street. They must be so proud. I suppose everyone is just hoping that one day they will be the next person to meet me. Then they could get their own poster, or milk carton. The UK needs to catch up with America. They do everything bigger and better.

Look at them. Little do they all know, I am here. Here with them now. It is such a rush to walk among them. I like that. I am among them. I should use that in the movie. This must be a great release for them all from the boring lives they lead. That the pubs of the country have laid on an all celebrate me day. They probably didn't know when to do it. The Blackout has given them the perfect opportunity.

I don't know why, but it almost makes me not want to work tonight.

Standing here, watching all my fans as they spend time together. It almost feels a shame that I have to single some out for stardom. They all deserve my attention tonight for the trouble they have gone to. I finish my drink and go back into the street. There are a lot of bars on this street. There are probably more people outside than inside. I think I need to use that to my benefit. I check my watch. It is 9.40. I am not going to make it to ten o'clock Blackout. I will have to leave that for eleven. I carry on walking between the bars. They all have different offers. One place even has a drink called The Blackout. It is made up of Haribo sweets, and five shots of your choice topped up with something called Kopparberg Cider. All for a tenner. That must be good value. I should be getting a cut of that too. I need to be advertising the sweets and the alcohol. I quite like the fact that someone has taken the time to make me into a drink. The others are probably a drink too. Guinness. I would be a good advert for Father Harry. It is the black and white thing again. With the white collar. Something all in black for the ONE. Maybe a vodka and coke. Maybe my movie should be in black and white? It would be the first good black-and-white movie. Another first for me. That is one.

I follow the guy down the alley way. He is stumbling all over the place. He keeps walking. I check around me. There is nobody else. He leans up against the wall and wait, why is he taking that out? Here? This isn't the time or place to start playing with yourself. I start to walk up behind him, but there is a river of pee coming backwards. Now I know what he was doing. The bars are probably too full of me to get to the bathroom. I step back a little and wait. I am not standing in the guy's pee. He zips up and turns to continue walking. As soon as he is pee-river free I am behind him and cut his throat. He hardly moves. I am sensing he has been drinking The Blackout. I grab him and place him on the ground and then step back. I lose my breath for a second. He is Father Harry. I couldn't tell as I was walking behind him, but that is who he has come as. For some reason I quickly look behind me. There is nobody there. I just had the feeling that someone could have done that to me. How weird is that? Who would want to work with me? I stand looking at him. There is something about seeing Father Harry like that. It is creepy. I check my watch.

It is just gone ten. I should have really thought about that. I don't really want him to be discovered yet. What if it starts a frenzy? What if everyone comes out of the bars to see him? Hoping I am still here and I would work with them. Especially The Blackout bar, it is my best opportunity. I look around me. There are a few old bins and pallets. I put them around him. He looks more homeless than anything else now. I reach down and take off the collar. It is eye-catching. I don't know why, but people react differently when they see that little piece of white card. Especially if there is a trickle of blood running down it. Again, another soon-to-be classic look! I am amazing, I see the movie in everything.

I go back to the main street. Things are getting even busier. It is like people don't really start coming out till about ten o'clock. I just walk up and down the road. This is what I always envisaged it would be like. Fans adoring me everywhere I turn. It makes me want to scream out that I am actually here. I imagine this is everywhere though. Everywhere around the country! I have seen dozens, maybe hundreds, of the ONE and Father Harry. There are a lot of schoolgirl costumes with blood everywhere. That must be for the girls. They will be so happy about that. I made them all minor celebrities. Seven and Seventeen may be even major celebs. I can't believe they are even selling plastic nail guns and knives with my name on. So many people are carrying them.

The world has not forgotten me. The world worships me.

That is all I needed to know. That makes all the hard work worth it. I walk down to the first bar I went into. It is heaving. I go up to the bar and order a drink. A bottle of Stella. I do like

Stella, I have decided. Maybe I need to endorse them first. They will then be the best beer in the world. None of this probably stuff. Oddly he didn't give me another free drink? He must have recognised me? Which is odd as I am practically the only person in here. I check my watch. I have ten minutes. I look around the room. There are so many of my fans in one place. So many! I love the fact that the girls in the school uniform all have numbers on. The fact that ninety per cent of them are all seven or seventeen makes me think that I may have spoken about those two above all others. They probably both went down the reality TV route. *Big Brother*, something like that. I check my watch again. Two minutes. When the lights go out I have probably two and a half minutes before I need to be out and heading to the door. I put my drink down and move more into the centre of the room. Everyone is dancing around me. It is great. I am sure a couple of them are starting to cop a feel as it is dark.

They start a countdown from ten. That was handy, saves me looking at my watch again. I join in the countdown as loud as I can. It is so exciting. Then bang, the lights are off. The room gasps, but there is no music. The DJ is obviously pausing for effect. It is working. I think everyone has stopped breathing for a second. Then the George song comes on. There are screams everywhere and I haven't even started. They can't all be working, can they? They are not all imitating me? Had the same idea? I look around. I can make out in the darkness they are only pretending, all with the fake knives and nail guns.

I start to put an end to their pretence.

I cut the throat of the girl nearest to me. There is a laugh from people that can make it out in the darkness. I keep moving forward, working with people at every turn and getting to their throats when I can. The smell of blood is everywhere. They must all be able to smell it, but they are just laughing. Another girl is in front of me. I stab her straight in the neck. The drink she is holding drops to the floor. This makes people look again. I think that makes it more real for them. Who would waste a drink? Even if it is probably the best beer in the world. I carry on towards the door, randomly plunging my knife into anyone that I walk past. I can hear the song playing. It is an amazing choice. It is me. I like the fact that he has captured who I am, how I am feeling and who the world probably expects me to be.

It is being drowned out by what I would say is real screaming now. I can tell the difference even if they can't. I head for the door. The bouncers have obviously recognised it too as they are heading inwards as I head outwards. In fact, a lot of people are heading out now. They are probably like me. Only went in for The Blackout song. I head straight back up the street towards my hotel.

That was the event that I needed to make Halloween my own. Yes, that is enough. Impactful and memorable, that is what I was going for. In a place it can be repeated every year. Pubs around the country will be staging those parties for centuries to come. I almost regret Father Harry in the alleyway now. Regret is a strong word... I don't regret anything. It just wasn't as classy. The Alphabet Killer needs a little class about him. Like Jack. I should have probably left it with The Blackout Party. That would have been better for the fans, I am sure of it. Given he was in hiding. They will probably put it down to a copycat so I don't need to worry about it.

The smell of blood is really in my nose. It has hit me hard and, well, made me hard. I would have loved to spend more time at the party with some of those girls. But I would have been mobbed. They wouldn't have been happy to just watch. It would have turned into an out-and-out orgy. I get to my hotel and get into the lift. I think an early night and then head to M. I have some shopping to do first to set—

A hand comes into the lift before the doors close. I push the door open button. I am courteous like that. I think it is always good to help people when you can.

"Hey, thanks."

"No problem."

She stands next to me in the lift and presses floor eleven.

"That was wild. Did you enjoy it?"

I can feel myself nodding at her.

"I really did." I really, really did.

"Hi, I am seventeen by the way." She is smiling from ear to ear as she says that. She didn't need to tell me. The school uniform and the number around her neck kind of gave it away. Plus she is almost as hot as seventeen. It is probably why she dressed as her.

"I can see. Great outfit! You have done her proud. My name is Edmund Carson. The ONE." Pause for dramatic effect.

"The Only."

She is smiling at that. That line will make all the girls go weak at the knees. She knows it is really me. I can tell…

Chapter 13

"You are welcome, more than welcome." I can tell she is still going. She will be having multiples of multiples. She was not a virgin though, definitely not a virgin. You can tell by the way she moved. She knew how to keep me interested from start to finish. Not many girls do. I always expect the nerves kick in at some point.

"It was lucky we were only a few doors apart as well. That way you were able to come to mine.

"Ha ha! Yes, and come in mine." Very quick. I do like that about a girl, and being hot as fuck helps as well. This is going to be something that she tells her friends for a long time to come. The night of The Blackout Party, she got to spend it with the real Edmund Carson. There is a headline right there. A real one. None of that fake news.

"Okay, so are you going to tell me your real name now? I can't keep calling you seventeen." It is not fair on Seventeen. Although I did think of her a few times while we were hard at it. A little role play is good.

"Really? Is that your name? Or are you still just stunned about what just happened?"

"Really? Gosia? I can't say I have heard it before." I thought she said oh gosh ahhh. Like posh girls do. I get up and fetch a bottle of water from the fridge. I fetch one for her too and leave it on the nightstand. I think she is still probably too weak to move. She really did give it her all. I do like someone who gives their all. Must have been the excitement of seeing me everywhere tonight. I can imagine the amount of guys that will get laid tonight because of that. I would have sent half the women in this town home wet.

"I must say, Gosia, you have helped to remind me what it was all about. This is what I love to do. I got a little crazy a few days ago. You will no doubt hear about it in the news or on the Dark Web. I forgot what real lovemaking was." Lovemaking, should I have said that? She is now going to think that was love instead of just fucking.

"For a moment there I forgot what everything was. I felt like I was losing touch with reality a little. I am sure all stars go through it from time to time, but tonight, the party, the atmosphere and you, you brought me back on track. Especially with the whole gymnastics bit. You must really work out. They say every hole is a goal, but I have never had a girl want to flick between the two of them as much as you. It must be true what they say about foreign girls. They can teach you a thing or two.

"No, not a lot really. I think I am just naturally fit. I haven't worked out in years. I am more one of those blessed people.

"No, you are right. Not everyone is like me. Not even tonight? And there was a lot of me tonight.

"Really? That is interesting. That's how you knew it was really me in the lift? I suppose there aren't as many hot Edmund Carsons out there as me." She is good at this. She knows exactly what to say. They rehearse this type of thing, don't they? Normal people, they rehearse what they would say if they bumped into a superstar. I mean, I never have, but other people have. It must be so exciting for her to put it into practice.

"I did enjoy tonight. The Blackout parties are an amazing idea. It may even replace the name Halloween in years to come. Become an Edmund Carson holiday celebration." I don't want to sound too cocky about the whole thing. Of course it will change the name. It already has. The DJ wasn't shouting Halloween party.

"No, I don't mind if they still don't report it. My fans will be searching the Dark Web for me." I mind a little, but I am not going to let on. I don't want her telling the press that I am upset about anything. I mean, just because I am not in the paper doesn't mean I am not in people's hearts.

Fuck me!,

That is another one. Another one I need to write down.

"No, it won't last forever. You can see how much people want me. Tonight shows that, doesn't it?" I lie back on the bed next to her.

"No, I have a plan. This was just part of it. To make the holiday my own! As I said, I lost my way a little bit. Now though, now I am back on track. You see, the trick is to keep them… Fuck!"

Fuck! Fuck! Fuck!

The trick was to keep them guessing. Then I have gone and hooked up with a hot girl and left my DNA everywhere. There was so much DNA at the party they would never have known it was really me. Especially after I left the message in Annan. I can't fuck it up already. I get up and head into the bathroom and get a towel. I run it under the hot tap and then head back into the bedroom.

"As I was saying, the trick is to keep them guessing. Then I met you in the lift and couldn't resist. You were looking so hot. Which means I have now left my DNA all over you!"

"And in you, yes." Smart arse. Sexy, but a smart and firm arse.

"You don't mind if I wipe you down, do you?"

She doesn't mind. She is almost orgasming at the thought of it. I start to wipe her down with the towel. I wipe all over, every nook and cranny, my nan used to say. Now I am regretting that Gosia was a gymnast. There isn't anywhere that she didn't have me. I make sure as I wipe I clean out every place I have been. I can feel her trembling as I do. This must be getting her excited all over again. It makes me want to satisfy her again. I am just that type of person.

"That is better. That way they won't be asking you for a DNA test.

"Ha ha! I am sure there are a lot of girls wanting to ask me for a DNA test too." She is so quick and so funny. That is what I like in a girl. All the memorable ones are quick, funny and caring.

I mean, they were all hot or else they wouldn't have been there, but there is more to a relationship than hotness. Wait a minute, what the fuck am I saying? Hotness is the key to any relationship. You just need to be a little hotter than your partner and then it will work. It is why they all put out for me on the first date. They all think we are close in hotness, bless them.

I lie back on the bed. I am careful not to touch her.

"Oh yeah, as I was saying, I have a plan. It is a good plan which is going to take a lot of effort on my part and also it is going to take a lot of patience.

"I know it is not something I am not known for. But I feel as if it is going to be one of my legacies. You know, like the School and the Hotel. Something the world will remember forever. I have to step it up for the fans.

"It will be worth it, thank you." She is exactly the type of person that I am doing this for. The grateful.

"Yes, exactly like tonight. That is a good example. When people think of what was formally known as Halloween, they will be thinking Edmund Carson."

I need to get going. That was the plan. The plan wasn't to get caught up with some girl in a hotel room for the night. Although I am sure I am not the first star to say that. I need to go. I get up and start to get dressed. I pack my bag as I go. She is making a few sighing noises. I don't know if it is still orgasms or the fact that she is upset at me leaving.

"I would have loved to. Looking at you naked on the bed, believe me, I really would love to. But I have one more thing to do tonight before I head to the next, official one." I give her a smile that lets her know the next step is a secret.

"Doing you would class as official also." It wouldn't, but she is cute. I get my shoes on and take another look at her on the bed. Fuck, I really need to take more notice of what I am doing. She may be DNA-free, but the bed is not. I bet all that blood was on me from the bar, wasn't it? Which means they can link this room to the bar? Then they can link her to me? They will work it out.

"I think I need to do something.

"Yes, about the sheets. You and I must be thinking alike." I knew we were on the same wavelength. You could tell, even when we were hard at it, she was going exactly where I wanted her to in bed.

"It would be the quickest way. Are you sure you don't mind? I mean, you would have to get up and go back to your old room?"

She is nodding. I like her. She is really nice.

"Okay, that's the plan then. Don't hang about too long though."

I walk over to the little fridge again and get all the little bottles of alcohol. I empty them all over my side of the bed. I then set fire to the bottom of the blanket. She is smiling. She doesn't move as if to show me how brave she is. It does make me smile.

"See you later, Gosh ahhh." That made her giggle I walk out of the room and head towards the lifts. I press the button and then stop.

Fuck!

When there is a fire the lifts cannot be used. There are signs in all of them. I would be trapped in the lift. Stairs it is. I start to walk down them. I now regret the eleventh floor even more. The alarms are going off as I hit the bottom floor. I head out of the hotel and back to the crappy old car that I have from Scotland. I should have really asked Gosia if she had a car I could have borrowed. I am sure she would have. I get in and start to drive.

I already know where I am going. That is the best thing about having a plan. You don't have to think about what is next. There is no confusion. I carry on down the road. These places opening twenty-four hours a day is so commonplace now. It is like we are turning into a nation of people who don't want to sleep. Which is good if you want to work at this time of night. I keep driving. It is only thirty minutes away. I am glad I didn't have too much more to drink. Last thing I need is to be pulled over by the police and lose my licence. It is only a provisional licence as it is. I pull up outside the diner. There are only a couple of cars in the car park. That is a good sign.

Ironic it is a diner. I am keeping to the same theme as the original Alphabet Killer outing in Birmingham. Working with people that work in the food industry. That guy probably supplies the food for here as well. Millionaires always have their fingers in lots of pies. That's a great line too. Millionaires and fingers in pies in the food industry. I really should be writing these down. It is a good job I have a great memory. I go inside the diner.

I pick a booth by the window so I can see if anyone else is coming. The menu is almost the size of the table. It must have a million types of burgers on there. The waitress comes over to serve me. I order an atomic burger and a beer. Not sure what an atomic burger is, but it was the first burger on the menu. She wanders off to the kitchen. I caught her name on the tag: it was Sandra. Sandra in a diner! Wasn't she in that dancing movie? Sandra? *Grease*, that was the name of the movie. I think she was a blonde though.

What the fuck am I saying!

Have I gone so mad that Sandra, *the* Sandra, wasn't the first thing that came into my mind? Sandra Bullock. That is who I should have been thinking about as soon as I saw the name. My memory is shit. Sandra Bullock is the second hottest woman in the world.

Wait, did I really say second?

Has Miss Walker got so far into my head that Sandra is out at second place? What is up with me lately? I seem to be losing reality of the world. Sandra Bullock is still number one. She will always be number one.

The food arrives. That was quick. I suppose I am the only person here. I tuck into it. Fuck, it is hot. There are real chillies and everything on top of the burger. Hidden in the fucking bun. I guess that is why they call it an atomic burger. Like the bomb.

I pretend to eat some more as I watch Sandra head back into the kitchen. I don't think it was the Miss Walker thing. It was just that she didn't look like a Sandra. Well, not how a Sandra should look. Like the Sandra.

I take a big gulp of the beer. My mouth is on fire. I take another. That will have to do. I need to get in and get out of here. I suddenly have a craving for ice cream. It must be the chillies on that burger?

I get out of the booth and head towards the kitchen to follow Sandra. I can make them both out. She is talking to a chef-like person. Well, he is dressed as a chef.

I look around the kitchen. There are a lot of things in here that could cause me an issue. A lot of knives! Not sure why I am thinking that? Why am I thinking that? I need to make sure that I work with them quickly before they get too excited about me being here. I stand by the door and wait. She will walk back. She knows I am here, so she knows to come and get my plate as soon as I am finished. I wait. And wait. She does know that I haven't paid, right? She is still standing talking to the guy. I bet she fancies him. Probably trying to a get a little action while it is quiet. Why else would she work nights alone with some bloke? They will have worked it out together to spend time away from their partners. Finally she finishes talking with him and heads towards me. I stand behind the door and as soon as it swings open and closed again I am behind her. I grab her mouth and then slit her throat. The blood oozes almost immediately from her. The smell is strong. Really strong! She must have an interesting diet. Although diet wouldn't have been one of the words I would use when describing her. I let her drop to the floor slowly. I don't want to alarm the chef. As I lay her down, something comes over me. I feel like I did with Susana. I feel like I could, should, take a bite out of her. There is a hunger brewing inside of me.

It has been so long since I have had a proper meal. In fact, I can't remember the last time? I lean in. I lick. I lick her neck again. I feel a shudder. I shouldn't bite. I need to stop. I am not that person. I am not an animal.

I stand up. Maybe I should ask the chef if he could rustle me up something. Something real from her that is not the same. Something without half a pound of chillies in it would be a good start. The smell of her has made me hard, but that is normal. I don't want this eating thing to make me into a weirdo. If I am going to eat the least I need to do is to cook it first.

I stand up and compose myself. My fans don't want that.

I look back into the kitchen area. I need to get from here to the chef without being seen. That is going to be hard. He is cleaning up at the sink, and it is a much bigger kitchen than you would have thought. I think I need to just go for it.

Fast and furious. That is an odd thing to say. Wasn't that a film? I push the door and walk as fast as I can at him. As I get closer I realise where fast and furious came from… and why I was looking around the room. The guy is a dead ringer for the bald one from the film. He is fucking huge! Muscles and everything!

Fuck!

I am behind him. He sees me in the reflection in the window. He has turned before I manage to get my knife high enough to get his neck. It is a long way up there. I plunged it straight into his stomach. He doesn't make a sound. He just hits me.

Fuck, that hurt!

I can feel myself lifted off the ground. I am actually flying. How hard did this guy hit me, with my knife still in his stomach? I land on the floor. At least I landed on my back. I raise my hands to my head to check it is still there. It is. I feel fucking dazed he hit me that hard. The adrenalin must be the only thing keeping me from passing out.

He is shouting something at me! I can hear him shouting, I just can't understand the words. Has he knocked them out of my head? He takes my knife out of his stomach. He has my knife now. He keeps walking towards me. He is still walking towards me. Walking? What is this fucking guy, a robot? Is he one of those robots made of silver? The time-travelling robots!

I scramble to my feet. I am so glad he hit me that hard now. It has given me time to get up. I start to move backwards. I am looking around for anything that I can use to stop him. I grab a pan and throw it at him. He knocks it away with ease. I swear his hands are bigger than the pan. What the fuck was I thinking? He is still fucking coming. He is screaming at me now. I am sure I made out my name in there somewhere. It is good that he recognises me, but this isn't how you get an autograph.

"Stop shouting at me... I don't understand you."

He is really mad now. It is a good job he doesn't move that fast. He is probably mad that I messed this up. I don't think any of my fans want that. I am still going backwards; he is still coming forwards. It is like we are going round in circles. I can smell blood. I mean, I can really smell blood. That is not Sandra's blood. It is sweeter, richer. It is the type of blood you imagine all over a cheese and onion sandwich. Hold on a fucking minute. I hold my hand up to my eye.

It is my fucking blood!

I am bleeding all down my face. This guy has cut my eye or my head, something like that. There is a lot of blood. Fuck, I am hard again now but at the smell of my own blood. I don't need that. What is he, a fucking boxer or something? I look around again. There are knives, but I am not sure I want to get that close.

I almost freeze. I can hear a click. He has a gun. A chef with a gun? I am looking directly at him as I move backwards. He doesn't have a gun. I look around me. I definitely heard a click. It is a kettle. I don't think twice about it. I grab it and throw it at him. It hits him square on the head and the hot water flushes in his face. He is screaming now, louder than before, but I think he's screaming at the kettle, not me. At least he has his hands covering his face. I grab the nearest knife and run at him. I stab him in the chest, twice. He pulls up his hand and gives me my knife back. Right in my side.

Fuck!

That fucking hurts. He fucking stabbed me. Why would he fucking stab me? He hits me again. How the fuck is he still standing? I am on the floor again. I pull the knife from my side. There is a lot of blood. I can't deal with that now. It fucking hurts, but I can't deal with it now. I can see him. The knife is still in his chest as well. He isn't moving now. At least that is something. He is just standing there like one of those rock creatures in *The Lord of the Rings*. He is big enough to be one. So are his hands, my God, they are like shovels.

I scramble back to my feet. The blood is really pouring now. My head, my side, it is fucking everywhere. He hits really fucking hard. His hands are by his side. The knife is still in his chest. He hasn't taken this one out. I am not even sure he has noticed it. He isn't moving. I don't like it.

"Are you…"

He falls to his knees. I jump back. I thought he was coming at me again. He then just slumps forward, face down, the knife still buried in his chest. There was such a bang I was expecting it to come out the other side.

I just stand there. I am not so sure he isn't going to get up. I am exhausted, I wasn't expecting that. It takes me a few minutes to get my senses back. My head is a little dizzy.

Right, I need to crack on. I go and look for the lights. It takes me a while, but I find them by the back door. I should really always go there first. It must be so they turn them off last thing. Although when is last thing for a twenty-four-hour diner? Christmas Day? No body works on Christmas day. I turn them off, all the outside lights and main diner lights. It leaves just a few in the kitchen.

I then go and get Sandra. She is out front. I don't want anyone coming to the door and seeing her like that. Attractive as it would be that Edmund Carson worked here, people will want a show and a meal and I am not cooking for the masses.

I sit her up next to the giant. I then sit him up too. I sit him up slowly as he is fucking heavy. I am still not sure he has been worked with though. He has that look on his face as if he could move again at any moment. I have made them comfortable. I need to look after myself now.

I head over to the sink. I can see my reflection in the window. I can see the blood as it has dripped down my face. He has cut me across the eye. It doesn't seem to be bleeding as much as it was, but it is still a good cut. It is a good-looking cut as well. It makes me look hard. I pull up my T-shirt. Fuck, that hurt. Being stabbed is not a good feeling. It is right in the side. He is obviously not a professional with a knife. He was off by at least twelve inches. I will have to tell him when he comes round. Always aim for dead centre. You would think that chefs would know that.

"Do you have a first aid box?"

Neither of them give me an answer. I guess it is a little early, especially for him. He moved so slow it could be a month before he wakes up. When you are that big I suppose you don't need to move for many people at all.

I look around the kitchen. I find it. It is a big one. I suppose you have to be prepared for anything, working in a kitchen.

"It is a good first aid box." I go through and find some wipes, some rubbing alcohol and some sticky stitches. My nan used to say in her day there were stitches they were real stitches with a piece of cotton a real needle. That must have fucking hurt. Sewing your skin like that.

I mean, Jack was a doctor of some kind, because he was good with a needle and thread? Now they are all sticky stiches, I am glad about that.

I clean up my face first. It is important in case anyone else turns up. It is a good scar, straight across the top of my right eye. I can already see that I am going to get a black eye as well. I use the sticky stitches. Seven of them! I probably only need four, but the girls will appreciate the look. It means I am willing to go the extra mile for my work, no matter the personal risk to myself. I then take of my T-shirt. I apply the rubbing alcohol.

It fucking burns!

I could have really done with a bottle of Scotch or something. That is what they do in the movies. They soak it in it, don't they? It is clean. I use the rest of the stitches. There are at least a dozen. I then put a pad over it and wrap my waist in bandages. I could have been a doctor. My nan always wanted me to be a doctor. I am a natural. I put my T-shirt back on. The last thing I need is him getting jealous as Sandra can't keep her eyes off me.

"Thanks, Sandra. It does look kind of cool.

"You know, I was thinking the exact same thing. Girls, well, women, they like a guy with a little flaw in his looks. It makes them look rugged and hard. Gives me another look: bad boy! I mean bad man. No, I mean bad boy. Bad man makes me sound like a bad man. Bad boy is more boy band idol, isn't it? That is more me.

"No, I said bad man." She must be going a bit deaf the love. I don't have a cape or anything. Why would I say I was Batman?

"He did give me a good fight. I tell you, when he hit me I thought I was going to see stars.

"Yes, like you have tonight."

She seems a nice lady, very polite. A bit too talkative for me though. I don't blame her. I bet you don't get to see many stars this time of night in a Birmingham diner. Drunks. I would guess most of the people she meets are drunks.

"I don't really know. I just knew I needed a B." Of course I planned it, but I don't want to give anything away. These waitresses can talk for England. The last thing I need is to slip up and then she gossips to everyone that comes through here.

"Yes that is right, the Alphabet Killer thing. I am glad you said that. It must mean that people are following despite the press." I know they are following. I am just making conversation while I decide what to do next. Plus the pain is a little too much. I seem to have been standing still for a while so it doesn't hurt.

"No, you are right, I am further on. I am just trying to throw them off the scent a little. Give me a bit of time to plan my grand finale.

"Oh, I do have a plan, Sandra. I say I do. I have a concept anyway, which is halfway there." See, the more I talk the more it is easy to slip up. I need to watch that.

"Even better than the school. It always has to be bigger and better.

"Yes, better than the hotel too. Hey, you heard about that? That was about the time of the Blackout. I did wonder how many people actually got to learn what Alan and I did there." I hope Alan is doing better.

"I guess so. True fans always have a way of keeping up with their idols. I love that you are a true fan, Sandra. I only meet a handful of what I would say are true believers." Believers. Beliebers. Like that singer. I wonder if my fans have a name? Carsons, Carsonites, Edmundtonians. They all work.

She is right: true fans do have a way of keeping up with us and need to be treated as such. I can't just leave them in the kitchen for the night, can I? They deserve better than that. I head back into the main diner. There are no cars outside and the lights are off. Nobody is coming. I just need to make it all happen quickly. I go back into the diner.

"How about I fix you two something? You know, for working so hard with me? How about I fix you a nice salad and a bottle of wine?"

She is nodding. I think he is stirring as well, but I sense it will take a bit of time so I will have to make the salad myself.

I head over to the fridge. It is full of ingredients. In fact, most of it is salad. I thought I would find ham and chicken?

I look around. There is another fridge. I open it. It is not a fridge, it is a freezer and all the burgers and steaks and chicken are all in there. There is no fresh meat. It is all frozen food. That can't be very healthy.

"Sandra, don't they cook anything fresh anymore?

"You are kidding me... They wouldn't do that?"

I take another look. Frozen egg omelette? She is right again. Five minutes in the microwave? It only takes three minutes to make the damn omelette. How lazy is that? No, no way do they have frozen beans on toast? What is the world coming to? Lazy, just lazy. Do people not want to put effort in anymore? No wonder those chef guys are cleaning up on the TV. People don't remember how to cook food.

"No, Sandra, I am not going to be heating anything up. It is not healthy for you. A nice salad and a bottle of wine it is."

I go back to the first fridge. I take out all the ingredients including an avocado. I don't like it, but I know it is trendy now. I find a big bowl and chop everything up and place it all in it. I then find some olive oil and salt and vinegar. My nan used to say it is a Mediterranean thing. I don't know, but I do like the taste of it. I then take it out to the nearest booth to the kitchen. I fetch some plates, knives and forks and place them down too. I then carry Sandra to the table.

"There, that is better. I bet you don't often get to sit at the table and take a rest. On your feet all night, I am sure."

I am not sure why I said that. I kind of feel sorry for her a bit. I mean, having to work nights just to have an affair with the chef. I go and fetch him. Fuck, he is heavy. That is not helping with the pain in my side. It will make her happy to spend a dinner with him. I didn't catch his name, but he is not awake yet. I drag him to the table. I manage to get him into the booth. Steve. His name is Steve. It is right there on his tag. That's odd, he didn't look like a Steve when he was coming towards me. He looked more like a Sven or Gregor. I thought he would have a name that sounds like he could be a mountain man, with an axe. Not that he needs an axe. He could probably punch a tree down.

"Now, Sandra, isn't that better?"

She is smiling. Smiling but not all the way as if I had…

"I am so sorry. Yes, I said a bottle of wine, didn't I?" I go back to the kitchen. I find two little bottles. They don't have big ones. I empty them into two glasses and stick a couple of spares in my pockets. I take them back to the booth and hand the glasses and the spares over, bar one.

"There, that is better." She is happier now I can tell. It must feel like a real date, instead of sneaking moments of passion in the kitchen when nobody is looking. I really should put some candles out, but I don't want to draw attention to them yet.

It will be a nice surprise for their co-workers to see in the morning that they have finally shared a date. I am sure they have all been wondering. Will they? Won't they? People do like a good romance. I unscrew the bottle I have kept.

"Here is to a fun-filled night." I clink their glasses and down it in one. It was not really for that. I hoped it would help with the pain. I don't think it is strong enough for that. He is awake now, I can tell. There is a smile in his eyes. Waking up to dinner with the one you love will do that for you. I should surprise Miss Walker more with things like that.

I go out of the front door and back to the car. I need some sleep. It has been a long night. I just need to find somewhere to sleep now. That is not as easy as it sounds this time of the morning. I wish I still had the Q7 I could have crashed right here. I start driving up the road.

That was a lot for one night. A lot of fun. But I know one thing. I might have lost my way a little but now I am back, back to my fucking best.

That is L and B done.

Again!

Chapter 14

The twelve days of Christmas. It is sticking in my mind since she said it. Is that the first twelve days on the Christmas calendar starting on 1st of December where you open the door and get the little chocolate? That is nowhere near Christmas? It can't be from Christmas Eve to New Year's Eve as that is only eight days. Is it from the 20th? of December? Does the twentieth actually mean something? I get my phone out and start looking it up. Some say from the 20th? To the 4th January, but that doesn't make sense? Something to do with Europe and three kings, but if I look into that, that would be the sixth of January. I just think it is twelve days over Christmas. Well, December to January. Wait, they have a terrorist version of the twelve days of Christmas! What is that about? It is Christmas.

Fucking idiots!

Do those people not respect anything? Somebody needs to do something about those people. People are people. It is that simple. You want to prove a point? Go to war. Don't sneak around like school kids pulling little girls' pigtails, and running away and hiding again. Stand up and have your say.

This nonsense would be over in a week if you did. I would help with that!

I read the song, the real version. I think he is just giving her little presents to whet her appetite. Because he loves her. That is what girls like. Stick with the little things first. Although it is mainly food to start with. Maybe she was a fat girl. Or maybe she was a skinny girl and he was trying to feed her up. There are some weirdo's out there that actually do that.

This would be a nice touch to my retirement from the limelight. I could dedicate the whole thing to her. She will love that. If I do, should I do it with food she would like? Giving someone salad everyday though isn't great. Cucumber, lettuce, tomato, onion I don't even think there are twelve things in a salad.

I should still do it for her. It would become almost a sign-off as we start our new life together. I send her a text just so that she knows she is on my mind.

"I am working on your Christmas present", with three kisses. Maybe I should have send twelve to give her a clue.

No, that will keep her happy. I am sure she will know that it is going to be something spectacular. Is it too spectacular though? The Alphabet Killer and the Twelve Days of Christmas? Is that too much of a challenge for me? Is it too much for my fans? Will they cope with the excitement? I need to consider that some more. Besides, I have fourteen left. So do I end with the twelfth day or do I leave something special for the end? As if you thought it was all over. It is now. That's what they do in the movies, don't they? I need something for the cinemagoers. They will be thinking, well, he did that. It is time for him to retire... and BANG! There was a little something you didn't expect. I am always going to be remembered as the something you didn't expect.

I think I need to complete M. Then I will give the twelve days some more thought. I get out of the car.

Fuck!

That still fucking hurts. Only when I move though. It is green brown and red now. That can't be good. I think I am getting a fever too. I don't have time to be sick. Fourteen. Fourteen more. It feels like it has been a long week already. I am glad it is Saturday. I do like the weekends, but I need to make more of them like normal people. I have been working for so long now sometimes I forget to take the weekend off.

All this trying to leave them guessing is becoming as hard as the work. It is hard enough just keeping below everyone's radar. I am lucky people don't socialise as much as they used to. My nan used to say of a night-time all the neighbours would sit on their steps and talk all night, taking turns to make cups of tea and stuff. Nowadays everyone has those I thingies and an Internet... that is what she said. An Internet! I am sure she thought it was an actual net of some kind. She was right though. Everyone is so busy with their own lives they don't really care about their neighbours.

It is a great stadium, with a hotel right next door. How good is that? It is a shame they are not playing at home today. It would have been good to see them play again. After losing to Derby the other week I am sure they need some time to recoup. Besides, I think they play at lunchtime on most Saturdays. It would be a bit late now. It is a good hotel though. I can see the football ground from the car park and it is ten minutes to the centre. It is one of the major cities. I can be lost in my work in a major city quite easily.

Fuck!

Even walking is hurting it now. I check in to the hotel. They are so polite on receptions. Nothing is ever too much trouble. It must be hard to be nice to people all day, especially some people. Some people are just out-and-out rude. But she couldn't have been nicer to me. She was almost shaking with excitement that I was there. Good-looking people always get that response, I am sure.

I head into my room. These rooms are all very similar. It is nice to treat myself to a hotel every now and again though. I mean, some people are very warm and receptive when I come to stay with them. But it always makes me feel as if I am forcing myself on them. Even more so, when they have kids! I suppose it is hard to keep guests and the family all happy.

I look over to the dresser. They always have those fliers now about what is going on in the local area. I sort through them. There is something about a horror night. I suppose that was for Halloween. It is a bit late now. There is a Turkish restaurant. It looks nice enough. I do like a good kebab. I am still unsure what it is, but I do like one. I put my bag on the bed. I then go to the zip.

Something is wrong.

My hand stays on the zip. Something doesn't feel right. I need to go. I grab my bag and run out of the door. I head towards the lift.

Fuck!

No! The stairs. It has to be the stairs. I run down the stairs. It fucking hurts as I run, but I know I need to get out of here. I am into reception. I hear someone shout out my name.

Fuck! Fuck! Fuck!

The press must be here. I run towards the door and out of the hotel. I am in the car park. There are people in the car park. One of them is running towards me. What the fuck is going on? He is diving straight at me. I punch him as hard as I can. He falls to the ground. That was amazing. That must have looked really cool for the others. There is another one coming. What the fuck is their problem? Why are they running at me? I start to run towards my car. Why am I running now? He is gaining on me.

"Fuck!"

He rugby-tackles me to the ground. I drop my bag and start kicking out. He is screaming. I manage to grab my knife and get it in his back. He releases me straight away and starts screaming. I plunge it in again, straight into his neck. There is blood everywhere. He is spurting like a fountain. I manage to get to my feet. There is a crowd starting to form, but nobody is coming close to me now. They are all mesmerised by the guy on the floor. I have my knife in my hand. I am looking directly at them. They are moving more backwards than forwards. They are shouting but not coming forward. I grab my bag and get back to my car. I throw it on the back seat and then get into the car. I can still hear them screaming but from a distance. There is a lot of screaming and pointing. They must be pointing me out to the press, but I can't see real cameras anywhere? Some of them have their phones out. Maybe that is what the cheap press people use, or now they want selfies?

When I am being attacked by the press they want selfies! Fucking fans, always the wrong time at the wrong place. I pull away. I am straight into traffic. I keep driving. I can hear them. I can hear the sirens. They are everywhere. It sounds like they are coming from all directions. I am doing fifty. It is as fast as I can go. What are all these people doing, driving on a Saturday night? The sirens are getting louder. They are getting closer. I look, but there is nowhere to pull out. I can't get past any of this traffic. I am fucking stuck in the flow. The flashes of blue are everywhere. They are lighting up the town centre. The sirens are on top of me. I should just stop the car and get out. I need to get out. I am fast. I am faster than them. I pull over into the next place that I can. It is too late. They are here.

They are here. Wait, they are here. But they are not stopping. They go past me. I count at least ten cars and that is just what is in front of me. I am sure they are on other streets as well. All flashing their lights and making sure everyone knows they are coming. I grab my bag and get out of the car. They have all gone straight past. I am in the crowds of people, and walking. It may be late afternoon but everyone is still shopping which is good.

What the fuck just happened? How did the fucking press know I was in Manchester? What was up with those people? Don't they know I am in pain? I look down at my shirt. It is bleeding again. What the fuck? The stitches must have all burst. That fucking guy, and I worked with him and everything. Why did I do that? I have made him famous and he fucking ripped my stitches out.

I can hear more sirens. They are getting louder again. What if they turned around? What if they were just picking the press up and now they are hunting the car? I need to get off this road. I need to get off the streets as soon as I can.

I carry on down the road. I am not running. I am just walking fast. There is a train station up ahead. I think it is time to get the train. Piccadilly? I thought that was in London? I get closer to the train station.

Fuck!

Two police cars pull up right outside. What the fuck is going on? It is like they don't want me to leave Manchester? Maybe I should have chosen somewhere a little less predictable. Maybe somewhere the girls' hands don't shake. The one in the hotel, she was very polite, but her hand was shaking when she checked me in. I can see it now. She must have known who I was and then got herself all worked up. I turn around and head back into the crowd. The train is off. I am not leaving that way.

She probably called the press there and then? Poor girl! She is probably up at the room now, waiting for an autograph or something more. She would be waiting for something more. She was young, reminded me of Amy Bunting from school. Pretty little thing gave good head, if I remember.

Fucking sirens!

Even more sirens. They are getting even louder now. I run up the next street. There is nothing up here. Just houses. I can still hear them.

Fuck!

What am I going to do? What am I going to fucking do? I turn as I see a man and his wife coming out of their house. It is my turn to run at them. They spot me. They are running back into the house. I am on top of them. My knife drags all the way down his back. He has fallen over in his own hallway. She is screaming. I am diving at her now and my knife rips her throat out. I run back to the door and slam it behind me.

FUCK!

I am in so much pain. The blood is oozing out of my side. He is still moving. I jump up and slit his throat. I then collapse on top of him. I take a breath. My side is fucking killing me. It is making my head hurt. I roll over onto my back and just lie there. I am still catching my breath. I look around me. It is a nice hallway. Small but nice.

If I don't move, it doesn't hurt, although I can feel it throbbing under my T-shirt. I hope that is not all my blood leaving my body. I look over at the woman. Yeah, I am going to need to leave some blood in my body.

I am going to have to sort it, aren't I? Before there is none left. I look over at the couple. They aren't with me yet. I am just going to have to sort myself. There are suitcases in the hallway. I just noticed that. They were obviously going somewhere. I hope this doesn't make them miss their flight. There is an airport up the road. I am sure they still have plenty of time.

I stand up. It fucking hurts so bad. I can hardly walk. I lean against the wall and work my way into the living room. It is fucking hot in here. Why is it so hot in here? I don't think I am going to find anything in here, although that sofa does look comfy. I am going to need to rest there as soon as I have sorted this. I am going to need to rest. I am fucking boiling. The kitchen is at the other end of the room. I head to it and start going through the cupboards. I find whisky and a first aid box. It is just plasters and bandages. I keep looking I find a sewing box and a needle and cotton. I think I am going to have to do this old style if I want to stay alive. That may be a little overdramatic, but I don't feel like I am going to get over this. I grab the whisky and open it. I am going to have to take a swig. That is what they do on TV when they are shot. I feel like I have been shot. I take a swig. It is fucking awful. I don't know how they do it. I take off my shirt. It is not good. The blood is seeping. At least it has stopped oozing. The hole does look smaller than it was, but the colour is not good. It is now green and red everywhere. There is yellow stuff as well. I don't think that was inside me. Where the fuck did it come from? I feel like I am going to pass out from the heat. I don't know if it was the running, but I am sure I am starting to sweat all over now. I grab the tea towel off the side, wipe my face with it and then soak it in whisky. I then put it on the—

"*Fuck!*"

That fucking stings. I feel like I have been fucking stabbed again. I wipe around it as much as I can. My eyes are fucking leaking. I knew it was cheap whisky. I look down. It looks cleaner. I take another swig of the whisky. I fucking hate whisky. I then spill some on the wound. They do that on TV too. I think I am supposed to let it dry before I sew it up. I take the sewing box to the living room, along with the bottle of whisky. I slump onto the sofa. I take another swig. It is warming me. Like I need fucking warming. I need some ice. Ice all over my body. I take out the needle and thread, and I love the fact that someone has already threaded it. She is obviously a crafty woman. I am not sure I would have been able to do that.

"Thank you." Just in case they are already awake in the hallway.

I look at the needle and at the hole in my side. I am not sure I can do this. I know they do on TV, but that is all special effects. I don't feel that great. I take another swig. I then drop some more on my side. Fuck, it stings. I quickly stick the needle in and do the first stitch. Fuck, that hurt. I swig at the whisky again. It is making me feel sick. I pour a little bit more on there. And then do it again. I pull it as hard as I can. It hurts. It really hurts. I take another swig. One more, it needs one more. I do it. I then collapse on the sofa. I take a swig. That is enough. I don't feel well. I am not going to be moving far. I manage to get myself to lie down. I place the whisky next to the sofa. I can feel it taking over me…

I open my eyes. It hurts. Opening my eyes hurts. I don't think I can see straight. I try to move my head. It hurts. Moving my head hurts. It is so hot in here. It is so hot. Is there a fire, am I on fire? Where am I? Why is it so hot? I look up at the ceiling. I am not sure where here is. I try to sit up. My stomach hurts. Why does it hurt? I look down. I don't have a shirt on. Where the fuck is my shirt? What the fuck is going on? Someone has been sewing my stomach! The needle is still fucking in there. I am trying to look around the room. The sweat is in my eyes. I can hardly see anything.

Jack!

It is fucking Jack. He is here. He has been sewing my stomach. I can't sit up. What the fuck has he done to me? I need to get to him. I am not going to be worked on by Jack. I am number one. He, is number two. Two only because I let him. He needs to remember that.

"Jack!" He will know I am awake now.

"Jack!" He has probably run. I am sure he has. I try to get up again. I am almost stuck to the sofa, someone's sofa, it is not mine. Where the fuck am I? I am not at home. I turn my head to look around the room. This isn't my house.

"Put a shirt on, Edmund." What? what the fuck is that? Who the fuck is that? Mum? Mum! What is my mum doing here? Why is she heading into the kitchen? I try to get up again. This isn't her house why is she going to the kitchen? I manage to half sit up. That hurts. I feel sick. My head is throbbing. I can see her. I can see her in the kitchen. What has happened to her face? What is up with her face? She looks like she has been in a fire or something. Is the house on fire? I am on fire. That is the heat I can feel. I feel my skin burning. Does my fucking skin look like that now? I need a fucking mirror and quick. What if I am ugly, I need to think about my fans. There is whisky next to the sofa. I hate whisky. Has Jack been drinking whisky while he was sewing me up? Is that why the needle is still in my fucking side? How fucking responsible is that! I get to my feet. If he is still here I need to work with him. I have to know what he has done to me. I feel like he has poisoned me. My mum is in on it as well. She will know where he is. I crawl along the wall, but I get to the kitchen.

"Mum."

She doesn't turn. She is still washing the dishes. Fuck, he is here too. He is at the table reading the paper. He is always reading the paper.

I make it to the table. I need to sit down. I can't stand, I feel dizzy. Sick and dizzy. I think I am shivering. How am I shivering? I am so hot.

"What are you doing today, Edmund?" He doesn't move the paper. He never moves the paper. What the fuck is going on? I need to answer him. I need to pretend everything is normal. They will slip up and tell me where Jack is then.

"Nothing."

He grunts. What the fuck is he grunting at? I don't need to put up with that shit. I try to stand. I can't. My legs won't let me move anywhere. I can't move.

"Where do you think you are going?"

How did he know I was trying to move? He can't see me through that paper, can he? I am looking at it. I don't see a hole. I can't even make out the letters. He lowers the paper. What the fuck? I try and jump back, but I can't. What the fuck is up with his face? He looks like Mum. Scars everywhere. What the fuck is going on?

"I said where are you going, Edmund?"

What? Why is he asking that?

"I was going to…"

"Going to what? Lie down? Take it easy? Work with someone? Learn the alphabet? What exactly are you going to do, Edmund?"

What? What is he going on about? Why is he shouting at me? What the fuck have I done to him? I think he has gone mad. Dads aren't supposed to shout at their kids. Doesn't he fucking know that?

"Dear…" Now she says something.

"He needs to hear this. He needs to know what a disappointment he has become. He needs to know what he has done. To everyone. Someone needs to tell him."

What? Who is a disappointment? He can't mean me? Why would he think I am a disappointment? I haven't done anything. What does someone need to tell me? I don't have to put up with this. I get to my feet. It fucking hurts. He is still talking, but I am not listening. I haven't done anything. I head back to the sofa and lie down. What is he on about... Oh no. I sit up. I have to sit up. I get to the edge of the sofa and throw up. It just keeps coming. I don't remember eating that much food. It is something Jack has put in my stomach. That was why he was sewing me up. He has fucking poisoned me. Bastard.

"Jack!" I need to deal with him.

I stop throwing up. I can feel there is more. More will come. I lie back down. I can't move. The shivers are getting worse. I can feel my body shaking. I need something to take the pain away. I try Jack's whisky. I try some more.

Fuck!

I spit it out. What if it is poisoned? What if that was what he was doing to me and I have just helped him work with me? It burns my throat. I am back lying down. I don't have the energy to move. I can hear them arguing in the kitchen. They never argue. They are talking about me, I can tell. He is upset about something. I thought he would be proud. Proud of what I had done. Proud of everything I have achieved.

I open my eyes. It is dark. I mean, really dark. There is not even a light on. I am shivering. I am cold and hot at the same time. That can't be good. I need to find a blanket. I need to get warm.

"That's what your plan was to do today, Edmund?" It is him. He is here again. In the dark. Why is my dad sitting in the dark? Sitting over me in the dark. I am trying to move my head, How long has he been there? I try but I can't. It hurts too much. My head is fucking killing me.

"I said—

"I heard what you said, Dad. I am not well. What else would I have done?

"No, you are not well, Edmund. That is evident."

There is something about the way he said that. Why is he mad at me? I think I can see him out of the corner of my eye. He is sitting in the chair. In the dark. At least that is the shape of him. What is up with him? Where is Mum?

"I need something, some medicine or something. Where is Mum?"

He doesn't reply. Isn't it his job to reply? He is my dad. He is supposed to make me feel better.

"Where is your mum, Edmund? Where do you think she is?"

I don't know. That is why I fucking asked him.

"You don't need medicine, Edmund. You deserve this! You deserve what is coming to you. You deserve more."

I deserve what? To be sick? Why would he say that? Who says that to his son? What kind of dad is he? A shit one. I knew he never cared about me. It is all coming out now isn't it.

"Does it hurt?"

Of course it hurts! I am on fire, my skin is burning, I can't see straight, every bone in my body is aching, I feel like I am about to die and he asks if it hurts?

"It is your turn, Edmund! Your fucking turn! Think of all the people you have hurt as you lie there. Think of all the lives you have ruined. The mothers, the fathers you have killed. Think about every fucking last one of them."

I try and turn towards him. What is he going on about? I haven't hurt anyone. I have made people's lives better. That is what I do make everything better. I made them famous. Without me these people would have been nothing. With me they are some ones. They are all someone.

"I haven't…"

He is up and over me. I am trying to hold my hands up to grab hold of him, to stop him. I can't. I am too weak to lift them. Jack, Jack has done this to me. He has poisoned me, for him. They are in this together. He is grabbing at my arms. My chest. He is coming for me.

"You haven't what, Edmund? You haven't hurt anyone? You haven't murdered anyone? You have killed them all, Edmund. You have killed us all, Edmund, hundreds, thousands. Your mother, your father, your grandmother…"

What! What the fuck? I know I didn't.

"I haven't! I haven't killed my nan."

"Of course you killed her. You think she was proud of what you did? You think she wasn't hiding in shame away from the rest of the world? She couldn't hold her head up again after what you did. What you did to those families. Those schoolchildren, Edmund. You may have well slit her throat yourself, you are so fucking good at it!"

His hands are round my throat. He is trying to strangle me. I am fighting him off. I am not strong enough to fight him off. My dad is going to kill me. He is going to kill me…

My eyes are open. I shake. I want to jump up, but I can't. I can hear them. I can hear the sirens. They have woken me up.

I can hear them. The darkness has gone. It's not night. The darkness has gone, but the fever hasn't. It is still there. I am still aching all over. I need food. I need something to help me. I need someone to help me. I turn my head towards the chair. I don't know why, but I expect him to still be there. I don't want him to be there. My whole head hurts as I turn my head. He is not there. Why was he saying that stuff? Why would he think that I would do something like that? I would never hurt my nan. I can still hear them. I can hear the sirens. Has he called the police? Is he sending the press here? He would do that. He would do that just to get back at me. Back at me for never taking that job. That is what this is all about. Why would that bother him? He didn't pay for my bike.

I use every piece of strength I have to get to my feet.

Fuck!

I collapse. I don't have the energy. If they are coming then this is it. I can't do anything about it. I should have been wearing something different. I should have been stronger. This isn't how I want to be remembered.

They are getting further away. They were close, but now they are getting further away. He hasn't called them. I crawl to the kitchen. I get to the cupboards. I know I saw some food there. Anything. I find some soup. I drink it straight out of the tin. I can't get up to cook it. It is not enough, I am still hungry I open another. I need to have food in me. My nan always said that. Feed a fever. That is what she said. I can hear her saying it. She would have looked after me. I look around the kitchen. I can see the laundry. There is a blanket. I manage to get up and get it. I cover myself as I lie on the kitchen floor. I am shivering. I pull it closer around me...

What am I doing on the floor? How long have I been here? I look up and it is dark again. It must be night-time again.

"Don't you have something to do?"

I look up. He is at the table. He is reading the paper in the dark. I can't see him, but I know he is behind there. I don't answer him. I am not sure what he wants from me. Why would he read in the dark? How can he read in the dark?

"I said don't you have something to do?"

The sweat is still running down my face. There are tins of empty soup next to me. Someone has been looking after me and feeding me soup? It will be my nan. She must be here too. She wouldn't let me go without food. She cares about me.

"The Alphabet."

What does he know about the Alphabet? Is that why he is here. Is that why he is giving me a hard time? He lowers the paper. He has that look again. He has that look that he is disappointed. No, not disappointed. He is angry.

"You thought you would murder your way through the alphabet, didn't you? Thought it would make some kind of statement to the world after everything you have done. Edmund, after everything you have done, you thought that was the way to what? Make things better? Make them remember you? What do you think you are actually achieving, Edmund? What the fuck is going on in that sick and twisted mind of yours?"

He must be delirious. Jack must have gotten to him too. Jack is trying to get me off my game. He is trying to belittle my accomplishments. He is making no sense whatsoever.

"You know what you need to do, Edmund. End this. End all of it. I am only going to tell you once."

Doesn't he think that is what I am trying to do? I was trying to do that as soon as possible. Why is he shouting at me? He is up again. He is standing over me. Looking directly at me. He is thinking about hurting me again isn't he? I can see it in his eyes.

"You have time, Edmund. You have time to end this. End this pathetic attempt to get some attention. People don't want it, Edmund. They don't want you, Edmund."

He is leaving. He is just going to leave me on the floor in the kitchen. He calls himself a father.

I give him a minute. I then take my blanket and crawl back into the living room. I get to the sofa and climb on. I cover myself with the blanket. He is still here, I can feel him. He is in the chair. I am not looking at him. I can hear him. I can hear him. He is still going on about what I have done. The people do want me. The Alphabet is not pathetic. It's genius. Everything I do is genius. Wait till he sees what I have planned.

He must have me confused with someone else. He is saying some horrible stuff. Who does he think I am? Who does he think I have become? He keeps talking about ending it. Ending it how? He wants me to end it. That is all I am trying to do?

My eyes open again. It must be nearly morning. I can see the light coming through. I feel worse than I ever have. I can't see. I am so hot, but I can't take this blanket off. I just keep shivering. I feel my head. There is a towel on it. I am sure there must be. I am so hot, but my head is cold.

"There, there." I know that touch. I know it is my nan. I can feel her kiss the top of my head. I knew she would look after me. I knew she would. She would have sorted my dad. I am sure of it. She never really liked him.

"Nan.

"Don't talk, Edmund. You will be okay."

I can hear her, but I can't see her. I knew she was here. She made me soup. I know she did. I wish I could see her. She is wiping my head. I can feel myself get better as she does. I can feel it working. It is all I needed. All I needed was her to make me better. I grab her hand. She squeezes it as I lie there. I feel myself drifting off to sleep for the first time in days. I can feel myself relax.

"Hi."

My eyes open. I know that hi. I always know that hi. My eyes don't hurt as the open. That has to be a good sign. I move my head and it doesn't feel like I want to die. That has to be another good sign.

"Hi." I smile at her. I knew she would come at some point. I must have texted her the address when I was out of it. Or my nan did. No it was me, it would have been a small cry for help, I am sure of it.

"How are you feeling?" She comes over and sits next to me. I don't want to show her that I am weak. I am not weak. I sit myself up. Even that doesn't hurt as much as it did before. I still feel a little light-headed, but I think that is going to be from lack of food and drink. I must have been out of it for hours.

"I am better." I look around the room. They are not here. I look over to the kitchen they are not there either. He knows what he said to me. He didn't want to be around when I got my strength back. Him, and Jack will be long gone now.

"That is good. Do you know what you need to do?

"I do. I need to prove him wrong."

She is nodding at me. How did she know that was what I was thinking? I do hope I wasn't talking in my sleep. You never know what you might say? Last thing she needs to hear are some of my conquests.

"And how you are going to do it?

"Yes! I am going to own it all. I will prove to him I am bigger than he ever thought. I will end this. I will end it and no one will ever forget me."

I need to end this. I need to ensure that he knows that I have a purpose and I am loved by people. That is why I am taking their holiday I am taking all the holidays. This wasn't just about the Alphabet; this was about signing off. I always said that. Why doesn't he listen? This was all about a remarkable ending. Something that will go down in history. I will show him. I will fucking show him. I will show everyone.

I need to go home, back to my own town. Something is calling me back to my town. I know they will be proud of me there. They will understand why I have done what I have done. That is a place to start!

Wait, my town?

That begins with M... Fuck I am good.

Chapter 15

I am glad I took a few days to recover. I can't believe I was out of it for five days. Five days, they just disappeared. I needed to make it up to Kevin and Sally too for leaving them on the floor for five days. I have eaten well and have started to feel like myself again. A little pain in the side but better. My father's words are not disappearing though. Who does he think he is talking to me like that? I will show him. I will fucking show him who I really am. I know what train I am taking. That was it, wasn't it? That is what made me run from the hotel. It didn't have anything to do with the girl at all. It was the fact that I was in the wrong town. Towns and counties are the same thing, right? I mean, Middlesex is a town, right? It counts. Who names a place Middlesex anyway? I mean, some places I understand, like Newcastle. I can see that it is named after a new castle. Northampton, Southampton – simple, they must be north and south of Hampton.

Did someone have Middlesex there? And that is why it was named Middlesex. Isn't all sex Middlesex? I mean, it is in the middle. Even girl on girl, or boy on boy is Middlesex.

I get on the train. It doesn't matter about the county, does it? I mean, some counties and towns have the same name. Like Northampton and Northamptonshire? I don't think there is a place called middle though? And surely it would be in the middle, wouldn't it? There is a town centre. Maybe that used to be called middle?

As it is my town, that counts, my home town. That is where I need to go. I can feel myself being drawn there. The train starts to pull away. I am glad I didn't get to work in Manchester now. Well, not really work. I am not making Kevin and Sally part of it all. They deserve better. I told them so. They won't have seen me at my best.

I get off the train and pull my hoodie from the bag and put it on. I don't need to be recognised tonight. It will feel like the second coming for some of the people that live in this town. I should have really kept an eye out for the sign. The one that always says something about the town. Twinned with or birthplace of. I am sure they will have added me to it by now. If they are looking at statues in Glasgow for me, then they are sure to have one here.

I am glad we lived close to the train station. He said it was all about the commute into London. That's why he made us live here. It has always been all about him. We weren't important, he has showed me that. I will prove it to him. It is not all about the Alphabet; I can be so much more. I will be remembered, for so much more than the Alphabet. He won't be remembered at all.

The train station is about a ten-minute walk to my house. It feels strange being here. A lot has happened over the last, what is it, a few years since I have been here? It must have been. I get to my street. I feel strange standing on it. I start to walk down towards my house. I know my house isn't there anymore, I am not mad. I remember the accident. As I get closer I can see a fence around the hole in the ground. I walk up to it. There is a sign on the fence saying it is now private property. Someone must have bought the land. I thought I still owned the land? I know I got insurance money, but does that mean that the insurance people now own it? There are a few bunches of flowers left at the foot of the fence. I look down at them. They must be for me. How weird is that? People are leaving me flowers at my parents' house? Laura. I don't think I even know a Laura? Sarah as well. It is no good just putting their name on a card. If they want to meet me then they need to leave an address or telephone number at least. My fans still love me. I suppose that is the main thing.

I turn and start walking back up the lane. I don't want to be seen standing there too long as they will put two and two together and start calling the press. Either that or chase me for selfies. I think I have had enough of people tackling me for selfies for a while.

I pass Mrs Green's house. She has one of those mobile homes in the driveway. They look amazing. I should have had one of those. I should really pay her a visit. I go up to the door and knock on it. There is no answer. She must be out. She is probably on a date. Someone is going to get a good night from her, I am sure of it.

I leave. I am going to walk to my nan's old house. It is only fifteen minutes away.

I walk past my school on the way. I thought it would have had a plaque or something by now. Maybe there is, but it is inside, inside above reception or in the school hall. That would be good for the students. To know a celebrity once went to this school. I had some good days here. I met her here. That was a high point. The high point! That was life-changing.

I wonder if she comes back here often. It must be a place of amazement for her too. Knowing now what she managed to get out of here. Me.

I carry on walking. It would have been good to be here on a school day. Maybe go inside and meet a few of the students. It would have been good to show them exactly what they could have become if they put their mind to it.

I get to my nan's house. It is all boarded up, all the windows and even the front door. Someone has put graffiti on the front door. Edmund Carson FU. That is so cool. Obviously a fan of the work I did at the girls' school. They remember what I wrote on the chalkboard. That is nice. Nan would have liked that.

I would have liked to have been to the house once more though. One more day with her there. I was so happy with my nan. I know I didn't have the fame I have today. But I was happy. We had some fun days together. No matter what my dad thinks, she was proud of me. She was always proud of me.

I should really go and see her house too. She only lives around the corner. I presume she has sold it because of moving, but it will bring back memories. Great memories. I turn the corner. It is boarded up too? Why is her house boarded up? Unless she hasn't sold it, and boarded it up herself? Maybe she was planning that we come back here all along. Be close to my nan. I was thinking somewhere hotter myself, but it is a possibility. She is so thoughtful. She has always been so thoughtful. Putting me first that is always a good sign in a relationship.

There are flowers on the doorstep. I go and pick them up. There is no card, but I am sure they will be from my fans. They do that though, don't they? I mean, she hasn't lived here for a couple of years and they are still worshipping her because of her boyfriend. I guess it is out there now that we are together. There were probably rumours before we even left school. I put the flowers back down. I wonder if they got them in Sophie's shop. It is good to think I am still supporting the local businesses. I have done so much for this town. Really put it on the map. The bank down the road is probably booming as well because of my relationship with Melanie. I start to walk back towards the train station. I have a feeling in my stomach. It is like a churning feeling. Seeing the two houses like that, all boarded up, it is like I am walking down memory lane for the last time. We won't come back here again. Once this is complete, I would expect we would be jetting between holidays and living somewhere hot, like Spain. I will have to control myself in Spain when we are together. Is there ever a good time to approach the thought of an orgy with your girlfriend?

Without knowing it, I have walked home again. How did that happen? I don't think I was aiming to walk here. I am back in front of what used to be my house. I am not going to forget it. Forget where it all started.

I suppose when they make the movie though they won't use this place. It will be shot in a studio somewhere. I touch the fence. I have that strange feeling again. It feels like goodbye. I suppose it is in a way. I am going to be so busy with the press that I won't have time to come back. I turn and walk back up the road. I do like the mobile home thing that Mrs Green has. She must be planning a trip of some kind. That would be nice for her. I am sure there are still a lot of men out there that she hasn't met. Not many but a few. There are still no lights on in her house. I walk around the back of the road towards the canal. I wonder if she is in bed and that is why she didn't answer.

What a surprise I would be for her. I go into her back garden and to the back door. It is locked, but there is a window open. I think it must be to the back of the garage. I flick the latch. It opens up fully. People are very trusting round here. Very trusting, or she knew I was coming. She didn't want to make it easy for me. She is a little tease. I think there is a saying, one my nan used to say about always leaving a window open for the one you love. She loves me, it is only natural.

I don't think we ever had any criminals in our street. It was just not that type of place. We were all brought up better than that. I climb through the window. It is the garage and I head into the house. It hasn't changed much. I go into the kitchen. I stand and look at the kitchen table. It is still the same one. Of course it is. She wouldn't have ever wanted to change it. I imagine it is the talking piece of the house. She will tell everyone I had her on that table. She would probably get a fortune if she decided to auction it. I head up the stairs past my old room and down to hers. I push the door gently.

She isn't here. The bed is all made. I often wondered what Mrs Green's bedroom would look like, and now I know. I walk over to the bed. I feel the sheets. They are proper silk. I am not surprised. The amount of action this bed must see, anything that can help with momentum has to be beneficial. She must get knackered.

I take off my shoes and lie down. There are mirrors on the ceiling. Mirrors on the ceiling! I only thought that was in the movies. She really is something. I get up and look in her wardrobes. She has a lot of clothes and shoes. There must be like a hundred pairs of shoes. I look through the drawers. She has so many pairs of underwear. Bras and pants. They are all clipped together too, so she is always wearing matching underwear. She likes her black all-in-one things as well. There must be a dozen, at least, all in one drawer. They have poppers around the ladies area. That must be for ease of access.

Is she a hooker or something? Who else has this much underwear and rarely keeps it on? She didn't charge me but then why would she? Until then she probably never had a real man before. Even hookers need some real loving every now and again, I am sure of it. I hear a car pull up. I jump off the bed and go over to the window. It is a taxi. Mrs Green is getting out of it, alone. It must have been a slow night for her. Either that or she has already done someone at his house, been paid and finished for the evening. Or her house. You never know, she may be into women as well. Maybe that is why she has so much underwear. She shares it with another woman now. I would not be surprised if I ruined her for men. I should have looked around for a strap-on thing. They enjoy that. I am not sure why though? I never have. I mean, if you want a dick then have a dick. Don't strap one on a girl and... oh, unless she wants a dick and the boobs. Maybe lesbians are all about the boobs. Mrs Green does have a nice pair, with all those little bumps around the nipples like mini nipples. They get just as hard, nice to run your tongue over, making her shiver as you give them a little nibble.

Oh fuck!

She is almost at the top of the stairs. I think I was lost in the moment then. I go and stand behind the bedroom door. There is not a lot of room here. If she kicks the door in it will knock me out. She doesn't. It opens gracefully. Gracefully, that is the word that comes to mind when she opened the door. I think it is the silk sheets. Don't know why, but all I can think about is sliding around on them with her. I am hard as a rock at the thought of it. She is standing looking at the bed. I am behind her. My knife is at her throat. She doesn't move. She can feel it, I know she can, and she can feel the steel against her throat as well. She has two things about to stab her at the same time. She doesn't say anything. Nothing! She isn't running or struggling, or anything. This is weird. This is really weird. It is like we are frozen, just standing here looking at the bed. She can feel it throbbing in her back. She will have been waiting to feel that again. I know I don't need to introduce myself.

It feels like we have been here for ages. What is she waiting for? Have we been standing here too long? Was there someone else in the cab I didn't see? Is she waiting for someone else to come upstairs? Is she expecting me to join into a threesome with her? Maybe this is what she likes. Maybe I am not the one who was supposed to break in. Maybe she likes this fantasy stuff. How long have I been fucking standing here? She drops her bag on the floor. It brings me back to reality.

I slit her throat from ear to ear. I then pull her back away from the sheets. Not sure why I did that. I guess I didn't want her to get blood on those sheets. They will be a bugger for her to clean tomorrow. I have one arm around her waist and her head has fallen back on mine. My other hand drops the knife.

The smell of the blood is so strong, sweet and strong. Exactly how I imagined it was going to be when we were downstairs on the table. I am like a rock. Harder than I think I have been for weeks. I almost feel dizzy the amount of blood that is heading down there. I hope that is not because I lost so much blood. My hand starts to wander. I can feel her nipples, all of them. They are hard. They are very hard. My hand wanders south. I can feel it. Even through her underwear she is wet. I mean, really wet. I knew she wanted me. I wonder how many nights she has fantasied about me returning. Leaves a window open just on the off-chance. Was it leave a light on? Is that what my nan used to say? Leave a light on for the one you love?

She knows I am not the type of man for courting. I am the type of man for fucking. That is who I am. She will be relishing the feeling in her back again. I move over towards the bed. I hold her with one hand and pull the top sheet off the bed before laying her down. She is smiling. She is not all here yet, but she is getting there. I start to undress her slowly. She is savouring every minute of this. I know it. She is naked. I stand back and look at her. She is hotter than I remembered. I get undressed too. As soon as I do I am on top of her. She whispers in my ear.

"I know you have. I am sorry I was so long " I knew she had been waiting for me. I slide right inside her. She makes

282

that sigh. The sigh that you know she has been waiting for so long. It feels great. It feels like it has been so long since I have had this. I am thrusting hard. She will like that. Shows I really want to be doing it. She moves like a professional and she learns. I love a woman that learns. Last time we were together she was all about the kissing. Now there is nothing. She knows I don't like that. That is a real professional. With every push there is another sigh. I think I am so hard it must be deep inside her. She is loving every minute of it though, I can tell. Whether it is the smell or not she looks so much hotter. These sheets really do help. I will have to get some for my love nest. I can feel an explosion building up inside her. It has been a long time coming for her. I can feel it building up inside me too. We both wanted this. We both needed this. I look at her directly in the eyes. We go at the same time. Oh, that feels good, so good. I am still going it feels like there must have been a cupful in there. I am even getting the light-headed feeling. It is not often I get that. Better even than the first time on the kitchen table.

I slowly pull out so that she keeps going, and lie next to her. She is still panting, I can hear her. She sounds like she has run a marathon.

"I would say even better than the first time.

"That is a good point. Imagine how good it would be if we had been doing it once a week since then." She wouldn't have been happy with once a week. I don't think she would be satisfied with once a day. Well, she would have been satisfied, but she would have wanted more. Women always want more of me. It is only natural.

"Where have I been all this time? Now that is a question.

"Yes, everywhere. It has been an interesting what, a couple of years, since I have been here?" Has it really been that long? She remembered me as if it was yesterday. It probably was for her. Nothing in her life has happened.

"That is hard to believe, isn't it? I suppose it has been.

"I think you get into the limelight and time just flies.

"Thanks. I am still hot. I was just thinking how hot you are too. You must have been working out since I was last here. You look amazing. You have never looked better."

She will like that, a bit of flattery. In this light though she could be what, thirty, thirty-five? I have always had a thing for older women, even if she is pushing the other side of forty.

"How is it that you are still living on your own, and single?

"That is nice of you to say." Only ever had two men in her life. One died and one left her for fame and fortune after one amazing afternoon in the kitchen.

"It has been a good couple of years. I have really enjoyed it. I think I will miss it all."

There is a silence. I think it is me and her. I just realised what I said. I will miss it. I can't stop thinking about it. I am going to end this. But not the way he thought. He dissed the Alphabet as if it was nothing. It is not nothing. All the work I have been doing feels like it is building to some kind of climax. I mean, I know what a climax feels like, I have had so many. I have given so many more. But it will be on my terms. I will ensure I wow people in the end.

The fame will carry on long after this, it is just that the work will change. It will more about movie deals and book signings. It is a type of retirement but not real retirement. You don't have to retire forever though. I would like to think I will make guest appearances. Just when the public has started to forget you, you come back with a bang. That is me. I will be always waiting for my next opportunity to delight the audience. I will miss this though, spending time with all my true fans like this. Intimate. I doubt I will have that again, not once I have a family and settle down. I am the committed type of man. I am a one-woman man. One woman at a time, of course.

"Sorry. Yes, sorry, that was a bit rude. I was lost in my own thoughts for a moment." Her smile is sweeter than I remember. It gives me that warm feeling.

"The future actually, and what it is going to bring.

"I am sure it will be great. It will just be a change of pace. Something that I am not used to." It will be a real change of pace. There is silence again.

"The immediate plan? Now there is a question. I am glad that you asked." That brings me back. That is what I am here for.

"Well, to be honest, I have something to prove. I don't want to really go into it, but I have something to prove. My thought is I could do something with Christmas. Make Christmas my holiday. If I can do that, nobody is ever going to forget me. Nobody can ever say that I haven't accomplished everything if I take the one time of the year everyone looks forward too."

"Yeah, I have already taken Halloween too, but the world expected that. Hell, they had parties everywhere in my honour. What I want is to do something so great that he, I mean they, will be thinking about me from Halloween to Christmas."

Nearly slipped up then. I don't want it getting back to my dad that I am mad about this. I don't want him thinking he can take credit for anything I do. I was going to do this anyway. I was always going to make it more. Always.

"Yes, like a season. I love that. The Season of Carson." I can see that becoming a thing. Spring, summer, autumn and Carson! It sounds good to me. The Carson Games. The Carson Gardens. It works on every level.

"My plan? Oh, my plan, yes, I am not one hundred per cent there yet. I had some ideas. Whatever I do now though it has to be bigger than what I have been doing.

"Yes, bigger than the Alphabet. I have proved that is possible. I have proved I can do anything and everything." She has been following me, hasn't she? She will have been searching the Dark Web. For more than just dates.

"I can't believe that you just said that. You are not the first person to mention the twelve days of Christmas." Clearly that is a sign. I am a believer of fate. That has to be a sign?

"You are so right. It could soon be known as the Twelve Days of Carson." My twelve days. Another marketing dream for my book and my movies. I will have done half the work for the advertising team. Christmas presents galore. Is that enough to shut him up though? Is it a big enough event? Why is what he said bothering me? This isn't about him.

"It is all about the brand and the followers, isn't it? I have had a gifted career at understanding that point." There I go again, saying had a gifted career as if it is over.

"I have a gifted career that is what I meant to say. Knowing what the public wants and what makes a great event. They love that about me. It is why I am so popular." I think I covered that up well. I don't want her to think that I have any doubts about my future.

"I don't know. Maybe one day. One day they will think about Father Harry before they think about Father Christmas." I can see that. It is religious, it is Christmas. I can really see that. With this I am going to change the world. The whole world.

"Ha ha! I guess we both do come late at night, leaving our friends fully satisfied." Such a line. I will have to use that in the film. The film and the book.

"Yes, back to the twelve days. I think I could do it. Do you know the song? It is a song, isn't it? Or a hymn. Do you know the hymn?"

She does. She starts singing it. I could make the words a little better. I need to work on that. Does it really need to be my true love gave to me? Why can't it just be my name? My Edmund gave to me. It works. It has the same amount of beats. She will know I was doing it for her then as well. Not just that but when people sing it to their loved ones, I will be right there too. The thought of me all over Christmas.

"That was very good. I think you are a natural singer." I wasn't really listening to her, but it wasn't making me cringe. I was just thinking how I could really make it my own.

"No, not really, I didn't spot anything wrong with the twelve days." It was just twelve days, wasn't it?

Oh fuck!

Shit, she is right. If I follow it to the letter of the law it is twenty-three different type of birds. I need fifty people to work with and I need to find five gold rings. That is if I just copy the song to the letter of the law. That is a lot of, well, a lot of everything. How am I ever going to deal with all that? In such a short space of time. There is no margin for error. Not that I ever make a mistake.

I can't forget that whatever I do I still have to travel. I have to travel and it all has to be in line with the Alphabet Killer. I am not giving up on that dream, I am just going to make it better. That is what I do. I make it better. I told him that. He should have listened to me. I can do both I am that fucking good dad.

If I do this it can't be about a bunch of birds. I am not running a butcher's shop. That's not me. Besides, I don't like the thought of hurting some innocent birds just for this. I am not a monster. No, it has to be bigger and better than that. They already have the old twelve days of Christmas, if that is what they want. The world will need something Edmund Carson style. Something they will never forget. Something that makes they hang my picture on their wall every year.

"It is a lot. I hadn't really given in a lot of thought until just now.

"Yes, I suppose you are right. I really need to start thinking about it. Seriously thinking about it. You are hot, great in bed and on fire today, aren't you?" If I am going to prove my point I should be kicking this all off in about a month, so it is going to be a really intense month of preparation. I really need to prepare. Is it a month? Might be a few weeks. I lost a week there, didn't I?

"I am not really sure. I was looking it up before... just before there are a lot of views about which twelve days they are. I don't think it really matters " I am sure it does matter for some people. But I am making this my own. It has to be special.

"Yes, this is part of the Alphabet Killer. This is M, my home town. I am not giving up on the Alphabet I will be the first person in history to do this. I am capable of doing both. I am the only person capable of doing both."

She is laughing at that. I knew she would get it. I am glad I included her now. She may have been forgotten in my whole story, but now she will play a critical part in the movie and the book. I can beef her part up a bit with regards to making the plan and everything. She deserves that. Twice she has put out for me over the period of a couple of years. Not many women can say that. Most woman are one-night-stands in my world.

"Are you sure?"

I get my phone out and look at the diary. She is right again. I don't know why I needed to check it out. I trust her. She has been nothing but right so far. I could do that. I could really do that.

"Friday the 13th. I can take Friday the 13th back for myself too and finish the Alphabet on Christmas Eve, leaving Christmas for the fans." That is genius. It is pure genius.

"Hold on a minute." I run the alphabet through my head using the song again. I do it twice just to make sure.

"No. I have thirteen left to go. N to Z is thirteen destinations." Maybe she wasn't right.

"Do you know what, I was saying that very same thing? I don't know who to. But yes, I was saying the very same thing." We are so in tune tonight. Not just in the sack but really in tune.

"They will think I am done. That will really throw them. The twelve days will be done. Then, as you say, like all the great movies of our time, just when you think the hero is dead, he comes back with one last bang. Z. Although I will need to find somewhere with a Z." I am sure there are some. I should have probably looked at that before I started the Alphabet Killer. That I could work everywhere in the country. The world will all be celebrating the fact that I completed the twelve days of Christmas and then as another special present to my fans, Merry Christmas with a Z, with a Zing! I need to use that: Merry Christmas with a Zing.

"Any other great ideas? I should have come to see you months ago." That made her smile.

"Ha ha! Just one, but it will cost me? Cost me what?" As if I didn't know. Women are good at selling their good ideas for sexual favours, aren't they? I am sure they all do it in one way or another.

"Whisper it to me first." I lean in.

She does. It takes her a little while. I think she is saying it slowly and husky on purpose, blowing warm air into my ear to tantalise me into giving her something more than a kiss. Not that she will have to ask for too long as I am ready to go again. I feel re-energised at the thought of it. The idea is good. No, it is not good, it is great.

"That is another amazing idea, and yes, it is so worth the price. Worth the price and more." I kiss her. Really kiss her. I kiss her so hard that it will start her dripping all over again.

That is a great plan, and it will help with everything that we well she was concerned with. This is really going to happen. I am going to have it all the Alphabet the holidays.

People won't be able to have any thoughts during their days that don't include me. Surely that is what every superstar wants. To be forefront in everyone's mind every day. . But it will wait twenty minutes. Maybe thirty-five. It is the second time within an hour. I only get better and longer with time.

M…

My home town, done!

Chapter 16

"So at last we are twelve days from Christmas... It begins." I like the comment "It begins". I think it will look good on the movie posters. Edmund Carson... It begins. It begins, Friday 13th. This date will be remembered for one thing and one thing only: me. Wait, it begins can only be used for the first movie? It will be more like... He returns Friday the 13th. He's back. The return of... They are all good. I am so excited about this. It has been a month in the planning and working with so many people. Some who have made it on the trip, some not so much. They just didn't fit the profile. This is going to be great. No, epic, it is going to be epic. I don't know what I was ever worried about. I said I could do it and I can. That will show him. I will make him as proud as Mum and Nan are.

"Yes, I know. I know it is a little cramped, James. I know we should have rotated everyone as well." If he tells me that one more time I will be rotating him out of the window at one hundred miles an hour. I will be happy to let some of these people be introduced into the world. It is getting a bit cramped in here. They are driving me mad too, keeping me up all night with the endless chit-chat about boys and fame and where they will be this time next year. It is not all about them. They just don't seem to get that. I walk to the back of the motor home and open the door to the bedroom.

"Listen, it starts today. So we only have a few weeks and then you will all have been introduced to the world." There are a few grumblings of "I can't wait", and "pick me first". They each know their roles so I don't know why they are grumbling. I am not changing them just because they are excited to get on with it. We are all excited. Most of us have been excited for weeks.

"Thank you, Mrs Green. I am so glad you came on this trip with me." At least she is seeing sense and helping me to keep the rest of them in check.

"No, Elle, we discussed this. We need to be different to the original song. It needs to be in my style. I can't just go and hang a partridge in a pear tree. People probably wouldn't even notice that." I checked. Partridges are really small. I am not sure you would even want to eat one.

"Yes, Rachel, you have told me that already." I am regretting letting her come along for the ride. If I hadn't been so horny that night I would have driven straight through Northampton and Grafton Street.

"I know it wasn't a pear tree. It was a *perdrix*, the French word for partridge. He meant to just give her a partridge."

I close the bedroom door. It doesn't shut them up, but it does muffle them enough to give me a little piece of peace. I sit back on the pull-out sofa. It has not been a bad bed since it got so cramped back there. But not for long. He returns, the Alphabet Killer. He returns tonight and the twelve days of Christmas begins. The world is speculating, I can feel it. There is a buzz around the country waiting for it. I know. The last time they heard from me was Manchester. My DNA is all over that. I am sure they will think I am done. Dead somewhere. I lost a lot of blood there. It will be in the hallway on the sofa in the kitchen. They will think I am done. Until tonight. Tonight. The return.

"They will get it, Sarah. Trust me. The world knows the radio DJ from Norwich. He has a TV series, he is a chat show host and even had a movie out." It is so funny, it is cool and something that they won't forget. It would have been better with the real guy. Like all stars though he lives in Hollywood. I will have to speak to him about it when I get there. Just to let him know that if he was here, I would have definitely used him for the part.

"It will probably relaunch the guy's career in Hollywood. I mean, the movie he made was what, six, seven years ago and he hasn't done anything since. Well, not that I have seen anyway. So if he has made a sequel it wasn't good." I do think sometimes that people think I don't think about other people. When he plays his own part in my movie he will thank me for it. People will see that. I am all for making other people's dreams come true.

Besides, I have had to sit outside his station for three days just to work out who is going to give me the best opportunity to work with them. That is real commitment to the cause.

"I have already done it, Olivia. I have set the tree up in the park. The pears, the partridges, they took me at least three hours to thread onto that thin piece of rope. It looks good, trust me." I should at least be happy they are all so supportive. They all want me to do this. They all want to be part of this.

"I wish you all could have come along and seen it. But I did not want to bring too much attention to it. Okay, a little attention with the Christmas fairy lights. It is the start so it has to be a little special. I just need to switch them on once he is in place." I guess they are worried. Worried that should anything happen to me, they are not going to get their moment in the spotlight. It is understandable given that most of them were working the streets when we met. They must think this is the big break they have all been waiting for to stop them being hookers. I needed people that wouldn't be missed. I don't want the press getting hold of the idea that I was about to do something big with M. I just thought about that. It was clear that Kevin and Sally weren't part of it, and Mrs Green is just missing in her motorhome. They aren't even going to be thinking about here. They will think I am still on M.

I guess Richard Gere could play my dad in the movie. Not that he deserves it. Not after the last time we met. He said some pretty awful things to me. I will show him. This will show him. He will be apologising to me and to Richard. Richard has a history in turning these ladies around to be stars. I mean, look what he did for Julia's career. She is not a hooker any more. She is a legend of a movie star now. Probably stopped turning tricks long ago now. Although the latest news from Hollywood is that there are a lot of people having to sleep around for jobs. I would never do that. I would never treat women that way. They can sleep with me because I am hot as fuck not just for a job. Although if they want to give me a job that is fine.

He probably looked a little bit like me in his early days, Richard. I would so love to go into those snooty shops and make that kind of scene. It would be so cool. I will definitely do that when I get to LA, take Miss Walker into the stores, they will know she is a lady already though. I will have to get her to play it up a bit, just for fun. Dress down. Definitely not wearing that black dress. I am sure she has some not so hot clothes somewhere in her wardrobe. I have that sudden feeling in my stomach again. That one that tells me a change is coming. All of a sudden as if thinking about her has given me it. That can't be right? Can it?

No, my head has just jumbled up all my feelings. It has crossed my feelings that it is all coming to a glorious conclusion. Is conclusion the word? Glorious achievement, with the end of my career and hers. She is my end. She is what all of this has been done for. Next year, next year is our year. We will be both out of work and ready to start a new. Not completely out of work. I will just not be touring anymore. Worked for the Beatles.

I can't wait to surprise her at New Year. New Year's Eve, to be precise! I want to turn up on her doorstep at midnight and give her the news. I am sure my mum used to call it first footing. If a dark-haired man walks across your threshold on New Year's Eve then good luck will come to you for the whole year. That is what I want. I want to tell her the news that all of this part of my life is over and now it is time for us to start a new chapter. It is time for us to have little Lake and District Carson. I can write and look after them while she still works at the school. Until production of the film starts of course and then we will all have to be in Hollywood. In Hollywood, living the life that I always imagined that we would.

No, this isn't the end! This is just the beginning, the beginning of...

Fuck!

He is already in the park. I didn't see him approaching. I am out of the motorhome, hoodie up. I almost have to run to catch up with him as the tree is about three quarters of the way through the park. I picked one that is really out of the way and secluded so that I could decorate it properly without being interrupted. I am hoping the lights do the trick though. It needs to attract attention when I am done.

I am looking around. There is nobody else in the park. There hasn't been the last few nights either as I have followed him home. I am getting closer. He stops and turns. Why is he stopping and turning? I am almost on top of him. He looks like he is about to say something, but my knife comes out and I stab him four times in the stomach. He grabs his stomach and I whiz around to the back of him and pull his head back and cut his throat. That will stop him saying anything. I catch him as he begins to fall, and drag him up onto the grass and towards the tree. It is less than a minute before we are out of sight from the path, and in the thick of the trees. That was quick work, really quick. I am conscious that working outside, you have to be fast. Anything could happen. I drag him up to the tree. There was no way I was going to find a real pear tree. I walked all the parks and I couldn't find one anywhere. I am sure they still have them. I place him at the bottom of the tree. I take my knife out. I need to add to the carving I have already made. I carved the Twelve Days of Christmas, and Day One, Friday the 13th into the tree. So they know I own Friday the 13th now. It is mine. There is nobody bigger than me. I carve "It Begins" underneath. I do like that. I think I may even make it the title of my first movie, which I will release on Friday the 13th just to make sure they understand what is to come. That is my date now.

I tie the rope hanging from the tree around his neck. I place the pillow case over his head and ensure that the printout is front and centre. I go to the other end of the rope and pull.

Fuck, he is a damn sight heavier than I thought he would be. I keep pulling though until he is part of the tree. I then tie the rope to the tree so that he stays there. It looks good. Even the face mask on the pillowcase looks good. It can only be him. Everyone in Norwich and the world will know it is him. I switch on the lights. That looks amazing. I can imagine this is how all trees are going to look like in the future. No more of this angels and glass balls. It will be all about the pears, partridges and DJs. I should have probably got some of those old style records, the black ones, and hung a few of them around also. It is bright. It will get the attention of everyone as they walk through the park. I take a quick selfie with him and the tree and then get back to the mobile home.

"Yes, it is done. Alan Partridge in a pear tree in Norwich, what is not to love about that? You should have seen it, Rachel, you would have been proud.

"I know, a Partridge. I just thought I would add a couple more just for the people who didn't get it." I was always going to go bigger and better, she should have known that. It is good. I signal the return and the start. I knew I could fuse both of these together. Nobody else could have done that.

"Yes, we are off to Overstrand! It should take us about an hour and by then it will be Saturday the 14th. It will be the second day of Christmas!"

I am out of the park and on the A140 within ten minutes. It was a good plan of Mrs Green's to do this overnight and hit two days in such a short time. In and out and people will then be anticipating my next move. I love this planning too. I am all prepared for the scenes. She is a sharp woman. I guess, because she is older she has to plan more ahead. I mean, she is in her forties already. She must know that there isn't much time left.

That will be the reason why she bought this motorhome. To try to get out and about a bit more, see the world before it is too late. I bet she never thought it was going to be with me though. That must be all her dreams come true. I am so happy for her.

We arrive in Overstrand and I go directly to the bed and breakfast.

I leave them all in the motorhome and head in. It is just as I expected: nobody about. I wanted to stay in the fancy place up the road. Big old Victorian home but they would have had a night person for sure. These people just give you the key. Nice pub though. I can see myself coming back here again. Not any time soon, but one day. I go back outside to the motorhome.

"Okay, James and Olivia, you are on. This is your time to shine." That's another good one. Time to shine! I really need be writing these down. I am on fire today. It is so good that I have them prepared. They are dressed the same and everything. It had to be black though. I wanted white, but for some reason there still seemed to be blood leaking through. I didn't want to ask, but it is clearly the wrong time of the month for Olivia. I take them in one by one. Straight in the side door, and my room is the first one on the right. I did tell them I would be arriving later. It works a treat.

I lay them both on the bed. I then turn them to face each other and make them hold hands. I think holding hands is very important. I think it is almost as important as kissing. It means you belong together. And you are not afraid to show it to the world.

"Yes, James. Almost like the first time we met. Although you were both were wearing a lot less clothes." It must be odd for any of their friends, wondering where they are. When I found them they were both fast asleep in their beds in Southampton, and what, two weeks later they turn up in bed again out by the coast. I am sure people will think they went on holiday, but generally you brag about these things for a while, don't you? Tell people you are not going to work? Off somewhere warm. Not somewhere like Overstrand! It is fucking freezing out there.

I go back out to the motorhome and pick up the cage. The cover is still over it. That is good as it does keep them quieter for some reason. I take them into the room and place them on the end of the bed. They are not turtle doves but doves all the same. James and Olivia are wearing matching turtleneck black jumpers. They will get it. Anyway, as Rachel said, it wasn't actually turtle doves. Turtle doves are just lovebirds and that is what James and Olivia are. Lovebirds. I take out my black marker. I just want to make sure so I write on the wall. "On the second day of Christmas my Edmund gave to me…" That will help them realise what is going on. Plus it will start them changing the words to the song. I am their Edmund and I am her Edmund so it works on so many levels. I don't need to finish it, they will see the two turtleneck-wearing lovebirds. I head into the bathroom and wash myself. I need to remember to always take the opportunity when I can as it is hard to wash in that bathroom on the motorhome. The shower is so small I could hardly get Mrs Green and me in there at the same time. I go back into the main room. They are whispering. Excitement will have gotten the best of them, I am sure.

"Promise me something, guys. If you start fooling around while I am out of the room, before morning you will get dressed again. I don't want to spoil the picture. The landlady is bound to come in at some point.

"Thank you." I knew they wouldn't let me down. They probably want this more than I do. Can you imagine Edmund Carson calling you the lovebirds? That must be almost worth a reality TV programme all by itself. I take a selfie with them both and then sign the wall, the door and then the bedcovers. I want to leave a little something for the owners just to say thank you for the room. Plus I need to practise my signature whenever I can. I am going to be signing a lot of stuff in the very near future.

I know they won't be able to keep their hands off each other and I am not really worried about it. The sign on the wall and the love doves in the cage will be enough for the press. They will love it. I leave them and get back into the motorhome. I have that urge for social media as I sit at the steering wheel. I haven't had that for a while. It must be a sign I am getting back to my best. This is the kind of thing I do well. I guess I just wanted to be able to share this with the world before I move on to the next place. They would have loved it. Everyone would have loved it. Imagine seeing that scene on Twitter and wondering where in the world are they? It would be like a treasure hunt. I need to capture that feeling in the press when I am making my movie. I have to capture the excitement of another Edmund Carson creation. Like that artist guy who just pops up every now and again. Painting on walls of banks and things. He knows how to market himself.

I can hear them all in the back of the motorhome. They know that they are two less in there now.

"So we can stay up here in Overstrand for the evening. Maybe pull into a campsite and head into Cromer tomorrow for some crab." I don't like crab, but I hear it is famous and I am sure that some of them will like it.

"Or we head down to the Cotswold Commons?

"Yes, Rachel, Somerset way." I may have to step up when I work with Rachel. I had her in my head as a maid milking, but that is like three, four days away. She is going to drive me mad by then with her constant know-it-all approach to everything.

"Cotswold it is then. Yes, we can see if they have Cornish cream teas.

"And pasties. I must say, I do like a Cornish pasty myself." I have never travelled with this many people before. It is exhausting. They are all want, want, want. And what do I get in return? The odd blow job and a quickie on the couch. It is hardly worth it. I won't be one of those celebrities with an entourage, I tell you. Me, maybe Miss Walker and a couple of hot hair stylists and make-up artists for the cameras, and that is it.

"Yes, Rachel. They all know it is not Cornwall. So they probably won't be Cornish pasties. It is just closer to Cornwall than say East Anglia is. So there is always a chance." Yes, I may have to let her go early.

It is time for us to go. It is a long drive and it is good to have some distance between you and your launch. The roads are going to be packed with fans this time tomorrow. All trying to get a look at the new scene. Is it a launch? Relaunch it is more of a relaunch. The excitement will be hard for them all to contain in the morning. Sometimes I wish I wasn't me so I could enjoy it all with them. It must be really special. I will have to spend some time with fans before filming to make sure that I do the feeling justice.

N and O, plus two days of the season formally known as Christmas.

Done! It is going to be that easy!

Chapter 17

Painswick! It is an odd name for a place to visit. I don't know why, but I have it in my head that I imagine Painswick to be something to do with candles and hot wax. According to the magazines it is supposed to be a pleasurable pain. Some of the movies I have seen agree with that too. Pleasurable for men more than women. Not something I want to find out.

It was a strong start, the first two days. I think that people will be happy about my return. I think it will shut him the fuck up. I am ending the alphabet my own way, and by telling people there are only ten days left I am also giving a deadline. I am telling the world I am not afraid of anyone.

It is very beautiful down here. Some of it reminds me of the Lake District. Hills and fields everywhere, very green. Although it would be a funny name to call your child. Pain Carson. Instead of District Carson. Although now I say it, it doesn't sound that bad. Pain Carson. I will have to keep it for Miss Walker. It will make her laugh.

I pull over into a picnic area. It is still early. Nobody is going to be around at seven fifteen a.m. I go back and lie on the sofa bed. They are all quiet. They must all be asleep

Driving a long distance will do that to you. It is not a bad idea. I could do with a few hours myself. I lie down and take advantage of the peace and quiet…

Fuck!

What was that? I jump off the sofa bed. I go to the front window. It was just some twat honking his horn. I check my watch. Two twenty. Fuck, I must have been tired. I only meant to have a couple of hours. I am hungry, I know that. I can see about two vehicles in front of me someone has set up a burger van. That will do. None of this was here when I went to sleep about six hours ago. I hope he hasn't set up as he knows I am here. Imagine the amount of business that would get him. I get up and go and fetch myself two burgers and a can of drink and bring them back to the motorhome.

"No, Rachel, you cannot smell onions. I didn't have onions." Why didn't I ask for onions? I do like onions on a burger.

"It is just for breakfast. I assure you, I will look for Cornish cream teas and pasties as soon as we get on the move." One of them could have popped out and got food if they were really hungry, rather than expecting me to do everything. It is not like they are busy just lying around back there.

I guess I have the rest of the day and the night to myself. That is good. I like this having a plan idea. It means you can plan some quality downtime as well. Sort of re-energise yourself for the tasks ahead. That is what the movie stars do, isn't it? Make one movie and take a couple of months off. I should have done that more over the years. My trouble is I am too dedicated to the work, let alone my over commitment to the fans.

I switch on the radio in the vein hope that something has broken on the news. It hasn't. They don't mention me at all anymore. Don't they realise that this plan of theirs hasn't really changed a thing? In fact, it hasn't changed anything. All they are doing is depriving the public of entertainment. They are going to feel pretty stupid after the book goes to number one and the film is a box office smash. Especially the papers, as I could have used some of the clippings in the movie, to show I was always following the press and listening to their comments. I could have made the news famous.

It is odd, there are days when I don't think about the press at all. Days when I understand that it is more about the work than about them. Then there are days when I just feel sorry for them. All of those poor journalists that are now out of work. The TV news shows that probably shut down. That is why they are showing old runs of black-and-white TV programmes like *Z-Cars*. To keep the public entertained. Shows like *Criminal Minds* have probably been given their own TV channel by now. They are just trying to fill the void that I have left.

I finish my burgers and go and lie back down. I take out my phone. Let's see what there is to see in Painswick. In truth, all I know is that it is near the other letters. That is why I picked it.

It is Queen of the Cotswolds, apparently. That's nice. The *Harry Potter* woman did some filming here once. She is minted now, maybe we should work on a book together. It has a nice church so that is good. I will run past it later just to have a look. Father Harry always likes a good church.

St Mary the Virgin. That would have been a difficult conversation to have with your husband, wouldn't it? I am not sure I would have taken her on holiday to Bethlehem after she told me she was pregnant. She didn't even lie and say it was his. That would have been easier than saying I was visited in a dream and now I am knocked up. He stood by her though – fair play to him. I think I would have gone to Boots the chemist and got one of those DNA tests. I would have tested myself and then all the other blokes that were in the village while I was down at my carpentry shop.

Painswick has some nice gardens as well. They do like their gardens out in the sticks, don't they? Always making a fuss of them!

Wait, it was in the *Domesday Book*. What the heck is a *Domesday Book*? And don't they know that doom is spelt D–O–O–M? I click on the link. It is something to do with taxes and William the Conqueror, or Domus Dei, Latin for the house of God. He really is everywhere. I don't know how the house of God and taxes have been mixed into the same thing. I am sure if I ask people though they will say that both have pretty much fucked up the world. Maybe that is why it is called Painswick. Both cause a lot of damn pain. I google it, it doesn't come up with anything.

It says here that Painswick is in the *Domesday Book* as a place called Wiche, a dairy farm. I didn't see a dairy farm on the way in. I should have been looking for that though as I could do with one in a day or two. I prefer the taxes and house of God thing. Not somewhere you make cheese.

I could just eat a cheese and pineapple hedgehog. Just the thought of cheese has me wanting one of those. Like the one I had at my birthday party. I bet they have some good cheese here too. I need to do that. Maybe get the cheese and take it home to Miss Walker. You can pick up pineapple chunks anywhere nowadays. We can have one at our New Year's Eve party.

I must also remember to invite Uncle George before it gets too late. It would be good to have the whole family together for a change. I text him. I am sure he will come. I hope he sorted out the stains on the car. I am sure he has.

"We have the whole day, Rachel." She is right though; if we are not going to waste our day off we need to get moving.

"We aren't going to be going far. Let's get some food and rest up while we get the chance for tomorrow we work." That has them excited. It has me excited too. Well, happy. I am not excited. Although it has been a couple of days, I may have to give one of them a treat later. Maybe a couple of them? That will fill the rest of my day.

"If you want to." It is still a little early, but if they want Christmas songs let's give them Christmas songs. I get one of the tapes that Mrs Green had put out and put it on. Got to love a little bit of "Santa Baby". They are not half bad singers. That should keep us going for a while…

"Time to go to work, ladies." I do feel as if I have had some me time and relaxed. This whole planning thing meant the girls have been ready for at least a week. All I have to do is put them into position. Besides, we have spent the last thirty hours eating cheese and watching TV. They didn't eat as much as I thought they would? They really aren't as hungry as they make out. Those pasties were a complete waste of time, and if Elle and I hadn't have been creative with the cream we wouldn't have used half of it.

I would have thought Mrs Green had a different taste in DVDs though. I mean, we all enjoyed them but *Only Fools and Horses, Fawlty Towers, Porridge…* I don't know why, but I always imagined her as a blue movie type of watcher. Or even a blue movie star. Maybe some deep throat, or *Debbie Does Dallas*. I like the idea of a girl doing a whole state. I would have thought Mrs Green would have done too. Mrs Green does Georgia? I am almost sure she would have already done my neighbourhood.

I do like a nice church. Especially one where I can drive a motorhome almost to the front door. Is it a door or a porch? I don't know why, but I think it is a porch. Either way, the grounds are big and, luckily for me, very tree-lined. Nobody is going to disturb us. I did say that I was going to swap Rachel out, but she has been good the last day or so, very supportive of the quest. Sometimes it is good to have intelligent conversation, someone to stimulate you! Sometimes I need stimulating in more ways than one.

I go to the back of the motorhome and open the door. I really need to get something for the smell in here though. I have been going through air freshener at a rate of knots. Although I suppose it won't be long before they are gone. Not that I even managed to get enough cast yet. That is an odd thing to say, "cast"? I suppose they are though. I suppose this is my real director debut. Creating multiple scenes around the country. I should have probably thought about that before taking yesterday off. I could have worked last night in town. We could have gone carol singing. That would have been a great disguise. I can just see Elle as a carol singer.

"Elle, Sarah, Trinity, it is your time to shine." I knew that would get a round of applause. Turning into a bit of a catchphrase as well, time to shine. They will be telling the press that, without a doubt. I lean over and move Rachel out of the way, then Sandy and Lorraine. I am a bit concerned about those two. Every time I split them up they seem to find themselves on top of each other again. I mean, I don't mind, but I am not sure all the others will be happy about a couple making out in front of them. Even if they are two hot girls!

I grab Elle. For a blonde she is pretty hot, and I am sure that if I asked she would dye her hair for me. Her collars and cuffs don't match. That is why I let her have a go yesterday. She is only pretending to be blonde. It is odd that I choose a blonde, brunette and redhead for this, isn't it? Maybe it was the variety. I could have dyed their hair to match the dresses, but that almost feels a little tacky to me. Besides, the blue white and red dresses go. And Trinity is a redhead with a red dress. I take them in turn up to the church, making sure that Elle is in the middle as she is the only one wearing a wedding dress. I am amazed at how many wedding dresses there are in charity shops. Do women do that on purpose to piss off the old man? I mean, he is hardly going to be happy after spending thousands on a dress to find out you gave it to a charity shop. Maybe that's what they do when they get divorced? Let's face it, most people get divorced at least once or twice nowadays.

Trinity needs to be on her left and Sarah to her right. That is it: blue, white and red. I go back to the motorhome and pick up the L signs and the berets. I even managed to string some onions together. I really am getting quite good at this threading lark. My needlework parallels Jack's, I am sure of it. If not better than his.

They are not going to miss that as an example, are they? Blue, white and red with berets and onions. All I need is a bike and a baguette and you are practically in France. I stick the signs to them, put the berets on their heads and put the onions around Sarah's neck. Wait!

Fuck!

That is where they could smell the onions from yesterday. It wasn't the hamburger... I thought they were going mad. I must have left them by the heater or something. I am surprised I couldn't smell them, but that place does need a good airing. Maybe I could drive down the road with the doors and windows open at the same time. I am sure they won't get too cold if I do.

I lie down next to them and take a couple of selfies. I don't think I need to write on the wall for this one. Three French Hens, or a French Hen Party to be precise. It is pretty much self-explanatory. Besides, if they check the DNA they have all been French-kissed in the last couple of weeks by me.

I get back in the motorhome and switch on the oven. I put it on low to just warm it up before heading to Quedgeley. It is only fifteen minutes up the road which is good. It will only just be technically Monday by then. The Asda next door isn't twenty-four hours on a Sunday either which makes it easier with less traffic as I will need to get in and out if I am going to work on a roundabout. I start the drive.

Something feels different though. While this is simple, as I have a cast to work with, they are all going to be gone in a couple of days. I don't think that was as exciting as it normally is.

I know one thing: I didn't work enough. I didn't try hard enough. I was distracted by Mrs Green and this motorhome. Some days I didn't even work. I just lazed around having sex and taking time out. I blame the girls. They spent their time keeping me entertained and horny.

I suppose if I had got enough we would have been talking seventy plus. Where else would I have put them? I mean, they are being good about all being cramped as it is. I need to start to think a little bit more outside the box. I need to start thinking about something that has the same impact but with less people to work with. Still the Alphabet stroke Edmund stroke Father Harry style though.

Something along the lines of the pie I made is a good start. Although that was for my own amusement, I guess, as it was one of my favourite nursery rhymes from my nan. But it shows that you don't need the numbers for the effect.

I get to Quedgeley. This is busier than I thought. What are all these people doing at gone midnight? I head into the Kingsway area and pull into the Asda car park. This is a stretch. I think trying to combine this was a stretch. The problem is I am always trying to do that for my fans. It is just who I am. I push myself for their entertainment. I suppose it is why they love me so much.

I blame Rachel. She was the one that told me that calling birds were actually Colly birds. Something we now call blackbirds. Then all I had in my head was the four and twenty black birds baked in a pie. Hence the pie. All set before the king. I should have kept with the four calling birds.

Why the fuck haven't I just been using birds?

I should have done that for all the bird ones and then I would have probably had enough people to work with. Why am I thinking about this now? I can't go back to it now. I have started. I should have thought about this a month ago.

Why didn't Mrs Green tell me about that? I swear I am not sleeping with her again, no matter how much she begs me. Last night was the last time. Not many women get the pleasure of me for a whole month, and we did some pretty freaky stuff. She begged me too. That was her reward for the good advice. But she should have been working harder for me.

I watch as the traffic goes round and round the roundabout. Like a teddy bear. Where the fuck did that just come from? Like a teddy bear! It is not even a roundabout; it is a garden, round and round the garden. I am going nursery rhyme mad. It's the four and twenty blackbirds. They have my fucking head pickled.

This isn't going to work. This roundabout isn't going to work. I think I need to go to the backup. I need to go to Kingsway Farm Park next door. There were lots more trees in front of the Kings School and community centre. I pull out of Asda and head over to the park. This is right. This will be better. No traffic. I pull over to the side of the road and head back to the bedroom.

"Yes, it is getting a lot less crowded in here all of a sudden." It is only five less, but I guess, if you are at the bottom of the pile, five is a lot.

"Yes, Rachel. I know there is a limit to how many people should be in one of these things and we are still over it." For a hooker she knows an awful lot about health and safety. She knows an awful lot about everything.

"Sandy, Lorraine, Linda and Caroline, you are on now." I give them the wink.

"Sorry, yes, it is your time to shine. Thank you for reminding me, Rachel."

I think that will make the rest of them happy. I start to drag them one by one to the edge of the park. Caroline feels like she hasn't been eating, she is almost wasting away. I am sure I remember her being a little bit bigger than this? She has probably been dieting. To be fair, they probably all have over the last month, just to grab my attention. Girls do like to look their best around me. The cassocks are a nice touch. I lay them out, facing Kings School. I then fetch the hymn books and place them in their hands. Four calling birds. Singing chicks. That is what the song meant really. Now for the final piece, I go to the oven and fetch the pie. I place it on the ground in front of them. Four and twenty black birds baked in a pie. Someone will get it. The press will get it. Set before the king. Kings School.

Shame they are not blackbirds though. I just couldn't get any. I mean, I tried. I lay in wait for a whole fucking day. I set up a box with a stick on a piece of string propping it up with bread laid underneath and around the box, waiting to see if the birds would go underneath. They wouldn't. Even with all the bread that I laid out. I am not upset about that really. I don't think I could have done anything to hurt a little bird. Besides, I made the gravy with black food colouring, and most things taste like chicken anyway. They won't notice the difference. I step back. It looks good. But it doesn't have the same feel. It doesn't have the same feel as it is not live. There is no rush of adrenalin. All I am doing is placing people on the ground. Will they think the same? The fans, will they think that it was too simple for me? They are used to a certain calibre. Calibre, where did that—

"Mate, what are you doing?"

Fuck!

That scared me. I was lost in my own little world then. I turn. There is a bloke standing about two feet away. I quickly look around. He is alone. That is good. He is not press and he doesn't seem to have a camera. He is looking directly at me though and then at the girls on the ground and then back at me.

"Hey, are you him? Are you… fucking hell!"

He recognises me, which is good. It is good to know I am not out of people's minds. But for some reason, he turns and starts to run. I run after him. It is the least I can do, have a selfie or sign something for him. He is screaming. Why is he screaming? There isn't going to be any press around in a park at this time of night. There is nothing around here. I am gaining on him in seconds I reach behind me and pull out my knife. I am going to have to work with him just to stop the screaming. I can't have the press finding the girls in the park. Elle and the other girls will still be at the church and I am sure they have yet to have their fifteen minutes of fame. They need to be discovered first. There is an order to these things. I dive at him, one hand grabbing his shoulder and the other plunging the knife into his back. He really screamed then. Maybe it was just one last call to the surrounding neighbourhood to get them to call *The Times* newspaper. It is a sharp knife. It almost slices straight down his back. Reminds me of butter, when a hot knife goes through really cold butter. I never thought about it like that before. I get on top of him and cut his throat. That will ensure he doesn't make any more calls for the press.

I am fucking knackered!

I can't remember the last time that I had to run that fast. I can't remember the last time that I had to run. Oh yeah, Manchester. Well, I didn't run; I just walked really fast. I fancy some toast now. With hot butter. I wonder why that is in my head.

Fuck!

I look around me. I am sitting here almost inviting the press to come see me. There is nothing and no one. Well, it is gone midnight on a Sunday. They are all probably nursing a hangover somewhere. From celebrating my return.

I was fast. It didn't take me that long to get on top of him. I look back at the motorhome. It is close enough. It is close enough to get him back to it. I don't need to waste the work. That is not like me. I am a true professional.

I grab him by his arms and head back into the motorhome. I lay him in the back with the others. They will fill him in with the details once he wakes up. He is never going to believe what he has just stumbled into. He is never going to believe his luck. I go and sit back at the wheel. I enjoyed that. I enjoyed the running even if it did nearly kill me. I pull out and join the traffic. I enjoyed it, but the last thing I need is someone else coming along and trying and getting in on the event. Well, that is not exactly true. I do need some more people to work with but not here. Not when I am mid-event. I need them to help me out by turning up on the downtime. I need to be more visible on the downtime so they know I need some support. My fans will help me with this, I am sure of it.

P and Q and the third and fourth day…

Fuck!

I turn the vehicle around and go back to the park. I jump out and take a couple of selfies with the girls and set off again. What was I thinking? I almost forgot again then. That was his fault for distracting me. I need them all, all the photos. How else am I going to include them all in my book?

P and Q and the third and fourth day of Merry Carson.

Done!

Chapter 18

Ross-on-Wye! I wonder if it was named after a guy called Ross who lived on the River Wye. Maybe even on a boat. That makes sense to me? There must be a place somewhere that has a list of meanings for towns. I need to research that for my movie. It will be good to have some points of interest in the story. Educating entertainment, Infotainment, I just got that now. That is clever how those words were put together.

I think this is the first time I have been somewhere that has two castles. After visiting both of them yesterday I thought I would have found some inspiration. I didn't. It didn't even say if the two castles were at war with each other? That would have been cool. A huge war. It could have been to do with King Ross, and why he did whatever he did? Maybe that's the why? These towns always mean something.

I am still not happy that my fans are getting the best of me with this whole twelve days thing. I was thinking it was because of the adrenalin, but I am still not sure that is it. It is not exciting me, and if it doesn't excite me it won't excite them. It is too simple. I need to make it more... I don't know, just more.

I am an artist, after all. I may be going through a period. Artists do that, don't they? They go through a period of change. What do they call those things that artists have? A muse? I think that is what I need: a muse to inspire the creative side of me. A muse would get my head and my heart beating faster. It would make me think differently? Miss Walker was never really that. She was more the voice of clarity and direction. I guess that is because she always had her own agenda to deal with at the same time. How she was going to trap me into marriage and have a baby.

Fuck!

She is on track now. She is on track more than me? And she knows I am working towards her plan. All she had to do was plant the idea and keep coming across. Fuck, she knows what she is doing. She is a clever woman. Maybe I am her muse? How the fuck did that happen?

 If I am going to have a muse of my own she needs to be someone a little more flamboyant. Now that is a good word. Flamboyant. Today is a good day to find me some of that. Today with what is ahead of me, I need to start thinking more that way. More creative, abstract! *Ob shay da* or something like that the French would say. That will get my heart beating again. Where the fuck are these words coming from today? I am on fire.

I am not waiting till tonight for the fifth day of Christmas. I mean Carson. It will need to take place in the day, well, at least late afternoon. I don't want to get myself caught out by the nightshift. The nightshift is probably quiet, so they would notice me more. I don't need that. Not today. Not when I am so close. Eight days. A week. Eight days a week, why is that in my head? There are only seven days in a week? Eight days a week and something about being in love She has done that too. Come up with something else to stick in my head so that I don't forget her. She is good.

A good haircut and a close shave are needed first, and a suit. I think a suit is as good a disguise as the vicar collar sometimes. Maybe it isn't the collar? It might just be people reacting differently to someone wearing a suit. People are always more polite to a well-dressed man.

I get out of the motorhome and smell the fresh air. I am really appreciating the fresh air after sharing that place with all of them for so long.

I do love the fact that they all have these camping places out in the sticks. Broadmeadow Camping and Caravan park right in the middle of town, but the town is out in the sticks. Nobody ever expects that, a town in the sticks. Countryside. My nan always called it the sticks. I guess that is because there are a lot of sticks in the countryside.

Although I sense we are going to have to part-company soon. I am sure there are fans everywhere looking for it now, my motorhome. I have probably made them a collector's item again. Sales of motorhomes are going through the roof. My fans will be getting the same one as me to help me keep away from the press, I am sure. Either that or to steal my limelight. No, what am I saying? They want me in the limelight. I am their idol.

Day seven, I think. We are good till day seven. Maybe till day eight, depending on the eight? Ate? Ate eight? Now that is a thought. That has been worrying me for a little while. But that could really work.

After all, that is why Seven is the scariest number. Because Seven Eight Nine. Ha ha! I am not sure why that sprang into my head. It is not even one of mine. I think it is one of my nan's jokes. She was never good at jokes.

I come out of the trailer park and take a walk into town. I did say I wanted to be more active in the day, didn't I? The weather is quite good considering it is nearly Christmas. I do like the fact that people have their lights up everywhere, really getting into the swing of it. I hope I am helping with that, inspiring them all at this time of year. I can't help but whistle Christmas songs. It is a good day. I wonder how many fans have sent me presents. The post office is bound to be under pressure from them all. I will have to do some free advertising for Royal Mail at some point. As a thank you for all the hard work.

I am looking for someone flamboyant as I walk. I don't think the people of Ross-on-Wye are known for flamboyance? By the looks of it, most of them can't spell flamboyant. I stop at the first local pub. They are advertising food. I am really hungry. I could really do with some liver and onions. Real liver and onions like I made for Miss Walker in that little cottage she had. That was a lovely day place. One of those cottages up in the Lake District will be a perfect holiday home for us. A little bigger, of course. With a hot tub.

Odd that I have not fancied eating with any of my friends in the motorhome. I don't know if it is the smell or not? Something isn't getting my creative cooking skills working. They are nice people though. They have really been helping me through all this and coming up with suggestions on what to do. Rachel knows everything. Just about everything about everything. You wouldn't have thought it when you first met her. But I never judge a book by its cover. I am listening to her advice.

The next couple though, after tonight, they are worrying me. I don't want to be known too much for religion. I have told her that, but that is the problem when you are messing about with a religious festival. Well currently a religious festival. I don't want the Alphabet Killer to be known for religion. If anyone is to be known for it, it should be Father Harry. I think the whole days six and seven need work. The six days of creation. People won't get that. They just won't. I know she said that is what it really meant. I prefer to believe it was all about the wedding food. I don't want to hurt any geese though, but I do prefer it.

The seven holy gifts as well? What if my fans aren't churchgoing people? I didn't even know there were holy gifts? And they weren't even real Christmas gifts. There wasn't a jumper or a pair of socks to be seen. No, I need to be thinking more away from religion. Although I could have done with the eight beauty things. It was a good one. I can see myself blessing everyone on a mound. A mound is a hill, right? That I could have done. Kind of like an open-air concert. My fans would like that.

I go inside the pub. There is nothing that is going to get my creative juices flowing in here. It is a typical old-fashioned pub. I place my order and it arrives within ten minutes. Must be pretty slow in here today. I start to eat my lunch while watching people walk up and down the street. A cheese and onion roll and a pint of the local beer. There was no liver and onions on the menu. I should really start to order Coke when I come to these places as the beer is always an acquired taste and I have not acquired it. I just get confused when I get to the bar. I always think that ordering something local makes you feel and seem like you are a local. I know if I have Real Cornish anything in Cornwall they just smile. They think you are one of them. Real Scottish taste in Scotland does the same thing. Although real Scottish taste is normally deep-fried something. Even in the north they always have the real stuff. Real Honest Ale! That one worries me a little bit. Are they trying to point out that it is real ale or trying to point out they are really not lying about the fact that it is real ale? My nan would say they protest too much. So it probably isn't even ale in the first place.

Fuck!

I nearly choked on my cheese and onion. That is her! That is my inspiration. Small, dark-haired, and she is wearing some really trendy, hippy-looking clothes. I take a swig of my drink and then run out of the pub to follow her. So many colours in her coat and her long, flowing dress. That is hot. Now that is someone who knows fashion. Not my fashion but the flamboyant type of fashion. You know she has creative juices in her. I bet she tastes amazing. All herby with a touch of sweetness. I am hard just thinking about it.

I follow her down the road until she enters a shop. I then follow her in. The shop is called Happy's. She heads out the back and then comes back into the main part of the shop without her coat on, and goes behind the counter and starts talking to the girl who is already there. She has a hot body as well. I could tell it was there under the coat. But now, now it is in front of me. Well, behind the counter in front of me.

She strikes me as the type of person who would work at a place named Happy's. She is cute, bouncy, the type I could throw around in a good session. That is a good thing for a muse. To be able to please their master. I browse the walls. There are wigs and accessories and jokes, lots of jokes. Like fake poo. I am not sure that is a good joke? But I am sure some people would laugh at it.

"Can I help you, sir?"

I turn around and she is standing right there. Right there in front of me. She has the most amazing green eyes. They are stunning. Something else I wasn't expecting. I wasn't expecting her to look so good up close. She smells good too, I can tell from here. I just want to smell her all over, now.

She is my muse. I am just a natural at finding these people. I attract the gorgeous people. My nan was right. I am a babe magnet.

"Swans." What? Why the fuck did I say swans? Swans aren't even next on the list. Why didn't I say geese? Or goose? That would have made more sense. Looking at her got me all hot and confused. Is that what a real muse will do for you? Is that what I do for Miss Walker? Of course it fucking is. I make everyone hot. Women fall to pieces in front of me and now I am doing it in front of her.

"Swans the inflatable kind, or just normal?"

What the fuck?

"You have inflatable swans?"

She smiles at me. Her smile is almost as dazzling as her eyes. She turns and heads towards the other side of the shop. I follow her. Is my tongue hanging out? Either that or my mouth is wide open because it suddenly feels all dry inside. It needs something hot and rich rolling around my tongue to cure it. She does have inflatable swans and they are big. Why would she have inflatable swans?

"We don't sell many in the winter, but they are popular in the summer."

She hands one to me. I want to say why, but the words aren't coming out.

"It has been about ten years since the fighting swans video, but we are still one hundred per cent a swan town." She can read my mind. Why are they a swan town? Why didn't I know that they were a swan town? Why didn't Rachel tell me about that when she told me about the two castles? I need to look that up at some point.

"Thanks. I don't suppose you have ten of them?"

"Ten?" She looks shocked at that. People don't normally ask for ten inflatable swans, do they?

"Yes. It is for my little sister's birthday. She just loves them. I thought of putting them in her room before she wakes up. It will be a lovely surprise for her."

She is smiling. I am smiling. I am smiling as I have no idea what I just said. That is just nonsense right there. Nonsense coming out of my mouth but it is creative nonsense. She is a muse. I even managed to avoid the obvious don't order seven. That is just genius. She is off, and comes back with the swans.

"You are in luck. We do have ten." She places them on the counter in front of her. That was fucking simple, and easier than seven holy gifts.

"Is there anything else I can help you with?"

There are so many answers to that question, most of them will involve us locking that door and being naked. I am even considering a threesome as the more I look at her mate the more I think this could be a first. That is how creative she has got me feeling. In a joke shop, imagine how much fun you could have, but what the heck, I may as well go for the obvious.

"Do you have anything with regards to geese?"

"Geese... Now you have me. I don't think we sell inflatable geese." She looks over to the counter and her friend. I smile at both of them. It was always going to be a long shot. But a muse has to earn her reward.

"Abby, we don't, but we do have those eggs. You know, the golden ones?"

Abby is a pretty name. She looks like an Abby. The girl behind the counter comes around and heads out the back. Abby follows her. It takes a little while, but they appear again carrying a box.

"We have these. They are golden eggs. They are actually supposed to be dragon eggs from *Harry Potter*. But they don't say dragon on them. They open up and play a nice tune. Something a little girl would like." She opens one. It is a nice tune. Very ballerina. It will be good for my little sister.

"Geese lay golden eggs, don't they? Maybe that is what you could tell your little sister? They do in *Charlie and the Chocolate Factory*." They are both nodding. I find myself nodding too. They are right. My little sister will like that.

"I think she will love them." It does work, doesn't it? My little... What the fuck? I don't have a little sister. Why am I thinking that! Insanity must be part of this shop. Or am I losing the plot? Now I have geese laying golden eggs for my little sister and yesterday I baked four and twenty blackbirds in a pie, made with chicken and black food colouring. I do, I need a holiday. A long holiday in Spain with loads of dark haired girls.

The fans will get the point though, won't they? The point about the geese that lay the golden eggs. It is enough, isn't it?

"How many would you like?"

"Ten, I guess."

They are both smiling. Probably weren't expecting this much business in such a short space of time. They box everything up for me. I hand over the cash. She was my muse. She is my muse. She was inspiring, creative, everything I am looking for. The door opens again and a couple of other people come in. I am not going to be able to have a threesome with all these people watching. Besides, they might complain if we close the shop in the middle of the day. Jokes seem to be popular in Ross-on-Wye.

I am halfway towards day six and seven within minutes of meeting her. That has to mean something. We were meant to be together. That is what it means.

"We could make a mask for you if you want to visualise the geese as well?"

I was nearly out of the door. They must have both been itching to talk to me some more.

"Sorry?" I turn back to the counter. Abby is back on this side. She wants me. She was trying hard to think of something to keep me in the shop. She is practically dragging me back in with her eyes. It is understandable as I knew we had a connection. She knows it too. Chemistry is chemistry.

"We can print out masks. We do them for people that want to look like celebrities and, you know, stag dos and hen parties so they all look the same. We can print any picture in any colour and make it into a mask."

She is amazing. That is sounding more and more like a plan. That will definitely be enough. I can place the mask on them. There is no mistaking that.

"I think that could be quite fun. I could put them on her teddy bears."

"Ahhhh." They both say it at the same time. Both their heads tilt to one side too. I think that is the come and get me tilt. They are almost opening the neck up to me. I am going to have to buy ten teddy bears too now. I must be the best big brother ever. They will know I am the best big brother ever.

"How old is she, your little sister?"

"Charlotte? She will be ten tomorrow." That makes sense. That is why I want ten of everything.

"Ahhhh." They are at it again. I should have used this whole family thing before as it seems to work a treat. Girls like this caring crap, don't they?

"It would take us a while to do ten, if you could come back later?"

Oh, I could come back later. That look in her eyes tells me I will not be the only one coming later.

"Yes, that shouldn't be a problem."

"I lock up about eight?" She was so keen to let me know that. She practically said, I am here till eight. Alone. I lock up, alone. Come do me. Alone! She didn't want the threesome thing. She wanted me all alone. Her friend is going to be so disappointed. But that is why they were out the back for so long. They were deciding who gets to do me. First.

"Sounds perfect." I turn and leave. Yes, she knew what she was saying. Wouldn't be surprised if she doesn't head home to shower and change now.

I head back towards the campsite. I passed a Next clothes shop on the way here. I pop in and get myself some clothes for this afternoon. This has been a remarkable hour. I had a nice lunch, a piece of inspiration that I just can't put into words other than I have a muse! And now the bones of a new plan. I even have a date for this evening, which doesn't happen every day. I so need to go out more in the day.

Rachel will not be happy as the two options we had were more traditional. She is a traditional type of girl. She didn't even want to do back door stuff when we were in bed together. I say bed. The pull-out sofa in the motorhome. I will have to break it to her gently. Like I did on the pull-out sofa.

I get back to the motorhome and put the clothes on the side. I head over to the bathroom and get my clippers. I am going to have to do this in the living area as there is not enough room in there. I am thinking a number four all over, including the beard. It will give me the designer look for sure. It will give me that cool but still a bit rough look. Abby will love that. I start to shave. There is a cheer from the other room. They are in full swing today and they can already sense how hot I am going to look.

"Nope, nobody is leaving us today. Well, no full body..." That got me a laugh. The fifth day of Christmas, this is a piece of bravery and includes everything I like about the Alphabet Killer. It is Rocio type of bravery that makes the Alphabet

Killer a star. He is not afraid to push the boundaries and laugh in the face of the press and the police.

"I know, Rachel, it is not the true meaning. But where was I going to get a goldfinch from? I am not even sure they exist anymore."

They do, I looked it up but I didn't want to share that with her. I am not sure my fans would have got it either. I didn't know that a goldfinch had five rings around his neck? They won't know that either. Not all of them. Besides, Elle had a much better idea. It was well worth the price I had to pay. Twice with cream! Lots of whipped cream.

"Yes, as you asked. I am still considering the food for the wedding, Rachel. Rachel you know I am not comfortable with too much religion. People will start to believe I have favourites and at no point in the world has having a favourite religion turned out well for anyone." There are only two more after this that were meant to be prepared for the food for the wedding. Days six and seven. The more I think about it, the more I should have done that. It would have been a lot easier. Just put up a banquet for the first seven days. It would be like the last supper. That looked like a good party.

I wonder why the milkmaids were invited to the wedding party though. The lords, ladies, pipers and drummers I understand, but why invite a milkmaid to a wedding? All I can think is the lords were doing them all. They do that sharing thing in high society, don't they? That is what the servants were, weren't they? Practically sex slaves… I should have some of them. When this is all done, I am going to get me some servants. Hot ones.

I finish the all-over shave. I think that is it. I rub my head. There are bits of hair flying everywhere. I really need a shower, even if it is in the tiny shower. I am beginning to really hate that thing.

"I know a shaven head does suit me.

"Yes, Mrs Green, so does the suit, suit me." I know what she is thinking, but I am not putting out again. The only person that is getting me today is Abby. I think for the inspiration she has given me alone she deserves at least one orgasm... Although I am not sure how I would be able to stop her at one. Once they start there is no stopping those things.

I head to the shower and then stop. No point in showering till I have them.

I go into their room. They are worse than kids for keeping this place tidy.

"Thank you, Rachel, it does look better up close." I count again, sixteen. Sixteen actors is getting me halfway through the maids are milking unless I can come up with something better. None of these are lords or ladies though. That is going to be a problem. I don't even know how many lords and ladies there are in the country? I know the lords have their own House in London. So there must be a few. Come to think of it, some of them are ladies – ladies of the night – but I don't think that counts. Lords and ladies of the night does have a familiar ring to it. Wait I am that good maybe I am a lord of the night. I like that Edmund Carson lord of the night. That is going on a T-shirt.

"Yes, Rachel, I am still going with the rings.

"I know it is not traditional, but it also needs to be popular and I don't think hurting a poor goldfinch would make me very popular, do you? The RSPCA would have a field day in the press about that.

"I do admit it would be realistic, yes." I go back into the kitchen and pick up the wire cutters.

"Yes, Rachel." I go back into the room. She is really going to keep me on top of this whole tradition thing, isn't she?

"I think Elle had a great idea. Five gold rings in a box, still on the fingers of the owners, is almost a classic. I can see that on the big screen. The police stumped by who is who. There is a whole mystery about it. They love that sort of thing."

She has a point. It is not going to keep them stumped for long. I guess they just run the prints in the computer and it pops up with who it is? It would take less than ten minutes. Mystery solved. I lean in as she wants to whisper something to me. I am sure it is going to be a ploy to take her into the other room for some alone time. They have all done that over the last month.

I knew she was clever. She knows that I am running out of friends to work with and coming up with ideas to help.

"Okra? I can't say I have ever heard of it."

She carries on explaining her idea. I guess it would be a little closer to the truth. I do have a bigger box as well. She made me buy it when we were discussing the goldfinch the first time around. I can't say I ever wanted to put one in a box though. I couldn't even catch a blackbird.

"The sum of the whole is greater than the parts, you say? No, I cannot say that I have heard that before." I haven't. I am not even sure I know what she is talking about now. I don't want to look stupid in front of her so I just agree.

I stand back. I do like the idea. It will help as well with the ninth day of Christmas. I will just need to find one, and a piano. I remember my nan saying it now. Isn't it funny how little things bring back such memories? She used to say to me as we sat there that I needed to make them dance.

"Rachel, I think it is a great idea."

She is happy. I can tell. It will make up for not listening to her on day six and seven.

"And you don't mind playing your part?"

She doesn't. I can tell. If she did she wouldn't have told me about it.

"Okay." I lean back into her. She says she has another idea. It may just be my aftershave drawing her closer to me. It is not. It is another great idea.

"Genius, Rachel, absolute genius. I woke up this morning worrying how to get past five, and between you and Abby four hours later I am practically at ten."

There was a look from all of them when I mentioned Abby's name. I need to gloss over that. I forget how much they don't really appreciate anyone else getting quality time with me. Especially someone who is not in the motorhome team. Oddly, they are happy to share as long as we are all here. They must just like to see and hear me in action.

"The Brad Pitt thing as well is genius. Maybe he will be remembered for something. I had forgotten all about that film."

I grab Rachel and take her into the other room.

"Thank you, really, for all your help. I can honestly say I don't think I would have been able to complete it without you." I could have. I just want to ensure she gives good feedback to the press when they meet her.

"No, it doesn't hurt. I have done this before. It is hard to talk afterwards, you know, until you are reunited, but it doesn't hurt." I lay her on the floor and give her a kiss. A real one, just so she knows how much I appreciate the effort she has gone to. It will be a nice touch for her story too.

I get up and fetch my knife from the side. I give her one last smile and then I slice hard at her neck until her head comes off. It is quite easy actually. I expected her neck to be a little tougher.

I pick up her head. She has left her mouth open. Does she think that I should put the rings in her mouth? She said to place them in her neck like the goldfinch. She was very clear on how to sew them in as well. So why would she leave her mouth open?

Oh, you don't think…? I look her straight in the eyes. Yes, now I know what she was thinking. She was trying to leave one last gift for me and for her. That is just wrong though, isn't it? I can't do that once her head is off her shoulders. Can I? It is called giving head though, isn't it? It isn't called giving head and shoulders. So that must mean it is okay to, wait, isn't head and shoulders some kind of a shampoo?

No, no, I can't! I don't have time. She is a little tease though. Right down to the last minute before she becomes famous, she is trying to tease me.

I place her head on the sofa and then go back into the other room and collect five gold rings off the girls. I make sure I choose them all from different girls. I suppose their families will recognise the jewellery straight away and think it is something of a trailer. Like a movie trailer. I am telling the world that they are with me now so this is just a taster as you know they will be coming to a town near you soon.

I go back into the other room. She is leaking a bit onto the sofa. I need to stop that as it will go straight through the box. Nobody wants a leaky present. Not even them. I go up to the gas cooker and turn it on. I need to sear the open wound. That's what they do isn't it. On TV and in films they sear the wound to stop it bleeding. I carry her over to the cooker.

"It will help, trust me." She does trust me. Why wouldn't she? I am everything she would ever want.

"It will probably stop you feeling light-headed too. I know how I feel when all my blood rushes south. Dizzy as fuck sometimes. There is a lot to fill down there if you know what I mean." She does she has swallowed it whole before.

I start to sear the wound. It must be tickling her a little as I can feel her ears wiggling. It takes a couple of minutes, but it is done. I take her back to the sofa. Suddenly all I can think about is BBQ food. Where did that come from? BBQ ribs would go down a treat now.

I fetch a needle and thread. I am getting quite good at this now. I then thread the gold rings into her neck like she asked. I can tell by the sparkle in her eyes this is exactly what she wanted. It is a good-looking necklace. It was good that I took her head from just above her shoulders too. That made rooms for the rings. I take one last look and then place her in the box.

"Okay, shower time."

"No, I am going alone this time." Insatiable. Some of them are absolutely insatiable.

Ten minutes later I am out of the shower. I didn't even play with myself, which has to be a first for me especially as the thought of Abby was running through my mind. I get dressed and wrap the present. I wonder if I will get my own wrapping paper. I mean Disney have their own, and they are just a movie studio. I could have different scenes on them. It will really jazz up the winter holiday. I pick up the card. It is one with a goldfinch on the front, and a robin, I think. It has a red breast. I think that is a robin. It is very Christmassy. I probably should have left a card at each place. They would have been good collector items. I can imagine them then being reprinted and sold at Christmas – if they still call it Christmas after this. Edmass is good. Edmass the winter holiday!

I write... "Have a good one. Love Edmund". It is important to use the word love when you talk about your fans. They love me so I should love them in return, and tell them as much as I can.

I check my phone. The police station is in the middle of town. I may as well drive closer, leave the motorhome round the back of the church where nobody will see it and walk there. Then I can walk over to Happy's to see Abby.

I should time it so I can go straight from the police station to Abby's. It will be better. It will be just before the nightshift come on and as Abby is closing. We don't want to be disturbed. She deserves quality time.

I sit back on the sofa. The dry part that doesn't have Rachel's blood on. I wish I hadn't wrapped the present now as I do have time and Rachel really wanted to do that for me. She might leak a little I don't want that on my new clothes. I get up and put an episode of *Only Fools and Horses* on. It is okay and everyone else seems to like it. It is the one called "To Hull and Back". I don't think I have ever been to Hull. It doesn't look like the type of place I want to go to either. It is a bit grey-looking for me. I have watched all of these now. A whole month in this thing means I had a lot of spare time. This episode is one of my favourites. Only they would be stupid enough to throw all that money out of the window at the end. I sit and watch it with them all again.

I end up watching a couple of episodes to kill some time.

I like the series. But I am not sure why they didn't leave it at that point when they walked into the sunset. Surely that is what it was all about? It was the perfect ending.

"Right, gang, time to get this show on the road. That is enough of the Trotters for one day."

I get back behind the wheel and head into town. I pass Morrison's and head to the back of the church. It is as good a place as any. It is really out the way as well. No fans will find me here. I pick up the present and head into town. This is good. I do like walking among them, especially with a day in my hand, in plain sight. They just don't know it. Imagine how they are going to feel when the movie comes out. Yes, hiding in plain sight is the easiest way of doing this.

I walk up to the police station. It looks deserted. I wonder if my picture is on the wall in there. My heart is beating at a million miles an hour. I open the door and walk into the reception area. It is not deserted; it is quite busy. It really is a little reception area. It looks like there are at least four people in front of me, which is a lot for a sleepy little town? I do hope that there isn't some kind of crime wave going on. I hope my motorhome is safe? I sit down on a bench and then place my present next to me. The desk guy clocks me and I clock him back. He goes back to talking to the coloured lady in front of him. I take out my phone and place it to my ear.

"Yes, yes, just one minute." I then step back outside, closing the door behind me. I put my phone back in my pocket. That is genius. The whole I have a fake call bit. I am a genius. In, out and delivered in less than a minute. That is how you entertain the masses. I am a fucking legend. It is no wonder people adore me. Speaking of adoring me. It is time to head towards Happy's.

R and the fifth day of Edmass.

Done!

Chapter 19

"Hi."

"Hi, can I help? Hey, it is you. I didn't recognise you there for a minute. It is a nice haircut. Looks really good." I can tell by the look in her eyes that she has just wet her pants. She made the 'really' stand out then. She is probably orgasming already just from looking at me. It is understandable. I am hot as fuck.

"I was just about to close up."

"Yes, sorry. We spent the afternoon at the park and time just got away from us. My mum wanted Charlotte out of the house while she made her cake." My mum made her a cake? My mum can't bake a cake! She always goes to the bakery in town. Charlotte wouldn't want to eat one of Mum's cakes.

Abby heads out to the back of the store and comes back with ten geese masks. They are really good. I must remember to sign the other four. They will become great collector items. Maybe I should just sign all of them. It would be a nice gift for Edmass. Just difficult to choose favourites to give them too.

"There you go. That will be just forty quid."

I take the money out of my wallet and pay her. I watch her as she places the money in the till really slowly. She doesn't want me to leave, I can tell.

"You must be the best big brother ever." She is right, I knew I would be.

"Oh, I don't know about that. I do try my best."

She is smiling at me again. I have been thinking about that smile all afternoon. In the shower she was doing more than smiling with that mouth, and yet I didn't play with myself? What was I thinking? I guess I was thinking I want the real thing.

"I am just trying to do my best since our father passed away." I am so good at this, how I slipped our father in there, mine and my little sister. Fake fucking little sister!

"Ahhh, I am sorry to hear about…" The head is tilting to one side again. She has stopped mid-sentence? Her eyes have suddenly become wide open. I think she has just recognised who she has standing in her shop. That is what I was waiting for, a shared moment. My knife goes straight into the exposed neck. She knew it was coming. The smile didn't move from her face, and her eyes stayed wide open so she could see everything as it happened. My knife slides out as easy as it slid in. The explosion of blood into the air is amazing. It has splashed over both our faces. That is fucking hot. I almost wish I had been on that side of the counter with her now. Holding her, I breathe it all in from here. It is exactly how I thought it would be. She drops to the floor, gracefully. I need to focus. It is always hard with that smell in the air. Everything is hard with that smell in the air. I walk over to the door and change the sign to "Closed" and pull down the blind. I then go and find the switches and turn the lights off. I go around to the counter and sit her up. I take a big lick as I do. That really is the stuff. Feels like ages since I have tasted something that warm and sweet. I knew there would be a little spice in her too. She has the look of something hot and spicy. That is the problem when you work with people weeks ago but keep them around. They just don't taste the same. I think they stop putting the effort in. She is not with me yet. I leave her to take it all in. The shock must be huge. I come around the counter and walk around the shop. I didn't get a real good look last time I was here. It was more about Abby and her friend. I need to remember when I am working to take some time for me. It can't all be about work and the fans.

This place is amazing. I head out of the back where I presumed the store room is. It isn't a store room; it is a fancy dress room. There must be a hundred, maybe two hundred costumes out here. I start to look through the rack. Why didn't I think about this before? I could be anyone! The Alphabet Killer could have been any character in history or fantasy. What a time to come up with that idea? I think about this when I am eighteen in?

I head back into the shop. She will be awake by now, I am sure of it. I go around to the other side of the counter. She is smiling up at me.

"Hey."

I knew it. She will have been excited to see me.

"Yes, thank you, I got the invite. You didn't need to crick your neck to invite me to do that. It is what I do best. Okay, it is what I do second best."

That made her laugh. I knew it would.

"Yes, that was me. You felt a tickle? You smelled so good that I couldn't help taking take a lick. I hope that is okay?"

Of course it was. I go in for another as she invites me. I can hear her giggling as I do. She has probably been dreaming about this for years but never thought I would come to her.

"No, I don't. You knew that already though, didn't you?

"I think I would have liked to have had a sister. But I was an only child." That is almost a sob story right there.

Is she interviewing me as I lick her? That is not news. Maybe it is her attempt at chit-chat. Women get nervous about talking to celebrities. I need to ensure I allow for that. I stop licking her. I have to. Not just because she probably feels that it is getting a little weird, but there is only one place I should be licking her that much in her mind. It really is because if I don't I can feel myself going in for a bite.

"I am sorry. You just taste amazing."

She likes that. I can tell. A bit of flattery always goes down well.

"I didn't know it was a fancy dress shop as well."

"It does inspire me. I was actually looking for inspiration, that is why I followed you, and you have really delivered, haven't you?" That will give her a buzz too. To know she helped on this journey. Telling her that will also make sure that she gives me good feedback.

"The geese and the swans, yes. I have a plan for both of them now. Rachel, this friend of mine, she has helped me out too.

"No, you don't need to worry about her. In fact I just dropped her off in town." I will never learn about naming other girls, will I? They get so protective and jealous over me.

"I know. I was just looking around. I think there are a lot of things here that are going to help me no end. I love the Heidi-looking wigs. They will be great for maids that are milking. Really give some class to the scene.

"You are right. I should make a list of everything else that I may need and start collecting it all."

I lean over and give her a kiss. I don't think she was expecting that. She thought I was going in for another lick. I can tell as it took her breath away. Poor girl is hardly breathing.

"I have wanted to do that since I saw you from the window of the pub.

"You have been thinking about that all afternoon? I bet that was a long wait." It was. I do feel for her. But now she knows that I am worth the wait.

I get up and start walking around the shop, trying to clock everything as I do. I am covered for the geese and the swans. We have a plan. I grab the Heidi wigs. They will do for the maids. I carry on looking.

There really isn't anything for lords or ladies. There are quite a few recorders. I go out the back and pick up the sack I saw and place the wigs and the recorders in it. I am thinking they may come in handy for the piped piper. The Pied Piper, now that is a thought and a good one. I head back out to the fancy dress area. There are a lot of costumes that could be the Pied Piper or Robin Hood, or Peter Pan. They are all very similar. I pick up all the ones that could work. I can sort them in the motorhome. I carry on looking through the costumes. Some of these may come in handy. I mean, if I want to walk around in a major town then a disguise is always helpful. I am not sure about a clown though. Imagine, the press finally catch up with me and I am dressed like a clown. That is not going to go down well at all. I stuff a few more costumes into the bag. Ones that I think may come in handy. One in particular I know will help me open a door or two.

I head back into the main shop.

"I love having my own costume department. I should probably have come somewhere like this a lot earlier."

I carry on walking around the shop. Inflatable sheep, inflatable cows... Inflatable cows, that's exactly what I need. I bet I could have got hens, blackbirds and everything if I had explored these places more. All the research I did and I didn't think of the obvious. Just go and buy the props.

"No fucking way is that a thing! Sorry, no way is that a thing. I try not to swear out loud. I keep those words more to myself."

I grab one off the shelf and open it.

"A clockwork exploding drummer! That is amazing!" They are like the toy soldiers that you see every Christmas. I wind it up and set it on the floor. It starts walking and hitting the drum. It is so cool. I love it. I watch as it makes its way across the room. It nearly gets to the other side of the room and then Bang! Well, more a poof than a bang, but it falls apart. I go over and pick it up. It has a reset button and it pulls itself back together. I love it. I really love it. I go back to the shelf. I count how many there are. There are fifteen, fifteen. I have spares...

"Abby, this is the best day ever. I didn't think it was going to be, but it is the best day ever...

"I agree. I can think of something to make it even better too."

She is right. I am ignoring her. That is not good after everything that she has done. I place the drummers in the sack. Hey, the sack. It is his sack, isn't it? I just realised that. A big black velvet sack. Probably a list in there with naughty and nice written on it. I will be on the nice list, she will be too. Hopefully with a hint of naughty.

"As I have his sack, Abby, and his outfit I need to ask you the question: have you been naughty or nice this year?" I pick her up and help her round to the main area of the shop.

"Ha ha! That is a good answer. You were planning to be nice up until the moment that you saw me, but now you want to be really naughty." That is enough to get me started. I start to strip her. Slowly. Girls like that. She is trembling every time I brush close to her. It is understandable.

"Wow." I knew there was something special under there. Something that screams I am a weird and wonderful goddess. She is so hot. I am almost nervous, almost! She is naked. I take a step back and look at her. I think that is a Christmas present for me. Edmass present, Edmass present for me.

"I mean, wow, just wow. I don't think I can stop myself from saying that." She can tell I mean it. She is smiling harder than I have ever seen her smile. It takes me less than a minute to be naked and on top of her.

"No, Abby, there is no rush. We have a few hours until day six and I am only going an hour down the road." She likes that. She likes the fact that I have quality time to spend with her. She likes the feel of me entering her even more, I can tell. I knew she was damp already. I start going at her slowly. I am going to take my time. Deep and slow. We have all night. This

feels fucking amazing. I think I will be doing this all night…
Doing her all night…

"Abby, Abby! Wake up!"

What the fuck happened? It is almost five A.M. I am up, and I get dressed as quickly as I can.

Fuck!

I was supposed to be in Stroud. This has really dented the whole in and out overnight thing. That is totally screwed now. She isn't moving. She must be knackered. I am not surprised. She really gave it her all. I knew I shouldn't have gone for twice. I knew it was a mistake I always get sleepy after the second time, and then she wanted to cuddle as well. She was just so fucking hot.

"Okay, you sleep it off. I wish I could stay, but I can't. I need to get out of here and on with day six." I grab my sack and head towards the door. That is heavy. I take some money out of my wallet and leave it on the counter. I look back at Abby as she is laid out almost lifeless on the floor. I must have done a real good job on her last night. She looks dead to the world. I head out the back and find a cloak from one of the costumes. I bring it back and cover her up. Last thing she needs is to sleep in till midday and the people in the shop see her naked. Although I am sure they would be happy about it. It is a real treat. She wouldn't want all the customers to see that though. It is reserved only for a special few.

I leave the shop and head back to the motorhome.

Fuck!

I hope she doesn't think the money was for the sex? I am not treating her like a hooker. It was for the goods. She will understand. Thank fuck it is still there. My heart was in my mouth there for a second that they would have left to start looking for me. I have never not been home before. I can imagine the panic they must have been feeling. Especially knowing what day five meant. I should have come back to let them know.

"It is okay. I am back now.

"I am sure you did all fear the worse, with the press everywhere. No, I just delivered day five and went to visit a friend. I just fell asleep on their sofa. I guess I was more tired than I let on." I nearly said her sofa. That wouldn't have gone down well.

"I know. Eight more days and then we can all sit back and relax." I start the motorhome and go out towards the west side of town. It is not the direction I want to go, but it is the road less travelled. I am sure the world's press is in town already given that I delivered day five almost half a day ago.

Fuck that was close. Too close.

I could have really messed up there. All for the sake of another quick leg over, well, not quick. That wouldn't have gone down well with the fans at all. Imagine that is how all this ended.

I keep saying that. I am getting concerned about that. I am really conscious about how this is all going to end. I have never been worried about that before. Is it really important how you retire in this game? True legends always retire at the top of their game, don't they? That is what I need to do.

I head towards Stroud. I have the masks and the eggs. It is a simple scene. I just don't think I am going to be able to do it this morning now. It is getting light already. I drive until I am about five miles away but still in the countryside. I am not going any further today. It is far too light, and doing this in the daylight is bound to draw too much unwanted attention. I need to park up. I find a deserted road surrounded by trees. This is it. This is the place. That is as much as I can do.

Fuck!

It is going to mean a long drive on Christmas Day. There just aren't enough places in the country beginning with the letter Z. Not that there are any beginning with the letter X either but I have some workarounds for that. I think.

I go back and lie on the sofa. I take out my phone and text Miss Walker. I don't know why, but I feel a little guilty about last night. I think it was making a mistake this close to the end. She wouldn't be happy about that. This will be our story, our story to tell the world. It will be just as important for her as it is for me.

I just text her: "Thinking about you", and end it with three little kisses. They like that. They like the little messages out of the blue. I put my phone down and close my eyes. I may as well sleep as there is nothing else I can do today.

Fuck!

Fuck, fuck, fuck, fuck, fuck seems to be my only word today. For the second time in a day I have overslept. What is up with me? I must be tired. Is this getting to me? Am I starting to feel the effects of overworking myself? I have to be really careful about that. Stars are always burning out. They never come back the same either.

It is already mid-afternoon. I only wanted to sleep till lunchtime.

"I know. I must have been tired, Mrs Green."

I know what she was getting at. She was getting at the fact that, she thought I was up to something else last night and the 'I fell asleep' line was just a cover-up. I am going to ignore it. I don't need to justify myself to her.

Tonight is a pretty simple night. I just need to get between here and Tewksbury. But first I am going to have to blow those swans. Seven of them. I really should have thought about that more when I was with Abby and got some kind of pump to help.

I go over to the side and pick up the seven swans. They are big. I think they are going to almost fill this place up. I need to be careful about that once they are blown up. I am going to need to work around them. I place them back on the side and then go to their room and the back of the trailer.

"I swear, every time I come in here it gets messier." They are very sheepish in their responses. I start to move the six I have earmarked for the geese and the guy from the park and the rest of Rachel into the living area. Her body is still hot. Even without its head. I am sure she wouldn't mind. I wonder if she could still feel it from the police station?

These girls are really working hard on trying to impress me. Some of these girls must have lost what, a stone? Maybe even two?

"Yes, you are all looking at lot better." Even Mrs Green has lost a couple of stone. Her boobs don't look as good now though. She should really watch out for that. Men don't like them when they start to get a bit saggy. I should have a quiet word with her about getting implants. They will keep her going for a while on the old dating scene. A nice double D not that I know what D size is. I just know people like them.

"I was just moving you so that I can throw the swans into the other room. I don't really have time to sit and blow them all up this evening in Tewksbury. I need to get ahead of the game. I can't afford another slip. I think the travelling is taking its toll as well, and I don't want to have a slip in days. That goes against everything I am trying to achieve. Besides, Boxing day isn't as good as Christmas day. Don't you agree?" I can tell they do. Deep down I do think that Mrs Green is a supporter. She knows it will be good for a kid from the neighbourhood to achieve this level of stardom. It will bring fame to the whole town.

If I think about it, none of these people care what day this gets completed. By Christmas they will have all probably signed contracts with the press or managed to get their own agents who will help sell their story of the time they spent with me. Mrs Green will do the best out of it. She has the original stories and she has been here through all of this. Through the nights collecting the girls and bringing them back to the motorhome. She was there for the knife fight in Haverhill. And Stacey at Stonehenge. I can't believe people still don't know that the place is just fake. It is just a money maker for the government. No, she will do okay from it all. She will be able to tell all their stories. I can see her becoming one of those loose women on TV. Well, looser woman.

I grab the first swan, open the packet and start to blow. This is going to take fucking ages... I blow again.

Three fucking hours! Three hours just to blow up seven giant swans, and put some rope around their necks. I had to stop. I thought I was going to pass out. I am so sure that Brad Pitt doesn't have to blow up his own swans. None of them offered to help either. I would have thought one of them would have been interested in helping. They could have put it in their autobiography. It would have been a nice twist. But no, nothing!

At least it is starting to get dark, which is good. I clamber over everyone and get to the cupboards. I am starving. I check through the fridge and pull out some bread and cheese. I don't have any onions as I gave them all to the French hens. This will have to do. I am going to make a promise to myself. Before this is all over I am going to have to have a really nice meal. I mean, a real meal with all the trimmings. Edmund Carson style! As a treat to, well, me. Edmund Carson style. I like that for the cookbook. I will have to remember that. I was going to start writing all this down. Why haven't I done that?

I sit with my sandwich and a Coke and switch on the TV. The DVD is still playing from yesterday. I don't mind. It is just something to watch while I have an hour to myself. There are a few giggles from the gang as they watch, but I ignore them. I am not happy. They could have been more supportive today. They could have helped me with the fucking swans for starters.

"It is time."

I head into Stroud. I looked this place up when Rachel was talking about the six days of creation. There is an exhibition on in the museum in the park. I was going to do something around that. But then I saw that they had a secret garden. I love a secret garden. Oh shit, it is like in the *Notting Hill* movie. Wow, I just remembered the girls watching that in the school. Maybe that is why I picked it. I thought it was something to do with ducks or geese in a secret garden, but no, they sneak in there, don't they? In the movie and sit on that bench. I need to watch that again. I am sure Miss Walker and I can watch it over Christmas. It is bound to be on.

I pull up in the park next to the museum. It is ten o'clock already so there is nobody around. I get out of the motorhome and walk over to the secret garden. It is about eleven steps from the motorhome. That is the type of distance I like. I am not sure why it is a secret garden. The door isn't locked, and it is signposted the secret garden. I can make out in the dark that it is a pretty garden, with a few pretty statues. I go back into the motorhome and just take them out one by one and place them sitting in a circle in the garden.

"Yes, Mrs Green, a secret garden. Just like I am your little secret."

I am not sure what she is on about. I think she was probably hoping for something a little more special for her. I am not sure why? Just because she put out a few more times than the others doesn't mean she gets special treatment. She should be giving me special treatment. Again.

I go back into the motorhome and collect the masks and the eggs. I place an egg into each of their laps and ensure they all have masks on. I was going to make them sit on the eggs, but if they fall over now as they can't balance that will spoil the scene. Besides, Mrs Green and at least two of the others might lose the egg if they sat on them. Some days it felt like throwing a sausage up Grafton Street. Carl Carnegie used to say that about some of the girls in the school. That was mean I shouldn't have said that. It is funny how I remembered him when I was working outside. If he hadn't have swum to France that scene would have been perfect in Brighton. It would have made me even more of a legend than I am there at the moment.

I then go back into the motorhome and drive away. It is that simple. That simple and that boring. I guess that is why I was feeling a little strange about it all. I could have been delivering milk or post. Am I nothing more than a glorified postman now? I didn't feel like I needed to work for it. But it does help, the fact that I can be in and out of a place.

I get back on the road and start heading towards Tewksbury. I fear this is going to be pretty much the same. In fact, I know it will be. I am almost prepared and Rachel and Ross are ready. Well, the swans are ready and all I need to do is secure Rachel and Ross to them.

I am sure they would have made a cute couple in this scene when they get to Tewksbury. Well, if she hadn't lost her head, that is. But let's face it, she isn't the first woman to lose her head over me. She won't be the last either. I just got that. It is Ross and Rachel. Oh my God, that is another connection, isn't it? She dated Brad Pitt for a while, didn't she? I am starting to think like an A-lister, always trying to work with A-listers.

It takes an hour, but we finally arrive closer to Tewksbury. I am going to let them sail into there. It will be more dramatic for the town. They will love it. People will be taking so many pictures from the pubs on the river.

I pull up by the riverbank. There is nothing else around. A riverbank in the middle of winter. That is such a shocker. Mad dogs and Englishmen or was that summer. I can't remember I know my nan used to say something along those lines for weather. I go to their room and take the swans out one by one and throw them on the ground outside the motorhome. I then go and fetch Rachel and take her outside. I tie a swan to each of her arms and her legs. I then go and get Ross and do the same. Well, to his two legs, and I tie both his hands together to one swan. It will look like he dived in. A little more manly for him. He will like that.

"No, I don't think it will be cold." Maybe I spoke too soon. He is not that manly. I don't think it will be cold. I think it will be fucking freezing, if I am honest, but I don't want to tell him that.

"Listen, you don't hear Rachel complaining, do you?

"No. That is a fair point." It is a fair point she doesn't have a head so it would be hard to hear her complaining.

"It was her idea. I think she is a huge fan.

"Yes, of both of us. The whole head in the box was from that film. She practically begged me to be in the scene of the seventh day. And then it is the movie *Seven*. On the River Severn! Not sure why it has an R in it, must be the English spelling. But all of it adds up, doesn't it?" Yes to twenty one you smart arse.

"I don't know. Maybe she was always mistaken for that Jennifer girl. That will be where the obsession started. You know how popular the whole Ross and Rachel thing was. How lucky that she ended up in a scene with Ross? I mean, you could not write this shit, I tell you. Genius!" All of this will be amazing for the book. I could write this shit.

Right. They are both tied. That was simple.

How the fuck do I get them into the water now? I drag Ross over first. I get him to the edge of the bank and try to roll him in. It isn't working. I try pushing. That isn't working

354

either. It would be a lot fucking easier if he wasn't tied to three large inflatable swans. What dick tied them on?

Fuck!

I am going to have to drag him in from the fucking river. I take my shoes and socks off and roll up my trousers. I then put my toes in. It is fucking freezing. It is a good job that he is face down and can't see this shit. I am fucking shivering. My eyes are nearly crying it is that cold. I manage to get him in. He slowly starts to float out a little. That is one.

I quickly get up and go and drag the rest of Rachel to the water's edge. She is even harder to get in. It is the fourth swan that's making this even fucking harder. I pull and pull some more.

FUCK!

I am in the fucking river. I pulled and she gave way. I am sure she must have been holding on to the side and then let go on purpose. I am fucking soaked, soaked and fucking freezing. I stand back up and pull her in full. I give her a little push so she is next to Ross and then I get out and back on to the bank.

Fuck that is cold. I am fucking shivering. I can hear him whingeing about it from here. I don't know what he is whingeing about though. In a day or so he will probably be in a five-star hotel, paid for by *The Times* newspaper. I have to go and shower again in that damn motorhome. For the last time fucking time, I tell you. That thing is going, and soon!

I watch as they float down the river towards Tewksbury. It is a sight to be seen. It is going to be a surprise when they meet, the two of them swimming under the water. I will have to remember to get them snorkels when I am making the movie. So they can see where they are going. And flippers. They will be able to steer better with flippers.

It has been a fucking lifeless day six and day seven. I am glad they are over. I am better than this. I am so much better than this. I can't be remembered as a postman. That is not how this ends.

I need to prepare day nine before I complete day eight or I will just not have time to get it all done. And it needs to be fucking better than this.

S and T and the sixth and seventh day of Christmas.

Done!... Achieved. I don't want to say done. It doesn't deserve it. I want to say achieved.

Chapter 20

Verwood. Do you think it was very woody around here at some point and then they lost a couple of ys? Maybe they gave one to Ross? That is why he was on it. V is another unpopular letter for a town. I was very lucky that Verwood was this side of the country though. Imagine if I had looked while I was in Tyneside or something. That was really handy.

I just can't rock up in this town in the early hours after Usk though. I need a plan. The traffic could really screw me up with that distance. I head into Morrison's. There are a lot of Morrison's. Feels like there is one in every town I visit. Maybe I should have had a conversation with them about some advertising. I have spent a lot of money with them over the last few years. They did something about Shine too didn't they. I remember the song. That would work well. Time to Shine with Edmund Carson. I do like the old market place in here. Looks like a real market.

I find what I am looking for, Okra. I am not sure they do look like that. I go back to the motorhome and head down to the grand piano store. It is about two miles away. That is handy. Venable's Grand Piano Store! It is like they were waiting for me, isn't it? I mean another V in a V. That can't be a coincidence? They probably opened it as soon as they clocked on the Alphabet Killers plans. It will make them a fortune.

I am not worried about any of the press looking for me today. They will all be in Uxbridge or under something. They will be hiding in bushes with those big lenses. I guess that is why I haven't seen them anywhere? With The Blackout in place I suppose they can't get caught photographing me? They have probably been following everything that I have done from the shadows. That will be how there are songs about me and everything. The press are probably the ones leaking it all onto the Dark Web? All in the hope that the ban gets lifted soon?

No, nobody will be looking for the Alphabet Killer in Verwood. But the press are probably here already. They need to understand the amount of work I have had to put into this, the planning. I will have to make sure that it comes across in the book and the movie. The fans will get a real feeling for the commitment I have for them.

I get to the store and go in for a walk around. There are a lot of security cameras and locks on the door. That is going to be an issue to get back in here later. How much is a grand piano worth anyway? A hundred, maybe two hundred quid? I walk over to one. Twenty fucking grand for a piano? Twenty grand! No wonder they have the name grand right there in the title. I would want it to play itself for twenty grand. Oh, this one does play itself.

It must be like in all those old horror movies when the piano just comes to life. That is the one. That is the one I will have to use. A self-playing piano. I think I am going to have one of those in my house in Camden when we get there. That would be so cool.

I look around the shop some more. I ask the guy if he has a restroom. He does. I go to it. That is it. That is the best way of getting in here. There is a window big enough to get through. I reach up and take it off the latch. I leave it closed. Hopefully nobody is going to notice that. Besides, I am never going to be able to fit a piano through it. Why would they even look?

Okay, I have the place. I just need to find a lady to work with. I think I may as well go back to Usk for that. There is bound to be a lady or two there as it is still out in the countryside. That is where ladies hang out, I am sure. All hunting and horse riding.

I don't agree with hunting though. Not for the poor animal. Poor thing, minding its own business and then a group of dogs and people on horses come chasing it across the fields. No, I don't agree with it. Every life is important. People need to respect that more. Maybe I can be an ambassador for that once I retire. Famous people do that don't they? Work for good causes. I am that type of person.

Usk is a two-hour drive. This is real commitment tomorrow. Commitment to try and get both of these days done overnight.

I get back in the motorhome and head in that direction. I stop as I reach Farnham. There is a huge sign about a Christmas fair in Weymouth. It is a four-day thing from Friday to Monday. There is an actual funfair and everything. That is not what caught my attention though. It is going to be opened and attended by the Lord of Weymouth. The Lord Mayor of Weymouth, to be precise! He is a Lord of a W. Lord of a W! That has to be worth a look? I head in that direction. I have till tomorrow to get to USK, so it is not as if I don't have time. It is about thirty-five miles. Only takes me forty-five minutes. I class that as a success on these roads.

Is that a fucking isle? No way! Weymouth has its own isle. Isle of Portland, wasn't that a kids' show? I am sure I remember Portland as a kids' show. It only has a town called Weston on it. Weston with a W as well! I need to go back to that Morrison's and put the lottery on as the world is falling into place. It is a long way to Y, but I could do it. It would be worth it.

Besides, I owe him!

I drive onto the isle. I have never been on an isle before. Not that I remember. I head to The George Inn. Uncle George would want me to visit there. I am hungry. I can't live on cheese sandwiches and cans of Coke. I grab my baseball cap and put it on. It helps that people wear them a lot everywhere these days. I can't believe I forgot it when I went to the pub the other day. That was stupid. I need to be more careful. Slipping up now will mean that I am not remembered for it. The Alphabet or Christmas. They will say that I failed on both. That is not me. I am not going to fail this.

I go inside and order some food and a Weymouth fruit cider. That will help with the local thing again. It isn't bad. I ordered a shepherd's pie too. It says home-cooked and made with local beef and veg. All of that makes me look like a local. The food comes in ten minutes now that is service. It is a good shepherd's pie. Has baked beans in it too, it gives it that sweet touch, almost like my mum used to make. She used to always grate cheese on top too. That would have been good. I miss a bit of home cooking. It seems I have been eating out for years now. I think I will do a lot of home cooking for Miss Walker when I retire. Especially after the cookbook has come out. I can imagine I will be throwing lots of dinner parties too. Maybe even host my own cooking programme, the fans will love that.

I pick up the local paper and start to read it. It helps people not notice me if I am behind it. I don't need a selfie buzz around here today. They will know that I am going to work here at some point. It restricts the view from half the people in the room which isn't a bad thing either. It has the Lord Mayor's whole agenda. He is on the isle on Sunday. That is perfect. I need to find out where he lives though, or at least where he is staying. I didn't see many five-star hotels on the way in. If I am going to work with him, I am going to have to follow him home. I can be down here Saturday afternoon. I will have to keep an eye on him and where he lives.

Sunday he is judging the bake-off competition and a cider-making competition. An afternoon of cider and cakes, that doesn't sound too bad.

I finish up my food and head back into the car park. I have parked in the corner by the tree so I am not in the open. I need to lose this tomorrow. I have been too open about my cars. They are not paying me to advertise them either. No, I need something a little faster to help with the distance. I get in and head back up towards Usk. It is a long drive, but for the first time I have a plan. I can see the light at the end of the tunnel. That is another one of my nan's sayings. I am going to waste all these if I don't write them down. I just need to be locked up in a room for a while with nothing but and pen and paper.

It takes most of the day to get back. People must be travelling home for Christmas. They must have broken up for work or something there is so much traffic on the road. I park up just outside the town and walk in. It is getting dark, but it will give me a chance to walk around. I looked up the town of Usk. There isn't a lot to it. Although there is a prison, which I thought was interesting as it doesn't seem like there would be enough people in the town to fill it. I would have liked to see what a prison looks like. My dad went to Alcatraz once. He said it was amazing, on an island too. Wait, now that rings a bell. Haven't I heard that somewhere recently? Yes, I am sure of it a prison has just been built on an island?

I wonder if they do tours and stuff? They could make it a bit of a tourist attraction or something?

I have lucked out with the main attraction in Usk. That is the right word, isn't it? Lucked out means lucky? There is only a farmers' market in the middle of the town. The maids they will be milking in a farmers' market. I walk through the town. There is little else here. A couple of bars, but I am not going to risk some company today. I head back to the motorhome and call it a night. I need to be energised for what is to come.

"Okay, today we are going to complete day eight and day nine. It will leave us three. Just three more days of Christmas, or whatever they will call it in the future.

"Thanks. Yes, Edmass is good. Carson is good too.

"No, I think Carsonmass is just pushing it a little."

There is a lot of cheering and laughing from everyone. This is their day, and finally I can get rid of this motorhome.

It was a good idea. I just wish I had employed a cleaner at the same time, and I cook. I have been leaving them food for weeks and they are hardly touching it. I step outside for some fresh air. I really need it. I look around me. I am not as far in the sticks as I thought. I am off the road, but it looks like there are a lot of farms and big estate houses. I look around. They are big houses, really big.

Lots of money for those houses. You would need to be a lord and lady to own a house like that! That is it, that is who lives out here. They will all be their country homes. How do I do it? How do I always end up it the right place at the right time? Lords and ladies everywhere. Now that is a plan. I head back into the motorhome. I need another shower. I am going to take one here, but if I get the chance I am going to ask one of those lord and ladies if they have a guest room with a hot fucking shower.

I shower and get dressed. I have just realised that I have dressed as him. I didn't mean to. It just happened. The ONE is making an appearance in the countryside. Is this part of this worried thing again? If something goes wrong today and the ban is lifted and the press find me then at least the first photo of me to be published in what, a year, six months, will be a classic photo, a black-and-white photo. I put my knife where it belongs. This feels right. Being dressed like him. This feels like home to me. I need to remember this for the calendar. I can see the ONE in a field, behind a tree or something for the month of July. It will show my playful side.

I leave the motorhome where it is and go for a walk. I leave the hood down but keep my cap on. I don't want people putting two and two together and getting four.

I keep looking left and right as I walk. Any one of these could have a lady living in them. I carry on walking until I watch as a Land Rover pulls out of a long driveway. There is a bloke in the front seat. He is on his own. He could be a lord. All dressed in the country style of clothing, that tweedy stuff. I cross the road to get a better look at the house. There is still a Land Rover in the driveway. Now that is a sign: if they can afford two of those cars then she must be a lady. She is going to be there, doing whatever ladies do.

That is the house where I am going to get my lady from. I need to take the long walk around though. I can't risk her seeing me walking up the driveway. She could call the BBC or anyone. There is a public footpath at the side of the property. I am not sure why people buy houses where anyone can walk through their land. When I have my country mansion I am going to have iron gates and security. There are some right weirdo's out there. You have to be safe. There are lots of bushes that should cover my walk. It will be good as long as I don't bump into any press hiding away. I walk up and come to the property from behind the barn. I would have made a good spy. I know how to do these things. I am just a natural. Always three steps ahead of everyone else.

There are three dogs. Big fuckers as well, but they are all in a kennel outside. It looks a nice one so at least they look after their animals. They will definitely be country lords and ladies. I walk past the barn. I count three horses. She is definitely a lady. Who else would have three horses? I mean, you can only ride one at a time, but to buy two friends for her horse, that is real money. Or is it one per dog? Is that how it works?

I head in towards the house. I am going to love my country home, with a flat in Chelsea or somewhere like that. That is what they will have. The lord and lady that live here. A flat or an apartment in an expensive part of London. I try the back door. It opens. That is a good sign too. It is good that they are all trustworthy neighbours. The last thing you need is untrustworthy neighbours. It is a lovely house. I can hear the radio playing in the kitchen. Just like my nan. She liked to listen to the radio when she was home. I must have caught her singing along to Abba at least a million times.

I creep in and stay close against the stairs, waiting to understand the layout of the house. "Dancing Queen" was her favourite. That one and the one about the train station. I can hear someone in what I presume must be the kitchen. I can smell something too. I think it is fresh bread. Is she making her own bread? Do ladies cook? I did wonder what they did all day. For some reason I thought it was open fairs and lunch with royalty. I need to be careful it is not a maid or something. I take a peek. No, that is no maid. She is older, but she is hot older. Hot like something you would have to have a lot of money to impress. Having a title must get you a whole other class of woman. That bread smells amazing. The smell is filling the whole house. That is all I can think about now. Fresh bread and butter!

I am just going to have to go for it. I take another look. It is a big kitchen. I am thinking back to that diner now. What if she is actually a lot bigger and it is just the distance that makes her look small? I can't go through that again. I almost died. I look around the hallway. There is a table with a house phone, and a vase which has roses in it. Who has a house phone nowadays? You would think rich people would have a mobile, with a butler to carry it around for them. I reach over and knock over the vase. It smashes on the floor. The water spoils the rug on the floor. I don't think the water was very clean. It has really made a mess of that.

"Hello?"

I knew that would get her attention. I can hear her coming closer. Is she wearing high heels as she makes bread? That is real class. I bet her underwear matches and everything. Posh girls always have matching underwear. I am ready. As she turns the corner, I am behind her. One slice at her throat and she is done. It was a clean slice. I grab her and pull her close. The smell of her blood oozing out mixed with the fresh bread is making me horny. Horny and hungry at the same time. The blood does smell rich. I knew it would. I carry her into the kitchen and place her gently on a chair. She is a lady. I can't have her falling on the floor. I look around the kitchen. The bread is on the side. It must have been fresh out of the oven. That is what makes the whole kitchen smell just wonderful. I take a look at her as she sits in the chair. She is a different quality. Something that tells me I have to treat her with respect. I can't wait to see that look in her eyes. The look in her eyes that is grateful that I arrived. Grateful as she knows what is going to come next. Her.

"Do you mind if I help myself to that lovely smelling bread?"

She is not awake yet, but there is no way that I can last until she wakes up. I go over and take one of the loaves. I find a bread knife and cut myself a large slice.

I taste it. It is as good as it smelled. I devour the first slice as if I hadn't eaten bread before in my life. As I do, I spot the butter on the side. It is under a glass dome. Surely it should be in the fridge? Is it healthy to have it just sitting on the side like that? I cut a few more slices and then butter one. That is heavenly. Wait, no, not heavenly. I take the other slice over to the lady as she sits in her chair.

"Do you mind?"

She still isn't awake. I thought she would have been excited to spend time with me now she knows that I am here. I am sure she won't mind. They never do. I dip the bread into her neck. It is still pumping so it fills half the bread for me. Oh, that tastes good. It tastes real good. I can't remember the last time I had fresh bread.

"You know, this is really quite good. Okay, it is better than quite good. It is amazing. You should sell this bread. You would make a fortune." I don't suppose that she needs the money. But it would be a good second income. She still isn't awake. I look back at her. She is just sitting there. That look is not in her eyes yet. I thought it would be by now? She looks very wealthy. Something almost regal about her. It is a shame it was such a lovely apron, she has made a right mess of it now. They are probably designer clothes as well.

I walk over and find a big towel. I take it over and wrap it around her neck, just loosely enough to stop the blood trickling down her clothes. I look at the floor. There is blood on the floor, but it is a tiled floor. I stand looking at it for a minute. It has me fixated as if I had forgotten something. I am glad it is a tiled floor. For some reason I am really glad about that. I need it to be a tiled floor.

"I think that we need to go." I have that feeling again. That feeling that I may have just done something that I shouldn't have. I have that feeling that I could have ruined everything. I could have, couldn't I? What if someone comes looking for her? What if she has servants? I should have checked that. What if she was making the bread for some fete she was opening? They may be expecting her? I can't do day eight any earlier. I can hardly rock up to the farmers' market when it is in full flow.

I need her to disappear until tomorrow. Disappear being the word. I pick her up and place her over my shoulder. I take her to the front door. There is a key rack on the wall. I can see the keys to the car. I pick them up and we head out of the door. I place her in the passenger seat and head back into the house and into the kitchen. I need to sort this place out. I find a mop and bucket and start on the floor. I manage to clean up all the blood, well, nearly all the blood, all apart from the chair. I take the chair and put it in the back of the car. I can't leave evidence of what happened. It is too early. I don't want the press here, not today. They will get their fill soon enough.

It needs to look like she just went out shopping. I go back into the hallway and pick up the vase. That should do it. I look down at the floor. That won't do it. I roll up the rug. That has to come too. It is too much of a mess. I take it out to the car and place it with the chair. I go back into the kitchen and pick up the half of the loaf and take it with me. They will do DNA on that. I am sure. She will probably have secret service people working for her. This way they will think she only made two.

I head back to the car and drive it off the driveway and down to the motorhome. I park it on the field side of the motorhome so that nobody from the road can see it. That should do it. She has disappeared, as far as anyone is concerned.

"It will only be for a couple of hours."

She still isn't speaking. I am sure she should be awake by now. I undo the scarf a little to check her neck. It might be too tight or I may have cut a little too deep. I check. No, it is fine. She should be fine.

"Is everything okay?"

Still nothing. Maybe she hit her head or something. Maybe she is a bit dazed and confused. I feel her forehead. It does feel a little cold. I should just give her some time.

I leave her where she is and head into the motorhome. I need to blow up the inflatable cows and make sure everyone has their wigs on. They are all happy today. I can hear them talking among themselves. They are all ready to work tonight.

What the fuck is that? It is almost a battering noise on the motorhome. I look out the window. The rain is coming down so hard. I don't think I have ever seen rain like that before. Where did that come from?

Fuck!

That reminds me. I was going to take a shower. I needed a hot decent shower. I miss having my own en suite at home. I miss… home. Odd thing to say? Does she remind me of my mum is that what it is. Why am I thinking of home?

I suppose I could go outside for a bit? Stand and let the rain hit me hard. It is a bit cold for that. Besides, what would happen if I got a cold and had to take a week off? I don't have anyone to step in and cover me. I really needed to look into the assistant thing, but I didn't. I am always taking too much onto my own shoulders. Now it is too late. I will be retiring in a few days.

I start on the cows. They aren't as big as the swans so I don't even bother asking the rest of them to help me blow them up. Not that they would. I then go into the bedroom. I take the wigs and place them all on their heads. It looks quite fetching actually, for blondes that is. They look like maids. Although Frankie already looked a little bit like a maid. Small waist, and ponytails, with nice boobs. Although this weight loss thing has made them shrink a little. Sometimes the girls go too far with this appearance stuff. Some men like a bit of meat on their girls. Not me. But some men I am sure. Normally skinny men.

I go back to the main area and take a look out the window again. She hasn't moved. She looks like she is watching the rain. She is probably upset about not being able to go horse riding. I am sure it will clear up soon. Once she is finished with the press tomorrow she will be able to take them out for a ride. She may even have time to take out all three.

I go back and sit on the sofa. I am not sure what else I can do today now. I don't want to walk into town in this weather. I will get soaked. This is the worst storm I have ever seen. I switch on the TV. I will be so glad when I can get a normal life back. Well, not normal, it will all be parties and openings. Movies and book signings, but what it won't be is dodgy motorhomes and third-rate hotels. Five-star all the way. I was born for five star.

Eight hours! Eight fucking hours and the rain has not eased. It is still coming down as hard as ever. This is going to be an issue. I don't really want to leave them outside in this.

The wigs could come off and the cows could fly away. They could probably get pneumonia or, worse, a man flu...

That is something you don't see every day: a cow flying away. It would be a funny sight.

I think there is a brolly in the drawer. That would help one of them stay dry but not the eight? Besides, how can they milk and hold an umbrella at the same time? That is just nonsense.

I sit looking around the motorhome. It is my last day in this motorhome. I think it is the longest time I have lived somewhere since I left my nan's.

Fuck!

That is it. They don't need to leave. There is room to leave them in here. I will just park it up at the cattle market. My fans will understand. It shows the caring side of me. They will love that.

I count. There are three seats on the sofa, four at the dinner table and then one in the passenger seat. That could do it. I just need to make sure they stay in position. I need a new nail gun. I am so going to have one in my garage when I retire. Two. You can never own too many nail guns.

I start to put them in place. The dining room table is easy and it looks good. They are so light to move around. I think all the work I have been doing lately has really toned me up. That will be good for the calendar and the pictures. The girls will love it. It has made me stronger than I have ever been.

It is done. They all have a cow in their laps and their hands in, well, nearly the right place, with the help of Sellotape. Maybe the nail gun wouldn't have been as useful for an inflatable cow. There is a beauty in the fact that the world is expecting it. The wigs and the cows will do most of the work for me. As soon as they count eight, they will know I have been here. They won't think someone else has done this.

I don't have a lot of choice other than to drive down and walk back. I don't think that the lady should drive, not if she has been dazed and confused all day. That is no good for her. I can use the brolly to get back. It will help a little bit with the rain. I would have preferred it to be one of those big golfing ones that my dad had and not one you can fit in your bag though.

I set off. I need to make it happen fast as I don't want the lady to be found, or wander off. In her condition she could go straight to the press and that would not be good. I head into town and to the farmers' market. It is an easy approach. I just go straight to the car park and then park up. It feels too easy. A lot of this has felt too easy.

"I think this is it, guys.

"You are welcome. I really wouldn't want you to be out there in this type of weather either. This way when the press arrive, the picture will still be fresh and you will all look as good as you look now." They do look good. They look like a family. I think that they are all a family really, aren't they, the people that I work with? A club, if you like, with only a few elite members. I need to remember that. In the future people will pay to be part of a club like that. We could hold elite parties and everything. I wonder if you could get different levels of membership. They would subscribe in the millions. Everything from just a quick meeting to working with me to the full Edmund Carson package. The ladies will all pay for that.

"Yes, I am sure that you will all be famous." That is the reason right there. That is the reason to pay to be in this club. All of these people will go down in history and be remembered every Christmas from now on. There grandchildren and great grandchildren will be talking about this.

I go and grab the brolly and then head to the door. I take one last look at the scene. It isn't everything that I wanted, but it will do the job. I head out into the rain. It is bucketing it down. I start down the road. I then stop and run back to the motorhome. I go inside.

"Sorry. I was having a real moment then."

I grab my bag and pull all my stuff together. I left the money, the clothes, the sack with the toys on costumes in and everything in the motorhome. That would have been embarrassing. Imagine if we had to stop somewhere on the way to the piano store and I had no money. That would have been bad in front of a lady. Five minutes later I am back in the rain. I run with all my bags and my brolly back to the car. It takes me five minutes. I am soaked. I get into the car. I should have really kept a towel to dry myself.

"Hey, you. Do you mind if I borrow your towel?"

She doesn't say anything. I can't believe that she is still dazed. I take the towel anyway. I need to at least dry my hair. I take my hoodie off and throw it on the back seat. That will help too. I dry my hair. That is better. It stops the rain falling down my back. I place the towel back around her neck. It will help clear the mess up a bit now that it is wet.

I then start the car. It is one of those push buttons. I do like them, like the Q7. It makes travelling a lot easier if you have a really good car.

"Okay, let's get this done."

Still nothing from her. I wonder if I should have brought some smelling salts, or should I take her to a hospital or something? Maybe there is some real damage there. It won't take her long to go through one of those CAT scan things.

"Is there anything I can do to help?" Still nothing!

I start to drive. There is no point going to the hospital. She probably has her own cover anyway. Rich people do that. They don't use regular hospitals. They have private hospitals and private care. I will need to get that cover for me and Miss Walker. We can't be using normal hospitals with the fans. There would be too much excitement.

I warm the car up and put both our heated seats on. That may help with warming her to me. I know when you feel warm and toasty you feel more comfortable, and you relax and start talking…

It has been forty-five minutes and she still hasn't said a word. I wonder if it is the address thing. Maybe I am addressing her wrong?

"My lady, I am sorry if I have upset you?" The use of the words my lady may help with breaking this silence. Still nothing! I can't think what I have done to upset her. I mean, I treated her with dignity from the beginning. I placed her on the chair and then cleaned up the house for her. I even mopped the floor for her. I mopped the fucking floor.

I don't know what it could be. Maybe she was looking forward to the bake sale? Or maybe she is a mute. I didn't think about that. I lean on the wheel and make a sign at her. I am sure this was some type of sign language. Nothing. I try again.

I think it is sign language. I put my thumbs up, that is universal in any language. Nothing!

"Fuck you." That is the easiest way to deal with it.

I carry on driving. She is doing this on purpose. Rich people are so snooty. They think they are so above us. I am rich. I am a fucking millionaire, for Christ's sake. We should fucking compare bank accounts, love. I will speak to anyone. I speak to everyone. I treat everyone equally.

We carry on driving. I am just going to ignore her. I reach over and turn off her heater. She doesn't deserve to be warm and toasty now.

It takes another hour and a half before we get to the shop. It is on a corner which is good as it means I can get to the back of the store. There are no overlooking houses. Nobody is going to be worried about a piano shop.

I park up. At last the rain has finally fucking stopped. I go outside and go to the window. I push it. It is open. I knew they wouldn't look at the latch. Nobody is worried about you robbing a piano shop. Either that or they are all trustworthy neighbours here too. It is good to see that.

I go and fetch her from the car. I don't speak to her. If she is not speaking to me then I am not speaking to her. I take her to the window. I jump up and push it. It comes open straight away. Result. I try and lift her up to it.

"Grab on."

Fuck!

I said I wasn't going to speak to her. I lift again. She is just not helping. I am trying to get her just to go through the window. I try again. She keeps falling down.

"Don't you want to do this? Is a piano not good enough for you, my lady?"

I thought this would be right up her street. She has probably being playing the piano since she was little. The least she can do is put some effort in.

"The chair." Why didn't I think of that before?

I put her down on the ground. I don't care if she is a lady. She should act like one. I head to the back of the car and get the chair. I put it under the window and then try to carry her and lift her up and put her through it.

"FUCK!"

Now we are both on the ground and the chair leg is broken. She must be heavier than I thought. The bread was all for her, wasn't it, not for a fair? She is eating three fucking loaves a day. I wish I hadn't worked out so much now or else I would have noticed how fat she was. That will be all the bake sales that she goes to too.

What the fuck am I supposed to do now? She is a waste of time. I stand up and leave her there. I go back to the car and fetch my knife from my bag. If I can't take her in in one go she will have to go piece by piece. That will fucking teach her for not helping me out. I stand over her. It is a shame because if she had been more of a lady I would have spent more time with her. I don't mind the older woman, and she would have never had a real man, just a rich snobby one.

I could take the legs and throw them in, and then the arms and then… What am I going on about? I only need her hands. I bend down and take both of them off. That was tougher than I thought it was going to be. I can climb through the window. I look down at the lady. I am not sure what to do about her though. She doesn't deserve to be in the scene. Not after the way she has treated me today. I think she is common, not that common is bad. But she doesn't deserve to be treated any better than a common…Wait, is common the word? Isn't it common her? She is a common her. Yes, that is it.

I go to the back of the car and take out the rug from the hallway. I lay it out on the ground. I collect her and roll her in it. I then go and place the rug under the window where the chair was. She is a common her and she deserves to be treated like a common her person. Like the ones they do in the movies. I don't ever remember those gangsters being called common him though?

I step on her and climb through the window. I step on her again as I climb back out and go back to my bag. I pick up the Okra and my marker. I then climb on her again as I go through the window for a third time. She will not be giving me any good feedback. I can hear her story to the press now about the night she spent with the legend Edmund Carson. Is it bad that you get one or two bad reviews? People won't believe it, will they? They will just think it is because I didn't shag her. She is probably the first woman I have worked with that didn't get the full experience. I wouldn't give it to her if she paid me.

This is Christmas anyway. People don't think bad of other people at Christmas. They will probably make rhymes about her being a Grinch and that will be all her fault.

Fuck!

No, they won't. It will be all about the dancing. Cut a rug, cut in a rug and dancing. I fucking amaze myself sometimes how my life comes together.

I head to the self-playing piano and try and open the lid. It doesn't open. I look around. There is a switch. I turn it on. The lid comes up and it starts to play. That is so cool. I love that. It must be a big party piece. I turn it off. I don't want it to draw a crowd to the shop. Although I could pretend to play for them. They would never know it wasn't real.

I take the hands and my knife and take off one of the fingers. I place it on the reception desk. I then take my knife and the lady's other nine fingers off. I go back to the piano and I turn it on again. I place the fingers on the keys and then quickly turn it off again so they are trapped in the lid.

I am lucky the piano is white. I take what is left of the hand and write "Play me" on the piano. I then place nine pieces of Okra on the top of the lid. They will get the lady's fingers' gesture, I am sure of it. Once they speak to her as well then they will understand. It won't be a pleasant conversation for them, but the press will spin it in the right way for me.

I go back through the window. I jump out.

Fuck!

I forgot she was there. She didn't even speak to me when I jumped on her. That is how mad at me she is. Right up her own arse, isn't she? I should probably do her up it just to show her that I am bigger than this. It would show her how big I am and I would make it hurt.

No, I am not that petty. Each to their own. She will look back at this moment with regret. She will regret the time she could have had with me.

Instead she is cut in a rug... I think it is genius. I have given a whole new meaning to the phrase haven't I?

U and V and the eighth and ninth day of Carsonwinter?

No Carsonwinter doesn't work. Ed Winter. Sounds like that Jack Frost guy very Christmassy. Either way U and V and the eighth and ninth day of Edmass…Oh what the hell it was better than six and seven and I so excited about the isle. They are…

Done!

Chapter 21

Sunday is the day of the bake-off. It is also nearly the end. Tonight and then tomorrow and then a trip up north and the twelve days of Christmas are done. The Alphabet is nearly done as well. All but one more day. I can't believe that has gone so fast. Everything has just fallen into place. As I got here yesterday it is like fate is opening the door for the conclusion of it all. It did seem odd yesterday though. I haven't been on my own much over the last month. Seemed very quiet.

I had thought about baking before, well, before the Pied Piper anyway. But as I got here, the stands and the cakes and the pulley systems, well, they are all laid on for me. Why wouldn't I? The fans will get it. I can spell it out for them. In fact, I will spell it out for them. I am just that kind of artist.

It was a result that the lord mayor lives in Weymouth, although he lives in a normal kind of house. That was a shocker. I thought a lord would have had a mansion or something.

Maybe the queen doesn't pay them as much as she used to. I mean, they must be on a few hundred grand a year, I am sure of it. It is not hard work. Yesterday he had to judge a cow and pony show. I mean, surely you just pick the fattest cow and the smallest pony.

They do seem to love him though. That chain that he wears it is a bit of a symbol of power. Like the collar. Is it too fancy a Christmas present for Miss Walker? I could see her wearing it. It is not like the necklace Richard gave Julia though. She seemed to like that one too. Wait, they were both wearing a suit too. Richard Gere and the Lord Mayor. The suit does make a difference. I am going to have to remember that when I am on one of those judging shows or in LA.

I head off to the show. He is going to be there from two o'clock. I quite like the idea of a cake and cider afternoon. Not too much cider though.

As I arrive, the place is rocking. Can you say rocking to a fete? They do love these things down south, don't they? They are all into the traditional. I do feel a little bit sad about the lady yesterday. Having spent the afternoon at one of these things. I do get how it would have been nice for her. I do get why she may have been a little bit mad about missing it. But she had to realise that being part of this, part of my story, was going to be more for her. She will be dining out on that for months. Dining out, I haven't said that since I was at my nan's. She would have loved this. I would have loved to take her to one of these. She would have won today. Her cakes were really good. Her sausage sandwiches were awful, but her cakes were lovely.

I go over to the main tent. It is big. There are all types of events going on in here today and he is at the centre of all of it. There is the bake-off and the cider competition. There are various jam competitions. Tomorrow is winter fruit and veg and local beers. Winter veg must be all the stuff you put in stews and cassaroles? I bet the farmers are having a field day. In an actual field, on a day. I just got that.

I walk through the stalls. I know them all. I walked this whole tent last night. They do love their cooking and cooking stalls. There are pots and pans and tools of all kinds just to make a cake. This is where the inspiration came from. I had other ideas, but this, this is almost the penultimate night. Like the penultimate episode of a series. Where you leave them all thinking, wow is that the end? It is not the end. I don't think there will ever be an end.

I try a couple of the ciders from the stalls as I walk around. The fruit ones are nice. The ones that look like dishwater aren't. They only give you a little thimble full though. Just to whet your appetite. Wait, is that what it is? Is your appetite on your tongue? I never knew that.

I head out of the tent and over to the fairground and watch the tractor pull. There is another hour or so till he judges the show. I wouldn't want to miss that. It is his last event of the day.

I think I could have been a farmer. I could have worked outside. I am not sure about when it is raining though. I am sure they wouldn't work in the rain either. I watch as they pull logs about and the cranes do some dancing to music. I bet they do that a lot on the farm, just to show off to the women. It would get you laid. It is very impressive.

It is time to head back in. I do. I watch the lord mayor wander through the stalls one by one. He has quite a following. They all look like ladies as well. He doesn't have one with him so maybe he is single. I am sure a few of these women will be offering him a bonus if he picks their Christmas cakes or current buns. Oh, I could do with a current bun right now. It has been ages since I have had a current bun.

I look up at the stage. It is dangling above our head on a whole system of pulleys. It really inspired me last night. Really made me think about what they would like to see. The fans. Yesterday when it came down with all the trophies on it, it was such an event. That is what they will have been missing. And it will be fresh. Fresh with new friends I have worked with that they weren't expecting. Back to my best. They will never believe the story of the lady then.

I carry on and watch him as they get down to the last three. Even I can see who is going to win this. She is hot. She is that cook hot. Like the one on the train. She is that type of hot who knows that she likes cakes, and all you can do is think about covering her in chocolate and licking it off. Oh, and dipping strawberries everywhere, strawberries shouldn't be dipped. Nigella, that is who it is, she is Nigella hot. I watch. Yes, I was right. He pinned the number one rosette on her chest. I wouldn't have minded doing that.

Maybe I should go home with her for tea first. I am now thinking of all types of fruit with chocolate body paint. I could give her a few hours of my attention.

I stand around waiting for him to leave. She is still here too. She is going to miss her opportunity and it is like he doesn't want to go. He spends the next hour walking around with people, tasting the cakes and the cider. I see his driver come in. It must be time. It is a good job there is only one road out of here. I go to the car and wait for him at the top of the street. He takes another forty-five minutes. His driver must be really pissed off at him. He was probably round the back of the tent with Nigella. I don't have time to do that now. She is going to be so upset about that. She could have had a real man. I will have to ask him how she was.

I follow him. He only lives in Weymouth, and his driver will drop him off. I would have thought his driver lived with him. Like a butler. Lords should have butlers, right? Like Batman. If Batman was English he would have been a lord. Or a knight. Oh, *The Dark Knight*. I get that now. Hidden meanings, they are everywhere today, aren't they?

I wait till the driver disappears. I go up to the door and knock. He answers and as he does, I raise my knife and stab him straight in the neck. It is so fast he doesn't even scream with the excitement of seeing me on his doorstep. I push him backwards and get into the house. He is on the floor. I step over him. If he is anything like the lady then he is just going to ignore me anyway. I walk into the house. I am walking on tiptoes. Why am I doing that? I am not a fairy? I am actually checking around the corner. There doesn't seem to be anyone else here. I go from room to room, but not like I normally do. More like I am creeping around the house. What is that about? No, nobody is here. That was weird. What made me do that? Is this due to that panic thing again? Panic is a strong word. Maybe I am worried that I am not going to be able to achieve it. I suppose all artists feel like this before they break a record or achieve the ultimate goal. I go back into the hallway.

"Yes. Yes, it is me." Well, there is a surprise. I go and pick him up and bring him into the living room and place him into the chair.

"To be honest, I met with a lady a few days ago and she was a bit of a bitch...No that is too strong a word. Didn't speak to me at all. I just thought it was something about class. I didn't expect you to want to talk to me either.

"That is very nice of you to say. No, I don't think legend is too strong a word." It is the word. But he knew that. That is why he said it. I like him.

"Yes, actually, yes, you are the lord. The lord from the song. I am glad that you keep up with the Dark Web. Do all lords and ladies do that?

"Just you. Well, thank you for the support. Yes, I have a plan. I know there was due to be ten. But I have to have my own spin on the song. Otherwise I would be just copying whoever wrote the original one all those years ago.

"You did? Yes, I was at the show. We are going back. Actually that is where, if it is okay with you, I am going to make the scene. It is a little Edmund Carson to have a scene. But what the hell, I am getting to the point of finishing the greatest run in history. It is good to let people know I have flair." That is a good word for me. Flair. I don't use it enough.

"I don't mind at all." Why would I mind? It is not often a lord asks you to share a glass of wine with him. I head into the kitchen. I could do with a nice glass of wine actually. I don't do that enough either. Treat myself.

"Hi, I am home."

What the FUCK?

Who is that? We aren't expecting anyone else. He didn't mention that. I can hear someone close the front door.

"How was the bake-off? Any surprises?"

I get back to the living room and stand beside the door from the hallway.

"Dad, are you home?"

As she turns the corner I am on her. I stab her straight in the back. She lets out a scream. It is faint, but it is one of those cute ones. Almost the same sigh she would make when having sex. But quieter. It will be the cold steel going into her body. It must be about the same. Something really hard and long entering her insides, making her sigh. Although my knife is only about ten inches! The smell explodes around the room. That is what I was waiting for. I pull her close and smell. It is amazing. What is weird is that I have worked a lot over the last few weeks but very rarely got the smell. I pull her close and then stop. What am I doing? Her father is in the room. You don't do anything like that with her father in the room. You have to respect your elders and this relationship. I place her on the sofa and go back to the kitchen and pick up the wine and two glasses. I take a minute to compose myself. He doesn't need to see that through my trousers.

I take them back to the lord. I pour the glasses and wait. I am not sure if he is going to be happy or not. I nearly got carried away there for a second.

"Really? That is good to know. I am sure. I am sure I will be able to fit her in somewhere." I suppose technically she is a lady, or a princess? Or maybe a lordette, ladyette? I don't want to ask and seem stupid. He is happy as long as I make her famous too. The whole family together. It is the least I can do after how nice he has been.

"It is just the two of you then." I scan the room. I can see that there are only pictures of the two of them.

"No, she is a very pretty girl." I look over at her. I didn't really get a good look at her before. She is a, a girl. I am sure of that. She isn't ugly, ugly. But she isn't really anything to write home about. She could be considered plain, I guess. I look at her again. Yes, plain is a good word. She will appreciate that.

"Very pretty." He is smiling. That is good. I think all dads must think that their daughters are gorgeous. I can imagine he is thinking when she wakes up she is going to have the surprise of her life having me in the room with them.

I suppose I could. I could give her a go. Bent over from behind she will look good. Long dark hair, the type you can tug from behind.

"Really never had a real boyfriend?" So she is a virgin. I don't think I have had a virgin before. I know most of the girls I sleep with have never had one so big, so it is like them being a virgin. But I don't think an official virgin. Do you think he is telling me that on purpose? He wants her first time to be with a celebrity. Doesn't he know that I will ruin her for other men? Once she has had me for her first, how is anyone else ever going to live up to me?

"So, if you don't mind me asking, where is her mum?

"Oh, I am sorry to hear that. I know what it is like to lose a mum at an early age. My mother had an accident when I was still young." That will put him at ease. To know we share an experience.

"Hey, you are awake?" I go over and sit her up. She doesn't have a bad rack. I mean, it is doable. Bouncy. I could play with them for a while. It feels like it has been a while since I have seen a pair that still look bouncy. The girls over the last month have been losing far too much weight, just to impress me.

"Yes, yes, I am. I was just speaking to your dad about you." She is giggling and tossing her hair a little. They are the, you can fuck me moves right there. If she knows the moves, then I doubt she is one. She is not a virgin.

"The scene, yes." I am back to paying attention to him.

"Yes, of course she can. I am thinking she can be part of the piper's scene. Maybe wearing a chef's uniform. You know, dressed all in white. I should have really got one of those hats.

"You do? Upstairs? A full white outfit?" How lucky is that?

"That is a good plan, my lord." I take a big swig of my wine and top his glass up so that he can keep drinking while I take her upstairs and get her dressed. It is like he is saying I want you to take my girl upstairs and do her. I am not the type of person to not take advice from a lord. So I go over and pick her up and do just that…

She was not a virgin. That was not her first time. It did make me realise that I have missed fully rounded boobs too. They just taste better. I take a shower. It is the best thing ever. I have been dreaming about a shower for weeks. An hour later we are downstairs and she is dressed in a pair of white jogging bottoms and a white shirt. I think it is his shirt.

"Sorry. We couldn't find the outfit that you mentioned." I don't even think he had one. He was just using that as an excuse for me to take care of his daughter. I think he can tell by the look on her face she was really taken care of. Her popularity will rise as soon as the world finds out what we did together. I am almost a little envious of the rise in fame. When you are already at the top it is hard work just to stay there. But these people, these people, they are climbing quickly from nobodies to somebodies.

"I think it is time that we get going, my lord."

I go and move the car onto the drive. It will be easier to get them into it. I then fetch them one by one and place them in the car. It is a good job it is dark this time of night. It gets dark really early down south, and up north.

It is only a short drive over to Weston. I have been here what, three, four times now and I am yet to go and see the sea or the sand. I was so looking forward to seeing the lifeguards in their hot red bikinis. I am not going to be able to see that now and I need to go first thing as soon as the clock strikes one minute past midnight. I need to be here for both days. Besides I am not sure that is what they wear in the winter. Bikinis would be a little cold. Being here for two days is what will make this special too. Creativity is my gift to the world. One minute past midnight. It is a long drive from here.

I head towards the tent. As I get close I can see the lights are off, and I switch mine off too. I don't need Eric seeing me approach in the car. I watched him last night. Why they would have a guard outside an empty tent, I don't know? I suppose there may be stuff in there now. Getting ready for tomorrow!

I pull over to the side of the road. I know where he stays in his little cabin. I need to go and deal with him first. I leave them talking in the car. I don't think I have ever worked with just a dad and his daughter before. I mean, I worked with families, well, multiple families, but I have never just had a dad and a daughter. Wait, not had a dad and a daughter. Worked with. I need to be careful in my interviews on this one.

I am keeping as low as possible. I will blend into the darkness. I wonder if that is why black is a classic. Just so you can stay in the shadows. I am underneath his window. I think I will wait. It is not that cold and I don't even know what is in there. Do security guys of tents carry guns? That would not be good. If not a gun I am sure they would probably be carrying a taser? I am sure it wouldn't affect me, but I am sure it would tickle enough to distract me from what I need to do. That would be a concern. I sit by the door. I can hear him moving around. Also sounds like he has the radio on. Must be a grown-up station as there is a lot more talking. It is a bit late for Jeremy to be on? Although after my appearance on his show he has probably got more shows to do.

I wait some more. It takes about twenty minutes and the radio goes off. I am waiting now. He is coming. The door opens and he walks down the steps and turns and locks the door. As he turns again I am straight in front of him. I stab him three times in the stomach. He wasn't expecting that. He grabs onto my shoulders. He looks like he wants to kiss me. That is nice. He is a sixty-year-old black man, which means he is not my type, but it is nice that he wanted to try. He is on his knees. Look, if I am not going to kiss you there is no point dropping to your knees, mate, as you aren't getting that.

I go behind him and drag my blade across his neck. Sometimes I feel it is not needed, but it does seem to make them talk and be engaged a lot sooner. I wouldn't want him to miss anything. In fact, I wouldn't want him to miss anything. Sod it, Eric can come to the scene too. I sit him back on the step.

"I will be back, Eric. I promise." Is that becoming a signature move? The whole stomach to neck thing. I seem to be doing that a bit. I have to watch out for it. Maybe need to patent that. Get royalties from those copycat people. I go back to the car and drive up to the tent. They are both excited. It is understandable.

"Let's get on with this. I think we have an hour or two till midnight."

I leave them and go into the tent for a quick look around. It is all dark. I really should turn the lights on, but it might draw attention. I need a…

I leave the tent and go back to Eric and bring him up to the tent. I can borrow his torch now. That is perfect. I am going to turn the lights on before I go. Just to get the full effect for the visitors tomorrow. I wonder if they will give it an award? It will deserve it. Not sure how I will collect it though.

I go for a walk around the tent. Oddly, it is not as dark as it should be. Maybe it is because it is a white tent. I take a walk around the whole tent. There are all sorts of things in here already. There is a pumpkin the size of a wheelbarrow.

Fuck me, look at that carrot. That has to be one fucking large rabbit that eats that carrot. Why would you make vegetables that big they will never fit in the oven so you have to chop it up anyway? It seems a waste of time to grow something like that to me.

I find the controls to the stage and try them. They don't work. It is going to need power, isn't it? They will need a generator to be up and running. I go looking for it outside. Well, that was easy. It was right outside the back of the tent. I push the button that says start and it starts. Some bluish lights turn on. That is good enough. I don't need the full lights. These must be some kind of backup lights. I head back into the tent and head to the stage again. I press the buttons again. The stage comes down. That is perfect. I go back to the car.

"It took a while, but I got it all working in the end."

She is looking at me. It took no time to get her working.

"If you don't mind, my lord, I want to put you in place first and then build the scene around you." I take the rope and him back inside to the stage. I take him to the middle of the stage and tie the rope under his arms. That is good. I then take the other end and throw it over the beam above the stage. It goes straight over and comes down the other side. I am good at this. I am almost a professional athlete.

I really need to reconsider this retirement thing. I am going to miss these scenes. I mean, I will always be on stage but staging the scenes. Giving the audience a surprise that is what I do best. That is what I was born to do. Am I really ready to give this up?

I pull him up and then tie the rope to the column next to the stage. I can't believe how easy that was. And it looks good. It almost looks like he is leaping in the air for joy with his hands up like that. That is exactly the look I was going for. Exactly the look. I go back out to the car.

"He looks really good, Aurore." I am still not sure that is her name. I am sure that was Cinderella or Sleeping Beauty or someone like that. I think she was just having me on. Unless she is a princess and that is what lords have?

"I just need to get the trays out and put the pipers in place." I head to the back of the car and bring out the first tray of pipers. It is a good job I made forty of these. It took more than a hundred pots of cream to fill them though. Cream is expensive too. No wonder my mum only used to put a little dab on my apple pie. I am sure they must have been upset on that stand this morning when they noticed they were missing.

I go back to the stage and start on the design. It is a simple one. I just hope I have enough bags. I am quite good with this piping thing. I could have been a baker. I could have been a master baker. That is what they are called, isn't it? I go back and collect the other two trays. It takes me fifty minutes, but I am happy. It is time to spell it out for them. I go and hide twenty-nine of the pipers. I don't want anyone to find them so I put them in the tractor field. I then make sure that there are ten pipers on the design. I space them out as if that is where they were working. One at the end of each point and one in each of the Vs. That is eight. I randomly place two more. I stand up and count them. Yes, it is clear there are ten. I go and fetch Aurore.

"Yes, it is time." She is almost creaming herself there and then. Wait, creaming herself. I just got that. White cream.

"No. I wish I did have time for that also. That would be a lot more fun. You were really good." She was average, but you never tell a woman that. I am sure I have improved her skill set. So as long as I haven't ruined her for more men she will get better. I undo her seat belt and lift her out of the car. Yes, she is having an orgasm every time I touch her. Even more when we walk into the tent.

"Yes, I know." It does look amazing. I wait for it. She is looking, she is looking. I pick up a piping bag and hold it to her.

"And this one is yours." I can see her brain ticking over. She is a clever girl. She will get it. I am sure she will have gone to private school. That is where all the rich kids go, isn't it? There it is. I knew she would get it.

"I know. It is a piece of genius, right?

"Lords Leaping over a Large Piped X piped by eleven pipers on the ground in Weston.

"Yes, yes, yes, I knew you would get it. X = Ten, for Ten lords leaping.

"Yes. And the X is for X as there isn't actually an X in the UK. Piped by eleven pipers. You are the eleventh piper. It is genius. I love these piper things. I have hidden the other twenty-nine as it is a really big X.

"Genius." I kiss her. I properly kiss her. Her dad will be happy that she has made out with such an artist.

"I never thought about that. It is like science. X = 10 LL over 11 PP in W. I am so smart. Thank you for pointing that out for me." The press are going to love that. I put her in place. I gesture to her dad and he gives his approval.

I then go and get Eric and place him on a chair next to the stage with his arms folded.

"It does look good, Eric. I am glad you agreed to be part of it." It does look good. So good that it had to have its own security guard. I take my marker and go up to the stage and add the equation she mentioned to it. That will keep them puzzled, I am sure of it. They'll probably lead with that on page one of the paper.

"I don't know, mate. I am sure they will probably give you the award for it. I say if they do, mate, keep it. Keep it and say it was a present from me for looking after the scene all night."

He does look great guarding them. I take out my phone and take a selfie with him, and then one with the scene and the puzzle. I think I am overexcited; I have taken like two dozen pictures. It is amazing.

Penultimate. Now it is time for the ultimate ending.

W and X all together in one scene and the tenth and eleventh day of Christmas. Done! Done!

Done!!

Chapter 22

This was a harder task than I thought it was going to be. I needed to put my feet up yesterday once I got here, just to take some time for me to reflect on everything that has happened. It was good for me. I need to do that more when I am retired. This is going to show him. It will go down as the greatest achievement in this field of work in history. The films, the book deals, they will only touch the surface of what this has really been. People will remember this forever.

The amount of time I have been spending on the road means I am so looking forward to some quality time off. Retirement does sound good. But I can come out of it. I hear that all the time, people coming out of retirement. It is more a statement of a break rather than the end, isn't it?

I could have picked better locations though. Looking at the maps last night I could have made this whole thing a lot easier. I didn't really think some of them through enough and just travelled by the seat of my pants. I am regretting using Leicester for L now.

Not at the time, as now I own Halloween. But that would have been a better drive down tonight. Now I have to travel back down to Cornwall after this. I can't believe there are only seven places in the UK that begin with the letter Z, and six of them are in Cornwall. Especially now that I am now in York. But I do own Halloween and Friday 13th. And tonight I will own Christmas. Nobody in my field has ever done all of that. I could have done something different for Y, I know. I should have done. But this is personal and I want my fans to know that I still listen to them. I want them to know that they could all get the chance to be personal with me. I couldn't find that Sarah woman from *The Times*. I am sure we will do an interview at some point so I can deal with her then. You would think she would put her address in the paper to taunt me, but I guess she was too scared to meet me in real life.

He has been playing on my mind for months though so I had to come to York. I may not be able to post on social media, but I have been following him on Facebook. I know where he is tonight. He is having a quiet night in with the family on Christmas Eve.

Well, the family and me, the Alphabet Killer.

Y and Z and then Boxing Day I need to go and spend some time with Miss Walker. I was going to wait till New Year's Eve, but why wait? Let's just get our lives started. I haven't seen her for what, I hate to think how long it has been? Seems like forever.

The world is watching. The Dark Web is watching, I can feel it. After the tenth and eleventh day they will know that we are close to achieving something great. I wouldn't be surprised if there are a lot of people in York hoping that I will turn up. They will all be holding their breath, anywhere beginning with a Y today. They must all be excited today. I must be the only person in history that can make a whole town excited at once. I exit the hotel. I am getting looks. I am not surprised, but it is a great costume from Happy's. Abby was hot. She was Miss Walker hot. Nearly Miss Walker hot. I wonder if I would have been better doing the alphabet in girls' names. I mean, I must have done that already, but Abby would have been a great place to start. She would always come first. To be fair I am that type of lover. They always do come first.

York looks a beautiful place. I may spend a couple of days here when we are retired. Really learn the history of the place. That is the type of thing you do when you retire.

This guy wasn't very nice to me. I don't know why, but I can't get that out of my head. I never can. People should be nicer to each other. That's what you remember. Like Al. Every time I check into a hotel I think of Al. He was down on his luck, but he still wanted to help me. The world would be a better place if we just treated people with respect. I will have to go back and visit Al at some point. See how he is doing.

It's walking distance to his house. People are wishing me a Merry Christmas every time they pass. I wave at the kids. Although it is really hot under here. I am dressed as the ONE and as him. All of this just so that I can carry the sack with the drummers into his house. Come to think of it, I have spares. I should stop and give some to the kids. That would have been a nice touch. Something they will remember forever. The first present given from me.

I can't believe some people are so stupid. They tell the world everything without even thinking about it. He maps his run every day, proud of the fact he is running ten miles.

Anyone can run ten miles. I could run ten miles right now and I am wearing two lots of clothes.

I can leave at night and blend into the darkness once I get rid of the top costume. I am sure that was the reason. Either that or it was another subconscious decision as I am so close I need to make sure I look good if I bump into the press.

I should be thankful he is a social media addict though. The app he is using, MapMyRun, shows where you start. He has shown me at least a dozen times where he lives, although sometimes he drives to a park and then runs there. There must be a reason for that?

Then he tells everyone he is looking forward to a family night in with a movie? I know it is Christmas Eve but really? Besides, who goes for a run on Christmas Eve afternoon? Shouldn't he be getting stuff ready for Christmas? This is a time for family. He should know that.

I walk up to his house. I intend on waiting for him inside. The lights are pretty. She must have only just put them on as it is not dark dark yet. I knock on the front door. His wife answers the door. Fuck, she is quite fit for a blonde. How did he ever get a girl like that? He didn't look like he had a big dick? He must have money. Money always brings them in. Becky that was her name!

"Ho, ho, ho!"

She is smiling. Who wouldn't be smiling when Father Christmas knocks on their door?

"Why, hello, Father Christmas, how can we help you?"

I think she may have a thing for old Saint Nick with that smile on her face.

"Well, hello, little girl. Is your mummy in?"

That really makes her smile.

That has put her at ease. I do like an easy woman. Flattery always works. I don't know why men don't use it more often.

"No, no, my mummy isn't home, neither is my daddy. He won't be home for a couple of hours yet. Is there anything that I can help you with?"

I am sure there is so much you can help me with... wait, you don't talk like that unless you are flirting. I mean, real flirting. She wants me. Can she see through this costume already? Is it that obvious?

"Yes. Well, actually I have a little present for you..."

I place my bag in front of me and stick my hand in. She is leaning forward. She smells lovely. I pull my knife from behind me and stab her repeatedly in the stomach as I move her backwards. She hardly makes a sound. She falls backwards and hits her head on the table in the hallway. Ouch, that has to hurt. That thud was a real thud. That is going to leave a nasty bump in the morning. She is out cold. That was easy.

"Mum, who was at the door?"

That will be his daughter. Sixteen or seventeen, if I remember? I am sure she will be a fan. I close the front door and head up the stairs. It's a nice house. He must be doing okay for himself. It explains a lot. Don't know why he feels the need to phone into radio shows though. Who does that in the middle of the day?

Well, that's easy. If you put your name on the door then it just makes my life easy. Alison's door is open. I can see her sitting at her dressing table doing her hair. She is pretty too. It must have come from her mother's side. I am behind her and cut her throat before she even drops the curling iron. At least I think that's what that is. It looks good anyway. She is dark-haired with curls? Where has that come from? They both have light hair. I knew she was too hot for him. She probably has another man somewhere. Her hair looks really good. Miss Walker is more the classic Sandra Straight. But maybe she should look like that too. How do you even bring these things up though? Do you fancy changing your hair? Women are funny if you criticise their appearance.

Wait, what the fuck! Screaming is coming from downstairs.

"Mum! Mum!"

Shit, I think that's his son. I really should have checked to see if anyone was in the house. I was just too focused on Darren's movements. I run down the stairs. He doesn't even turn. Why didn't he turn when he heard someone running down the stairs? I grab him as he bends over his mum. I cut his throat too. He falls next to her. He probably thought it was his sister running to help. I stand over them both lying on the floor. That was more intense than I thought it was going to be. And quick, so quick. I am a true professional now. I am a master of my craft. This just shows it. The speed I can work with anyone.

"Hello? Hello? Is anyone else in the house? Anyone? I am looking for Darren? Anyone?"

The house is silent, at last. I don't need any more surprises.

Now for the movie night, but first I need to ditch a layer of clothes. It is so hot in here. I do. I leave Father Christmas in the hallway and I go and explore his house. It's quite nice. Nice kitchen. I can see myself with a kitchen like this when we move to Camden. I take a couple of photos. It will be a nice conversation opener with Miss Walker. We can't rent forever. I go back into the hallway. They are still both quiet. I move them into the front room. I lay the mum on the sofa. I love the fact that it's all an open-plan layout. It is cool. Is the kitchen in the living room or the living room in the kitchen? I put the boy in one of the chairs. I then go upstairs.

"Hey, you are awake. That was quick. You will be surprised how long some people take. I guess you must have been excited." Of course she was. It is me.

"Yes, yes, I am. I am glad you recognised me. It's been a few months since I have been in the paper or anywhere on the media. I say a few, quite a lot. They don't report like they used to. The news is a bit boring now, don't you think?

"I know, right? I know. I can't understand it either, but it hasn't stopped me. I have been working all the same. I am sure if you are sixteen you have been following me on the Dark Web?" I wait for her reaction. She doesn't correct me so she must be sixteen. She looks legal age to me.

"I am on Y and twelve so yes, nearly done. She must have been holding her breath to see if I would come here before I completed it. She still looks like she is holding her breath now. Poor girl all worked up.

"It is the first time anyone has done anything like this. You will all be going down in history as much as I am."

I lay her on the bed. I sit next to her. She knows it was a good line. It is good to give her hope of fame too.

"Yeah, your dad and I go back a bit. He has some opinions about what I do or have done. They are a little unfair, to be honest. I just wanted to chat to him about them.

"He does? He is just that kind of dad, I guess... My dad was similar. Always had opinions on what I should be doing and when. My mum would try to shut him up sometimes, but it never worked. Parents, eh!" We are developing a rapport so that is good. That is good press right there, and with the youngsters. A whole new generation of followers.

"I love the curls, by the way. They are really doing it for you. It gives your body more hair. I mean, your hair more body." I was distracted for a minute then, looking at her body. She definitely gets her looks from her mother.

"Quiet night in for you all, wasn't it? Maybe I could join you? That was my plan anyway.

"Couple of hours, eh? Yeah, your mum did say." She didn't say. I just didn't want to tell her I have been stalking her dad.

"I wonder what we could do with a couple of hours."

I know that smile. I don't need to be invited more than once. I undress her as she lies on the bed. She is definitely eighteen. I would say she has the body of a twenty-year-old. Her mum doesn't look old enough to have a twenty-year-old daughter. I undress as well. Briefly I think about the mother. She looks hot. Maybe that's where I should be. They are always a little more comfortable, the more mature woman. But she is blonde and going to have a headache, I know that. Women don't like doing it with a headache, do they? She took a nasty hit on the way down.

"You are not, are you? I should have asked first." I don't know why I said that. I didn't ask Aurore.

"No. Good, I like a woman with a bit of experience." I am not sure I ever want a virgin. I like a girl to know what she is doing.

I get on top of her and start. Something is not right. I slipped straight in, but it doesn't feel right. This is clunky and awkward. Well, not clunky. Don't even know where that word just came from. It is awkward. It doesn't feel right. I don't understand. I come out of her. There is like a piece of string in her... woman's bits. What is that for? Shit, I know what it's for...

"You could have said before we started," I whisper in her ear. I don't want her to feel embarrassed.

"Near the end, eh?"

She didn't think that I would notice.

"No, I just can't bring myself to. I am sorry." I could just pull it out? Would it make that much difference? No, no, I can't.

"Listen, I will say I did and you can say the same.

"People won't think that. They won't think that you weren't pretty enough. Look at you. Of course you are pretty enough. And who knows, later it might be all cleared up and we can try again?"

That was a little disgusting. Nobody wants to do it at that time. I understand that she is worried that she will never get the opportunity again. I can't blame her for it really. I need to look at it from her point of view. But YUK! I get dressed.

"How about we just put your dressing gown on, and we go down and sit with your brother and mother? That way, should the moment take us we can start again?"

She is smiling again now. I am just the best host.

I grab the gown from the back of the door and put it on her. I don't want to go through all that bra nonsense again. It's too hard. They must be able to invent something easier to hold them in. Hers were quite firm though. She didn't really need it. I help her down the stairs. She must be weak at the knees from all the blood loss. I mean, once a month they just empty everything out. I wonder if they get transfusions or something if they lose too much. It would make a lot of sense.

"Oh, you are all awake. That's good.

"I was just helping her sort her hair. The curls are amazing, don't you think?" I take her over and place her in one of the armchairs.

"I know. Something smells amazing. Becky, what is it?"

I walk over to the oven. I open the door.

"Is that roast beef? It looks amazing. With mustard seeds around the edge as well? That's a great touch. Hand- rolled by you, no doubt?" That is some quality cooking right there.

"Rare. I am more a rare type of person. But the smell is amazing. It can't have been on for more than fifteen minutes? It is still pink

"You put it in just as I knocked on the door, eh? I think it will go down a storm. No, you sit down and relax. I think I know what to do from here... Leave it to me. It will be my present to you, to cook you all dinner."

The veg is all prepared and ready to go on. I turn it on. This will be something they never forget. The day Edmund Carson came and cooked dinner.

"It is okay, I know my way around the kitchen. My nan was a stickler for a Sunday dinner. It was my favourite meal of the week for me. She was an amazing cook." Sometimes that thought makes me smile. Every time I think of her it makes me smile.

"I will find them."

I look. I find the eggs, the flour and the milk. I put everything together with a pinch of salt and pepper and a little drop of water. Just twenty-five mil, that was my nan's secret recipe tip. I have never forgotten it.

"Normally I would chill the mixture for thirty minutes or so. But that beef will be well done if I do. Nobody likes well-done beef. Well, apart from my mum. She was weird like that. Really liked it burnt all around the edges.

"The trick, the trick is four eggs. Some people put one or two. Not me. I put in four every time. It gives it that flavour, and you cook it round the beef. It has to be round the beef to take in the flavour. Yorkshire pudding only takes what, twenty, thirty minutes."

"Where did I learn that? It was in an old cooking book my nan had. Kellogg's, like the cornflakes, I think it was called. Made in the forties, or something like that? Little red book. It had lots of great recipes in it. I will have to lend it to you."

I pull out the beef and place the mixture in the roasting tray. Yes, it had only just gone in. I can see the blood rolling around the bottom of the pan. That is making me even hungrier.

Fuck, I did say I was going to have a real dinner before all of this was over. There is never going to be a better opportunity. To be honest, I don't know if that is true. Because everything always works out in my favour. I am a charmed man. Charmed, charming man. Yes that is me.

"You know what would go well with this stuff?

"Exactly. You all do follow me, don't you? I am thinking, maybe you, Chris? I would normally say Alison, but I think she has enough going on at the moment."

I don't think I can get the blood thing out of my head. I mean, if her body is saying she doesn't want it why would I? I grab a bowl and walk over to the chair that he is sitting in. I open him up. He is very skinny. I think I have seen him go running with his dad. Probably keeps himself in good condition for the ladies. Why wouldn't he? He looks like his dad. He needs all the help he can get as he doesn't have the money yet. I pull him onto the floor.

"There are what, five of us? I think I need the lot. Heart as well."

I take everything. It is not often I take everything, but I am nearing retirement. So I need to make the most of this opportunity to show my cooking skills. It will start them talking about the cookbook. It is going to be all over the press. I wouldn't be surprised if someone isn't already stealing my recipes.

"Ha ha! I am glad he has a good heart. Hey, like that Irish singer bloke. He had a good heart. They are hard to find, so I hear."

"It looks good. Very tasty. I think it is a little like veal. The younger the meat the better it is. I tell you, the first time it was good. But I never knew how good it could be until I was in the Lake District and worked with my friend's son. I was actually heading there when your dad and I were on the radio together."

I take the food to the cooker. I have made sure it is saturated in Chris. It makes a great sauce.

"It helps with the flavour, you know. I think it's sweet and rich at the same time. Mixed with the meat, it is really good. Trust me, I know what I am doing."

I sort through everything, and pick the best bits to cook for us.

"Liver, kidney, heart, it is all good. I find the trick to slowly poach them on a low heat with just a little pinch of salt and pepper and at the last minute give it a blast. Just to make sure it's really hot when serving. All of this with the beef and veg, it will be amazing." I put it all in a pan and on a low heat.

"Okay, dinner will be what, twenty-five minutes or so. That's how long the Yorkshire takes. Yorkshire! Does it actually come from here? Is that why it has that name? I am so glad I am cooking it here now. Really make me feel like a local.

"A movie? Yes, that is what we said, let's look for one while that all comes together. You have a lot of DVDs. I didn't even know people had these things any more. It's all downloadable. Have you ever heard of Netflix, Amazon? Hell, if you want to break the law I know a lot of pirate places.

"No, that is fine. It is good you are law-abiding. There are some real classics here. You have a lot of black-and-white movies too. I was just talking to someone about black-and-white TV, classics." I am surprised he has such good taste. In women and in movies. I think we could have been great friends.

"*Die Hard*. Love them. *Logan's Run*. Now that is a movie. Did you see *The Island*? It was called something like that. Tried to make a remake of *Logan's Run*, but it wasn't any good. You can't beat the original.

"Okay, *Die Hard* it is. You can't go wrong with a bit of Bruce. My dad was a huge fan. We used to watch him in everything.

"He actually had them all on tape. Yes, tape. *Moonlighting*, now there was a series. Yes, with the blonde girl. I didn't like her. Maybe that's where it comes from. I ended up preferring the dorky girl on reception over her. Mister Pesto, or something silly like that." Now I think about it, the whole thing may have been about that blonde girl. Cybil something. She used to wind me up. Bruce could always do better, but for some reason he was fixated on one woman throughout the whole thing. Who would be that stupid to be fixated on one woman? Yes, that is why I prefer dark-haired girls. Well, I prefer Miss Walker. I settle for others.

"Talking of dads, is that him? He is home early."

I hear the car pull up on the driveway. Why didn't he just run from home today? Why would he drive somewhere to go for a run? That troubles me. I think I may have a word with her before I go to check his phone and his app to see who he is running with. Running is just running it doesn't matter where you start.

That was close. Half an hour or so later he would have opened the door to me.

"Now, let this be a surprise. I will hide behind the door. Don't give me away now…"

I go and stand behind the living room door. I hear him come through the door and take his shoes off. I should have taken my shoes off. I have just noticed they are all wearing slippers. She didn't say anything. I know stars are hard to talk to, but house rules are house rules.

"Shhh…"

I make sure that none of them call out. I know they won't. It will be a nice surprise for their dad. I can see the excitement in all their eyes. Becky's are practically sparkling all over the place.

"Hi, honey, I am home."

That is a bit corny. I do like it though.

I smile at them. They are excited about the surprise, I can tell. He walks into the room.

"Something smells amazing…What! No! No!"

He goes running towards his wife. I am surprised. I thought the kids would come first. I mean, she is hot, but aren't the kids the most important thing? He is on his knees in front of the sofa. He is trying to hold on to her. I creep up behind. I put my finger to my lips for the kids. Last thing I need is them giving away that I am here. I stand behind him. I plunge my knife into his neck. He screams. He screams a little bit like a girl. He grabs at my hand. All that does is make me move the knife about. Doesn't he know that won't help him? I take it out and plunge it in again.

"Hi, Darren. We have been expecting you."

Now that is a line. I am going to have to remember that for the movie. I like it when the line is good. We have been expecting you is good. He falls to the floor. He is kicking about a bit. I almost feel sorry for him. I thought he wouldn't have wanted that. It makes him look a bit silly really. Like one of those flapping fish. I leave him there. If he is happy to embarrass himself in front of his family then that is his problem. None of them looked that silly. I wonder how her headache is. It must be pounding. Maybe I should get her a tablet or something?

"Darren, a little catch-up as you are late. I am making us a fabulous dinner, and then we are down for a *Die Hard* movie.

"Tonight, I have decided, is all about forgiveness. You know, I was a little mad at first. I was mad about the fact that you called me out on national radio. And you were ahead of the game with the Father Harry thing. And not very favourable about the way I work. But then I realised, I realised, that wasn't your fault. The press have not been very good to me. Sure, at first they were. I was followed, praised, worshipped even. But then they got bored of me. Again at first I blamed them. But it wasn't them, it was me. I wasn't entertaining enough. Sure, I tried to keep it fresh, but it wasn't enough for them. They are a fickle bunch, I will give them that."

I go and check on the beef.

"It's good you have a glass door. You are not supposed to open the oven while the Yorkshire is rising. Another trick my nan used to teach me.

"This is nearly done. I hope you like it rare? Anyway what was I saying? Oh yeah, the press. The press started to be unfavourable to me. And that's when you spoke up. You spoke up when they had started this hate campaign about me. Is hate too strong a word? Maybe! You were only led by what they made you believe. And here was me bad-mouthing you for a while. I thought I should come here, work with your family to show I do not hold a grudge against you. You know, that Yorkshire is really rising. I love that. There is nothing but flour, eggs and milk. A little bit of salt and pepper and it climbs the sides of the oven. I love how that happens." I am not telling

411

him the secret recipe. They can't know it just because we have shared some moments. Let's see how he is when he comes around.

"Does everyone like all of the veg?

"Cool. You know, I think dinner in front of the TV. That really screams family night in to me. As a kid I always lay in front of the TV with my dinner. When my parents let me anyway which was most of the time. They were good parents, all in all. Which I am sure you guys are. Darren, Becky, I have to say, you do have some great kids there."

I fetch five plates from the cupboard and lay them on the side to start dishing up the food.

"I am going to take the meat out before I start dishing up. Is that okay? I like it to rest a bit. It actually absorbs the juices more."

I bet I sound like a chef to them. The amount all that stuff is on the TV, I have picked up a lot of the lingo that they use. That is going to come in so handy for my cooking programme. Come dine we me, Edmund Carson.

"Good. You know, Darren, your family were very keen to work with me. We were almost done in a matter of minutes. They are a credit to you. They really are."

I take the meat out of the oven and rest it on the side. I walk over to Alison and whisper in her ear.

"Are you going to be okay with a roast dinner? I could make some soup or something? Maybe some crackers? They always help me sort my stomach.

"Cool."

People generally want soup when they are ill, especially when their stomach is all upset. It can't be very nice for her. I am glad I am not a girl. I can imagine that it must piss her off a bit, once a month. It is no wonder men need to sleep around more. They are never out of action. Must be like having a car that breaks down for a week every month. You would need another ride.

"So, five roast dinners with all the works coming up."

I dish everything up. That Yorkshire is amazing. I keep the best bits for my plate. I deserve that. Little bit burnt and crispy at the ends. Really takes the beef flavour in. The sauce from the heart and kidneys with the Yorkshire looks amazing. I could have been a chef, I know I could have. Full-time. I put all the plates on the coffee table including my own and sit Darren up.

"There you go. We are going to watch *Die Hard*. It was Chris's idea. Hope that is okay? I knew that you wanted a movie night in.

"On Facebook? Actually I am a follower." That will impress him. Probably make his year. It will impress his kids too.

"I read it this morning. I did want to say congratulations on all the running by the way. That is real dedication, to be out of the house for a couple of hours a day." I look at Becky to see if she has clocked what I was saying. She has. I can tell it in her eyes. There is almost a fear in them. As if I shouldn't be mentioning it. It is their business I know. I shouldn't really be interfering. Besides he isn't going to do any better than her.

"Yes, we are already on Y and clearly number twelve. I know it hasn't been fast, but it has been amazing, hasn't it? Have you followed it all?

"The world has. I knew the press thing doesn't really matter when you have real fame like me. People find a way of getting their Edmund fix." They know exactly how to speak to celebrities. Ensure that you let them know how important they are and all is good.

"They are over there in the sack. They are a little gift for you all when I leave. You know, when I have set the scene.

"I know, there are some things I have done that will definitely go down in history. I was thinking that exact thing on the way over here. Some of these places will never be the same again. Some dates will never be the same again." I can see from their faces they agree. I own them all now. I have the dates and I have made myself a UK-wide treasure by visiting all my fans. I need to ensure that I visit some of those places when I do my first tour.

"It needs some salt. Did you put any in the veg before you started?"

I get up and go back into the kitchen.

"No worries. Not all people salt the water first. Anyone have a need for anything else? Pepper? More mustard?

"No. No problem. Wait, wine. Red sounds perfect. Rioja. Think that will do."

I open the wine and grab three glasses.

"Alison, I would offer you some, but that is really your parents' call."

They are shaking their heads. No wine for her. I sit back down with my back to the sofa and dinner in front of me. I pour three glasses. I pass one to Darren and his wife.

"A toast. I just wanted to say that there are no hard feelings. The past is the past. It's all about the future now, yours and mine. I hope you are all as happy as I am." Well, as happy as I intend to be once I have retired and start raking in the movie money. Although I am quite happy now. It does make me think about this whole retirement thing. Is it really for me? This is a great night in. I clink both their glasses and take a big swig of the wine. It is good. I must remember this wine. I tuck in. This stuff, this stuff is delicious. If I was a cook by now, I would have a string of restaurants and TV shows.

"I tell you, the mustard on the beef, that's a magical touch. Really gives a bit of heat to the beef. I am going to have to do that again."

I don't know why people ever have gravy though? This sauce from Chris is out of this world. Maybe I should have made them some? They aren't complaining, and I didn't see a gravy jug anywhere? It is how food should be cooked. The blood really gives it depth. I guess that is how someone invented black pudding. A few sausages and some blood spilled. I eat the lot and some of theirs. They don't seem very hungry. I guess it's the shock of being here with me. I get up and close all the curtains. I then move the coffee table over and lie down in front of the TV. I pull Alison down to one side and Darren on the other. Chris and his mother are still in the chair and laid out on the sofa. They look so comfortable. I am sure I saw Becky sneaking a look at her phone. Probably sending a quick text to her friends to tell them what an epic night in they are having. You don't get a celebrity coming round for dinner all the time.

"This is what I call a family night in."

We lie down to watch *Die Hard*. It's a real family movie. It is a Christmas movie. It's always Christmas, isn't it? In all of them. Other than the one with the bomb in the park. Oh, and the one where he is older and his kids are older. It was good, but the first one is the best. We watch the whole movie. We laugh and jump all at the same time. It leaves us all with a real Christmas feeling, I can tell. Although it was loud in places the sirens and things. They almost felt real.

"That was great. I loved that. I forgot how good the movie was. I forgot how good it was just to have a simple night in as well." I give them all a genuine smile. I really enjoyed that.

"Ha ha! Celebrities are always throwing stuff out of windows, aren't they?

"No, I have never done that. I should be more adventurous." I am not sure I want to throw a chair out of a window.

"Oh, and the bear. I love the bear too. Although I bet he was stoned in the back of that limo." I should take one of those home for Miss Walker. It would be a nice Edmass present. I get up. Wow, I think my head is spinning a bit. I am sure I can still hear the helicopters from the film.

"I think I drank most of that whole bottle. I don't think any of you helped." Alison did. I swear I saw her nicking a few sips when we were lying together. I don't think her parents really cared. It is not often you get this type of company. Besides, the alcohol probably helps with the girl pain.

I go to the sink and wash my face. That Rioja is strong stuff.

"I think I have stayed long enough. I should leave you all to cuddle up and watch another movie. I need my rest anyway. It's about a six-hour drive tomorrow."

"Yes, Chris, and the real Santa is coming tomorrow. I am sure you have all been on the nice list." He is a funny kid. I hope he has been on the nice list. I hope everyone is this year. Although when it is my holiday. I will be rewarding the girls on the naughty list more than Santa ever did.

I take out the DVD. I can, I can still hear helicopters, and there seems to be a lot of noise outside. I wonder what the fuck that is. I fetch *Logan's Run*. I place it back in the player. This is a quality film. They will really enjoy it.

What the FUCK is that?

Before I hit play I can see my name on TV.

"Is that my name on TV?" I look around at them all.

They are nodding.

"I am glad you think so. I thought I was drunk for a minute then. I am on the TV?"

They are all cheering. Have they lifted the ban for Christmas? That would be an amazing, amazing gift for the world. I take it back. I take back everything I said about the government. What a time to do it. What a time to bring happiness to the world. Christmas is officially mine. I turn up the volume.

"The police have confirmed the notorious world-renowned serial killer is inside this Yorkshire house. Their belief is that he currently has at least four hostages."

What the fuck?

I don't have any hostages? How the fuck did they know I was here? That is the noise I can hear, isn't it? All of that is going on outside this window. I recognise that fucking street. They are not supposed to be here, not now. Is this some kind of joke? That is what it is, isn't it? Some kind of joke.

"Guys, is this some kind of joke? Are you trying to wind me up?"

It is probably a video or something. I swap the channel to trip them up? I am on that channel too. I switch again. I am on that channel too. I keep going, I am on every channel. I am on every fucking TV channel. The world isn't reporting anything else. It is all about me!

"I am on every fucking channel!" I let those words sink in and then I look at them all again.

"I am on every fucking channel. At last, every fucking channel." I run into the hallway and fetch the drummers. I don't have time. The press are already here. They are going to be banging down the door to get a look at the twelfth day of Christmas any minute now.

I add twelve of them around the living room. I throw the rest and the sack and the Father Christmas costume under the stairs. That is not how I want to be remembered. I am wearing the perfect costume for tonight, aren't I?

"I am on every channel!" I shout as loud as I can. That is amazing. I knew I would be, I knew it. I knew that Friday the 13th, Halloween, the twelve days of Christmas, they were all going to make it for me. They have made it for me, haven't they? This is it. I am back!"

They are all nodding. They are so happy for me, I can tell.

"I said, I said the Alphabet Killer, he was going to make it. He was the one to bring them back to me. He was the one that was going to make me a worldwide mega star." That will show him. That will show my father. I told him I was going to make this end my way. In style. Edmund Carson style.

"Fuck! I am only on Y!" I look over at them all watching me dance around the room. I didn't finish it. Why did they turn up today?

"Why did they turn up today? I am only on Y?" They don't think they have won by turning up early, do they? They haven't stopped me.

"Becky, you are right, you are so right. They are probably going to give me a police escort down to Z. That is real respect, isn't it? That is real fame. I bet Jack didn't get a police escort." What was I worried about? She has nailed it.

They are, they really are excited. They had to be so excited about the whole thing they couldn't wait. They will probably help me pick someone out also. A local celebrity to end the Alphabet on. Where does that woman live that does the TV programme *Countdown*? It will probably be her. That would make a perfect ending. Hot and good with letters. Although sometimes she does look blonde.

This, this right here is all worth it. It is really worth it.

I go back to the TV and listen to some more.

"Police sources tell us that Edmund Carson was expected in York sometime today due to an event that has been blacked out over the last few months. We have been told that once he is in custody the police will release his full activity over the past six months. Which, if true, will be the most anticipated police briefing of all time."

Of course I was. They are not stupid. They knew I was coming. The most anticipated police briefing of all time. All time. Jack is going to be so proud.

That is the phone. The phone is ringing. Is that on the TV or…? I turn the TV down. No, it is the actual phone.

"You are right, Darren, it is probably for me." I walk over and pick up the phone.

"Hi."

"Hello, am I talking to Edmund Carson?"

"The ONE, the Only." They will like that. That will be good for the book and the movie. The guy on the end of the phone, his heart must have skipped a beat at that.

"Hi, Edmund, this is police inspector Stephen Murphy. I was just wondering if you were planning to come out of the house this evening and come and meet with us?"

I put the phone down.

I can't think about going out there like this. I need to freshen up a little. There will be press. I turn the TV up some more. There are press, I can see them. There are loads of press. Wait.

"Chris, is that the front of the house?"

He nods at me. I should take a look.

"Yes, if you want to." Alison wants to take a look also. I think she just wants to share the limelight. She knows that the world's press is out there, and to be seen with a superstar is going to be amazing for her. I pick her up and take her to the window. I am a great host. I hold her in front of the window so she can have a better look. There are blue lights flashing everywhere and spotlights and everything. How long have they been out here? They must have been setting up while we were watching the movie. I look back over at the TV. I can see me on the TV and Alison. She is looking good. It is a good job that she has done her hair.

The phone rings again. I take Alison back and then answer it.

"Hello?"

"Hello, Edmund. It is police inspector Stephen Murphy again."

"Hello, Stephen."

"I could see you with Alison. Is Alison coming out with you?"

I wouldn't have thought so? Surely they want me out on my own. It is more of the big reveal moment. This is my moment, isn't it?

"No, I don't think so. I will be coming out alone. Alison is not feeling her best. A little girl trouble, to be fair. Are the press there?" I know they are. I was just testing. I want to make sure they are front and centre for the event of the decade. A decade or a century, I am not sure which one is bigger?

"Yes, Edmund, the world's press is waiting. They are all here. They have been waiting a long time for you."

I knew it. I knew it wouldn't just be the English press. The world is waiting for me. Thank God for the Dark Web.

"Okay, I won't be long."

I put the phone back down. I go to the sink and wash my face and hair. It is a good job I had a shave this morning. It was only because I was wearing the fake beard. And the ONE costume was a good plan. No, it was a great plan, as if I knew today was going to be the day. I must have had a moment. This is how the world will want to see me again. I stand and look at my reflection in the kitchen cabinet.

I am so good-looking. I have always known that. I am a good-looking man. The world will always forgive a good-looking man.

Forgive?

As the word hit my head I feel sick. I feel like something has upset my stomach in a matter of seconds. How did that happen? I didn't feel sick before.

It was the word, the word forgive.

What would they have to forgive me for? I have done nothing but entertain. I have done nothing more than ensure that the UK takes back the crown from the world. The film industry will come back to the UK because of me. I am almost royalty, so why would the word forgive come to mind? I am still staring into my reflection. It has been a long time. All of this, all of this work, it doesn't feel like it. It feels as if it was only yesterday I was peddling to school and then taking the bus over to Caroline's school. So much has happened. My parents, my father will understand now, won't he? He will understand I had a plan all along. I forgive him for the words he said to me. Maybe that is how the word forgive fell off my lips. My nan, she will be so proud. She will be looking down at me and smiling. My time as the ONE, Father Harry, the Alphabet Killer. That time has flown by and they are all with me. They will always be with me.

I will still be the Alphabet Killer, won't I? They will let me finish this, won't they? This doesn't count as a success for them. This counts as a joint ending, doesn't it? They are doing this to ensure that I finish it.

Feels like I have been staring at myself for ages. I take my phone out of my pocket and take a picture of my reflection. I want to remember this moment. I want to remember when the world came to help me get across the line.

"They will let you. They will help you."

I know that voice. I spin around. She is here. She is standing here in this house with me, with them. She is not even looking at them; she is looking directly at me. She is wearing her black dress. She will always be wearing that black dress. Forever.

"You're here?" There is a lump in my throat as I say that.

"Of course I am here. Where else would I be?"

I walk over and kiss her. I kiss her like it was the first time we kissed. She kisses me back until she pulls a little bit away from me.

"It is time."

I know it is time. I can do this now. Now that she is here, there is nothing that I can't face. We stand and just smile at each other. This is the moment I should have taken a picture of. This is the beginning.

"Do you have it?"

Oh, she means it is time for that. That makes me smile even more.

"I do. It is in my pocket." I take out the box with the ring in it. I start to go down on one knee. And then I stand up again.

"Not here. We should do this out there. In front of the world."

She is smiling even wider. But she is shaking her head.

"Edmund, this is the time. What is out there is for you, and you alone. You deserve this moment. We have a lifetime ahead of us to announce our love." My smile is bigger. She is remarkable. She knows how much this means to me. We are about to start the rest of our lives together in the mainstream entertainment circuit. This is private for us. I go back and kneel in front of her.

"Miss Walker." She doesn't need to hear the words again. She drops to her knees too and I place the ring on her finger. She kisses me. Really kisses me. Then gives me little kisses all over my face. She knows this is my time.

We both stand up. I let go of her hand. I go over to the DVD player and turn on *Logan's Run*. I mouth the words Merry Christmas to them all and then go back to see her. We stand by the front door.

"Are you ready, Edmund?" my heart is beating so fast. I know everything I have been working for has been leading to this moment but I can't still help think that I am not fully ready. She is smiling at me. I don't think I will ever forget that smile. She is the most beautiful woman in the world.

"Are you ready, Edmund?" She has never had to ask me twice before.

"I am."

I grab the handle to the door. I turn to see her one more time. She has gone already. The box with the ring in is sitting on the table by the door that Becky hit her head on. I stand and look at it for a moment. I can't think why it would still be there. I look back at the door and then open it and step out to the night.

I stand on the step and look at all of them. There is so much noise, so much noise. There are flashing lights and police and press everywhere. There are ambulances as well. They must be in case someone faints. This is exactly how I imagined it. I walk into the middle of the street. I am throwing the odd little wave to everyone as I walk towards what I presume is the bulk of the press. There are a lot of flashing lights. There is a lot of shouting as well now. People are almost screaming my name. I knew that they would. It means the world to me. It will mean the world to her as well. I turn to look back at the house. I can see the curtains moving. She will be watching. This is my moment, but it is the start of the rest of our life. I can see the police walking towards me. I stop and look at the press. I know they are shouting my name, but it is so loud I can't hear everything they are saying. I drop to my knees in front of them, much like I did the first time we met in front of my parents' burning house. I take up the pose with my hands in front of me. The pose that made me so famous with the blanket around my shoulders, but now they will see the man I have become. I am almost praying towards them for all the dedication that they have given to me over the years. I feel my eyes close. They love that. They know it means I am really thinking about them. My hands go cold.

"Hello, Edmund."

I look up. There are two of them. One guy clasps my hands in handcuffs.

"Hey, why is he putting handcuffs on me?" I give him the look.

"They are needed. Edmund, the world is watching."

I look directly at him.

"My name is Stephen." It is the guy from the phone. I could tell by his voice. There is a loud cheer. It is a really loud cheer and lots of clapping. It brings me back round to remembering the press. I stand up. They are all cheering as they call my name. I can't make out all the words as it is so loud, but they love me. They all love me. Everything I was doing was for this moment. The moment that the world finally saw Edmund Carson in person.

"Sergeant Chacon here is going to read you your rights, if that is okay?"

I think I know my rights. I think he is probably going to ask me not to sign anything though. You can get carried away at this point and bring down the price of all your merchandise. That is probably what the cuffs are for. To stop me being tempted to sign things on the way to Cornwall. We are walking towards a car.

I glance behind me and they are taking Becky out on a stretcher. That must be due to the bump on her head. I hope she is okay. That was a nasty thud. Sergeant Chacon stops talking.

"Do you have anything to say, Mr Carson?" I like that. I like Mr Carson. I suppose I need to get used to it.

"Nothing really, Sergeant Chacon. Well, nothing other than what is your name, sergeant? I like to remember the names of the people that have been part of my story. You know, for the books and the movies. Everyone has to play their part."

He looks over to the Stephen guy who just nods his head.

"It is Alberto. Alberto Chacon, Mr Carson."

"Hi, Alberto, you can call me Edmund. We are friends now…"

We are not friends, but it will give the lad a little ego boost. I carry on walking and get to the car. The clapping is still going on. There is a lot of shouting. I swear I heard them shouting about Callington? I know I was trying to throw them off so that would make sense. The last time I threw them off was Birmingham. They want me to start all over again. The poor people in Callington were probably all expecting me for weeks.

"Mind your head, Mr Carson." He puts me in the back. I guess he is going to be my chauffer down to Cornwall. It is a nice car. He closes the door. I can nearly hear them talking outside. They are patting each other on the back. So proud to be part of my story I am sure about it.

I knock on the window and beckon him in. It is a long drive and we will probably have to stop a few times. I drank a lot of that wine so I am going to need a pee at some point. It takes a few minutes but he gets in the car.

"Sorry to keep you waiting, Mr Carson."

"No problem, Alberto. I was just worried that it is late and it is a long drive."

"A long drive, sir?"

"Yeah, you know, to finish becoming..." I stop. He isn't going to drive me to Cornwall. It must be ten o'clock so he will be changing shifts. I look at the handcuffs in front of me.

He doesn't have to. He was just pointing that out to me, wasn't he? You don't need a long drive, sir! I don't need to drive anywhere to finish the Alphabet.

I am up and my hands are over the headrest and over his head and around his throat still with the cuffs on.

I pull. I pull as hard as I can with my knee in the back of the chair. He is kicking and fighting as if it wasn't him who recommended it. Probably for the cameras, some of the press will have those long lenses and they will be pointing in here. A long drive, sir? The guy is a legend in his own right. I will have to make sure that makes the film.

He may as well have said look where you are. I looked where I was. I hear the crack of his neck and he stops moving. I sit back on the back seat. They are all still chanting my name.

This is it, without question. Without a doubt, I am the Alphabet Killer. The ONE, the only Alphabet Killer. I do like that.

The twelfth day of Christmas and the Alphabet is complete.

Who would have thought it? I have even just made black and white cool again. Wait, don't they call cop cars black-and-whites? I am sure I have heard that.

I knock on the window again to Stephen. He is still standing out there. I can see him. He looks over.

I mouth the words *Z-Cars* to him and put my thumbs up to him. He smiles. He knew it was coming.

I sit back in my seat. I can feel the wave of retirement coming over me. It is time for a rest.

The ONE, Father Harry and The Alphabet Killer, Edmund they all need a rest. At least this way they can just drop me straight down to Miss Walker's house and we can spend Christmas together. My nan she would have been proud of this. I wish she could have seen it.

Edmund Carson her ONE her Only.